P9-CFU-534

SAY YOU STILL LOVE ME

Center Point
Large Print

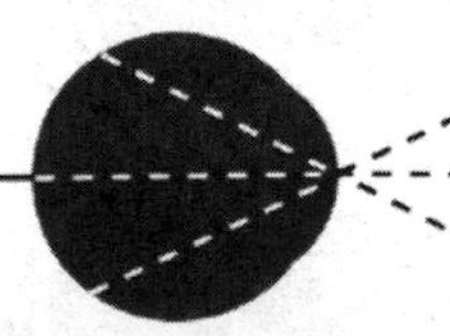

This Large Print Book carries the Seal of Approval of N.A.V.H.

SAY YOU STILL LOVE ME

A Novel

K. A. TUCKER

CENTER POINT LARGE PRINT
THORNDIKE, MAINE

This Center Point Large Print edition
is published in the year 2019 by arrangement with
Atria Books, a division of Simon & Schuster, Inc.

This book is a work of fiction.
Any references to historical events, real people, or real places are used fictitiously. Other names, characters, places, and events are products of the author's imagination, and any resemblance to actual events or places or persons, living or dead, is entirely coincidental.

The text of this Large Print edition is unabridged.
In other aspects, this book may vary
from the original edition.
Printed in the United States of America
on permanent paper.
Set in 16-point Times New Roman type.

ISBN: 978-1-64358-382-2

The Library of Congress has cataloged this record
under Library of Congress Control Number: 2019946713

To tail-chewing cats and sneaky psychics,
thank you for making both real
and fictional life more interesting

SAY YOU STILL LOVE ME

Chapter 1

NOW

A spoiled tart.

Or was it spoiled brat?

I purse my lips and try not to sneer at Tripp Porter as he drones on with a status update about the continuous permit delays, his monotonous voice flat enough to sink a yapping Jack Russell into a coma. Meanwhile I'm struggling to recall *exactly* what this arrogant ass called me at the holiday party. Of course, he was oblivious to the fact that I was standing on the other side of the pillar while he bad-mouthed me, his crimson bow tie hanging loose around his collar, his tongue flapping after his umpteenth gimlet.

It was the same night that Dad officially announced my leaping promotion to the newly created role of senior vice president at Calloway Group—my stepping-stone to president when he retires. With an MBA from Wharton and ten years of experience at CG between summer internships and post grad, he thought I was ready.

Clearly, Tripp Porter did not.

And by the thinly veiled smirk that curls his lips every time he looks my way, he *still* doesn't. But that could also be because he's under the impression that *he* should be in the senior vice president's role, and not reporting to the twenty-nine-year-old leggy brunette tart who once fetched his coffee.

Spoiled *tart*. That was *definitely* it.

Who the hell even uses that word, anyway?

I let my gaze drift around the room of suits—CG's management team, mostly wealthy white men in their mid to late fifties, afflicted with varying degrees of male pattern baldness—and wonder how many of them share Tripp's viewpoint, that Kieran Calloway has lost his damn mind, setting up his daughter to one day take over. That I should be finding ways to spend my trust fund, not wasting *their* time by dragging them into this meeting and demanding answers on two billion dollars' worth of projects.

Unfortunately for them, I'm not going anywhere. *And* I'm beyond fed up, because I heard the same bullshit update from Tripp in the last meeting.

"So what you're saying is that you've made no progress with the Marquee," I interrupt loudly, topping my blunt words with a saccharine smile as my French-tipped nails trace the walnut swirls of the polished table. We bought the struggling hotel for $120 million two years ago. *I'm* the one who brought the project to the table. *I'm* the one who pushed Dad to buy it, insisting it would make an excellent condo conversion. Dad leaned forward on it for *me*. And now, despite rounds of meetings and revisions to the blueprints, we *still* can't seem to get the city's approval for construction to begin.

I catch glances exchanged and brows arching around the table. *Some* of these people *must* share my frustrations, right?

"What *can* I say, Piper," Tripp begins, adjusting his navy-blue tie around his stout neck. *And there's that condescending smirk again*. "I've already told Kieran that we should sell it and cut our losses. The groundwork for this project wasn't set properly, and it's taking more time to fix the mess than I anticipated. I've got a meeting with the city on the twenty-ninth to get to the root of the problem."

I was the one overseeing the project until my promotion and when I left, it was on track. It doesn't take a genius to hear what he's implying—that the "mess" is thanks to *my* poor directive.

I grit my teeth to keep my composure. "That's nearly a month away."

"Yes, you're right," he says slowly. Annoyingly.

"We're now six *months* behind schedule," I emphasize sharply. "The investors are inquiring." I don't have to tell Tripp, or anyone else here, how irate that makes my father, who prides himself on our remarkable track record for reliability and on-time completion.

Tripp sighs heavily. “I don’t know what to tell you, Piper. It’s the earliest meeting date that old shrew Adriane Guthrie would agree to. You know how inflexible she is. Well, maybe *you* don’t, but ask your father.” He reaches for his phone and begins scrolling through his messages, as if this conversation is over.

I wasn’t going to do this until after the meeting, in private. But since Tripp is hell-bent on making me look like some clueless bobblehead, maybe everyone around this table is in need of an education.

“I spoke to Adriane this morning. We had a lovely chat.” I smile sweetly at Tripp, whose indifferent gaze has been replaced with suspicion. Adriane is a clever older woman whom I sat next to at a dinner event a few years back; we bonded over the same tastes in books and movies, and the same unsavory viewpoints about men like Tripp. She’s always been willing to make time for me. “It seems you missed the last scheduled meeting—”

“Something important came up,” he smoothly deflects.

“—without the common decency to phone her,” I finish.

His bushy brows draw together in a deep frown; he’s no doubt quickly thinking up some bullshit reason for that.

“I also spoke to Serge,” I add. The senior

project development manager handling the day-to-day work behind this project, a guy who puts in twelve-hour days and has a bad habit of chewing on pens as he works.

Tripp's eyebrows arch.

"He was told to forget about the Marquee and focus all efforts on the Waterway project." *Told by you.*

"The Waterway project is the crown jewel for this company. That's where our focus is right now," Tripp retorts, his chest beginning to puff out as he gathers his confidence back.

"Yes. It's an enormous project. Too large, some are suggesting." Architecturally beautiful twin towers of mixed residential and hotel atop the city's waterfront market. "And we're still looking for investors for that, which means now is not the time to be dropping the ball on our other projects," I remind him tersely. "Mark?" I turn to my assistant, who sits beside me, studiously typing out meeting notes on his laptop. "Did Adriane's assistant call back yet?"

Mark clears his throat, struggling to keep a serious face. "Yes. She has tomorrow morning at nine available." The same time as Tripp's standing tee-off time. To be fair, I didn't specifically ask for a Friday morning meeting when I called Adriane.

"Perfect. We all know Tripp is free then." I turn back to Tripp, whose cheeks are flushed with red.

"Make sure you bring the right people with you when you go in to meet with her. And call me on your way back with an update, which I expect will be favorable. Unless you *need me* to come with you to the meeting to help get the final sign-offs?" From the corner of my eye, I catch a few smirks around the table. I don't acknowledge any of them, though, keeping my steady gaze locked on Tripp, my expression flat.

"No. Of course not," he answers gruffly.

"Good! I think we're done here, then." I force a chipper tone. I collect my phone and my notepad and stand, feeling a room of gazes drift downward to my emerald-green dress, the sleeves capped to show off my toned arms, the waist cinched to flatter my curves. Whatever they may think about me running the show, none have ever hidden the fact that they enjoy the view. I don't particularly relish the attention, but I also refuse to hide my femininity behind wide-leg trousers and bulky blazers because they can't keep their leering eyes away.

"See everyone at the next meeting." I stroll out of the boardroom with my head held high, making sure my heels clack extra loud for Tripp, in case he missed the part where the tart just handed him his ass.

"That was deeply satisfying," Mark murmurs, closing the distance quickly to walk beside me, his laptop tucked under his arm.

"Let's just hope it works," I mutter, the wave of adrenaline that spurred me on now giving way to anxiety as I wonder what Tripp's next move in this power play will be, and how I'll need to pivot. I swallow against the case of nerves and peer up at Mark, meeting his broad smile. "But yes, it was, wasn't it?"

Mark is tall—well over six feet—and wiry, which makes every button-down shirt he wears too baggy on his slender frame. I'd love to give him a few pointers in the wardrobe department, but our employer-employee relationship hasn't reached that stage yet.

We're quite comfortable in the "plotting together to trounce misogynistic jerks" stage, though.

He reaches around me to pull open the glass door to Calloway's executive wing—executive alley, we call it—and hold it for me.

"Thank you, kind sir," I offer dramatically, smiling as I recall the first time he did this, during his interview for the assistant's position. I had faltered at the threshold, surprised by the gentlemanly gesture. He immediately began backpedaling, promising through stumbled words that the move in no way reflected his beliefs about a woman's ability to hold her own doors open. He confided later that he was sure he had blown the interview.

Meanwhile I knew right then and there that,

while he had zero experience, he was the right person for the job. Polite, considerate, but also in tune with the twenty-first century.

"You're welcome, milady," he says without missing a beat and with a terribly fake cockney accent that makes me chuckle. Deep dimples form in his cheeks. He's attractive, with a full head of blond hair that he runs a gel-coated hand through each morning, at most, earnest blue eyes that lock on yours when you're in conversation, and a clean-cut jaw that makes him look a decade younger than his thirty-four years. If I were interested in dating, and *not* his boss, Mark might be a man who'd pique my interest.

But I *am* his boss, and I'm eons away from heading back down the let's-get-to-know-each-other path with *any* man.

Thanks mainly to the jackass in the custom-tailored navy suit lingering straight ahead.

I sigh heavily. If there is one person who can deflate my triumphant high, it's David Worthington. "When's my next meeting? Noon?" I ask Mark.

"One P.M." His gaze narrows on David's hand as it carelessly flicks the wooden blades of the delicate miniature windmill on Mark's desk—a gift from Mark's mom to celebrate his first desk job: a symbol of his Danish roots. A replacement of the one David broke a month ago, doing this very same thing.

Mark dislikes David—with a passion, I'd hazard—but he has yet to say anything openly. That could be on account of David being VP of Sales & Marketing.

Or because David's missing an assistant and Mark has been helping to fill the gap, catering to David's demanding and sometimes childish needs.

Or because David's my ex-fiancé.

"I'm gonna run out to grab sushi. Do you want me to pick you up some?" Mark offers, eager to get away.

"No, I'm good, thanks. I need to go for a walk soon anyway. I'll grab lunch then." Even with all the glass walls and windows, the air turns stifling around here after too long.

" 'Kay. See you in a bit." Mark nods politely toward David as he passes through to lock up his things.

I don't even offer that much, pushing through the door and into my office, knowing David will be right on my heels.

My office, much like every executive office on this floor save for my father's, is all glass—glass walls, glass door, floor-to-ceiling glass windows. It affords plenty of daylight but no privacy. I've attempted to create some with a decorative coat tree strategically placed to the right of the door and a six-foot potted palm to the left. A few key pieces chosen by an interior decorator—a mid-century-style writing desk, camel-colored leather wingback chair, and a Persian rug bursting with shades of fuchsia, gold, and navy—add panache to an otherwise bland space.

Entering my small corner of this vast building brings me comfort during the hectic, long days.

Except when David is in it.

"Running out to grab a quickie with his boyfriend again?" he murmurs as soon as the soft click of the door sounds.

I drop my notebook onto my desk with a loud thud. "Mark is *not* gay. You just *want* him to be, because you feel threatened by him."

David snorts, as if the very idea of *him* feeling threatened by a guy who doesn't own a Maserati and lives in a rented bachelor pad on the outskirts of the city is preposterous. "Oh, come on, Piper. The guy spends his weekends running around the park in tights. *For fun.*"

"He's an actor!" Mark was a theater major in college; not exactly a good fit for CG. When Carla from Human Resources passed along his résumé, she did it in jest, thinking I'd catch on quickly and toss it aside. It was my sheer curiosity that got him through my door for an interview.

"*Exactly* my point."

I shake my head. "You're an idiot. Besides, that Shakespeare in the Park production is renowned. Maybe you should go and see it before you judge. *We* built the entire place, after all." A city contract that we bid on and won, along with several awards in the years following. It was the first development project I ever worked on during my summer internship here.

David folds his thick arms across his chest and smiles knowingly at me. "So *you've* seen him perform?"

"I'm going this weekend."

"What time? I'll come with you."

"Shouldn't you be interviewing some poor fool for your assistant's position? And, by the way, Mark is not picking up your dry cleaning, so stop asking him to." David knows I'm lying about going to see the play, that I enjoy theater about as much as I enjoy golf, which is exponentially less than, say, sitting on hold with the tech help desk or waiting for my nail lacquer to dry.

"Not for another hour." He grabs my apple off my desk and settles into the chair across from me, legs splayed.

"Try not to scare this one into early retirement, too," I mutter, focusing on my computer screen as I scroll through my calendar and then my emails, opening one up to read.

"Oh, don't worry. I'll make sure this one is *much* younger." He bites into *my* apple, and I do my best to ignore his penetrating gaze.

How I fell under the spell of David Worthington, I'll never understand. I guess it was for the same reason most women fall for him at first: the thick, coiffed blond hair, the playful azure-blue eyes, the square jaw, the straight white teeth, the muscular body that he treats like a temple with daily workouts and zero refined sugar. Physically, he's an Adonis, and from the first day he strolled through the doors of CG three years ago as the new executive, he had my attention.

Add the fact that he's Ivy League educated, whip-sharp, charming, born into the right pedigree, and highly successful, and you have a man who always gets what he wants. For a time, that was me. For almost two years, in fact. But then he slipped that gaudy two-carat diamond bauble—that spoke more to his taste than mine—on my finger and the polished veneer gave way to the ugly reality that David is a classic narcissist.

I realized that somewhere between him putting a deposit down on a house he knew I didn't want, telling me about his "guys' Vegas weekend" trip while he was already *on the way to the airport,* and strongly suggesting that our marriage would fare better with only one of us working at CG.

So I set the engagement ring on the dining room table and moved out. It was an easy decision but a tough life lesson, compounded by the fact that I have to see him almost every day. *Literally*. His office is directly across from mine. I look up from my desk and *there he is*.

He devours half my apple before I finally snap with irritation. "Seriously, what do you want, *David?*" His name is a curse upon my lips.

"Any highlights from the meeting?"

"You'll get the meeting notes by end of day. And why weren't you there, by the way?"

"I had a call with Drummond."

"Right." Our potential anchor tenant for the Waterway project, the draw for other retail space leasing. We need them to commit before our project unveiling next month. "How'd it go?"

"Ninety percent there." He pauses. "I heard Tripp's still being a dick." At least his voice has lost its obnoxious edge.

Maybe it's because I miss sounding off about work to David, or maybe it's because I have no one else to talk to about it—venting to Mark wouldn't be appropriate—but I abandon my computer screen and lean back in my chair. "It's like he *wants* the Marquee to tank out of sheer bitterness."

"More like he wants *you* to tank." There's no love lost between David and Tripp. It was Tripp who objected vehemently to my father going external to hire a then thirty-two-year-old David from a New York firm, pushing for Dad to instead bring in one of his cronies to fill the role.

David frowns in thought. "He's been here for, what is it, twenty-eight years now?"

"I don't care if he laid the first brick to the

very first building we ever developed, there's no excuse for the way he's been acting."

He holds his hands up in surrender. "All I'm saying is that he's *finally* seeing the writing on the wall. He'll never run this company and he's not liking it."

I can't help the snort. "He's getting paid enough to fake liking it." The old toad has a new luxury sedan every year and lives in the swanky estate community of Ferndale with his third wife. He's far from hard up.

David smooths his index fingers over his eyebrows. It's a small tell of his, something he does when he's thinking, without realizing it. I used to always tease him about it. "Have you said anything to Kieran yet?"

"I'm not running to my *daddy* about issues with Tripp." What would that do, besides prove that I'm not ready to be in this position, let alone take over when he retires? "It's on me to handle, and I'm handling it."

He aims and tosses the apple core across the room, into my trash can. "Where is the silver fox today, anyway? I thought he was back from Tokyo already."

I smirk, my gaze drifting to the closed office door at the end of the hall. My father, an arresting presence in any room, is more attractive and fit at sixty-six years than a lot of men two decades younger. Which is why he has no problem finding women *three* decades younger to date. "Industry meeting."

"Oh, right. He's shooting eighteen at Bryant Springs. He told me about that."

I roll my eyes. Of course he told David. My father tells David *everything*. They text like schoolgirls. David is the son Kieran Calloway never had, despite the fact that he has a son. Rhett, my older brother, a guy who wants nothing to do with the corporate world. Or my father.

My father was joyous when David and I announced our engagement and furious with me when I ended it. There was a point, right after the breakup, when the very air circulating around David and me was toxic, when I asked him to fire David. He told me he'd do no such thing because his quasi son is too *good for the business*. Then he kicked me out of his office for even coming to him to suggest it.

I considered quitting out of spite, but decided I'd already given David enough of my past; I wasn't going to lose my future because of him, too.

Silence lingers in my office.

And then David sighs wistfully and waves a hand between us. "This is nice, isn't it? Us, talking like this again?"

"Yeah. It is," I concede.

"Let's do it again sometime. Like over dinner tomorrow—"

"No." I stand and round my desk, heading for the door. It's the only way I'll get rid of him. "It's over and you know it."

"It wasn't *all* bad times, Piper. I seem to remember you enjoying some of it *a lot*."

I turn to find his heated gaze drifting over my legs, my hips, my chest, before settling on my face. His lewd thoughts are practically scrawled across his forehead.

My cheeks flush. "*That* part was never our problem." It's one instance where David has never been selfish, though I think it may have more to do with him wanting glowing reviews when his conquests kiss and tell. And it was easy to ignore our deeper issues when the wild chemistry between us drowned everything else out.

That last time we were together, *after* I called off the engagement, when I came to collect my last few things and he begged me to "talk" . . . well, that was a moment of sheer stupidity on my part. One I'll never repeat.

David finally heaves himself out of the chair. "You just have to stop being so uptight about everything."

I take a deep, calming breath. Four months post-breakup and he has yet to accept an ounce of responsibility for our demise. "Who *you* are and who *I* am are not compatible. You'll do best with a spineless trophy, someone who'll let you walk all over her whenever you feel like it." I pull the door open. "Go forth and find thee thy perfect doormat."

He pauses at the threshold, a mere foot away, close enough that his Tom Ford aftershave fills my nostrils. That scent alone used to get my blood rushing. "You say that now, but I doubt you'll like it when I start dating again."

"Let's test that theory out."

"Fine. I'm going out to dinner with Vicki tomorrow. You remember her, right? That sexy blonde from the gym. She's been after me for years. Pretty sure she'll be staying over."

"Tomorrow, you say?"

"Tomorrow." He smiles smugly as he peers down at me, waiting for a reaction.

"Didn't you just ask me out to dinner tomorrow? Because having dinner with your ex-fiancée when you already have a date for that night is sleazy, even for you."

"I . . . We . . ." He stammers, caught in his lie. "I meant, *hypothetically,* I *could* go out with her."

I chuckle. "Sure, right."

"That's not the point." His expression sours.

"No, the point is that I don't care who you date, screw, or marry," I usher him out with a hand against his broad back, "as long as you accept that it'll never be me again." I push my office door shut with a heavy sigh.

I believe that, deep down inside, David knows

we don't belong together. He's just not the kind of guy to accept losing. It's not something his ego can handle.

But is this what my life has become?

Managing fragile male egos all day long?

I groan into my empty office.

The elevator corridor in the lobby is eerily empty when I step out onto the ground floor just before one P.M., though evidence of a recent pizza delivery lingers in the air. It won't remain quiet for long, as any number of the six elevators are surely about to open, delivering a small horde of tenants and visitors from the twenty-four floors above.

My heels click against the travertine as I march through the atrium, past rows of planters brimming with palms and ferns. Midday sunlight streams in from the glass dome above, broken up by an archway of crisscrossing beams. Our lobby is an architecturally stunning masterpiece, designed by Fredrik Gustafsson, the very same man at the helm of the Waterway project.

We own this building, though we occupy only five floors of it, renting out the rest to a host of companies in the finance, insurance, and real estate sectors. The land was part of a smart investment by my father, who began quietly buying up defunct industrial properties around Lennox's waterfront decades ago, around the same time that he began lobbying to city officials that the neglected area could be revitalized into an urban mecca. Slowly, he's had the ramshackle mills and warehouses demolished, the area rezoned, and, project by project, has brought the area—now pegged Augustin Square—back to life.

"Off to lunch, Miss Calloway?" a baritone voice booms as I pass through the security gate.

I turn to find Gus grinning at me. I've known the cheerful security guard with the Jersey accent since I was wearing pigtails and Mary Janes. He was getting on in age even back then. Now, his tight gray curls are a stark contrast to his deep brown skin. But, while he could retire, he's shown no interest in doing so.

Gus has become as much a part of CG as my father. When we moved buildings, my father specifically asked Rikell, the company that we contract our security resources from, that Gus come with us. And by ask, I mean he told them that if Gus wasn't coming, neither were they, to this building or any others that he owns.

My father isn't the easiest man to negotiate with.

Not only did Rikell obligc, but they gave Gus a promotion to supervisor, managing schedules and staff onsite, and having final hiring say on the guard staff. But still, Gus sits at this front desk, greeting every building occupant by name, breaking up the monotony of the daily grind in the most pleasant way.

"What's it gonna be today?"

I can't help but grin back. "Not sure yet. Something good." We're a seven-minute walk to the Pier Market, a long, narrow construct packed with vendors and a popular locale by the river, where you can find everything from fresh-cut flowers to lobsters to French macarons. Around it is an array of restaurants, peddling every culinary taste imaginable. I've gotten lost in the menus posted outside the doors on many occasions, drooling over the idea of a comforting moussaka or chicken biryani or green curry for lunch.

I always end up bringing back a salad.

"Oh, I'll bet." Gus grunts, knowing as much.

I make a point of leaning over to brush the dusting of fine white powder from his uniform shirt pocket. "Have you been eating donuts again?" Talk about embodying a stereotype.

"Not just *any* donut!" he scoffs. "They're these . . . oh, I can't remember what Basha called them, but they're covered in icing sugar, and have this plum jam filling inside." He smacks his lips. "I'll save you one next time."

My eyes narrow. "And exactly how many did you eat, Gus?"

"Just the one." He averts his gaze to a stack of papers on the desk.

"Four. He ate *four* donuts for lunch," says Ivan,

the young security attendant with a dark olive complexion and an excessively thick neck sitting beside him. He emphasizes that by holding up four fingers.

"It's a good thing you're leaving next week, you rat," Gus mutters before flashing a sheepish smile my way. "Basha said they were best eaten fresh."

"Oh, well then that makes *complete* sense." I shake my head. Ever since Gus's wife died of an aneurysm five years ago, his waistline has been growing at an exponential rate. Sometimes I think he's intentionally eating like this to shorten his days so he can join her in the afterlife. "I'm bringing you back a salad." I give the counter a pat, as if passing my judgment with a gavel, and then head for the exterior doors.

A man steps out from behind a closed door ahead of me and begins heading for the same exit. He's in simple business attire—black dress pants and a white button-down shirt that looks extra crisp with a gold tie—that clings to his solid, muscular body in the most pleasing way.

After spending two years with David, fit bodies alone don't immediately grab my attention anymore.

But there's something about this guy . . .

The way he moves, that slender nose, the shape of his forehead, that hair color . . .

It's been *years,* and he looks so different, but . . .

I frown and my feet falter as I watch him climb the steps. No. It can't possibly be *him*.

It can't be the boy who broke my heart.

"Kyle?" I call out.

Chapter 2

THEN

2006, Camp Wawa, Day One

"Is that where we'll be eating?" I crinkle my nose at the pavilion to our left. Two faded crimson oars crisscross the front, "Camp Wawa" scrawled across each paddle in white. The picnic tables lined up beneath the covering, on the other hand, look freshly painted, and in every color under the rainbow. There must be at least twenty of them.

My mom smiles wistfully at the structure. "Your cabin will pick a table and scribble all over it. It'll be yours for the summer."

"Sounds *great*." I eye the dozens of sparrows that hop along the tables. Pooping, probably. As birds do. I sigh heavily. "Is there still time to quit and go to Europe?"

"You're going to love it here, Piper. Trust me." Nothing I say seems to dampen the nostalgic buzz that's been radiating off my mother since we crossed an old one-lane bridge, about a half hour ago. "Being a summer camp counselor is a critical milestone. I wish more people got to experience it." She turns the car into the parking area, hand over hand before shifting back to the ten-and-two position, as if demonstrating proper driving skills. That's how she always drives. "You'll make friends for life here. People you can call up twenty years from now, for *anything,* and they'll be there for you. I promise, you won't forget these days, *ever*."

"Most traumatic events *are* hard to forget." I watch four teenage girls trudge past Mom's car like a pack of Sherpas, giant backpacks strapped to their bodies, fluffy pillows and sleeping bag rolls tucked beneath their arms. Their matching messy ponytails and cut-off jean shorts prove what my mother warned me of this morning when I entered the kitchen in a silky patterned sundress and jeweled sandals—that I'm highly overdressed for Camp Wawa's counselor orientation day. "And I've been to camp before, remember? White Pine? I *hated* it." Falling asleep to the sound of three roommates breathing for four weeks? Not a shred of privacy unless you locked yourself in the bathroom? No, thanks.

"That was *not* a real camp. Real camps don't put their kids up in suites and serve meals on fine china. That was Constance's influence, and I should have known better than to *ever* listen to her," she mutters bitterly, throwing the car into park. She and my dad's mother will only ever see eye-to-eye when they're both six feet under, their corpses facing each other. "And, besides, you've never been a counselor before. It's a whole different ball game."

I sigh. "But why does it have to be at a camp three *hours* away from home?"

"Oh, look! They still have the wishing well!" she exclaims, ignoring my grumbles, waving her lacquered fingernails toward a circular stone-and-wood structure. The lake peeking through the row of tall, scraggly pine trees beyond it is a dark, *cold,* uninviting blue. "This brings back *so* many good memories. I always looked forward to my summers here."

"You grew up in a whole different world than me, Mom." Public school and family camping vacations at state parks; a tiny two-bedroom farmhouse and sharing a room with Aunt Jackie; drugstore hair-dye boxes and Sears shopping sprees once a year for back-to-school. A station wagon with a gaping hole in the floor of the front passenger seat, if Gramps's stories are true.

It's a far cry from the life she married into, the life *I* know—of a sprawling six-bedroom luxury home, of private school that costs more than many people earn in a year, ski vacations at our Aspen chalet in the winter, and lazy summer days at our beach house on Martha's Vineyard, if we're not jetting off somewhere. I know I'm lucky, and I never take it for granted. But gratitude only goes so far. "If you're going to *force* me into this—and, by the way, I'm pretty sure there are parenting studies that speak out against this sort of thing—couldn't I have at least gone to White Pine?"

She glares at me. "You *just* said you hated White Pine!"

"Yeah, but at least the rooms are air-conditioned." The website for this place says I'm going to "become one with nature in a charmingly cozy cabin that holds ten campers and two counselors." Translation: packed into a crowded, stuffy shed for the next eight weeks. With bugs.

"Trust me, Piper. We're doing you a favor. It'll be good for you to experience another side of life. The *normal* side. I've tried my best to keep you grounded, but . . . this'll help teach you to be more conscious of our wealth."

I struggle not to roll my eyes. Mom's always talking about how we should try living a more "normal life," like "normal people." Ironically, the topic usually comes up as she's flipping through the catalogue for her next new sports car, or writing a check to pay the caterers for the latest party she's hosted, or pouring a celebratory glass of pricey cognac for my father when he closes his latest multimillion-dollar deal.

Hell, we drove here in her Porsche!

The truth is, she may not have been born into money, but she has slid into the role of a prim and proper socialite wife to a business tycoon husband so smoothly, no one would ever guess her modest upbringing.

Though, I fear that role is about to change to that of *ex*-wife.

"So making me do this has *nothing* to do with you and Dad wanting the summer alone to sort out the details of your divorce?" I finally dare ask, my voice cracking slightly at that last word. One I never imagined uttering in relation to Kieran and Alison Calloway.

Mom shoots me a look but doesn't offer an answer, drumming her fingers on the steering wheel instead. Her official stance has always been that marital problems are between the adults and not up for discussion with the children. The fact that I know about the "mistake" my father made with a redheaded architect in LA and that a divorce lawyer's business card slipped out of Mom's wallet a few weeks ago hasn't affected her refusal to divulge anything thus far.

"Mom . . ."

"I'm spending a few days at your aunt Jackie's and then heading out to the summer house so I can *think*."

"And are you going to let Dad visit?" I press, a hint of a pleading tone entering my voice. Their raised voices have carried to my bedroom more than once, as of late. My father, insisting that he fly out for the weekends so they can "work things out and move on."

My mother, insisting that he *not*.

"He said he was sorry, Mom," I offer more softly. It feels like the right thing to say in a situation that I'm still struggling to wrap my head around. It also feels like a last-ditch effort to avert what I'm guessing is inevitable.

Her eyes blink in rapid fire to fight the threatening tears from spilling. "I'm trying, Piper," she whispers hoarsely. "But what he did was—" Her lips purse tightly, as if to seal away the rest of that sentence from escaping, as if too much has already been divulged.

My chest tightens with this rare display of vulnerability from my mother, who keeps her mask of confidence and self-assuredness in place at all times.

What he did was break her heart.

I swallow against the forming lump in my throat and try a different angle. "I deserve to know if I'm coming home to a 'For Sale' sign on our lawn, don't I?" I haven't seen any real estate agent cards slip from her wallet as of yet.

It's a long moment before I catch the soft sigh and subtle nod. She clears her throat, and the calm, collected façade is back. "You and your father have a special bond, and I don't want to say anything that might damage that," she begins carefully. "Our problems don't begin and end with his . . . indiscretion." Her jaw clenches with that word. "Things have not been going well for some time."

"Is it because he works so much?"

"That certainly doesn't help."

For Kieran Calloway, time has always been a valuable commodity, awarded mostly to one business meeting or the next, and *never* wasted. He's rarely on time for dinner, and usually comes late to our family vacations and leaves early, granting us no more than five or six days at a time, half of that spent on the phone or his computer.

And yet, for as long as I can remember, he has *always* found time for me. I used to sit on his lap in his office and make him explain the latest building designs to me over and over again, a thousand "why" questions rolling off my tongue, his display of patience a rarity, seemingly available only for his baby girl. I remember looking out on the city as he'd describe with passion how he wanted the skyline and the downtown core to look one day, drawing in the air with his fingertip. I've *always* been in awe of him—of how he can take an idea and then convince all these people to help him make it a concrete-and-glass reality.

Now we go for days with our paths never crossing and, when they do, he's usually grilling me on my grades, my tennis scores, and any boyfriend who he needs to approve. Every so often, he'll poke his head into my room at night—his tie hanging loose around his neck, his face drawn from exhaustion—to see if I'm awake and, if I am, he'll settle down beside me and tell me about the derelict factory he just bought or the famous architect he just hired. Details of his day that my mother and brother have no interest in hearing, but that I absorb like a blanket of comfort as I curl against him, hanging onto every word.

"Just tell him to work less, then. He'll listen."

Mom chuckles, and it's an oddly dark sound. *Oh, you naïve girl,* I hear it murmur. "Your father is not an easy man to be married to, Piper."

I'm not as naïve as she thinks. I've read the papers, heard the whispers around school of kids echoing what they overheard their parents mutter about doing business with Kieran Calloway. I know that my father is successful because he is formidable. He can be a tyrant when it comes to getting what he wants, and a vindictive bastard when he doesn't get it.

He's just *never* been that way with me.

I let my gaze drift over the grassy fields and milling teenagers again, ready to shift the conversation away from our pending family crisis. "You're right. This is *so much better* than spending the summer in Europe with Ava and Reid," I murmur dryly. My best friends should be landing in Rome right about now, chaperoned by Ava's stepmother, a twenty-seven-year-old model who has no clue about her basic obligations as a parental figure. Ava plans on taking full advantage of that.

Mom sighs with relief. Happy that I'm relenting on divorce talk for the moment, likely. "You've always been a good kid, Piper. I just think you could stand to make a few new friends with . . . different priorities." Her forehead furrows slightly, her recent Botox injections keeping her disapproval from showing too much. "We wouldn't be doing you any favors by handing you a credit card so you can lounge by hotel pools and shop all summer. Your father and I agree on that much, at least."

"Well, I could have worked at Dad's, if he had found me something better than a *receptionist's* position," I argue.

"You're sixteen." Her platinum-blonde bob sways with her headshake. "Besides, you have your whole life to get sucked into that world. Right now, I want you to experience normal teenager stuff. And being a camp counselor will look *really* good on your college application."

I roll my eyes. "*Mom*. Grandpa has a *campus building* named after him."

"See? This is exactly the attitude I don't want my children to have." She waggles a finger. "And, who knows? You might decide that you don't want to work for your father, after all."

"You're kidding, right?" I've been fascinated with what my father does for as long as I can remember, and she knows it.

"Well, look at your brother—"

I lift a hand in the air to stop her, my annoyance flaring. "I am *so* tired of talking about Rhett." He's *all* we've talked about for the past nine months, since he decided Brown and the family business aren't for him, dropped out of college, and took off to Thailand to live in a hut and teach English. My dad has all but officially disowned him. It certainly hasn't helped with our family dynamics, either.

"I know. Just . . ." She sighs heavily. "Please *try* this summer. For me." Her normally glowing complexion looks tired and worn.

"Well, I'm *here,* aren't I?" I grumble reluctantly, but I cap it off with a smile, reaching back to pat my sleeping bag roll. "With my shiny new potato sack that I get to sweat in for the next eight weeks."

"And it isn't because of the car your father promised you at the end of the summer, if you agreed to this?"

My hands fly to my chest with my mock gasp. "How could you even suggest such a thing? I'm *deeply* wounded."

"Right."

"But just so you know, I'm getting the C70. With leather seats. *And* every other upgrade. Limited edition." Dad insists that my first car has to be a Volvo because he's convinced they're the safest cars on the market? Fine. I'm picking the most expensive model.

She chuckles softly and then leans in to plant a kiss on my cheek, her Chanel No. 5 wafting into my nostrils. "Come on. Let's get out of this car. I'm dying to see what's changed."

"We're bunking together for the summer." The stocky blonde girl presses a hot, sweaty hand against mine. She's manning the registration desk—a folding table set up on the grass beneath a maple tree, surrounded by blue coolers brimming with soda cans and boxes filled with red nylon bags and potato chips—and, by her solid stance and the tidy line of pens and paperwork, seems to be taking the job seriously.

"Hey . . ." I check the name tag affixed to her tomato-red camp T-shirt, tight across an ample chest and rounded belly. ". . . Christa." It's handwritten in unnaturally perfect, bubbly penmanship, the letters alternating between fuchsia and black, with powder-pink daisies drawn in each corner.

Obsessively neat. Crafty. A scrapbooker, likely.

"So, you've never been to Wawa before, right? 'Cuz I don't remember seeing you here." She does a quick once-over of my dress with her sapphire eyes. She's wearing jeans, though it's far too hot for them, even in the shade. The pink cast and dewy sheen over her otherwise pale skin tells me she's feeling the oppressive heat.

"No. But my mom has." I throw a thumb over

my shoulder, pointing in the general direction that my mother scurried off in like a child charging a playground, babbling about a totem pole. Noise buzzes all around us—piercing laughter, doors slamming shut, the relentless shrill of the cicadas, the annoying whir of a riding lawn mower. "She used to come here every summer."

"This is my *twelfth* year here. Fourth as a counselor."

"Wow." I do the quick math. That makes her at least nineteen years old.

She laughs, and it comes out sounding like a series of small snorts. "Yeah. That's probably why I'm *lead* counselor this year." She lifts her chin with that proclamation.

And very proud of the title, it would seem.

"So, anyway, boys' cabins are on the right side, girls' are on the left. We meet in the middle for all activities and meals." She thrusts a nylon bag toward me. "Here's your welcome kit. It has your T-shirts, flashlight, and counselor handbook. You'll need to read it, but just to highlight the most important rules—no cell phones, no altering of staff uniforms. Oh, and *obviously,* no smoking or drinking."

My hands go in the air. "No worries here." I hate cigarettes and I'm not much of a drinker.

"Help yourself to a snack," she says, gesturing to the coolers. "Our welcome meeting is at four in the pavilion, dinner's at six, ice breakers and bonfire start at eight." She rhymes off each item smoothly, like she's been doing it all day. "Breakfast is between eight and nine A.M. Campers start showing up at one. Tomorrow will feel like the longest day of your life." She taps a clipboard filled with signatures. "Activities sign-up sheets for the next two weeks. Every counselor has to supervise one activity per week. My word of advice—avoid archery." She pushes her T-shirt sleeve up to show me a small white scar marring her thick bicep.

"Noted. I'm actually more afraid of the drama session, though." I've never relished the stage, and a week of helping a bunch of kids muddle through their lines sounds agonizing.

I'm beginning to see why Christa was appointed lead counselor. I'm guessing she knows the ins and outs of this place better than anyone else and she's definitely giving off those "responsible person" vibes.

But what's it going to be like to bunk with her?

I push any dour thoughts that come with that aside. "So, how many counselors are there here, anyway?"

"Forty. Thirty-three returning, six campers who've moved up to junior counselors. And you."

My gaze drifts to where a small cluster of people collide with squeals and hugs, as if the yearlong wait to see one another has been excruciating.

And *I'm* the *only* outsider.

"Ashley!" Christa hollers at a girl passing by. "Come here!"

The tall, willowy girl trudges over in worn Birkenstock sandals, pushing loose strands of her frizzy strawberry-blonde mane off her face. The rest of it—reaching halfway down her back and seemingly as wide as it is long—is held back by a colorful bohemian head scarf, the emerald green in it matching the base color of her flowing floral tank top, and her eyes.

My gaze can't help but stick to her face—to the thick layer of brown freckles that coats her cheeks, her nose, her forehead—and I instantly take pity on her. I know one other girl afflicted with such freckles—Rachel, from my English class—and I've heard the cruel things guys say about her. When I get too much sun in the summer and the fine dusting of pale brown spots appears over the bridge of my nose, I always use concealer to hide them.

There's no hiding *these* freckles, though.

"This is Piper," Christa says. "I need you to show her around Wawa."

"Of course!" the girl exclaims in a chirpy, upbeat voice, showing off a set of braces with her wide smile before pressing her lips together, as if self-conscious. "What cabin are you in? We can drop off your stuff first."

"Nine," Christa answers for me. "Counselors

share the bunk closest to the door. My stuff's on the bottom."

I suppress my annoyed sigh at the thought of climbing up and down a ladder in the middle of the night to use the bathroom. I guess my new roommate doesn't believe in drawing straws.

"But first . . . choose." Christa slides the counselor activities clipboard forward across the table, warning in an ominous voice while pointing to the scar on her arm as a reminder, "And choose wisely."

I grab the pen and begin flipping through the clipped sheets, though I'm fairly familiar with my options after having spent hours going through the camp website last week. White Pine had stables for horseback riding, and its prime location near the coast of Maine allowed for scuba diving and sailing. But here, in the heart of upstate New York, camp activities are limited to the basics. Kayaking, swimming, hiking . . . They don't even have tennis. They *do* have badminton, though, and thankfully, a spot is still available, so I quickly scrawl my name down for that. Finding my second mandatory activity is not as simple. My options have been whittled down to knitting, archery . . . and drama.

I knew we should have gotten here earlier.

"Does it matter if I've never done something before?" How am I supposed to help a kid aim an arrow?

"You'll learn. And there's always someone who's done it before."

Ashley leans in over my shoulder to peer at the sheets, her button nose scrunched up. "I made everyone in my family scarves for Christmas last year."

"Knitting it is." I sigh as I jot my name down, wondering if it ever gets cold in Thailand. Rhett didn't come home for the holidays last year. Can you mail a scarf to a beach hut?

My mom appears out of nowhere then, rushing excitedly toward me. "Can you believe they still have the exact same corn roast pot? Oh, Piper . . . just wait until you dip a freshly picked and boiled cob into a pot of melted butter. You'll have it running down your chin and all over your forearms . . ."

I cringe at the thought of grease clogging my pores. "Gross!"

"I know!" She laughs out loud and then reaches out to offer Christa her hand. "I'm Alison Calloway, Piper's mom. I'm *so* happy she's spending her summer here. I've been telling her about this place forever." Her eyes are alight as she takes in Christa and Ashley, and I can see the wheels churning inside her head, can hear the excited voice whisper-screaming, "Piper's made her first lifelong camp friends!"

Don't get your hopes up, Mom.

"Please take care of my little girl for me. She's only sixteen."

"Mom."

"We will, Mrs. Calloway," Christa promises sternly, as if accepting a mission request.

"So *you* used to go here?" Ashley asks, her wide eyes taking in my mother in her silk tank top and coral capris, diamonds adorning her earlobes and fingers, a string of freshwater pearls finishing the look nicely. It's an outfit more suited to lunching at the country club than dropping her daughter off at what my father called a "low budget" camp.

"I did! *Many* years ago." Mom laughs, well aware of how ill-suited she is to her old life. "By the way, was that Russell I saw going into the kitchen? Because I *swear* it looked just like him, but that means he'd have been working here for, what, forty-three or forty-four years?"

"Forty-five years, this summer," Christa confirms.

"Wow!" my mom gasps with astonishment. "He was always my favorite. I have to say hello to him before I go. Which," she checks her diamond-encrusted wristwatch, "is really soon if I want to get to your aunt Jackie's by dinner."

An odd rumble and sputtering sounds behind us. We turn to watch a boxy pea-soup-green hatchback park next to my mom's shiny black Porsche. With its multiple dents and scrapes along the passenger door, the two of them side-by-side looks almost comical. I have no idea what that car is, but it's definitely old and not in a good, classic-car way.

The driver's-side door opens and a tall, lean guy emerges. He lifts his arms above his head and arches his back with an exaggerated stretch before reaching down to slide his wallet into the back pocket of his baggy black jeans.

A flock of people runs toward him.

"I didn't think Kyle was coming back." Ashley's emerald eyes keenly watch him.

"Yup." Christa sighs with resignation. "Why . . . I don't know."

Kyle. I file that away as I watch him take turns slapping hands with the guys and hugging the girls, his cheeks lifting with a broad smile. He's sporting a punkish hairstyle, his chestnut-brown hair short on the sides but longer on top and at the back, where a two-inch strip runs down the center. It's been gelled to stand on end.

I struggle to make out his face from this distance—he has on dark, shield-style sunglasses—but I have that odd gut feeling that when I do finally see him up close, he's going to be jaw-droppingly gorgeous.

"I guess they've relaxed the dress code since I was here last," my mother murmurs, and I can't tell whether she disapproves. She always has been a huge proponent of my school's uniform guidelines, which includes modest hairstyles.

The guy—Kyle—observes my mom's car a moment and then says something to his friends. *Who showed up here in that?* or something along those lines, I imagine. A few fingers point our way, and suddenly Kyle's walking toward the registration desk, his focus on us.

Maybe on me.

The flutters in my stomach tell me that I hope it's the latter.

Christa begins busying herself with the pens next to the activities clipboard, lining them up in a perfect row. Is she an obsessively neat person?

Or is she suddenly nervous?

At forty feet away, I note that Kyle is lean but has a muscular frame. At thirty feet, I'm able to size up his solid, angular jaw. At twenty-five feet, I decide his faux Mohawk suits the shape of his face just fine. At twenty feet, the sun flickers off his full mouth and I notice the silver ring through the left corner of his bottom lip. At ten feet, I realize he has my favorite type of nose on a guy—long and slender, not too prominent. At five feet, he slides off his sunglasses to show me irises the color of burnt sugar.

My gut was one hundred percent right.

"Oh! Look, there's Russell!" my mom exclaims. "Come on, Piper, I want to introduce you to him before he disappears again," she urges, hooking a slender hand through my arm.

"Uh . . . But Ashley is going to give me a

tour . . ." I stall, eagerly waiting to hear Kyle speak.

"I'll find you over there in a minute!" Ashley waves me off, her excited eyes glued to Kyle.

I guess that settles that.

With a small huff, I let Mom pull me toward the mud-brown building and the man in a black-and-white checkered cook's uniform, peeling carrots into a bucket at the picnic table. "Get on Russell's good side and he'll give you a double helping of his homemade chocolate pudding whenever it's on the menu," she says in a low voice. "And trust me, that stuff is currency around here."

"Just like prison."

"Hush!" She swats playfully at my arm. "Your aunt Jackie and I never had any money to buy candy at the canteen, so we'd trade our bowls to kids for . . ." She rambles on about SweeTarts and Snickers bars; meanwhile I glance over my shoulder.

Kyle is chuckling at something Ashley's saying as he shifts from foot to foot, a red nylon welcome bag dangling casually from his fingers.

"Piper?" my mom calls out, slowing. "What do you think?"

"Uh . . . Yeah, sure."

"Were you even listening to me?"

I meet her gaze. "No. Sorry. What?"

Frowning, she peers back to see where my

focus was, just as Kyle turns to find our eyes on him. He smirks and casts a small wave.

"Ahh . . . I *see,*" Mom murmurs knowingly. "So it's going to be the boy with the Mohawk, is it?"

"I don't know what you're talking about," I mumble, my cheeks heating. "And it's a *Faux*hawk."

Chapter 3

NOW

When I unlock and open the front door to my condo that evening, my mind is still swirling with memories.

Kyle has lingered in my thoughts all afternoon, like the constant prick of an embedded thorn—impossible to ignore. I was late for my one o'clock meeting and mentally absent for all of them, as a summer long since filed away into the past came flooding into my present. Even David, normally too self-involved to notice anyone else's struggles, paused his relentless press to confiscate Mark for his own needs long enough to ask if I was feeling all right.

My door connects with something solid just inside.

"Hello?" I holler through the crack.

"Piper! Hold on! Let me move that!" comes the responding shout.

Bare feet slap against the hardwood, followed by a series of grunts and the sound of a heavy object sliding across the floor, and then the door flings open and a freckled face appears.

"Sorry!" Ashley exclaims, panting. "I meant to move those earlier, but I got caught up with unpacking." She takes a deep breath, exhales, and then grins. "Hey, new roomie!"

I laugh as I hip-check the door shut and shimmy past the wall of stacked blue containers to set my purse on the kitchen island. "Is this *all* your party-planning stuff?"

"Yeah," she admits, smoothing over the lifted corner of a label marked "Ribbons." "I'll make it all fit in my room, though, I promise."

"No worries. How'd today go? Did security give you any problems?"

"Nope! They even met the movers at the service elevator." Ashley runs her slender fingers over her hair, attempting to tame the strawberry-blonde halo of frizz around her messy topknot, to no avail. The only day of the week that it's truly ever smooth is Friday, if she goes for a blowout at the salon. And if it's a humid day? Forget about it. Even that won't last an hour.

"Good. I stopped by the front desk this morning to make sure they remembered, but you never know with them."

"That shade of green looks amazing on you," she murmurs, dusting her hands over the ratty concert T-shirt she obviously threw on to unpack. The disheveled, frumpy outfit is so opposite her usual feminine boho-chic look.

"Thanks." I kick off my heels with a groan, stretching and wiggling my toes. I'm going to need to swallow my pride and start changing into running shoes for the fifteen-minute walk from work. "Is Christa home yet?"

"On her way. And she's bringing dinner, so don't order in."

"*Thank God.*" Christa is the general manager at a popular steak house nearby, with a staff of seventy-eight, open 364 days a year. On the rare occasion that our schedules cross paths over dinner, she usually brings a fully prepped meal, hot off the grill, saving me from day-old sushi and wilted salad.

I round the island and wander over to the adjacent living room, to take in the charcoal-gray velvet sectional. "So, *this* is the infamous couch." The one that sparked the colossal fight between Ashley and Chad that ended in their breakup. The one that Elton, Christa's severely cross-eyed Siamese cat, is currently perched on, calmly and methodically licking away at his paw.

"I told you it would be perfect for this room," Ashley says, her gaze assessing the space with a smile of satisfaction.

"It's starting to look like an actual home in here," I agree. When I ended things with David, I left with my bedroom set and two white leather chairs. Everything else was his and I didn't want any of it. My dad offered me this place—a spacious three-bedroom, four-bathroom penthouse unit in CG's newly completed Posey Park project. It's far too spacious for one person but it's close to work, so I happily accepted, having every intention of hiring Marcelle, my mom's interior decorator, as soon as I had time to care about things like furniture and artwork.

For all the effort I put into decorating my office, I've put in the opposite amount here. Almost four months have gone by, and the generous space still sits mostly empty and undecorated. Christa moved in last month and brought with her a flat-screen television to hang over the gas fireplace, a chunky oak coffee table that is heavy enough to break shins, and a four-person round-tabled IKEA dining set that screams of low budget.

Basically, we've been living like a couple of college students who found a penthouse to squat in.

But now, it's starting to come together. With some style, too, as Ashley's beautiful, *huge* sectional and geometric black-and-white rug complement my white leather chairs perfectly.

I sink into the couch to test it out. "*Oh* . . . I'm not getting up again tonight."

"See? I told you it was comfortable."

"*So* comfortable."

"And two people can lie down on either side, easily," she goes on, as if still selling the thing to me. "It's perfect."

"Oh, it is," I agree, adding more gently, "though I can see why Chad *might* think this was too big for your place." The tiny midtown bungalow that they were renting couldn't have been more than nine hundred square feet.

"It *was* a bit tight for there," she admits sheepishly. "But we could have made it work. He didn't have to be such a jerk about it."

I offer her a sympathetic smile. "Was he there today?"

"He showed up as the movers were carrying out the last load, just to make sure I didn't take anything I wasn't supposed to. Like his TV." She rolls her eyes. "I don't even know how to turn on that stupid thing."

"So, things didn't leave off amicably then?"

"I'm sorry, what? Did you say you wanted a glass of pinot noir to celebrate my move in?" Ashley sashays over to the kitchen island and pours two glasses of red wine from an uncorked bottle, artfully avoiding my question. She hands me mine and then takes a seat beside me.

We clink glasses and I revel in the first sip, savoring the meld of black currant and elderberry.

"So how are you *really* doing?"

She sighs. "I think this is really it, this time." Her tone is missing its typical chirpiness.

"You've said that before." In the five years since they started dating, Chad and Ashley have broken up a handful of times, twice while living together. It invariably unfolds the same way: Ashley has enough of Chad mocking her—her eclectic style; her oddly close relationship to Zelda, her psychic; the fact that she *has* a psychic; the "wasted" amount of time, effort, and money she puts into her fledgling event-planning business, a passion that he claims will never take off. He gets defensive when she calls him disrespectful and complains that he's sick of supporting her financially, then they have a huge fight and break up. The separation usually lasts two or three months, until Chad comes crawling back, asking her to give him another chance.

And she takes him back. She *always* takes him back because her confidence in herself is sorely lacking.

Her button nose crinkles. "Yeah, but this time feels different. More final, you know?"

If only . . . I reach over to give her shoulder a squeeze. "You guys have been trying to make it work for five *years* now. Maybe there's someone who you'd mesh with better?" Chad and Ashley are as opposite as you can get, and not in a good way. Ashley is all about organic foods, vegetarianism, and protecting nature, while Chad had a deer head—from a deer that he shot—stuffed and mounted above their bed. Ashley uses laundry baskets instead of dresser drawers to store her clothes, while Chad vacuums the vacuum cleaner. Ashley will spend hours on Pinterest, looking for ways to up-cycle a chipped teapot to avoid it going into a landfill; Chad is an engineer for an energy company—that Ashley has protested outside. Ashley spends a few hours every Thanksgiving working at a soup kitchen; Chad thinks the homeless are all lazy people looking for a handout.

Basically, Chad's a dick and Ashley's way too good for him. I don't know how they ever ended up together in the first place, or how they've given each other five years of their lives.

I suck back a large gulp of wine before I say any of this out loud, though, because it'll only make things awkward as hell when they reunite.

Ashley sighs with resignation. "Well, I guess the silver lining is that the three of us get to live together. Who knew that would *finally* happen, right?"

"Who knew . . ." I echo, tapping my wineglass against hers again. "And it only took thirteen years and a few jerks." More like, who knew that the Camp Wawa trifecta of oddly suited girls would last beyond that summer in the first place. But it has, through out-of-state colleges and boyfriends, polar-opposite social circles, contrasting priorities, and, at times, an abrasive rubbing of personalities. Ashley and Christa have become my two most trusted and loyal friends. Sometimes I'm amazed by that, but then I think back to that summer, to the aftermath, and it doesn't seem so crazy.

With a resigned sigh, Ashley holds out her

hand and makes a soft, tongue-clucking sound. "Here . . . kitty, kitty, kitty."

Elton pauses in his obsessive bathing ritual to glare at her.

"Why won't he come to me?" Ashley complains. "Cats love me!"

"Not him. He hates everyone." I savor another mouthful of wine. Christa was so desperate for a cat that when an elderly friend of her family was seeking a new home for Elton, her "loving and affectionate" blue point Siamese cat from "impeccable purebred lineage," Christa didn't think twice before adopting him and bringing him home to the condo she shared with her younger sister, Carrie.

And Ginger, Carrie's Jack Russell.

It didn't take long to learn that *loving and affectionate* are not the most accurate words to describe this animal and, after four months of vet bills to treat Ginger's scourged face and the discovery that Carrie's chronic sinus problems were in fact a cat allergy, Christa had to either give up Elton or find another place to live.

"He hates *every*one?" Ashley asks with incredulity.

"Everyone. People, other animals. Even plants. Basically, anything that consumes or produces oxygen."

"Plants, too?"

"Carrie stepped out to walk her dog and came home to every last houseplant uprooted and shredded." She claims it was a premeditated massacre.

Ashley's gaze flashes to the dozen or so potted aloe veras and succulents sitting in a box in the corner.

"Yeah, you'd better keep those in your room, with the door closed at all times."

"*So* weird." She eyes Elton, who's gone back to licking his front paw. "Is he still doing that weird thing with his—"

"Yup." Turns out Elton suffers from severe anxiety, which only surfaced after Christa adopted him. He spends half his day trying to outrun his tail and the other half attacking it.

"Too much inbreeding, I guess."

"Too much of *something,*" I murmur, letting my head sink into the plush cushions as I stare up at the seventeen-foot white ceilings. My nostrils catch a faint odor. "What *is* that?" I inhale sharply. "It smells like . . . cigarettes?"

"Seriously?" Ashley presses her nose against the cushion again, and then groans. "I've shampooed and doused this thing with vinegar, like, *five* times. I thought I got it all out!"

I frown. "Why would it smell like cigarettes?" Neither Ashley nor Chad are smokers, and Chad is too much of a clean freak to ever allow others to smoke in the house.

"Zelda."

My frown deepens. "Your psychic does house calls?" And *smokes* during them?

"No. In *her* house."

"I am *so* confused right now."

Ashley sighs with exasperation, and I can tell she doesn't want to tell me whatever I'm about to hear. "I bought this couch off Zelda and *she* smokes in *her* house."

"Wait a minute . . ." I hold my free hand up. "You bought a *couch* off your *psychic?* You told me it was brand-new!"

"Well yeah, brand-new for *me,*" she clarifies.

"Ash*ley* . . ."

"What! Ugh. Okay! So, Zelda sensed I'd be needing a new couch in my life soon and since she had just ordered a new one for herself, she offered to sell me hers. And look!" She gestures at our sizeable space. "She was right! And she sold it to me for five hundred bucks, even though she paid almost three grand for it last year!"

"Because she knew she wouldn't get more for it, reeking from smoke! Oh my God, this is making *so* much more sense now," I moan, gulping my wine. When Ashley said she bought a new couch and promised it would look fantastic in my place and "please, please, please, can I bring it because I can't return it," I assumed she had bought a floor model on clearance.

I shake my head at my friend. "*This* is why you and Chad had a huge fight and broke up, isn't it?"

"No, not *exactly,*" she says with a mixture of irritation and reluctance. "Chad was pissed, but I promised I'd get the smoke out and rearrange the living room to make it cozy. So he calmed down, and I thought everything would be fine. It wasn't until the smoke smell faded that we started to smell the urine—"

"What?" I bolt upright, nearly spilling my wine all over my dress in the process.

"It's all gone, I swear!" Her hands are in the air in surrender. "It was just one cushion and I replaced all the stuffing in it. But *that's* when Chad blew up. He said that I was stupid for trusting Zelda, and that she had conned me."

"And would you maybe . . . perhaps . . . agree that she took advantage of you?" I ask as evenly as I can.

"I don't know? No! I mean, why would she do that when she sees me *every* month? Honestly, I think she just forgot about it. Or figured it wasn't a big deal. It was probably her grandson. He's two, and I remember her saying they were having a tough time potty training him."

"Yeah. *Maybe*." I struggle to hide my skepticism from my voice. My dear friend's sweet, forgiving, glass-is-always-half-full nature is both a blessing and a curse.

Slowly, I settle back into my seat, though not nearly as relaxed. "Which cushion was—"

"I'll never tell," she says with wide-eyed earnest. "But isn't it *perfect* for this place?"

Finally, I have to laugh to myself, because the entire debacle is Ashley in a nutshell.

She joins in soon enough, shaking her head. "I know. I'm ridiculous."

"Just don't tell Christa," I warn. The last time Christa told Ashley what she thought about the "spiritual advisor" who bills our best friend two hundred bucks a month, they didn't speak for weeks. "And there had better not be any bad spirit juju with this thing. If weird stuff starts happening around here, the couch has to go."

She rolls her eyes. "You sound like Chad now."

Maybe he isn't a complete idiot, after all.

The sound of keys jiggling has Elton leaping off the couch and trotting toward the door. I cringe at the sight of his tail, the end of it a bony white stick where he's chewed off the hair. He meows—that unnatural woeful Siamese howl—in greeting as Christa plows through, her arms laden with two plastic restaurant bags. She has to turn sideways to manage past Ashley's containers. "Tell me you have more of that wine."

Ashley and I share a look. Christa rarely drinks and when she does, it's sugar-free, low-calorie vodka on account of her being hyperconscious about maintaining her figure. Halfway through college, she got onto an extreme healthy eating and exercise kick that helped her shed pounds. Since then, it's been what seems like a constant battle against her body's natural tendency to carry extra weight. She'll never be what society deems "thin," but she can fill out a vintage swing dress like no one else I know.

"Rough day?" I hazard as Ashley heads for the cabinet to fetch a third wineglass.

"Oh no, it was great!" Christa says, her voice dripping with sarcasm. She dumps the take-out containers on the counter and reaches down to scoop up Elton and hug him close. He returns the affection immediately, rubbing his pointy face against her cheek, his raspy purr carrying. "I caught my bar manager stealing bottles of Veuve."

"*Oh*. I'm sorry," Ashley says, her freckled face scrunching with sincerity as she holds out the glass.

Christa sighs heavily, then sets the cat down to take the wine and tuck her hair behind her ear. She's been wearing it layered and shoulder-length for years now, a style well-suited to her round face. "There's a vegetarian pasta for you, Ash, and a bloody slab of cow for you." She nods to me through a sizeable gulp.

"Gosh, that sounds delicious," I murmur with a mock-dreamy look. Christa might be the only general manager at a steak house who is genuinely disgusted by steak.

"So . . . how was everyone else's day? As much fun as mine, I'm guessing?" Christa's gaze takes in the disarray around the condo.

"Well . . . *I* for one am exhausted, but I'm happy to be here with you guys." Ashley collects cutlery and plates from the drawers and begins dishing out.

"That couch is perfect for this place, by the way," Christa says before another gulp, eyeing the new living room setup. "Where did you get it from again?"

Ashley's eyes flash to me. "Oh . . . just some local furniture store?" It comes out sounding like a question, but Christa is too distracted by her own frazzled nerves to seem to notice.

"Cool. Piper?"

"I made Tripp look like a fool." But that's not what I really want to talk about, what I've been *dying* to talk to somebody about. "You'll never guess who I saw in the lobby today. At least, I *think* I saw him."

They pause, waiting expectantly.

"Kyle Miller."

Their mouths hang open for a long moment, and then . . .

"Seriously?"

"Why are you just telling me now?"

"What did he say to you?"

"Is he still gorgeous?"

I hold my free hand in the air to stop the

onslaught of questions. “I’m not even sure it was him. He was ahead of me and then he went out the doors, and when I tried to catch up, he was just *gone*.” I couldn’t have been more than ten paces behind him, and yet he all but disappeared when I reached the sidewalk, my adrenaline racing through my veins.

I don’t tell Christa and Ashley that I spent the next hour wandering through the Pier Market, looking not at the tempting menus or the colorful wares, but for those familiar dark golden eyes.

“Wow. *Kyle Miller,*” Christa begins, exchanging a glance with Ashley.

“I know.”

“And you’ve *never* talked to him since that summer? Not even once?” Christa already knows the answer to that, but she asks it anyway, as if to confirm the gravity of Kyle’s possible reappearance in my life.

“How could I? He literally dropped off the face of the earth.” His phone number went out of service a few days after he left Wawa. My emails to him went unanswered at first, and then they bounced back. He’s nowhere on social media from what I can see, and I’ve looked more than once over the years.

Even now, thirteen years later, I can hear the twinge of frustration in my voice over how things ended between us.

How confusing.

How unfinished.

"What do you think he was doing there?" Ashley asks.

"No idea. He was in a tie, so maybe he's working for one of the other companies? Or maybe he was just a visitor." I don't know what's behind that door he exited.

"Do you think he knows it's your family's building?" Ashley asks.

"Oh, come on," Christa, ever the cynic, scoffs. "It says 'Calloway' across the front in giant, golden letters."

"That doesn't mean he'd make the connection," Ashley argues. "Did you ever tell him who your father is?"

I shake my head. "I don't think so."

"See? So how would he know?" Ashley's big green eyes get that dreamy look in them. "Wouldn't that be something, though, if he *does* work there?"

My stomach does a nervous flip. It's been thirteen years. Does Kyle Miller remember me? Does he still think about me as I do him? And if so, are those thoughts laced with fondness?

Indifference?

Or regret?

"Those were the days, huh?" Ashley finally lets out a longing sigh. "Remember Eric? Man, that guy used to drive me nuts."

Christa snorts. "That's because he had a *huge* crush on you."

"Couldn't have been *that* big. He never returned my emails, either." Ashley waves it off, but her face pinches. "I wonder how he's doing."

Silence lingers through the kitchen as we all drift into our own thoughts.

"What will you say to Kyle if you see him again?" Christa finally asks.

I shrug. "I don't know. Hi?" I swallow against the sudden swell of nerves.

And *Why would you hurt me like that?*

Chapter 4

THEN

2006, Camp Wawa, Day One

". . . they were, like, *best* friends, but then Marie hooked up with Carlos one night, even though she *knew* Jenny was, like, *in love* with him," Ashley murmurs from the side of her mouth, leaning in so I can catch her muffled words over the buzz of laughter and soft music. "It was a *total* disaster."

I covertly study Carlos, a stocky guy in a mustard-yellow T-shirt, standing across from us, laughing with his friends while he stokes the bonfire with a fresh-cut log. The two rivals for his affection sit equidistant to him—Jenny, the tall, lithe blonde on the picnic table to the right, and Marie, the petite girl with a jet-black French braid huddled with a group to the left. He's cute enough to garner the attention, I *guess*. He seems to be more interested in the brunette helping him now than either of those two, though.

"So, did they work things out?"

"No." Ashley's emerald eyes widen with emphasis. "And then Darian had Marie and Jenny bunking together this summer. Thank *God* Christa saw the list and made her fix the

assignments. Can you imagine how tense that would have been?"

I assume that's a rhetorical question, so I merely shake my head as I swat the mosquito on my knee—I should have changed into pants—and make a mental note to avoid accidentally stepping into any minefields around those two girls.

When Christa asked Ashley to show me around, Ashley took that not only in the physical "girls' restroom to the left, canteen closes at five, stay away from the weedy side of the lake" sense, but also as a rundown of key social connections and juicy gossip, and anything else she deems I might need to know about the people I'll be living and working with for the next two months. The amount of information she's off-loaded on me in tiny, private slips between the welcome meeting, dinner, and now is staggering. I'm doing my best to keep everything straight.

So far, aside from the Carlos-Marie-Jenny triangle, there's also the Kate-and-Colin bet—a pool going on how long it will take for the two senior counselors to hook up again after last summer's off-and-on-again fling. Based on the googly eyes and secretive smiles they've been throwing each other all evening, I'm considering throwing five bucks into the hat for tonight. And then there's the "Will Tom and Doyle finally come out?" question mark, regarding the lanky blond guy and his friend at the picnic table to the right of us, who were campers here for years and, Ashley swears, have been secretly dating each other for the past two summers.

I've also learned that Claire, the girl in the oversized fleece sweatshirt with muscular legs, is the resident waterskiing and wakeboarding instructor for the summer and so good that there's talk of her qualifying for the Pan Am Games; and that Olivia's dad owns four gas stations, which classifies her as "rich," especially with the brand-new Honda Civic she pulled up to camp in; and that Justin got into Columbia University for the fall with a full ride from financial aid that he's been bragging about.

In my circle of friends, no one would *ever* brag about needing financial aid for *anything*.

I've also been given the quick rundown on Christa. Apparently she isn't well-liked. Partly because she has a tendency to boss people around and she insists on *always being right,* but also because she's been known to rat out counselors. Now that she's been tapped as lead counselor—a glorified title for the camp director's personal gopher that she announces to anyone who will listen—people have been avoiding her at all costs.

And *I'm* the lucky one who gets to room with her for the next two *months*.

I'm sure there are plenty of questions floating

around about the new girl. Everyone's been nice so far, but I haven't missed the frequent curious glances, and there was that abrupt end to a hushed conversation between Ashley and two other girls as I returned with my burger, followed by embellished smiles.

I haven't offered much information about my life, so I can't imagine what Ashley would be saying about me by way of introduction. It's nice being a mystery. So different from back home, where it seemed half the school knew my name by the end of my first day of freshman year. Or rather, they knew my family name.

The *one* person I'm dying to get information on, though, the one I've been acutely aware of since crossing the threshold to take a seat at the pavilion for orientation, is the one Ashley hasn't divulged a single detail about yet. The one leaning casually against the trunk of a giant cedar tree, his hands tucked loosely into his pockets, his feet crossed at the ankles, talking with Olivia as she shamelessly flirts with him. The one I've swapped frequent glances with for hours now, allowing myself to admire that gorgeous face for a mere second or two before shifting away, so as not to be *too* obvious.

"So, what's that guy's story, anyway?" I finally ask, feigning disinterest. "You know, the one from earlier. Kurt or something . . ."

"Kyle," she corrects, her eyes immediately

locking on him, as if she's been aware of his location all along, too. "He runs this place. At least it feels like that, sometimes. He's . . . different."

"How so?"

"He's just . . ." She shakes her head. "I don't know how to explain it. I like him, don't get me wrong. But no one really knows much about him." She glances around and then lowers her voice even further. "He used to come here with his brother. He was this quiet, skinny little kid who didn't say much. Then they just stopped coming. No one saw or heard from him for forever, until he showed up as a junior counselor last year, looking like *that,* and I swear, *every* girl had an instant crush on him. Well, except for Christa." Ashley snorts. "She reported him for skipping out on his activity once and got him into major shit." She pauses. "Why? Are you interested?"

"He's decent enough, I guess," I lie, nonchalantly. *Decent* doesn't even begin to cut what Kyle is. And so different from Trevor, the guy I dated for almost five months this past year. Trevor was a senior, and six feet of brawny muscle, broad shoulders, and baby-blue eyes. He also turned out to be a pig masquerading as a nice guy—promising he wouldn't pressure me into sex, all while sliding his hand up my shirt and spiking my drinks at parties. When I figured out the latter, I dumped his ass. His ego didn't take too kindly to that. I mean, a sophomore dumping *the* Trevor Reilly? He ended up with another senior within two days, and told every guy who would listen to not bother with me unless they wanted serious blue balls.

"So, who has Kyle hooked up with around here, anyway?" Because a guy who looks like that doesn't spend an entire summer surrounded by fawning hormonal admirers and stay celibate.

"He was with Avery last summer."

My gaze surveys the crowd. "Let me guess, the one in the navy-striped shirt?"

"Yeah." Ashley frowns. "How'd you know?"

"Just a hunch," I mutter wryly, watching the leggy redhead with the bag of marshmallows as she carefully skewers several on the end of a long metal stick. Narrow hips, skinny waist, large breasts, long, glossy tresses the color of a fiery copper. She stands out from all the girl-next-door counselors around the circle, and she's easily the most classically beautiful female here.

Kyle doesn't sound as different as Ashley claims, after all. At least not as far as his choice of girls goes. "How old is she?"

"Twenty, I think? *At least* twenty. This is her second year as a senior counselor. Kyle's only seventeen." Ashley looks knowingly at me. "He must like them older."

Or more experienced. If that's the case, how

quick will he be to abandon the interest he seems to be showing in me? I mean, it's not like I'm saving myself for marriage, but I'm also not in a rush to rid myself of my virginity as if it were a hot potato. I want it to mean something when it finally happens and so far, I haven't met a guy who fills that requirement. Trevor Reilly definitely did not.

Will Kyle?

"So, what happened between them?"

She shrugs. "Summer ended, I guess. Plus, if you ask me, she's not the most interesting person, but I'm not sure it was her personality he was after." Ashley accepts a marshmallow roaster stick from a nearby guy with a smile of thanks. "She bunked with Christa last year. That didn't go over so well."

I fish out two jumbo marshmallows from the bag and hand them to her, while stealing another glance. Olivia, or "Miss Sunoco," is moving in on Kyle, her hips casually swaying to the languid beat of the moody alternative music playing over a portable radio, her long golden-brown hair flipping with every exaggerated laugh. Does he find *her* interesting, I wonder?

"He'll never go for Olivia," Ashley says as if reading my mind, her eyes on the two of them as she shifts a few steps to hold her stick high above the flames. "She's a total one-upper. You'll see what I mean soon. And she's *always* talking about money. About their big house, and their cars, and where they're going on vacation. Kyle can't stand girls like that. That's what Eric told me, anyway."

Noted. So I shouldn't mention . . . basically anything about my life around him. "Who's Eric?"

"Kyle's partner in crime. That one over there."

I follow the jut of her chin to a guy across from us, busy dousing himself with bug repellent. I'd noticed him earlier. He stuck by Kyle's side during orientation and dinner.

"He's cute." In a Ryan Phillippe sort of way, with dark blond curls that hug his scalp and a mischievous look in his eyes.

"He's a loudmouth and a goof." Ashley chews her bottom lip as if considering her next words. "Last year, Kyle told me Eric said I was pretty." She laughs nervously and shakes her head, as if brushing it off.

I frown. "You don't believe him?"

"Come on . . . Guys don't like girls with *this many* freckles." A flush crawls up her neck. "Especially not guys like Eric."

"That's not true." I can't deny that I pitied her for those freckles when I first saw her. But only hours later, I can see that Ashley has a lithe, natural way about her, and when she smiles, her entire face transforms. She's one of those people who, the more you get to know them, the more attractive they become, wild hair, freckles, and all.

I study Eric again. He's put down the can of bug spray and is now having a whispered conversation with another guy, their attention veering to Kyle and Olivia across the way, impish smiles on their lips. "Would Kyle do something like that to you?" Because playing on an insecure girl's emotions like that would make him a douchebag.

Ashley's brow furrows, as if she's giving that question serious thought for the first time. "No. I guess he wouldn't. I mean, they both joke around, but they're not mean-spirited."

"So then . . . you and Eric?"

"What?" She giggles. "No. We're not compatible. Eric's a Sagittarius and I'm a Pisces. It would *never* work."

I wait for her to crack a smile, or laugh. Something to tell me she didn't just invoke unsuitable zodiac signs as a valid reason for avoiding a hookup.

Her face remains serious.

"Anyway, Eric was messing around with someone else, like, a week after Kyle told me that, so he couldn't have been *that* into me—"

"Freckles!" Eric hollers, attracting everyone's attention as he marches toward us.

Including Kyle's.

I feel my body naturally stand up straighter.

"Stop calling me that!" Ashley's scowl quickly fades to a smile as Eric rounds the bonfire. "God, you're so tall now!"

With a wide grin, he wraps his arms around her, pulling her into a friendly hug. "Yeah. Late growth spurt, I guess."

They break apart and she playfully pokes him in the ribs. "You never emailed me."

"You know how it is when you leave here." His inky blue eyes flip to me. "*So?* Who's your new friend?"

Ashley waves dramatically toward me. "Piper, this is Eric. Eric . . . Piper."

He offers his hand and I take it, but the handshake quickly morphs into a weird slap-snap-flap move that leaves my hand frozen midair, my eyebrows raised in surprise, feeling foolish.

Eric frowns with astonishment. "*Wow.* You've *really* never been to Wawa before."

"Uh . . . no."

" 'Cause you know, there's a secret handshake."

"There's a *secret* handshake?" I echo, feigning shock.

He grins. "*Oh,* yeah, there's a secret handshake. Better learn it fast because you'll be doing it a thousand times this summer."

"*Ten* thousand times," comes a throaty male voice. I turn to find Kyle standing beside me, close enough that I can smell the mix of Deep

Woods bug spray and whatever hair product he uses to get his hair to stay up.

He must have broken free of Olivia's advances and made a beeline here as soon as he saw his best friend approaching. I swallow, forcing down the swirl of giddiness over that thought. "Ten *thousand*. That's a lot."

"It is," he agrees with mock seriousness. "Soon you'll be waking up to your hand doing the motions in your sleep."

"Yeah, *that*'s not what your hand is doing while *you're* asleep," Eric retorts, earning himself a swift punch to the shoulder from his friend.

Kyle turns his attention back to me, his golden eyes glittering with amusement. "Hey."

"Hey." A blush creeps along my cheeks. Knowing I'm blushing only makes my face grow hotter. I wish the sky would plummet into full darkness right about now.

"I'm Kyle." He holds his hand out and I eye it warily. A cute smile curves the corner of his mouth with the lip ring. "Nothing funny. Promise."

His fingers are long and slender as they slip over mine, his skin cool to the touch. "I'm Piper."

"Piper," he repeats, his hand lingering a beat or two longer than normal before he releases me. "I like that. It's different."

"It's *definitely* different." And it has come with an arsenal of unwanted nicknames. Pipe Cleaner, before my stick figure began to fill out; Pipes, courtesy of my brother; Piper the Viper, from opposing players on the tennis courts—that one's growing on me. And of course, there are also the gags. I've found more than one jar of dills in my locker this past year, and the guys' swim team has taken to trailing me in the halls while whispering some stupid rhyme about picking their pickles.

Kyle slides his thumbs into his pockets and lets them hang in that casual way. "So, how'd you end up at Wawa for the first time ever, Piper?" He's watching me so intently, his eyes—with a vibrant green hugging the pupils, I can see now—searching mine.

I have to clear my throat before I can manage words. "My mom used to go here, and she's a firm believer that everyone should experience being a camp counselor at least once in their life, so . . . here I am."

"Those damn parents, always forcing us to experience life and shit," he murmurs, his lip twitching with amusement as he reaches up to casually scratch the back of his neck. His sleeve slips, showing off the edges of black ink. Seventeen and tatted. Did his parents actually allow that? Because mine are vehemently opposed to it. My dad has basically told me that every tattoo is a digit lost from my trust fund if he finds out.

"So you get it, then." I smile softly.

His gaze flickers to my mouth. “I do.”

“Everyone!” Darian, our petite and energetic camp director, has climbed up onto one of the picnic tables. She claps several times, showing off toned arms. “Everyone, grab a seat! Chair, table, grass, wherever. Get comfortable!”

There’s a shuffle of bodies around the campfire as people settle in. I find myself perched on one end of a picnic table bench, next to Kyle. His jean-clad thigh softly nudges mine, momentarily distracting me from everything else.

“It looks like you’re all having fun, catching up. That is *awesome!*” Darian emphasizes the word *awesome* by throwing her arms in the air. My guess is that she was that spunky high school cheerleader in her former life. Somewhere in the last twenty or so years, she traded in her long blonde ponytail, short skirt, and pom-poms for a cropped cut, hiking boots, and a tennis visor that reads “Camper 4 Life!” across the front. “Now, I *know* I don’t have to remind you guys what the first day of camp is like, right? All the excitement and nerves can make for a long night. Kids are excited, nervous, homesick . . . which means they don’t sleep, which means *you guys,*” she jabs the air with her index fingers, “don’t sleep either.”

A chorus of groans sounds out.

“And then you’re up at the crack of dawn for an even *longer* day.”

More groans.

Darian holds her hands up in surrender. "I know, I know . . . But taking care of these kids and making sure they enjoy their week away is kind of why you're here, am I right?" She pauses, waiting for a few sounds of agreement. "And you all need to get a good night's sleep tonight so you're ready for what's to come. You catching my drift?" She casts a searching look around the group.

"No shenanigans?" Eric calls out with an impish grin, earning a few laughs.

"You got it, Mr. Vetter! No shenanigans! And I don't want to have to treat you like children by watching your every move. Listen, I know there will be times when you need to unwind a bit after refereeing and corralling kids all day. I get it. *I've* been there, too. But I expect everyone in their cabins by ten tonight, snoring softly, so you're bright-eyed and bushy-tailed when those parents and kids pull in tomorrow. Is everyone with me on this?" Again, her arms go above her head, her question seeming more like a practiced cheer.

Kyle leans in toward me. "Darian tries hard to be 'hip,' " he murmurs, his voice low, his mouth close to my ear as he air-quotes the word *hip*.

I take a deep, calming breath to balance my spiking heart rate. "So I'm noticing."

"She usually misses the mark, big time." He settles back, resting his elbows behind him on the picnic table, his long legs stretching out in front of him. "But she's all right, as far as bosses go. No one's allowed to be a dick to her."

It sounds oddly like a warning. Like, if you're a dick to Darian, you're going to have a problem getting along with the other counselors. Or maybe just with Kyle.

"Okay! So on that note, we do have a few new people in our group. One who is *brand-spanking* new to Wawa." Darian's hand flies my way and I instinctively tense at being singled out. "So, I think it's a good time to play our *favorite* ice-breaker game"—another round of groans carries—"and see what new things we can learn about one another. Come on! It's been a year. Stuff has happened. Besides, I'm sure there's still plenty you don't know about even your closest friends here." She claps her hands. "Okay! Two truths and a lie! Who's going first? Don't make me pick."

Someone shouts, "New girl goes first!" and a chant of "New girl, new girl!" begins.

"Okay, then! Piper, stand up and try to fool us." Darian nods encouragingly.

"Are you kidding me?" I mutter under my breath, squirming in my seat as forty-odd sets of eyes land on me. Two truths and a lie? What the hell do I say? Couldn't they have given me two minutes to prepare?

My mind has gone completely blank.

"I'm going first," Kyle announces, standing and taking a step forward, steering everyone's attention to him.

Darian doesn't object.

I let out a shaky sigh of relief.

"Let's see . . . two truths and a lie . . ." He slides his fingers over his chin in exaggerated thought. "This is my second year as a counselor at Wawa, I got caught up in an armed robbery, and I just got my fifth tat last month." He rhymes them off so smoothly, I'd think he had them long since prepared.

"One . . . two . . . three . . ." Eric, who's sitting on the other side of Kyle, counts out loud, his brow furrowed in thought. "Hey, Avery! Does Kyle have any ink on his ass? Or you know . . ." He waves a hand at his own groin area.

Laughter erupts.

"Don't pretend you guys don't walk around butt-naked together every chance you get," Avery throws back in a snippy tone, her face flushing to match her red hair.

"Yeah. But we don't get up close and personal." Eric's eyebrows waggle. "If you know what I mean—"

"Thank you, Eric!" Darian cuts him off with a warning tone. "Anyone want to take a guess? What *is* Kyle Miller's lie?"

Even I know this is his second year as a counselor. A general consensus of "Number

Two!" and "Armed robbery!" echoes around the campfire as Kyle waits patiently, his arms folded over his chest, a knowing smirk on his lips.

"Well?" Darian watches him expectantly, though, I note, with a touch of apprehension in her gaze.

Kyle reaches up and tugs at his shirt collar, stretching it to reveal a slender but muscular shoulder and the fresh outline of a tattoo in progress. "This will be number four when it's finished."

Eyebrows pop and looks are exchanged, and then a flurry of curious questions about the robbery erupt.

"We're going clockwise," Kyle announces, ignoring them all, settling back into his seat beside me. He nudges a surprised-looking Eric beside him with his knee.

"Dude," Eric mutters, peering at his best friend. "Seriously? When?"

Kyle shrugs nonchalantly. "I can't remember. Two truths and a lie, Vetter. Go."

Eric shakes his head and then, just like that—as if Kyle is the camp director running the show—he stands and rattles off his own three lines.

But Eric's words don't register for me. My focus is on the boy beside me, his elbows resting on his knees, his attention locked on the dancing flames. I have so many questions.

Golden eyes turn to me suddenly and I avert

my gaze to the sparse grass at my feet, but it's too late.

"You come up with anything yet?" he asks casually.

"Almost," I lie. "Thanks, by the way, for buying me some time."

He shrugs. "Being the new guy sucks."

I guess that would have been him last year, after so many years away.

Eric is done and everyone's shouting out numbers, most of them having chosen "one."

Kyle discreetly holds out three fingers for me and winks. "He's a shitty swimmer."

I guess he was listening to his friend, after all. Meanwhile, my attention is now on his wrist, on the ink peeking out from beneath the tan leather band. I jut my chin toward it. "What's that?"

Kyle smooths his thumb back and forth over the bracelet for a moment, his mouth working over words that don't seem to want to come. And then he unfastens the snap and stretches his arm out to settle on my bare knee, palm up. Waiting for me to see for myself.

I struggle to ignore the feel of his hot skin against mine as I take in the tattoo. Two rows, two numbers, with several decimal points following each. The second number is a negative.

"They're coordinates." I look up in time to

see the small, satisfied smile on his profile as he watches the fire. "To where?"

A few beats pass before he pulls his arm away and refastens the leather band, covering the tattoo. "Nowhere special," he says casually, leaning back on his elbows once again.

"You permanently marked your body with coordinates to a place that *isn't* special?"

The smile grows wider. "Maybe I did."

I shake my head but chuckle. I can't get a read on this guy, other than that he's lying and we both know it.

The ice-breaker game is rolling through the group swiftly and I really should be listening, but I can't seem to pay attention to anyone except Kyle.

"So, what's your lie going to be?"

"If I tell you, it kind of defeats the purpose of the game, doesn't it?"

His tongue slides out to flick his lip ring absently, drawing my attention to it. I've kissed three guys in my life and none of them had a lip ring. I wonder what it would feel like, to kiss Kyle.

My blood begins rushing at the thought.

"I'll know which one it is, anyway."

"Really . . . And what makes you so sure?" I ask playfully.

Another lip ring flick. "I'm a telepath." He turns to look at me, catching my gaze on his mouth. "I'll bet you."

"How much?"

Kyle shifts ever so slightly, bringing himself closer to me. "Loser has to eat five Fun Dips in under a minute. Winner buys."

"What?" I laugh through a cringe. "Is that even humanly possible?"

"Eric did it when he lost a bet with me. And he always loses when he bets me, by the way." The smug smile touching his lips is downright devilish.

I set my jaw with determination. I love Fun Dips. I love winning even more. "The doubles or the singles?"

"I'll let you get away with the singles."

"You're on."

An excited gleam sparks in his eyes.

It's Avery's turn now, and she hops off the picnic table to stand, showing off a set of long and slender but shapely legs. Everyone's attention is on her as she scoops her glossy red locks back with both hands, then tucks strands behind each ear.

But I'm stealing frequent glances Kyle's way, trying to catch any flicker of interest that may linger for last summer's fling. Did he sleep with her? Eric's joke implies that they've gone pretty far.

A tight, uncomfortable feeling stirs in my stomach with the thought.

But I remind myself that he's sitting beside me.

He came to *me*.

"Okay. So . . . let's see . . ." Avery swings her arms at her sides twice. "I'm changing my major to herpetology—"

"Lie," he murmurs without missing a beat.

"How do you know?" *And what the hell even is that?*

"Because she hates reptiles."

Ahhh . . .

"Especially turtles."

I frown. "Who *hates* turtles?"

"Exactly." His eyebrows pull together. "I need to be with the kind of girl who likes turtles." He pauses a beat and then peers at me with intense scrutiny. "Are *you* the kind of girl who likes turtles?"

I struggle to suppress what would no doubt be a stupid grin, as flutters stir in my stomach. "I *love* turtles." The chocolate pecan kind. As far as the living kind go, I'm indifferent. I mean, I'd swerve if I saw one crossing the road, but I have no plans to join a "Save the Turtles" advocacy program.

But this has nothing to do with turtles, anyway.

I swallow my nerves. "Actually, I have a bunch of them at home."

"Really . . ." His eyes narrow and I can't help but note the thick fringe of long, dark lashes. "How many?"

"A hundred and one." I struggle to keep a straight face.

Kyle lets out a low whistle. "That's a lot of turtles."

"We have a turtle farm."

His head falls back and he belts out a laugh that grabs everyone's attention, including Avery's, whose eyes narrow and dart from him to me.

"Something you need to share, Kyle?" Darian asks through a tight smile, her annoyance thinly veiled. I wonder if she feels the same way about Kyle that Christa does.

He holds a hand in the air, palm out. "I'm sorry, but have you ever heard of anyone having a *turtle farm?*"

"What the hell's the point of a turtle farm?" Eric mutters. "All they'd do is sit around in the sand all day."

"And swim," Kyle offers. "But you'd need a big pool, especially for a hundred and one of them."

"A hundred and one? You mean, like the Dalmatians?"

"*Exactly* like the Dalmatians, Vetter. *Exactly.*"

Eric frowns as if considering that. "Are the spots on their shells or their bodies?"

"Okay, boys . . ." Darian interrupts the Ping-Pong match of wit between the two friends. She points toward Avery. "Can we please focus?"

"Yes. Of course. I apologize," Kyle says somberly. "Please, Avery . . . continue telling us about your *cats*."

With another wary glare Kyle's way, Avery continues. "Their names are Snow and Coal."

"Because one's all white and one's all black. She said the same thing last year," Kyle mutters, and there's no missing the boredom in his voice. Whatever Avery may feel for him—which right now appears to be a fair amount of resentment—there's no love lost on his end.

"Didn't stop you from hooking up with her all summer," I retort before I can stop myself.

Kyle muffles another laugh through a fake coughing fit, earning a dirty look from Avery and a throat-clearing from Darian. "I see Ashley's been busy filling you in on everything you wanted to know?"

And now Kyle is fully aware of the fact that I wanted to know about him.

My cheeks flush. But I shouldn't be embarrassed, should I? Because, unless I'm horribly imperceptive, the signs are all there that this interest is mutual.

Avery has finished and people are now shouting out their guesses.

"I missed her third thing. What was it?" I ask.

"Probably that she has a sister who looks exactly like her, or something equally lame." Kyle waves a dismissive hand in her direction. "Do you have a sister who looks like you?"

"No. A brother, who looks nothing like me."

He is my mother's son, while I'm a much more feminine version of my father.

Kyle smiles smugly. "Now I know one truth about you."

Shit.

"Come on, Piper. I'm counting on you to come up with something more interesting than siblings and cats."

"Well, I'm sorry if I haven't been involved in any robberies lately."

An odd, unreadable look flickers over his face, but it's gone in an instant. "So then shock me." His eyes roam my face. "Say something that you wouldn't want to stand up in front of a group of strangers and admit to."

"Fine." My stomach flips.

"And let's up the stakes. Ten Fun Dips, two minutes."

"Fine."

"Fine." He smirks. He turns his attention back to the circle.

I feel compelled to ask him something—*anything*—to keep our conversation going. "So . . . do you have a brother?"

His fingers move for that leather band again, fumbling absently with it. "Yeah. One brother. Jeremy."

"Is he going to come here this year?"

"Nah." Kyle's eyes roam the treetops falling into darkness, now that the sun has dropped past them. "So, what activities did you sign up for?"

"Uh . . ." I struggle to think, his diversion away from his brother swift. "Knitting and badminton."

He cringes. "*Knitting?* That's the worst."

"Options were slim. You?"

"Kayaking and hiking."

I frown. "But those slots were full when I signed up, and you came after me."

"Pays to know people."

"Apparently," I grumble. "I've never even held a knitting needle."

Kyle nods toward the counselors. They're halfway around the circle. "Better start thinking up a good lie, unless you want to lose our bet."

We sit quietly next to each other—me, hyperaware of Kyle's every shift, twitch, and glance—and listen as one by one, everyone takes a turn standing before the crowd, attempting to trick the group. Most tries are unimaginative—answers people throw out just to get their turn over with and the attention off them. Then there are people like Christa, whose truths are so blatantly obvious—"I'm a Type A personality, I like to be in control"—that it's impossible to mistake the lie—"I drive Formula One race cars in my free time."

A few are good. A guy named Vince had everyone divided over whether he went skydiving last week or if a shark did in fact brush past his calf at Cocoa Beach during spring break. Turns out Vince is scared shitless of heights and would have to already be dead and tossed out of a plane in order to agree to skydiving.

Tom stood up and outed himself as gay—to a round of cheers, proving that many already suspected that truth.

And then there was Olivia . . . I got my first real taste of her and her "I spent New Year's Eve in Paris," "My dad said that if I keep my four-point-oh, he'll buy me a Range Rover when I graduate" truths, along with her "I met Harry Styles last year" lie. Apparently she met him *two* years ago.

As each person pauses to wait for the consensus, Kyle holds up one, two, or three fingers for me. And he's right, *every* time. I'm beginning to think there is such a thing as telepaths. At the very least, he has a natural ability to read people.

By the time my turn comes, my palms are sweating.

"Okay! And last but not least . . ." Darian makes a drum roll with her palms on the back of the cardboard box used to shuttle over wood scraps for the fire.

I stand, feeling everyone's gaze on me once again.

"Hope you like sour apple," Kyle murmurs, and I can hear the smug smile in his voice.

And I hope this doesn't backfire terribly on me.

"We have turtles at home, I'm crushing hard on Kyle, and I dumped my high school soccer team captain's ass for trying to pressure me into having sex."

Probably not what Darian had in mind for this ice breaker, but there you have it.

Eyes flash wide, mouths drop, and shocked, nervous giggles sound, and then people begin shouting out numbers. I stand with my head held high, like I'm unfazed, even as heat crawls up the back of my neck. Thank God for the cover of night, finally.

"*Okay,* that was . . . interesting." Darian's own eyebrows are arched as she looks at me, her words failing her. "Well, Piper? What's the lie?"

Taking a deep breath, I finally dare look over my shoulder and down.

Kyle peers up at me with a small smile on his lips, dipping his head once as if in approval. I guess I didn't *totally* fail. He holds up his index finger.

Number one.

I feel the triumphant smile take over as I turn to the group. "I'd *never* date a soccer player. They're a bunch of crybabies."

Laughter and jeers explode around the circle as I settle back down next to Kyle, my blood still racing through my ears, my eyes on the flames, unable to gather the nerve to meet his gaze.

Darian begins addressing the group—reminders

for where to be tomorrow and when—but I dismiss her instantly. With Christa as my bunk mate, I basically have a walking, talking agenda anyway.

"You do *not* have a turtle farm," Kyle mutters.

"I didn't say I did."

"Yeah, you . . ." His words drift as he realizes his own error.

"We have two snapping turtles living in our pond at home. They've been there since April." My mother has tried to have them relocated, but they've somehow eluded the animal control guys so far. "But thank you for the idea. I *never* would have remembered them."

He shakes his head in disbelief, and a soft curse slips from his lips.

"So . . ." I swallow away my nervousness. "Was that *shocking* enough for you?"

Kyle leans forward to rest his elbows on his knees again, making it impossible for me not to look at him, short of turning away. "Well, let's see . . ." He uses his fingers to count out. "The most fucking convenient truth, if I've ever heard one . . ."

I giggle.

He hesitates. " . . . a pretty ballsy admission . . ." But by the soft smile touching his lips, I'd say one that he's pleased with. Is that a slight flush in his cheeks? " . . . and then your lie." A frown touches his brow. "So who was he, then?" He tilts his head to meet my gaze, and for the first time I see a genuinely somber look.

My breath hitches at the beauty of it. "Captain of the rugby team," I admit. "How'd you know that part was true?"

He shrugs. There's a long pause. "Sounds like he was a real dick."

"You're perceptive." *Please don't be a dick, like him.*

Kyle's face splits with a wide smile. "So I've been told." His gaze dips to my lips.

I feel the overwhelming urge to find out if Kyle is as good at kissing as he seems to be at guessing lies, and the brazenness to make sure I find out on my first night at Wawa. "Hey, so do you want to—"

"Miller! Rematch time!" a guy yells out, pulling Kyle's attention away from me. A group of guys are jogging toward the nearby field, where a bright overhead light has been turned on to illuminate the grass. A guy bounces a soccer ball off his knee.

"Oh, you mean Eric. I don't play soccer!" Kyle hollers back.

"What? You scored five—umph!" Eric's words cut off when Kyle elbows him in the ribs.

"These guys don't know what they're talking about," Kyle dismisses, then stands and stretches, his T-shirt lifting to give me a glimpse of a narrow but chiseled waist and dark hair trailing south of his belly button, his jeans sitting below the elastic waistband of his navy-blue Calvin Kleins. "But you know, I should, uh, head over there to, you know, console all those crybabies."

I laugh. "Right."

"I mean, *I* don't play."

"No, of course not." I mock-frown.

He begins walking backward, away from me, grinning. "Because *I'm* not a crybaby."

"You're not. And by the way, did you want those *ten* sour apple Fun Dips with breakfast or lunch tomorrow?"

He gives me a gritted-tooth smile. "Canteen opens at ten thirty."

"Mid-morning sugar rush it is."

"Can't wait." He saunters away, Eric jostling him playfully.

"Oh my God!" Ashley squeals, sliding down to me. "I *can't believe* you actually said that in front of everybody!"

"I know. Me neither." And a quick glance around the group, namely at Avery's and Olivia's tight expressions, tells me they aren't exactly pleased by it. But I guess when the new girl strolls in and basically stakes claim to the boy everyone else wants on the very first night, that's bound to happen.

Crap, did I just guarantee myself enemies for an entire summer?

"I knew you liked him, by the way." Ashley

playfully jabs my ribs with her finger. "I could just tell."

She could tell, but she doesn't seem bothered or annoyed by the fact that I lied. She seems genuinely . . . giddy for me. It's at that moment that I decide Ashley is a friend I need to have this summer.

Christa sits next to Ashley. "Seriously? *Kyle Miller?*" Her voice drips with disapproval. Her expression isn't much better.

I'm immediately on the defensive. "And what's wrong with him?"

"He's a jerk."

"Not to *me,* he isn't." I give her a knowing look. *Judas.*

"He's irresponsible, he lies, he thinks everything's a joke," she says, listing Kyle's supposed faults on her stubby fingers. "He shouldn't have been allowed back here."

"But he was." I flash Ashley a wide-eyed "What the hell?" look.

"Something bad is going to happen one day, and it'll be because of him. Mark my words."

I can't help it. I laugh. "*Mark your words?* What are you, ninety years old?"

"So . . ." Ashley leans forward to effectively block Christa's face from mine and end a brewing confrontation. "What did you two talk about?"

I struggle to shake off my growing irritation with my new roommate. "Just . . . stuff." As if

I'm going to divulge anything within Christa's earshot. "We made a bet, to see if he could guess my lie."

Her eyes flash with excitement. "Who won?"

I look to the field in time to see Kyle peer over his shoulder at me, the sly smile touching his lips as infuriating as it is sexy. Ashley was right, he's just . . . different, and I can't put my finger on exactly how.

But I'm quite certain that I'm done for.

"Definitely me."

Chapter 5

NOW

"Five copies, single-sided, two staples in each, a half-inch apart." Mark's voice is thin as he relays David's scrupulous instructions sent to him last night.

"Ignore it. He can email the presentation to them." David has had weeks to hire a new assistant and he's dragging his feet. There is no way in hell I'm letting him dominate mine anymore.

I pause mid–pen stroke as the red light on my office phone flashes, indicating an incoming call. I muted the ringer long ago, the sound of it grating on my nerves.

"A. Calloway," the display screen reads. It's just like my mom to still dial the office line instead of my mobile. She's no doubt following up on her email from last night to discuss the merits of damask versus brocade window treatments. She got the summer house in the divorce settlement and has taken to redecorating every three years. While I always enjoy talking to her, now is not the time for that thirty-minute conversation. Not when I have no valuable input to offer anyway.

Not when I'm anxiously waiting on an update

on the city planner meeting from Tripp, hoping my power play has paid off.

I let her call go to voicemail.

"You know Tripp always has Jill call me to check your schedule, right?" Mark hovers over my desk, smoothly collecting one check requisition after another as I sign and approve payments to the various suppliers and contractors. "That way he can wait until you're tied up in a meeting and just leave a message."

I did *not* know that, actually, though now that I look back, he's always leaving me voicemails. That way he doesn't have to feel like he's answering to me. I shouldn't be surprised. *Coward.* "So he knows I'm going to be at The Port Room over lunch?"

"I'm sure Jill will tell him."

The Port Room is a private members-only establishment of rustic wood floors and broad leather seats, where I sometimes like to hold meetings for its comfort. The downside is that phone conversations while inside are forbidden.

And Tripp knows that.

"I guess I'll have to make sure to answer my phone then, won't I?" Because I want to hear what the weasel has to say, live. "And, let me guess, he's taking the afternoon off?"

"Jill moved his tee-time to one."

In my rush to pass the requisition on, the corner of the sheet catches my skin, slicing through. I hiss, sticking my index finger in my mouth to quell the sting and stifle the unprofessional curse that wants to scream out. "I should ask her to cancel it," I grumble bitterly. Though they're calling for 98 degrees this afternoon. At least the bastard will sweat in the midday heat.

"I bet Jill would do it for you."

"Care to wager five sour apple Fun Dips on that?" Not that I'd win that gamble. It's no secret that Tripp's assistant, a woman in her late forties who dons purple cat's-eye glasses and a librarian's bun, doesn't enjoy working for him.

He frowns curiously. "Fun Dip?"

"Never mind." I sigh, scrawling "Piper C. Calloway"—C for Constance, after my dad's mother—across the bottom of the last approval, giving the numbers a second fleeting glance. "Please tell me this is it."

"This is it."

"Thank God."

"Except for the others coming this afternoon . . ."

With a groan, I toss my pen to my desk and lean back into my chair, inspecting my wound. Who knew this role would entail so much mundane paperwork?

Mark pauses at my office door to eye me curiously. "Wild night?"

"No, not really." Though the bags under my eyes would lead one to believe otherwise.

"Maybe too much red wine. My head's a bit foggy." Ashley, Christa, and I polished off two bottles while reminiscing about Camp Wawa. I was in bed by midnight, though I tossed and turned until three, my mind and heart dwelling on the possibility that the golden-eyed boy with the Fauxhawk might have crossed my path yesterday.

I've almost positive that it *was* Kyle I saw.

"You want me to hit Joe's for a pick-me-up?"

I check the time. Ten thirty. I have an hour and a half until my lunch meeting—and Tripp's call, if Mark is right about his avoidance tactics—and a dozen reports to go through, and I'm suddenly stir-crazy.

Besides, I have something I need to do downstairs.

"No, I'll go. I could use a walk before I fall asleep in my chair staring at these numbers. Black, two sugars, right?"

"Yeah. Thanks." He frowns, as if surprised that I remembered. "You know . . . you're pretty cool to work for." The glass door to my office shuts before I have a chance to respond, but his words leave me with a smile. I think I know where that praise is coming from. It's well known around the company that the executive team, including my father, has an old-school mentality when it comes to assistants. A "you take care of me" way of operating, from a time when people still readily used the term *secretaries* and assistants were more like Depression-era work-wives, making sure their bosses were well caffeinated and properly fed, and that the real wives received gifts on wedding anniversaries and birthdays.

It's not that the executive assistants here are treated poorly—they're applauded and well compensated for their mothering abilities. But it's an archaic environment, one I can't wait to change.

My dad may have frowned when I told him I'd hired a male assistant, but he didn't try to dissuade me. And I've never treated Mark like someone who is here merely to fetch coffee and run the printer. Sure, he does those things, as well as book meeting rooms and set up appointments, but I've also enrolled him in tasks that teach him about the industry and prove that I believe he has a useful head on his shoulders. When Mark moves on, it'll be to bigger and better things, and I'll be happy for him.

I reach for my purse just as raucous male laughter carries from down the hall. A moment later, my father and David appear. "You're kidding me," I mutter, rolling my eyes, taking in the sight of them. They're wearing their usual Friday golf attire—tailored wool-blend pants and collared shirts—only this week they're dressed identically in charcoal gray and powder pink.

My dad raps his knuckles twice against Mark's desk as he passes—his standard greeting, one that always makes Mark visibly stiffen—and then strolls right into my office.

"Welcome back! How was Tokyo?" I haven't seen him since early last week.

"Exhausting. Glad to be home. Got my five-mile run in as the sun was coming up and then eighteen holes with my favorite guy." Dad has a gruff, steely voice, the kind that commands attention when he speaks and intimidates people. He also can't hold a smile for long, which only ups the intimidation factor. "And how's my daughter? Holding down the Calloway fort?"

"*Someone* has to." I smile wryly up at him. "You got some color."

"Did I?" He frowns as he checks his sinewy forearms, already golden and toned and coated with darker hair than the full, thick mane of silvery gray on his head. He wasn't always so focused on his health, having spent years carrying around an extra twenty pounds thanks to frequent steak dinners and daily cocktail hours. But a mild heart attack two years ago changed things. He'll still have the occasional scotch, but now his diet consists mainly of white fish and salads, and he has all but cut out caffeine.

He wanders over to the windows to gaze down over the city, his arms resting across his chest. No doubt admiring his life's work so far and what is yet to come. By the time he retires, Kieran Calloway will have made his mark on a city that half a million people call home, with everything from luxury high-rises to affordable condominiums, to retail and entertainment locations and even an architecturally world-renowned library.

Talk about a legacy.

"I heard about your problems with Tripp over the Marquee project."

Straight to business.

I spear a glare through two glass walls. It's wasted effort, though, as David's back is to me, his phone pressed to his ear as he bounces a tennis ball against his window.

I hope it pins him in the eye.

"I'm handling it."

"Are you?" he asks lightly, but I hear the dicey undercurrent beneath it. "I've known Tripp a *long* time. There's a certain nuance to motivating him."

"Does it involve a bottle of Hendrick's?" I mutter under my breath.

"I've left him a message this morning, emphasizing how important his role is in—"

"You didn't!" I burst, tossing the pen in my hand across my desk in frustration. "Don't you see how bad this looks for me?" It looks like I've run to my daddy with my problems because I can't handle them on my own. It's *exactly* what Tripp expects.

Unlike my girlish shrill, his voice remains

calm. "I'm not going to risk losing him for the sake of your ego, Piper. Calloway Group is not a one-man show. You need guys like him and David in your corner, whether you like them or not."

I take a deep, calming breath and try to match his tone, all while inside I'm screaming. "I'm waiting on a call from Tripp to update me on the meeting with the city planners, and I expect things to move forward smoothly after today—"

"*Nothing* ever moves smoothly in this industry."

"If I have to get more involved, I *will*."

The responding sigh is one that breeds tension in my shoulders. It means I'm about to get a lecture. Wandering back to my desk, he perches himself on the edge. "You *lead* them. You *guide* them. You *motivate* them. And you *rely* on them. You *don't* do their jobs for them, Piper."

"You can't motivate someone who doesn't respect you."

"Then *earn* Tripp's respect."

"*How?* The guy calls me a spoiled tart to anyone who will listen!"

He squeezes the bridge of his nose with his index finger, as if pained from a headache. "I'll talk to him."

"No, you will *not, Dad!*" I tack on a sigh and a calmer "*Please* don't," because my voice is bordering on hysterical.

He pauses, as if searching for another angle in this conversation. "Well, *are* you a spoiled tart?"

"What? No!"

"Good. I'm glad you know your worth. And *I* know that you are a brilliant young woman with the passion and the potential to continue leading the Calloway legacy like no one else. That's why I promoted you." He offers me a rare, encouraging smile before it falls off. "Now prove it to the rest of them." There's an edge creeping into his brusque voice. "I have no plans on going anywhere anytime soon, but as we learned two years ago, nothing is guaranteed. I want you at the head of the Calloway table *now,* with your feet in the fire, so everyone can start getting used to the idea of you running CG one day. But you still have *a lot* to learn, from me and from this executive team. That includes Tripp."

"Yes, *sir,*" I manage to get out through gritted teeth. "I just don't understand what value you see in him."

"I will admit that Tripp has let his false aspirations cloud his judgment lately. But he has been by my side for almost thirty years. That kind of loyalty counts for something in this business." Dad's gaze wanders toward the skyline once again. "How is everything with the Waterway project?"

I push aside my dour mood as I pat the stack of papers next to me. "Final design approvals have come in. Seagrum and Whilcroft have signed the loan papers."

"How short are we on financing?"

"We need another three hundred million to close the construction loan."

"How are talks with Deutsche Bank coming along?"

"Long and excruciating, but I think we're making headway. Jim is getting more numbers to them." Jim, our director of investments, is a tall, slender man with a perpetual five o'clock shadow and a keen financial sense, especially when it comes to negotiations involving that kind of money.

"And the unveiling ceremony?"

"At the art gallery on Fifth. Everything's underway for that."

"Keep me informed," Dad murmurs, reaching for the gift that arrived from my brother last week—made from recycled silver spoons, which I don't think was a coincidence given he always jokes that we came out of my mother's womb suckling on them—to study it with an incredulous look. "*That's* what this thing is for? To hold my *phone?*"

I let out a soft sigh, relieved at the sudden switch in topic, even if it's to a more personal one. "I take it Rhett sent *you* one, too."

"Yes, and I told Greta to toss it, but the damn woman never listens to me."

I smirk. Greta's been my father's executive assistant for almost twenty-five years. She's set to retire next year and he's already talking about doubling her salary to get her to stay. The truth is, I'm not sure my father can survive without "that damn woman."

"I have no use for tchotchkes," he mutters, fiddling with my iPhone perched within the cradle, shifting it this way and that.

"Works pretty well. And it's clever." In a kitschy sort of way.

Dad lets out a sound that *might* be approval—if he could approve of anything my brother does—before standing with a stretch. His hard gaze drifts to the office across the way. "You know . . . David really loves you."

I roll my eyes. "David really loves *David*." And I'll never be stupid enough to divulge anything to him ever again.

"Confidence is important in a man—"

"Dad."

His hands go up in the air. "You're going to be running a multi*billion*-dollar company one day. You need to be with a man like David. Not like that last waste of space."

"Who?" I frown, confused for a moment. "Wait, are you talking about *Ryan?*" My ex from four years ago?

Dad grunts at the name.

Waste of space . . . "He was a published author!"

"Who couldn't pay his own rent, if I recall correctly," he throws back.

"He could have been a lot worse."

"Yes, you're right. He could have been a criminal."

I sigh heavily. In my father's eyes, a man's worth is set by his family name, his bank account, and his shoes.

And I want to be done with this conversation. "Say hi to *Rita* for me."

He pauses, seemingly caught off guard. "Actually, we decided to take some time apart. She moved out."

I feel my eyebrows spike in surprise. "Since when?"

"It's been at least a month now," he says dismissively.

"A month!" They were together for almost a year! I thought this was the one he was going to marry. "You should have told me."

He shrugs. "I didn't think you particularly liked her."

Like would be too strong a word for my feelings toward Rita, but at least she's a full decade older than me, unlike the thirty-two-year-old interior designer before her. Thankfully that one was short-lived.

"I don't like the idea of you being alone at

night," I say instead. He was alone at home when he had his heart attack. It was sheer luck that he managed to dial 9-1-1.

"And I don't like *you* being alone, period," he smoothly pivots.

"I'm *not*. I have Christa, and Ashley moved in, too."

"At your age, you should be—"

"Enjoying my life." I smile as I firmly cut him off. "Marrying David would have been a *huge* mistake. And have you forgotten that he suggested I quit CG so he could take over?"

Dad waves it off with, "he wasn't serious."

I stifle my groan. "I would have been miserable, married to him. Is that what you want, Dad? For me to be miserable?"

Whatever rebuttal was formulating on his lips dies with a resigned sigh. "Tell the girls I say hello." Dad reaches for the door handle.

"You know who else is happy?" I tap the spoon sculpture. "*Rhett* is happy." My brother moved back from Thailand a year ago with his Thai wife, Lawan. They started an up-cycling shop in a charming town an hour outside of Lennox. I've only been out to see it once, but it seems to fit the composting, rainwater-preserving, recycling guru he has become.

Dad's expression sours. "Well, of course he's happy. His mother still pays his bills and he's always stoned."

Unfortunately, Rhett's altruistic lifestyle also seems to fit the pot-smoking, responsibility-shirking stereotype my dad still has him pegged for.

I can't help but laugh, even as I shake my head at him. "He doesn't smoke pot and Mom doesn't pay his bills." She just made sure he got his trust fund, something my dad was adamant about revoking until Rhett passed this "stage" in his life. "He's coming into town in a few weeks. I'm meeting him for dinner. You should come."

Dad doesn't miss a beat. "I'll be away."

"Maybe some other time, then." I'm not feeling hopeful.

"Give me an update on the Marquee approvals by end of day." He's swiftly moving for his office, a room three times the size of mine and David's, complete with solid wood walls, its own washroom, and mahogany wet bar.

With a heavy sigh—great, soon I'll be reporting in to my father *hourly*—I grab my purse and phone and march out the door, sticking my head into David's office long enough to tell him that the only thing Mark will be stapling for him is his goddamn tongue.

"So, I have a favor to ask of you . . ." I set the fancy coffee on the security desk in front of Gus.

"Whipped cream, chocolate sprinkles . . ." His brown eyes twinkle. "Must be a *big* favor."

It's quiet in the lobby for the moment, Ivan somewhere else and no one waiting to gain access to the building. Still, I lean in and drop my voice. "I saw a man in the building yesterday around lunchtime and I need his name."

"A *man*." His thick eyebrows arch curiously and I can almost see the wheels churning in his mind. Gus wasn't impressed with my relationship with David, a truth he's never shared out loud, but he never had to because the displeasure was plastered on his face every time David and I strolled in together.

"An old *friend* from summer camp. I don't know if he works in the building or if he was visiting. Anyway, I was wondering if you could scan your entry log. I'm pretty sure it was him." I hadn't even thought of asking Gus until Christa, ever the quick-thinking one, mentioned checking with security.

Gus's big brown eyes regard me curiously as he lifts the paper coffee cup to his mouth. When he pulls away, there's a whipped cream mustache left that he doesn't immediately wipe away.

I press my lips together to stifle my laugh.

"So what's this *friend's* name?"

"Kyle Miller." Just saying it makes my heart leap.

"Hmm . . . Kyle Miller, from summer camp." Gus finally wipes a napkin across his upper lip. "What does he look like?"

"Uh . . ." I try to reconcile my memories of the seventeen-year-old boy with the man I saw yesterday who, if it *was* Kyle, is now thirty. "About six feet tall, *really* fit, dark brown hair . . . and he has these pretty hazel eyes. Golden, really."

Gus's mouth curves in a thoughtful frown. "And was this Kyle Miller a *good* friend of yours?"

"Yeah." For a while, anyway.

"Decent guy?"

"He was." I feel my cheeks turning pink and I'm mortified. I can't remember the last time just talking about a guy made me blush and it's happening in front of our security guard. I need to get back upstairs and to work, like the executive I am. "So does that name sound at all familiar? Can you maybe check your computer?"

Gus's chair creaks as he leans his girth back in it. "Don't think I need to check the computer."

"No . . . ?" I hold my breath as I search Gus's face, looking for a flicker of recognition.

"Nope. 'Cause I just hired a guy named Kyle with dark hair and pretty golden eyes."

My jaw drops as a wave of shock rushes through me. "You *what?*" *Kyle's going to be a security guard in my building? I'm going to see him every day?*

Gus's deep laugh carries through the cavernous lobby. "Ivan's moving to Chicago, so I needed a new guard. Head office gave me a couple guys to choose from. I liked Kyle best. He's in training now. Starts Monday." Gus frowns. "Except, his last name isn't Miller. It's Stewart."

Wait. *"Stewart?"* My frown matches his. "Maybe it's not the same Kyle, then." As quickly as the shock flowed through me, a wave of disappointment barrels in.

"Only one way to find out." Gus juts his chin somewhere behind me.

I whip my head around so fast, a painful snap explodes in my neck. But I barely notice the burn of heat that follows, focused on the two uniformed men strolling side-by-side toward us. Ivan on the left.

And Kyle *Stewart*.

I inhale sharply.

It *is* my Kyle.

My stomach clenches as I watch him approach, much like it did that first time so many years ago. He's changed so much, and yet there's no mistaking him. He still moves with that casual, unbothered swagger. The punkish two-inch Fauxhawk has been replaced by a more mature and stylish cut, though his thick mane of chestnut-brown hair still has volume on top. He's grown taller, surpassing me by a few inches, even in my heels.

It's his body that has changed the most, filled out by weight and muscle in the best possible ways, his shoulders broad and strong but not bulky, his arms corded with muscle but not in an overdone way. His jaw is now hard and chiseled. His lip ring is gone, but the tattoo on his arm has grown, the ink sprawling over his forearm.

Those beautiful golden irises with rings of green, they haven't changed a bit. And they're locked on me.

"Oh my God! Kyle!" I burst out in a near-squeal, shocking both myself and Ivan, by the wide-eyed look he gives me. I clear my throat and add with a touch more dignity, "Long time, no see."

"Hey." Kyle's chest lifts with a deep breath as he watches me evenly. He doesn't make a move forward. Is it just surprise to see me here that holds him back?

"Seems like you already have a friend in the building," Gus calls out.

"Looks like it . . ." A slight frown pulls his brows together. "Sarah, right?"

"What? Oh, right. Funny." I laugh, waiting for his face to crack with a smile.

The moment drags on.

"Uh . . . Piper," I stammer, my excitement deflating instantly. "From Camp Wawa?" *You've got to be kidding me*. I don't look *that* different. And there's no way I meant *that little* to him that he's forgotten about me.

Is there?

I pause, waiting for a hint of recognition. "You know . . . turtles?" *Really, Piper? Of all the things you could use to try to jog his memory . . .* I peer into those eyes of his again, in search of the youthful, curious spark I remember. And realize that it's missing.

So is the friendliness.

"Right. So . . . you work here?" he finally asks, calm and collected. Sounding every bit the stranger to me.

"Yeah. This is my company. I mean, my dad's company, but I'll be taking over one day." I jab a thumb toward the "Calloway Group" emblem on the wall. Did that sound obnoxious?

Kyle's gaze drifts to the sign. "That's why that name seemed familiar," he murmurs more to himself.

Oh my God. Kyle truly *has* forgotten me.

The disappointment that comes with that realization is staggering. That I could have meant so little to him . . . My chest aches.

Silence lingers as Kyle and I face off against each other, with Gus and Ivan an ever-attentive audience to this painfully awkward reunion.

An elevator dings and voices sound, snapping me out of my trance. "I have a meeting to get to," I lie, feeling my face burn. *Yeah, a meeting with myself, to lick my ego's wounds*. Collecting my tray of coffees from the counter, I clear my voice. "Good luck with the new job. I'm sure you'll like working with Gus." I don't wait for an answer, heading for the bank of elevators, the speedy click of my heels a hollow echo. I jab at the button several times, urging it to open quickly so I can disappear.

Still, I can't help but steal a glance back.

Ivan and Gus are discussing something on a clipboard and Kyle seems to be listening, his back to me. I'll admit, he makes that dowdy security guard uniform look good, as if it were customized specifically for his body.

Suddenly he turns, just enough to give me his profile as he scans the newspaper sitting open on the desk.

I hold my breath, willing him to turn a bit farther, to look my way, to show me he hasn't dismissed me from his thoughts so easily.

But his focus never strays.

When the ding sounds and my elevator doors open, I dive in, suddenly wanting to be anywhere but here.

Chapter 6

THEN

2006, Camp Wawa, Day Two

Avery's perfectly shaped brows spike as I set the can of Coke and ten packs of Fun Dips on the makeshift counter—a barrier of plywood atop stacked wooden crates.

"They're for a bet," I say, as if that explains everything. Well, not the Coke. That's to help me survive the fact that they don't serve coffee to camp counselors.

"I never took those bets with him," she murmurs casually, her crystal-blue eyes on a clipboard of paper as she makes a few quick tick marks, her long red hair pulled to one side in a loose braid. Last night, I didn't notice how milky white her skin is, nor how long and slender her arms are.

"Yeah, well . . . I like Fun Dips." I shrug, because how else should Kyle's potential summer fling for this year respond to Kyle's summer fling from last year in a way that doesn't guarantee an enemy?

"Hope you won," Avery says, finally. She's wasted no time altering her Camp Wawa T-shirt, cutting off the sleeves and collar and cinching the waist with a knot, a style that makes the bulky red cotton thing not quite as unflattering and her waist look that much tinier in comparison to her chest. I noticed a few other counselors at breakfast had done it, too. I guess they didn't get Christa's speech about "the rules."

"I *did* win." I pull out a twenty from my jean shorts pocket, which should *just* cover it, and set it next to the candy. "And you'll want to order more razz apple." There were only nine, so I grabbed a cherry flavor, as well.

"We went through, like, *fifty* cases of Fun Dips because of those two fools last year." She jabs the buttons on the archaic cash register, the printer churning its tally.

Does she still like him? Is this air of indifference a cloak for her feelings? Why did they break up?

Did they sleep together? How many times?

I realize that I'm staring at her now, so I avert my eyes, letting them wander over the canteen's interior again. It's a modified mobile trailer with the wheels replaced by concrete blocks. From the outside, it looks like it belongs in the Louisiana bayou of a Disney cartoon, the typical white vinyl covered by cedar shingles painted a forest green and plastered with at least fifty kitschy metal signs. A loose string of patio lanterns dangles unevenly from the roof's edge. The inside has been gutted of all the traditional mobile home amenities to make room for a perimeter of thin metal shelves that house everything from licorice, candy bars, and chips, to cans of Coke and Dr. Pepper, to bug spray and sunscreen, to tampons and maxi pads. In the corner sits a chest freezer with a laminated sign listing available ice cream flavors. Tubs of dime candy line the front of the cash register, tongs and small brown paper bags at the ready to fill up.

"Does all this stuff actually sell?"

Avery snorts. "You kidding? Those candy shelves will be *empty* and the kids will be broke by Wednesday."

It can't be that hard for a kid to go broke, I note, scanning the prices. Definitely no candy discounts around here.

"Of course, Christa won't let *your* kids do that. She'll have a whole speech about saving money prepared for the first day." Avery laughs, a musical sound. "Who tries to teach money management to a bunch of eight-year-olds at camp? Just let them have fun!"

"That's right. You guys shared a cabin last year."

"Yeah . . ." The cash register drawer pops open with a ding, and she slides my money into the slot. "That was *fun*." Her voices drips with sarcasm.

I match it. "Well, I'm the lucky winner this year. Any tips on how to deal with her?"

"Pretend she's not there." She rolls her eyes, parroting Christa with, " 'You need to do' this, 'you need to do' that."

I laugh. Avery seems friendly enough toward me, even if it's at Christa's expense.

"*Seriously*. It's brutal. Just wait 'til you try to get out after the kids are asleep. She threatened to go to Darian because I didn't come back until, like, four one night." Avery shakes her head. "So I lost it on her. She stayed out of my way after that."

I frown. "So, we *are* allowed to leave our cabins at night?" Darian had alluded to counselors "unwinding" after a day of refereeing, but I forgot to ask Ashley.

Avery's eyebrows arch in surprise. "Wow. You *really* haven't been to camp before."

"Not really. I . . . no." There's no point trying to describe White Pine.

"Some of the counselors go out after the kids are asleep, to hang out for a bit. It's no big deal. There's always someone around if a kid wakes up. That's the one good thing about bunking with Christa—she always stays back. Which is great because *nobody* likes her anyway." Avery stuffs my purchase into a brown paper bag just as the air-conditioning unit mounted in the far window kicks in. A fresh wave of cool air blows into the shop, ruffling the dusty and tattered floral window valance.

It feels heavenly. “So, how do you get a job in here, anyway?” I don’t remember *canteen* being on the activities sheet.

“Seniority. It can get boring, but when it’s ninety-five degrees out and you’re not in the lake, you want to be in here.” Avery reaches behind her to grab a can of root beer. She takes a long draw from her straw as she eyes me, as if sizing me up. “Talk to Darian. There’s four of us taking turns in here, but she has a backup list. She might be willing to put you on it.” She hesitates. “Or, I could mention it to her when I see her next.”

“That’d be . . . great. Thanks.” I frown as I wonder why she’s being so nice to me, but quickly decide that it’s better than the alternative, whatever her motives may be. I grab my paper bag. “Enjoy the cool air. I’ll just be out there, *dying* in my own sweat.” I head for the door, my stomach beginning to flutter with anxious nerves at the thought of tracking down Kyle.

I’ve only seen him briefly since last night. The counselor meet ’n’ greet shut down promptly at nine forty-five. Counselors had just enough time to get back to their cabins and settle in, Darian’s curfew warning heeded. I crawled into my top bunk and expected to spend the night memorizing the knots in the pine boards above my head while obsessing over every little gesture, glance, and word exchanged between me and Kyle, but somehow drifted off to the rhythm of Christa's soft snores.

Kyle didn't make his grand appearance until the end of breakfast, sauntering in just long enough to throw a casual smile my way. Then he scooped up a bagel and orange juice, and strolled off with Eric at his side.

I haven't seen him since and, even with that quick but obvious flirtation, I can't help but wonder if he's now avoiding me, if maybe he's already lost interest.

The very thought threatens to sink my spirits.

"Hey!"

I glance back over my shoulder to find Avery grinning mischievously, showing off her perfectly straight, white teeth. "I'll bet Christa told you that you're not allowed to cut your T-shirt?"

"Um . . ." My wary eyes flitter between her face and the enormous silver blades of the scissors as she rounds the counter.

She laughs. "You look like you're worried that I'm going to stab you."

"Well . . . are you?" I ask pointedly.

"Relax. I'm not interested in Kyle anymore."

I feel my shoulders sink with relief and a sheepish smile form. At least I wasn't the only one sensing that awkwardness.

"Don't move," she murmurs, slipping her cool fingers beneath the collar of my T-shirt to pull the cotton away. She begins snipping.

I hesitate. "So, what happened with you and Kyle anyway?" What can she tell me about him that I haven't heard yet?

Her eyes flicker to me a moment. "Nothing really . . . Summer ended. He went back home; I started college. He's too young for me, anyway. It was fun, but that's all you'll get from Kyle. *Fun*."

"So he's a player?" My stomach turns queasy.

"No. Not that. At least, he wasn't with me." She tosses the bound cotton collar to the trash can and sets to work on my left sleeve. "He just won't let you get too close." She smiles secretly, snipping off my right sleeve. "But you'll have *lots* of fun. There." She steps back to admire her work. "Just tie the waist up and you might not die."

"Thanks," I murmur. "See you later." I push through the canteen's rickety door and am immediately hit with a blast of mid-morning heat.

Christa is loitering nearby, intently studying her clipboard.

I stifle my groan to offer, "Hey." *Great. Here we go . . .*

Her chest puffs out with a deep breath. "Hi, Piper." Lifting her chin, she strolls into the shop, offering me a tight-lipped smile as she passes, making no note of my deviant attire.

I frown curiously.

Until I hear her say, "I'm here to collect your count sheets." The air-conditioning unit has switched off for the moment, allowing her voice to carry clearly through the thin walls and poorly sealed window.

A sinking feeling hits me as I realize that Christa must have been outside when we were talking about her.

Must have heard the less-than-kind words directed toward her.

I quickly trudge off, guilt swarming my conscience.

“Can I drive on the way back?” I grip the bar as we speed along the narrow gravel path, the golf cart bumping and jolting as Ashley manages to hit every pothole so far, and there aren’t that many to avoid.

“Didn’t you *just* get your license?”

“I’ve had mine longer than you’ve had yours!” It’s not a wonder she failed the driving test three times before finally passing just two weeks ago, something she admitted to with a sheepish grin as she jumped into the driver’s seat.

“Fine. We’ll switch when we get to—ahh!” She jams on the brake just as Eric jumps out from behind a thick crop of bush. “Are you crazy? I could have hit you!” she shrieks, her face flushing instantly.

“Ahoy, fair maidens!” he booms, stalking forward in an exaggerated stiff gait, waving a stick in the air. “I seek you now by order of . . .”

He falters. "Maximus Decimus Meridius to commandeer said fine vessel hence forth."

Ashley rolls her eyes. "We don't have time for this." She gestures at the little trailer attached to our hitch, stocked with Tupperware bins full of plastic trash bags, toilet paper, hand soap, and flashlights. We've been tasked with stocking the girls' cabins and shower room before the campers begin arriving.

"Forthwith!" He takes a step forward. "Tout suite!"

I bite my tongue against the urge to correct him, as Madame Monroe's squeaky voice fills my head. My French teacher drilled the proper phrase into our heads by yelling "Tout de suite!" at the beginning of every class to rush us to our seats.

Meanwhile, Ashley's nose crinkles with confusion. "What?"

Eric tosses the stick to the ground and reaches in to scoop Ashley from her seat. As tall as she is, he still manages to throw her over his shoulder with surprising ease.

"Put me down, Eric!" she squeals, but she's giggling as she thumps her fists against his back.

Kyle suddenly appears from behind another thicket.

"Don't you *dare* . . ." I begin, my hands in the air to block him from any attempt to pull me off. Meanwhile, my heart is leaping in my chest with the thought of his hands on me.

But he slides into the driver's seat instead, reaching back to smoothly unfasten the hitch, releasing the wagon. "Hark! A captive!" he yells, and then throws the cart into forward. The electric engine whirls as we speed away, leaving Eric and Ashley behind with the trailer of supplies.

"What are you doing?" I say with a laugh. "We have to deliver those!"

He glances at his wristwatch, and I can tell that it's all for show. "You've got *tons* of time. Plus it's right there." He nods toward the girls' cabins as we pass the turnoff.

"Where are you taking me?"

"For a tour. Why? You worried?"

"About getting fired on my first day? Kind of."

He chuckles, shaking his head. "You're not gonna get fired. And, don't worry, Eric and Ashley will be done in no time."

"But if Christa sees that we're not—"

"Christa's busy driving people crazy in the rec center." Suddenly we're whipping around a bend in the path and I'm squealing with a mix of glee and fear, my body pressing against Kyle's.

"You're going to roll us!" I warn.

"These things don't roll. Trust me, I'm an expert."

"My brother broke his arm rolling one of these." Rhett and his buddies—drunk—decided to take a shortcut down a steep hill at the thirteenth hole and ended up putting the cart into the country club's duck pond. He's lucky it wasn't worse, though the tongue-lashing and financial penalties my father laid on him more than made up for the lack of serious injuries.

"Well, I'm a better driver than your brother." We wind around another bend and this time, instead of continuing along the path, Kyle veers off onto a wooded one.

"Seriously. Where are we going?"

He settles back into his seat, gripping the steering wheel casually with one hand, his lips curled up in a secretive smile.

I try to match his calm ease; meanwhile inside, my nerves are going haywire. Wherever he's taking me, it's away from the rest of the campground.

I train my gaze on the trees as the forest grows denser and the trail grows narrow. It stops altogether in front of a bramble of bushes and a sign that marks Camp Wawa's property line. Beyond it is a "No Trespassing" sign, indicating government land. Kyle shuts the cart off, hops out, and begins walking ahead. He pauses just long enough to look at me and call out, "What are you doing?"

"Uh . . . following you, I guess?" I climb off my seat. On impulse, I grab the brown candy bag from the storage container and then begin trailing him up a steep footpath, wincing as the evergreen branches scratch at my bare legs.

We finally break through the dense bush and are suddenly out into the open.

"Wow," I murmur, shielding my eyes from the blinding sun as I take in the vast expanse of blue water and trees below. We're on the edge of a rocky cliff. "This lake is bigger than I thought." From this vantage spot, it looks like it might go on forever.

"It has a lot of little bays." Kyle pulls a pack of Marlboros from his pocket and tosses it on the ground nearby.

He smokes? I'm not sure how I feel about that.

His phone, wallet, and sunglasses follow closely after. "If you can get in the boat on waterskiing day, you should do it. You'll get to see more of it." He kicks off his running shoes and socks.

"What are you doing?" I ask warily.

Reaching over his head, he peels off his Camp Wawa T-shirt, giving me a good, long look at his lean torso, cut with muscle and decorated with swirls of ink over the ball of his shoulder and along one side of his collarbone. "It's hot out."

I try not to stare at the way his board shorts hang off his hips, but I fail miserably.

And then Kyle takes a running leap over the cliff.

I gasp and rush for the edge just as he breaks through the water's surface, his body disappearing into the murky darkness with a small splash. He surfaces a moment later, his groan of content loud. "Oh, yeah. Damn, that felt good!"

"You're insane!" I shriek, my blood pounding in my ears.

He laughs and then swims out, pulling himself onto his back to show off his bare chest. He's at ease in the water, as if he's been swimming for years. "Come in!"

"No way!"

"Why not?"

"Because!" I gesture a hand out, as if that's answer enough. "How high is this, anyway?"

"It's only thirty feet."

Only. "There's rocks everywhere!"

"It's clear. I've jumped off it a hundred times. *Five* hundred times." His arms cut through the water as he treads, watching me steadily. "Oh. I get it. You're *scared*." The taunting is unmistakable.

"I am not," I scoff, though the height *is* daunting.

"Prove it."

"But . . . I don't have a bathing suit."

"Weak," he throws back, and I can see the smug smile all the way from up here.

Is this a test? Did Avery jump off this cliff with him?

It *did* look like fun. And I'm not afraid of heights. "No, what's weak is you trying to get me out of my clothes like this," I retort, matching his arrogance.

"I'd never do that. I swear." He pauses, treading water to lift a hand in the air, giving me a Boy Scout salute.

I roll my eyes at him, even though I doubt he can see it.

"Just jump in with your clothes on. You can change on the way back. It's not like you don't have a thousand camp T-shirts, anyway."

More like six, but his point is fair.

"Come on. I know you want to." He swims farther back, to give me space.

The water *does* look enticing and it's hot out.

And I'm feeling a rush of adrenaline with the thought of doing it.

And Kyle is waiting for me at the bottom.

"Oh my God, I can't believe I'm doing this," I mutter, setting my things next to Kyle's and kicking off my shoes. "You're *sure* there aren't any rocks?"

"Positive. Just take a run at it."

I take a deep breath and, before I can chicken out, I dart forward and leap.

I vaguely hear Kyle's cheer over my scream as I sail through the air, my stomach in my throat as I plummet, to plunge into the dark waters feet-first. It's shockingly cold the second the water envelops my body, but by the time I emerge, it's a refreshing cool against my skin, a balm for the summer heat and humidity.

I laugh, wiping drops from my eyes, exhilaration moving in where fear lived a moment before. I look back at the sheer wall of jagged rock looming over us. "I can't believe I just did that. Oh my God. That was *amazing!*"

"Told you so." Kyle smiles wide, his dazzling eyes flashing with amusement as he wades over to me. He's so close that our knees bump with each pedal of our legs, trying to stay afloat.

So close that he could easily kiss me, if he wanted to.

Does he want to?

I swallow the rise of nerves in my throat. Suddenly the thirty-foot drop pales in comparison to the bravery I'd need to summon to lean in, to press my lips against his.

"Did that hurt?" I ask, pretending that the silver ring had my attention all this time.

"Nah." His tongue darts out to flick at it and I feel my own lips parting. He's so close now, I can feel his breath caressing my skin.

"So, how do we get back up there?"

He abruptly shifts and begins swimming away. "This way."

My disappointment swells as I trail him, wishing I hadn't asked.

With easy, strong strokes, he cuts through the water and around a bend on the left, to a low platform of rock. His muscles tense and glisten as he hoists himself out, before offering his hand to help me pull myself up. My clothes hang heavily from my body as we pick our way around boulders and bushes, along a weedy, narrow path that leads up the steep hill. Kyle takes my hand at the halfway point where it's especially treacherous, his wet fingers wrapped firmly around mine to help me climb.

My thigh muscles are burning by the time we reach the top but I barely notice, enthralled by his touch, not wanting to lose it. I groan when he lets go, and duck to hide my embarrassment at the reaction while I wring out the cotton of my T-shirt. "I'm soaked."

"Sun's hot. You'll dry off fast out here." Settling onto the rock, Kyle reaches for his pack of Marlboros and slides a cigarette into his mouth. He notices me watching him. "You don't mind, do you?" he asks, his lips already hugging a cigarette, lighter paused midair to ignite.

I shrug. "Nah, it's cool." I sit down next to him.

He holds the pack out for me, but I wave it away.

He lights up and in moments, the acrid smell of smoke is filling my nostrils. Oddly enough, it's not bothering me as it normally does, and I find myself content to sit next to a shirtless Kyle while he puffs away quietly, his gaze drifting over the blue skies and the majestic lake.

So far I'm enjoying Camp Wawa a hundred times more than I imagined I would, this time yesterday. It might have something to do with my company, but I haven't ached for Europe once since I stepped out of my mom's car. "You said you come here a lot?"

He releases a ring-shaped cloud of smoke and watches it sail upward. "Still remember the first time I jumped. I was nine, and I tagged along with some older kids. I stood on the edge of that cliff for almost an hour, my knees shaking." He pauses, as if recalling that very moment, and then a soft chuckle escapes. "Thought I was gonna piss my pants on the way down. And when I did it, and looked back at that rock wall, I was *so* sure it was the bravest thing I'd ever do in my entire life. After that, I couldn't stop." He absently rubs a finger across the tattoo on his wrist. "It's the first thing I did when I got here last year. And I've been waiting all year to do it again. "

It dawns on me then. "Those coordinates are for this spot, aren't they?"

He winces against the sun's glare as he peers at me. "Look at you. You're kind of smart, aren't you?"

I shrug, feeling my cheeks flush. "Sometimes."

His stomach muscles tense as he eases himself back, one arm resting under his head, the other free to hold his cigarette to his lips. His eyes are closed against the sun's brightness, allowing my gaze free range over his lean body, already dry and coated in a thin sheen of sweat. He doesn't have the padding of muscles that Trevor had, but there were rumors that Trevor had been doping.

"What are you thinking about?" he asks suddenly.

I avert my gaze from his smooth chest to the sparse blades of grass between the rocky surface and think fast. "That robbery," I blurt out. "What was it like?"

It's a moment before he answers. "Crazy."

"But, like . . ." I fumble through the questions now churning in my head. "Where were you? A convenience store or someone's house?"

"A bank."

I feel my eyebrows pop. "Seriously? People still rob banks?" I mutter in disbelief, more to myself.

"The stupid ones do."

Stupid ones with a gun, apparently. "So, did the police catch them?"

"Oh, yeah. They caught 'em all right. They'll be going away for a long time."

"Were you scared? Did you think you were going to get shot? I mean . . . *I'd* be terrified."

His tongue flicks at his lip ring. "More in shock than anything."

"What did your parents say about it?"

"My parents?" He pauses, as if needing to think through his answer. "They were glad I was okay."

"No shit. Mine would lose their minds. Never let me out of their sight again."

"Understandable." He takes a drag off his cigarette.

And my eyes draw over the various ink on his body. "They're okay with you getting tattoos? Your parents, I mean."

"Why wouldn't they be?"

"I don't know." I shrug. " 'Cause you're only seventeen?"

"Ashley was pretty thorough." He smirks. "What else does she have on me?"

My face begins to burn. "Not much. Just that you came here when you were younger but then suddenly stopped. You and Avery were together last summer . . . and every girl here wants you."

"Not *every* girl," he murmurs after a moment. "Christa doesn't. Unless she has a weird way of showing it."

"Yeah, I don't think she likes you."

"So then, every girl except Christa."

I laugh. "Wow! Aren't *we* cocky."

He smiles through a puff. "Hey, *you* said it."

I let my gaze drift over the landscape as I absorb the hum of motorboats and nearby birds chirping. "I can see why this is your favorite place."

"You want to jump again?"

A rush of adrenaline spikes through my body at just the suggestion. With him, a hundred times over, until my throat is hoarse from screaming and my legs wobble from the climb back up. But

I'm not getting paid to go cliff diving and gawk at Kyle. "What time is it?"

He shrugs, not making a move for his watch or his phone.

"Don't you think we should get back soon? I mean, before anyone notices that we're missing?" I'll be surprised if they didn't hear my scream as it is.

"Do you always worry so much?"

"I'm *not* worried," I lie, because I'm betting Kyle isn't the type of guy who would be attracted to a worrier.

"Why're you here, anyway?" he asks around a mouthful of smoke, smoothly diverting the topic.

Catching me off-guard. "Uh . . . I needed a summer job?"

"Your mother dropped you off in a brand-new, fully loaded Nine-Eleven, Piper. Something tells me money is your family's *last* problem." And, by the tone in his voice, that's somehow a strike against me.

There's no point denying it. "Yeah, my family has *some* money." *A lot of money.* More than Kyle can possibly imagine, I'm guessing. I hear the defensiveness creeping into my voice.

So must Kyle, because he holds a hand up in surrender, murmuring, "Relax. I'm just trying to figure you out, is all. You seem out of your element here."

"Like I said last night, my mom went here when

she was growing up and she really wanted me to come for a summer." After a moment, I add, "And she thinks it'll look good on my college applications."

Kyle's lips twist in thought, seemingly pondering that. "Fair enough."

I wait for him to ask me who my father is, what my parents do that has made us wealthy, but he doesn't. I wonder if it's because he doesn't want to know, or doesn't care.

"So, why'd *you* come?" I finally ask.

"Because I actually *need* a summer job and this place beats flipping burgers at Johnny B's any day of the week. Plus, Eric is basically my best friend and everyone's pretty cool, for the most part anyway. The kids are fun." He takes another long drag, his mouth working around the *O*'s. He smiles slyly. "I had the best summer of my life last year."

"Because of Avery?" I dare ask in a nonchalant tone, though I'm dying to get his take, now that she offered me hers.

He snorts as he studies the end of his cigarette. "Because of *everything*. But Avery and I had fun, yeah."

That stir of jealousy sparks in my gut. I struggle to push it aside. "That's what she said."

"You two were talking about me?" There's no mistaking the surprise in his voice.

"I didn't bring it up. I swear."

"What'd she say?"

"Exactly what you just did: that you two had a lot of *fun*."

"Anything else?"

I open my mouth, intent on saying "Nothing," but I decide I'd rather go with the truth. "That you don't let people get too close." I watch him carefully for his reaction.

He seems to consider that. "I guess she's right, I don't. Not her, anyway. I knew right away that it wasn't gonna last past the summer, so I made sure to keep it easy. You know, so no one got hurt." He pauses. "It doesn't bother me at all if she ends up with someone else this year. I haven't thought much about her, to be honest."

What about *this?* Me? Has he already dismissed me as this year's summer fling? And will I be okay with that? I want to ask, but I bite my tongue.

His crooked smile tells me he somehow knows what I'm thinking anyway.

"This summer will be even better," I dare say.

"Oh yeah?" He squints against the sun as he studies my face. "And why's that?"

"Because *I'm* here."

He chuckles. "Now who's being cocky?" Taking one last haul off his cigarette, he butts it out on the stone and then sits up. He reaches for his shoes, a pair of suede Adidas that are literally falling apart—the seam on one toe broken, the ends of the laces frayed, the dark gray material severely stained.

"Can't let go of them, huh?" I tease.

"They're comfortable," he murmurs, but I note how his cheeks flush.

Did I just embarrass the guy I'm madly crushing on? *Way to go, Piper.*

I quickly backpedal. "I have a pair of tennis shoes like that. They're my lucky ones. I haven't lost a tennis match in them, like, *ever*."

His gaze is still on his grayed laces, but I see the corners of his mouth pull, in a tiny smile. A smile that says he knows I'm lying, punctuated by his quick glance at my pristine teal Nikes, bought just last week, along with two more pairs to choose from throughout the summer.

"We should probably get back." He yanks his T-shirt over his head.

As anxious as I am about getting caught shirking responsibility, I'm not ready to leave. "Not so fast." I reach for the brown paper bag and toss it to him.

He cringes. "I knew you had these."

"No, you didn't."

"Yeah, I did. I saw you come out of the canteen with them."

I frown. "Where were you?"

"Around . . ." He tips his head to gaze at me, his eyes twinkling playfully. "You're *really* gonna make me do this?"

"A bet's a bet."

With a groan, he dumps the packs out on his lap, holding up the cherry flavor with a scowl. "They only had nine razz apples."

He tosses it onto my lap. "I'm allergic to cherry."

"Really?" I frown. "But I doubt there's actual cherry in it."

"You willing to find out up here?" He gestures at our secluded spot, high up on the rock. "Because I'm anaphylactic."

"*Oh*. No. Definitely not." I shake my head for emphasis. "Let's prorate it, though. You've gotta do nine in . . . one minute, forty-eight seconds."

"You're taking this to a whole new level." Chuckling, he tears open the tops of the pouches, holding them upright between his thighs in a line. Setting the timer on his watch, he hands it to me, our fingers sliding across each other in the process, sending my blood racing through my veins.

I clear my throat to help calm myself. "Ready?"

"No."

"And . . . Go!" I press the tiny red button and the numbers begin churning on the screen.

With a curse, he grabs the first open pack and, tipping his head back, he dumps the powder into his mouth. His face twists horribly against the tartness. "Oh, God . . . I forgot . . . how sour these are!" he manages between swallows and cringes.

I howl with laughter. "One down, eight to go!"

He fires a glare my way, tosses the empty pack aside, and collects another one. "Just you wait—I'm gonna get you back for this."

I'm in tears by the time he finishes the last pack, just as the beep of his watch sounds. "I can't believe you actually did it!"

He rubs at his bottom lip with his thumb, wiping away at some residual powder. "I thought I was going to puke for a minute. My mouth hurts." He stretches his tongue out and waggles it around, showing off his green-tinged candy-coated taste buds, making me laugh harder. "Shut up and eat yours," he mutters through a smile, as he begins collecting the tossed packs.

"I haven't had one of these in forever." I wet the candy stick in my mouth before dipping it into the powder, and then pop it back into my mouth. My cheeks pucker, the cherry tart on my tongue.

I glance up to find Kyle's gaze locked on my mouth. "So *that's* what those are for," he murmurs, his expression contemplative, his lips parted. It's the same look he had earlier, when we were in the water.

When I was sure he wanted to kiss me.

I desperately *want* him to.

With a small, playful smile, I scoop more powder on my stick and suck it off, more slowly this time, repeating the steps several times.

Kyle dips his head. He's trying not to laugh.

"What?" I ask, and a touch of apprehension stirs.

"Nothing. It's just . . . your mouth, it's stained red."

"No it's not." I press my lips together.

He bursts out laughing. "Yeah. Like, *all* over."

Heat floods my cheeks as I silently curse, tossing the stick into the pack. Here I am, trying to seduce him, and now I look like a four-year-old who got into her mother's lipstick. "Yeah, well, your tongue is green." I furiously rub my palm against my lips, trying in vain to wipe the color off.

"Stop! Stop . . ." He's still laughing as he grabs hold of my hand and pulls it away, lacing my fingers within his. His eyes are twinkling with mischief as they settle on my mouth. "Actually, I like the red on you. Like, *really* like it." He leans in a touch but then hesitates.

I can't take it anymore.

I close the distance and press my mouth against his. Only for a second, long enough to feel the softness of his lips and the cold metal of his lip ring, and to taste the sour apple candy powder.

And then I remember.

I break free with a gasp, my heart rate spiking. "Oh my God! I forgot! I'm so sorry, I wasn't thinking! What do we do?"

He frowns with confusion. "About what?"

"Your allergy!" How far is the walk to the golf cart? Can we make it in time?

"*Oh*. That." He grins. "Yeah. I lied about that."

"What?"

He shrugs. "I *hate* the cherry flavor."

Relief bowls over me, even as I smack his chest. "Kyle! You don't joke about stuff like that!"

"I'm definitely regretting it *now*." His gaze drops to my mouth, lingering for a moment before he finally leans in.

The last kiss was fast and fleeting, driven by my impulsiveness. This one, though, is all Kyle. It's slow and intentional, his lips brushing over mine once, twice . . . before settling against them in a playful dance of soft presses and the occasional graze of his tongue. Only his tip, though, and only against my lips, moving fast enough that I barely catch it with my own. Each time that I do, I sense Kyle smiling.

Trevor *never* kissed me like this. He always dove right in—with passionate lips and busy hands. I thought he was a good kisser. I thought that was what I liked.

But *this* . . .

This is more like a game. Kyle is teasing me.

And I am devouring every second of it.

My breathing turns shallow as I match his tempo, my fists balled in my lap, heat beginning to pulse through my limbs and into my core. My fingers reach for his lap, but I hold them back, curious to see what he does next.

But he just keeps going with this torturous, slow pace for minutes that feel like hours, until he finally breaks free.

"Was the cherry that bad?" I whisper, my head swimming in a heady fog.

His golden eyes burn with heat as he smiles at me. "Actually, I think you've made me a huge fan of all things cherry." With a deep—shaky, I note—exhale, he eases himself off the rock and holds out his hand. "Come on. Don't want to get you into trouble on your first day."

Chapter 7

NOW

"How was it?" Christa settles onto the bar stool beside me, a stack of paperwork within her grasp.

"*Delectable,* as usual." I've never had a bad meal at Christa's restaurant, and I've eaten here enough times that odds say I should have had at least one overcooked steak or crusty pasta. I shove aside my dirty dishes, the small pool of red meat juices unappealing now that my stomach is stretching the seams of my dress. "You done for the night?"

"Just need to finalize this kitchen order, if I can translate Ian's notes." She shakes her head as her finger drags along the margin. "The man is forty-eight years old. It's time he learned how to spell. I mean, seriously . . . green *peepers? Baycan?*"

I lean over to read off the supply list that the kitchen manager pulled together. "Whatever you do, don't forget to order the *chivs* and *sore kreem*. Can't have the baked potato without the *chivs* and *sore kreem*."

She sighs, accepting the club soda that Sam the bartender swoops in to set in front of her. "I gave two of my managers the weekend off and now I have no bar manager, so I'm basically chained to this place. I may as well sleep here." She says that like it's a punishment, but I know Christa—bossing people around is the fuel to her engine.

"I guess I have the condo to myself, then." Ashley took the five o'clock train to her parents', where she'll be staying until Sunday.

"Can you feed Elton his dinner tomorrow?"

"If he's nice to me." I sniff.

"Can you feed him *anyway?*"

"Fine."

"He won't bother you."

"No, you're right. He'll pretend I don't exist." That cat has mastered the art of snubbing in a way few humans can match.

"So? What happened today to make you show up here looking like your dog got hit by a car?"

I slide my empty wineglass forward and Sam fills it wordlessly, with an extra heavy hand. I guess my dour face says I need it. I take a greedy gulp, feeding the warm buzz that's finally beginning to temper my mood. "Besides my dad telling me that I need to *earn* Tripp the Prick's respect?"

Her face twists with disgust. "The guy's a misogynist. By definition, he's incapable of respecting a woman. How are you supposed to do that?"

"Well, probably *not* by telling him to shove his golf stick up his ass," I mutter. The dick called at twelve fifteen—as predicted—and was momentarily speechless when I interrupted my lunch meeting at The Port Room to answer the call.

It started out well enough. He declared confidently that all necessary permit approvals for the Marquee would be in our hands by Monday, latest. I swallowed my pride and commended him for a job well done, and then requested that he send me the revised timelines and budgets by Monday, noon. That's when he had the nerve to flat-out refuse to request that amount of work of *his* team on a Friday afternoon, especially when the work would no doubt bleed into the summer weekend. Oddly enough, for a man who doesn't care to win *my* approval, he certainly cares about theirs.

So I snapped, in the most unprofessional way.

Frankly, it's nothing my father wouldn't have demanded, and probably not in terms any nicer, but for some reason I feel like I'm going to hear about it.

"He deserved it. Your dad should fire him." Christa clinks her glass against mine. "What about Kyle Miller?" Her eyebrows rise in question. "Did you have a chance to talk to security about him?"

I take a big mouthful. "Kyle *is* security. And he's now Kyle Stewart."

Christa's blue eyes are bulging by the time I'm done explaining today's run-in.

"*Kyle* is in security?" she says, her voice dripping with disbelief. "Do they give those guards guns?"

"No."

"Tasers?"

"No."

"I guess he can't cause too many problems, then," she murmurs with grim satisfaction.

"Can we please focus on how he didn't even remember *my name?*" Even admitting it to Christa is embarrassing. "I mean, I could maybe understand Penny or Pepper. But *Sarah?*"

She shrugs through a sip of her drink. "He was, like, sixteen."

"Seventeen."

"Fine. Seventeen. And he's a guy. And it was one summer, thirteen *years* ago," she rationalizes. "It happens."

I give her a flat look.

"Fine. You're right. Kyle should at the very least remember your name," she concedes reluctantly. "I was just trying to make you feel better."

"Exactly. So then it's impossible, isn't it? That he'd forget me completely?"

Because, even after all these years, with college and boyfriends, and my career and my engagement to David, Kyle Miller has always been a sliver in my heart, a shadow in my thoughts. A lingering "what if" that I have never been able to truly shake.

"I'd say so, given you guys got *fired* from Wawa together," Christa mutters. "Plus that whole thing with Eric ending up in the hospital."

"Exactly! So . . . *Sarah?*"

"I don't know. Maybe he got into drugs. Like, heavy stuff. Maybe he's a raging crack addict," Christa offers through a draw of her soda.

I let out a derisive snort. "Yeah, I don't think so." I just don't see Kyle—the version I knew, anyway—touching that stuff.

"Okay, fine. Head injury?"

"That made him lose his memory of that *entire* summer? It'd have to be a serious head injury. I don't think so. He seemed . . . perfect."

I feel Christa's hawkish gaze on me as I sip my wine and mull over the possibilities.

"So what if he doesn't remember you?" she finally says. "You were always too good for him. You're smart and beautiful and ambitious. Your family is corporate royalty. You're up *here*." Her arm stretches above us, as high as she can go. "He's down here." She grinds her toe into the hardwood floor, like she's squashing a bug. "He knew it back then, too. And now look at you both. You're going to be running the world one day and he's basically a mall cop."

I roll my eyes. "That doesn't mean we can't be friends."

"But that's my point! Why would you *want* to be? He disappeared and never called you! Why give that jerk another second's thought?" Her face twists with a look of disgust at the very idea.

"I don't know. Maybe I need closure?" I toy with the cocktail list, unable to summon the same level of anger. "At least he seems to have turned out okay. He has a decent job."

"Yeah, I'm guessing he didn't include Wawa as a referral." Christa snorts derisively, then gives me a knowing look. "And I'm not surprised he changed his last name."

"That's why I could never find him."

"I don't know why you kept looking," she mutters under her breath, ticking away at lines on her order chart.

I sigh. I know she's just trying to make me feel better, in her own way. But Christa always did judge Kyle too harshly.

I'm still hung up on the disappointing possibility that I could have been so forgettable to a guy who once upon a time meant so much to me. "Maybe he was playing one of his elaborate Kyle jokes. You know how he is. Or *was,* back then." How much has he changed in thirteen years, aside from his name?

"Or maybe he was pretending because he doesn't *want* to remember you," Christa says, in typical blunt, no-nonsense fashion.

"Or maybe he doesn't want to remember me," I echo, a thought that had already been lingering in the recesses of my mind but I didn't want to give voice to. I tip my head back and pour half the glass of my red wine down my throat, hoping it might help me swallow that bitter pill.

"You're in early today." David appears out of nowhere to charge through our building's exterior door. He holds it open for me.

I mutter my thanks, my eyes darting to the security desk, my stomach tense with nerves. Gus is there, wearing his usual wide smile, greeting employees as they swipe their badges across the pad. The seat next to him is vacant.

It's Monday. He did say Kyle was starting today, didn't he?

Unless Kyle walked out of here on Friday with no intention of ever coming back after discovering that I work here.

"Who are you trying to impress?" David asks.

"What?"

He shrugs. "You just look more done up than usual."

"I've worn this a thousand times." My mother brought the figure-hugging blue gingham pencil dress back from Paris a few years ago from a designer's trunk show. It's one of my favorites, not that David would remember that.

"Not the dress. The lipstick." He smirks. "You always wore that cherry-red lipstick when you were trying to get my attention."

"I did not," I deny. "What are *you* doing here,

anyway?" He's not usually in the office until just before nine.

"Had to get out of there before my date woke up. I forgot what a bad idea it is to bring them back to *my* place."

It's the first time David has admitted to sleeping with another woman since our breakup. I can't tell if he's lying, trying to get a jealous rise out of me. If he is, he's going to be disappointed, because all I feel is relief. "I hope she steals everything."

"Don't be catty. It's unbecoming," he murmurs smugly.

I catch the curious glances that Calloway employees are casting our way as we pass. David and I used to start our days strolling in together like this, albeit a touch later. By noon, half the company will assume we've reconciled. "Don't walk so close to me," I warn, edging away.

"Why?"

"I don't want anyone to think we're back together."

He sighs with exasperation. "Oh, for fuck's sake, Piper. I'll see you upstairs."

Gus nods politely as David speeds through the security gate with barely a glance, and then turns his big brown eyes to me. They're full of wariness, the question in them unmistakable. "Good morning, Miss Calloway. You look especially lovely today."

"Thanks." Maybe the cherry-red lipstick *was* too punchy for a Monday morning, especially when I rarely wear anything beyond a light layer of gloss.

"And how was your weekend?"

"Quiet. I spent it *alone*." Just me and Elton, who afforded me nothing more than a cross-eyed glare when I filled his bowl with overpriced canned cat food.

Gus seems to get my hidden meaning—that it was *not* spent making up with David—because I catch the soft sigh of relief that escapes him. "Good. Everyone needs a weekend to themselves every once in a while."

"So . . ." My stomach does an anxious flip as I steal a glance at the empty seat. There's a half-finished cup of coffee sitting on the desk in front of it, so Kyle *must* be here. But, after my first humiliating encounter with him, I don't want to let on that I care one way or another, even to Gus. "Do you miss Ivan yet?"

"It's an adjustment, that's for sure." Gus smiles warmly. "But people come and they go all the time. As old as I am, I've gotten used to it by now. I figure I'll just be thankful for the precious time I get with them."

Unless they were your first love and they fell off the face of the earth, only to resurface thirteen years later and not remember you at all.

Gus looks up at me expectantly, and suddenly

I feel foolish for standing here, chatting him up, though it's something I do every Monday morning. This time, however, I have an ulterior motive, and I'm afraid he knows it.

"I'll see you later." I wave my pass over the pad, wait for the light to turn green, and push past the metal arm.

"Have a good day, Miss Calloway," he offers as I stroll toward the bank of elevators, the click of my heels echoing through the cavernous atrium. I absently paw at the elevator button, my gaze on my phone screen, distracting myself from my disappointment with messages. The doors open and I step forward.

And plow into a solid body.

"Excuse me. I assumed it was empt—" My words cut off as I peer up into familiar eyes. "Oh . . . hey."

A few beats pass before Kyle responds with a soft "Hey."

"I . . . my phone. I wasn't paying attention," I admit in a stammer, before clearing my throat.

His gaze flickers downward to linger on my mouth for a moment, before flitting back to meet my eyes.

That's when I see it. The smallest upturn of his lips, the tiniest knowing smile.

It's just for a second. It's just long enough.

Actually, I like the red on you. Like, really *like it.*

I take a deep breath, as an odd mix of vindication and sorrow washes through me.

"It's good to see you again, Kyle."

"Good to see you, too, Piper," he finally offers, his jaw tensing as he peers down at me, though his eyes show a hint of softness that wasn't there before.

"Not Sarah?" I keep my voice light, casual, as if Friday's slight didn't leave a deep wound, didn't keep my mind spinning all weekend long.

The tip of his tongue catches the corner of his mouth, where nothing but a faint scar from his lip ring remains. "Yeah. I'm . . . That was . . . Sorry about that."

"How could you forget my name?" This time, I can't hide the hurt.

His lips twist with thought, as if considering how to answer. "I didn't," he finally admits, his gaze landing on his black boots. "I was surprised and unprepared. I was . . . a jerk."

"Yeah. You were." And the lobby at seven thirty on Monday morning is not the place to demand a better explanation.

His broad chest lifts with a deep sigh. "So, how are you?" His voice remains cool. Does he really want to know? Or is this just a formality?

I push aside that thought. "I'm good. *Great,* actually."

"Yeah, seems like it." I detect a sardonic flavor

in his tone as his hazel eyes roam the atrium's architecture.

"And you? You seem to be doing well." My gaze drifts over his uniform.

"Can't complain. Rikell's a decent company. I get benefits and holidays. You know, that sort of stuff." He folds his arms across his chest, making his biceps look that much bigger and more sculpted in the short sleeves of his uniform shirt.

And I catch myself staring at them, for far too long. So long that he begins shifting on his feet. "How many is that now?" I nod toward the sleeve of ink, even as my cheeks flush.

He stretches his arm out in front of him, slowly turning it this way and that, as if admiring his own tattoos. "I stopped counting a long time ago."

"I'll bet." I clear my throat. "Do you live in the city?"

"Summer Heights."

"Oh, yeah? Nice. We have a few buildings out there." It's a good half-hour commute by car—longer, by public transit—an area considered more affordable for young families and people just starting out.

"Yeah, well, we're renting for now. We'll see how we like it."

We're renting.

We'll see how *we* like it.

Of course Kyle's living with someone. He's

thirty years old. My stomach tightens as my gaze drops to his left hand. There's no wedding band. Not even a tan line of one. An unexpected wave of relief hits me, followed by that voice inside my head, reminding me that a missing ring doesn't mean he's not married. Or at least madly in love with someone: that the next step isn't inevitable.

I push that painful thought aside. "I just live a few blocks from here. With Ashley and Christa."

That earns a high-browed look. *"Christa?"*

I laugh. "She's gotten *a lot* better. Most of the time."

"That's . . . cool. I guess?" His gaze drifts to the security desk behind me, and I sense him searching for an escape. "I should—"

"Have you kept in touch with anyone from Wawa?" *Was I the only one you completely shut out?*

When his eyes meet mine again, there's heaviness in them. "I've seen Eric a few times over the years, but that's it."

"Oh yeah?" Despite the tension, I smile at the mention of that goof. "We were just talking about him the other night. How's he doing? Still a pain in the ass?"

Kyle's eyes narrow as he studies me for a long moment. "He's good. Listen, I should get back to work. I don't want Gus firing me on my first day."

"Says the guy who used to sneak off the second he saw any opening," I tease softly.

"Yeah, well . . . That was a *long* time ago. Shit happens. People change." His smile is sad.

"They do." Sometimes for the better, and sometimes not.

But which is it, for Kyle?

I feel the overwhelming need to know. "Hey, do you want to grab a drink sometime? Or a coffee, or lunch, or whatever. You know, catch up on things." On *every*thing.

A curious smirk touches his lips, but it's fleeting. "Yeah . . ." His brow furrows. "Let's keep it simple for now. You know, stick to hellos in the morning and goodbyes at night. That sort of thing." His voice is low and soft—almost apologetic—as he delivers me the verbal blow.

The sort of thing that strangers do. Not friends. Not even acquaintances. And definitely not what we used to be.

I swallow against the ball of disappointment growing in my throat. "Of course. If that's what you want."

"I think it's best for everyone involved." He takes a step back. "Have a great day, *Miss Calloway*." He shifts around me and strolls toward the desk, his steps even and slow.

I absently paw at the elevator button again and hear the ding to announce another available car, but I don't move, my feet weighted in place, my gaze locked on Kyle's retreating back.

It happens just as he's edging past Gus to take his seat. He turns and our eyes meet, and thirteen years seem to evaporate in the air between us.

Christa was right, after all.

Kyle may not have forgotten me, but he doesn't seem to want to remember *us*.

With my heels kicked off and my feet propped on a cardboard filing box, I quietly watch the last rays of sun creep over the Marquee building. Its rooftop is just visible. We had the hotel signage removed as soon as the deal closed on the building. Now it sits idle, the first few floors boarded up to keep out riffraff, giving vermin free rein inside.

Maybe Christa's right and I shouldn't give Kyle a second thought.

Or maybe I should *hate* him.

For breaking my heart thirteen years ago.

For treating me so callously last Friday.

For wanting to keep me at arm's length today.

But right now, all I have inside me are questions.

"Heading home soon?"

I spin in my chair to find my father standing in the doorway. He's swapped his pinstripe power suit and tie for a crisp white collared shirt—the top two buttons open—and a beige linen blazer and khaki pants. The subtle sandalwood aroma of his aftershave wafts in.

"Soon. But more important, where are *you* off to, Don Juan?"

The right corner of his mouth quirks. "A dinner meeting."

Dad never goes to business meetings without a tie.

"You need to trim two months on the Marquee's revised timelines—"

"I know," I say. "I've already asked Tripp to have his team tighten it. He said he'd have something to me by the end of the week. I'm pushing for an eleven-week reduction."

"Oh." My dad nods slowly, a flash of satisfaction crossing his face. "Good." He drags his fingertips along his chin in thought. I note the smoothness, even from here. Whoever he's meeting, he shaved in his office's restroom for her. "You and Tripp seem to be playing nice?"

"Seems so." I grit my teeth through an innocent smile. Tripp spent the two-hour meeting this afternoon glowering at me from across the table as Serge walked me through the revised plans post city approval. If looks could kill, I'd be split open on a spit and roasting right now.

"Interesting . . ." Dad's eyes narrow. "I didn't think being told to shove a golf club up his ass would motivate him so well."

Shit.

Of course the piglet went squealing all the way home.

I take a deep breath, set my shoulders, and brace myself for a tongue-lashing.

"I know you think I'm hard on you, and demanding. And maybe I am. But everything I do—*everything* I've ever done over the years—I've done only with your best interest at heart. You know that, right?"

"Yeah, Dad. I do."

He sighs heavily. "Don't stay here too late."

"I won't. Promise. Enjoy your dinner."

He makes a sound and turns to leave.

"Hey, Dad?"

"Hmm?" His eyebrows rise in question.

"Please tell me this one's at least forty?"

The smirk on his lips as he walks out doesn't bring me comfort.

Chapter 8

THEN

2006, Camp Wawa, Week One

“Ready for your first *full* day in the best place in the world?” Darian shouts, her diminutive stature looking especially grandiose from atop the picnic table. The morning sunlight is creeping over the tree line behind her, causing squints and hand-shields as both counselors and campers look on, their cereal dishes empty and forgotten.

No! I want to yell back. I could *kill* for a caffeine hit right now.

Darian wasn’t lying when she said yesterday would be long. Kyle and I came back from the cliff just in time to hitch the trailer to the golf cart and speed back to the pavilion. No one but Eric and Ashley seemed to realize that we’d left in the first place, and Ashley promised me she wouldn’t say a word to anyone, right before she asked why my clothes were damp.

We were shoveling our hot dogs into our mouths when the first round of children started arriving, a full hour early. Kids as young as eight and as old as fifteen piled out of their parents’ cars, many searching for familiar faces and gleeful when they found them. There were also a few with scowls and glossy eyes, pleading to go home as their frazzled parents marched them up to the registration desks.

Since then, it's been controlled mayhem. Greeting, smiling, identifying, collecting, and leading kids to their respective cabins like proverbial ducks, refereeing them as they fought over top versus bottom bunk, getting them to the various orientation and ice-breaker activities, coaxing them into eating their vegetables, ensuring they didn't burn their little fingers on marshmallows, and reminding them to brush their teeth and use the bathroom before lights-out, otherwise it'd be a trek in the night to the facilities.

The tears began as soon as the lights went out at nine P.M. First it was Izzy—the pint-sized platinum blonde who in her eight years of life had *never* spent a night away from her mother. The whimpers grew to sobs, then all-out wails, as she cried about wanting to go home and about missing her dog, Otis, and her dead dog, Rose. It caused a chain reaction, and soon we had four girls crying for home and the other six crying from irritation, and Christa and me tag-teaming around the cabin for two hours, trying to get them all to settle. By the time the last whimper sounded, I thought *I* was going to start crying.

When Izzy woke us up at four this morning

because she had wet her bed, a tear may have slipped out.

Whoever thought it'd be a good idea to give us ten eight-year-olds who are not only new to Camp Wawa, but also new to being at *any* sleepaway camp, deserves a punch in the head.

Or they could at least open the canteen now so I can grab myself a Coke, because I'm going to need it to get through this day. But how on earth am I going to get through this entire summer? Eight weeks, eight new sets of kids. Eighty little girls. What if they *all* cry themselves to sleep *every* night?

This must be why *camp counselor* looks so good on college applications—they know you've endured hell and lived to talk about it.

My gaze wanders one picnic table over, to where Kyle is tossing Cheerios at one of his kids' heads. The curly-haired boy of maybe ten keeps turning to try to catch his counselor mid-toss, only to giggle at the mock-stern look and shush from Kyle, who points toward Darian as if to say "pay attention."

Perhaps sensing my gaze, Kyle suddenly turns my way and our eyes catch. A crooked smile curls his lips and I feel a stupid, wide grin form, as I forget my exhaustion and instead focus on what his mouth felt like against mine yesterday.

I can still feel him there, still taste the mix of apple candy powder and, faintly, menthol.

Does he want it to happen again as much as I do?

Darian's sharp claps and boisterous voice echo through the space, pulling my attention back. "And the most important thing of all, Wawa campers, is let's have *fun!*"

"The yarn tubs are in the supply room. How many are there, Christa?"

"Three," Christa chirps from one table over, as she lines paint-filled squirt bottles and trays in a tidy row.

"Great. Find them and head on out to the pavilion." Darian's brow furrows with concentration as she directs counselors in Wawa's recreation center—a long, simple rectangular building of paneled walls and public school–grade linoleum, used mainly for rainy days and end-of-camp dances. "Ashley, Marie, you two know how to knit, right?"

Marie shrugs and then nods.

"Uh . . . *hello*." Ashley gestures at the blue scarf loosely wrapped around her neck.

"The stockinette stitch master! How could I forget?"

Ashley giggles. "I learned the garter stitch over winter."

"Ooooh." Darian's eyes widen with excitement. "I *love* a good Foxy Roxy scarf."

"In a soft dove-gray wool?"

Darian hugs her clipboard to her chest and closes her eyes. "You've always been my favorite, Ashley!"

I cast a questioning glance at Marie, who shrugs again, capping it off with a small eye roll and smile. At least I'm not the only one who thinks they're being weird.

"Okay, so you can show Piper the ropes, then?" Darian asks, switching back to leader mode.

"I'll teach her," comes a male voice from behind.

My heart skips as I turn to see Kyle saunter in, the sleeves of his camp T-shirt cut off to the seam, displaying the unfinished ink lines on his shoulder.

"Kyle, aren't you supposed to be covering . . ." Darian frowns at her master sheet, searching for his name.

"Hiking. Yeah, I was, but Jessica swapped with me."

"You know you're not allowed to swap!" Christa bursts out with irritation.

Darian sighs. "Kyle, you know the rules. It's camp policy, for child safety. I need to know which counselors are where at *all* times."

Walking past Christa—not giving her so much as a sideways glance—Kyle holds his hands up in surrender as he edges in closer, until he's towering over Darian's diminutive frame. "I know, I told Jess that. But she begged me to switch and I figured, if I could get hold of you to tell you, it'd be okay." He drops his voice in a mock whisper. "I think she has a thing for Mitch."

Darian's blue-gray eyes flicker toward me, a knowing look in them, as if *I* had something to do with this.

"They've already taken off down River Trail, but if you want me to run out and send Jess back, I can," Kyle offers innocently. "She could make it back in like . . . fifteen minutes. Twenty, tops."

Darian sighs. "No, I don't want to disrupt the group. Just . . . no more switches. I'm serious, Kyle."

I catch Christa's exaggerated eye roll.

"Of course! No problem." Kyle's fingers toy with the spiky hair atop his head, hesitating a moment. "Except for kayaking, okay?"

Darian groans, but Kyle's already talking again. "Because I kinda already got Mark to switch with me. I'm just not feeling confident in my swimming abilities."

One blonde eyebrow arches severely. "You? Not confident in something?"

He shrugs. "It's been a while since I've been swimming in a lake."

I frown. He just jumped off a thirty-foot cliff, into a *lake,* twenty-four hours ago.

I wonder if he can feel my penetrating "liar, liar, pants on fire" look.

Kyle leans in to scan the clipboard. "So could you just scratch his name off there, and add me in? And then you know where everyone is and it's all good. Right?"

Darian scans the board, then shoots a pursed-lip look my way before her gaze shifts up to his playful smile. It's a moment before she shakes her head, but then she's scribbling her pen across the page. "So Mark is going to do kayaking, and you are on badminton."

Badminton.

An excited flutter stirs in my stomach. *That's my second activity.* Kyle has switched his activities for the next two weeks to match mine.

"Just this one time. Make sure you know your new schedule. And . . . *coordinate* better from now on," Darian, not clueless, scolds softly, but caps it off with a knowing smile.

He drags his fingers over his chest in a sign of the cross. "You're awesome, Dare."

"I know," she answers lightly, but there's no missing the way her chest puffs up with a proud, deep breath.

Meanwhile, Christa is shaking her head, her mouth working over words as if debating whether to release them. By the annoyed look on her face, she probably shouldn't.

It's the perfect time for Avery and another girl to stroll through the door.

"Oh, good. You're here. The art supplies

are ready for you. You're going to be making origami!" Darian exclaims.

"Yay!" Avery holds her hands up in mock enthusiasm.

Darian thrusts a sheet of paper out to the knitting group. "Here's your camper list. One of you should get out there now to start rounding them up."

"I'll go." Marie grabs it and rushes off before anyone can suggest otherwise.

Kyle sidles up next to me as we trail Ashley toward a door marked "Storage. Staff only."

"Knitting? Really?" I tease; meanwhile my insides are screaming with glee. "I thought you hated knitting."

"Someone's got to teach you. And I'm good. Way better than Freckles."

"Yeah, right," Ashley says over her shoulder. "You know the garter stitch?"

He grins. "I know garters."

"*Not* . . . Oh my God." She shakes her head at him, her cheeks flushing.

He reaches out to give the end of her scarf a playful tug. "You know it's, like, ninety-four degrees outside, right?"

"It's a prop. I'm going to take it off, after I *wow* them."

Kyle pauses long enough to let me ahead of him, his hand skimming the small of my back in the process, sending shivers up my spine.

The storage room is long, narrow, and lit by one naked bulb. And jammed with supplies.

"Here's one," Ashley announces, tapping a Rubbermaid container that's labeled "Knitting" across the sides and top, her eyes lighting up with an odd excitement as they skim over the clutter. "But I don't think they're all marked."

"How's it going so far?" Kyle asks me, setting aside a container marked "Drama."

"Fine. I'm exhausted."

"Rough night?"

"The worst. They were crying."

"How many?"

"*All* of them."

He chuckles. "It'll get better."

"I don't believe you."

"Do you think any of us would come back if it didn't?"

He makes a good point.

Kyle pulls a white mask from a nearby box and presses it against his face, covering the top half, leaving only his square jaw and pouty lips visible. "You'll *never* guess who I am with this on."

I laugh. "That's the only musical I've ever been able to sit through." Though none of the actors looked as good as he does right now.

"Which one?"

"*The Phantom* . . . You know?" I gesture at the mask.

"Oh . . ." Kyle tosses it back into the bin and shuts the lid. "Never seen it."

"Seriously? You should go. I've seen it four times now. On Broadway, and then in Singapore, London, and . . . Vancouver, I think." I crack open a bin to find a colorful mess of pom-poms and Popsicle sticks and other basic art supplies. "My mother's a *huge* theater geek. Andrew Lloyd Webber actually spent a weekend at our summer house. She drags me to *so* many shows."

"Yeah, that all sounds rough," Kyle mutters, fishing out a ball of white yarn from an orange container. "Incoming! Two of three."

"Hey!" Ashley scowls as the yarn bounces off her forehead, but her annoyance fades almost instantly. " 'Kay. I'm gonna take this one out. You two find the last one." She trots out with her arms laden, but not before offering me an exaggerated wink.

Meanwhile my cheeks have begun to burn as I replay what I just said, wondering how obnoxious that must have sounded. "I'm not like Olivia, I swear," I blurt out.

Kyle chuckles. "Is that what you're worried about? Me thinking you're like the Gasoline Queen?"

"Nice. She's Miss Sunoco in my head. And, well . . . yeah."

Kyle shoves another tub aside. "I know you're not like Olivia. She goes out of her way to make it sound like her family is rolling in dough and rub people's noses in it. Meanwhile, here you are, going out of your way to pretend you're just like the rest of us."

"I *am* just like everyone else here!" *Except with an enormous trust fund.*

"Yeah, that's *exactly* what I was thinking, when I first saw you," he murmurs as he peeks in a blue tub full of paint bottles and brushes.

"So . . . what *were* you thinking?" I dare ask, avoiding his gaze as I pry a lid off a green tub to discover knitting needles. My stomach clenches with anticipation of his answer.

Kyle shifts to stand behind me, his body oh so close but not touching me. "Well, I definitely was *not* thinking that you're the prettiest girl I've ever laid eyes on."

"No?" I smile as a warm shiver runs down my spine.

"No way." He leans in, until his mouth is next to my ear. "And that first night by the campfire, there's *no way* I was wondering what it'd be like to kiss you." His hands settle gently on either side of my waist, as his lips skate over my cheek. "And last night? When I was falling asleep? I *definitely* wasn't thinking about you at all."

My breathing has turned ragged.

Voices carry near the doorway then, reminding us that we're not alone.

Kyle releases his gentle grip of my body and

slides around to face me, but not without a distinctive sigh of frustration. “I’ll take this one out. It’s heavier.”

“I can handle it.” Spiking tennis balls across courts since I was eight has guaranteed me slender but strong arms. To prove my point, I lift the tub. It’s awkward but manageable.

His fingers slide over mine, weaving their way through to grasp the handles, his hands warm and strong. His gaze drops to my mouth, and I hold my breath, hoping he’ll lean in and kiss me. “You’re coming out tonight after lights-out, right? It’s a full moon. We’re going up to the cliff.”

“To jump?”

“Don’t know yet. If it’s bright enough, yeah.”

A tiny thrill swirls inside at his insistence. “If I can get away. Avery said Christa’s going to be a problem.”

“Whatever. You heard Darian at orientation. As long as we’re not being idiots, she doesn’t care.”

I wonder if she’d think jumping off a thirty-foot cliff—at night—would qualify as being an idiot.

“Please?” he whispers, leaning in farther, until his mouth is a mere inch from mine, so close that I sense rather than see his smile, his breath kissing my skin.

He *must* be able to hear my heart pounding.

Finally . . . *finally* . . . he presses his lips against mine in a sweet, slow kiss.

"Did you guys see the other tub of paint in here?" Christa's sudden voice at the doorway makes me jump.

I silently curse her as Kyle takes a step back, weaseling the tub from my grip. "The orange one in the corner." With a wink my way, he saunters out of the supply room, leaving me light-headed.

"There's no PDA in front of campers," Christa scolds.

I grab the last container. "Do you see any campers here?" I throw back over my shoulder as I hurry out, not giving her a chance to get the last word in.

Through the small window beside our bunk, I spy two tall figures trudging along the path. Is one of them Kyle? We agreed to meet by the fork in the path toward the girls' cabins at ten. That was almost half an hour ago.

He's probably gone already.

I pull my weary body to a sitting position and pause a moment, to listen to ten little girls, breathing deeply. Kyle was right; tonight was nothing like last night's horrors. After a full day of sun and heat and excitement, the kids curled into their sleeping bags and didn't utter a sound. At one point I thought I'd have to carry Izzy from the campfire to bed, her tiny body melting with exhaustion into mine.

Below me, Christa is quiet as well, having

finally tucked away her book and shut her flashlight ten minutes ago. I know because I've timed it, and it's been the longest ten minutes of my life.

It's now or never.

With a stir in my stomach, I ease myself down the ladder and grab my hoodie and my bathing suit from my hook.

"Where are you going?" comes Christa's rushed whisper the moment my hand touches the door handle.

I stifle my curse. "Restroom," I lie, and duck out. I'm ten steps away when I hear her footfalls on the gravel pathway behind me.

"You can't just take off like that and not tell me."

I roll my eyes before turning to face her. She's standing just outside the cabin door, arms crossed, pajamas rumpled, her jaw set with hard determination. My guess is she's been lying in wait, knowing what I was planning and determined to foil it.

"I don't care if no one likes me because I follow the rules. We're here to take care of the kids, not get drunk and fool around."

"Who's getting drunk? I'm meeting up with Ashley and a few others. I'll be back soon." It's not entirely a lie, as Ashley said she'd come out.

"And what if one of our kids has to go to the bathroom?"

"They're in comas. They're not waking up—"

"But what if they do?"

"Then you take them! It's right *there!*" I gesture over my shoulder in the direction of the restrooms, not bothering to hide my annoyance. "I've got to go. I'll be back in a bit." I turn to leave.

"Don't hook up with him," she blurts, as if unable to keep it in any longer.

So this is really about Kyle. I sigh. "Why? Because you don't like him?"

"No." She closes the distance. "Because *you* don't know him."

I can't help it. I laugh. "And *you* do?"

Her brow tightens. "No. I just know *things,* okay?"

My curiosity gets the better of me. "Like?"

"Like . . ." She looks ready to swallow her tongue, keeping whatever's on her mind from spilling out. "You have to be around him for the next two months, you know."

Something tells me that's not what she was going to say.

Now it's my turn to fold my arms over my chest. *"And?"* Two months of seeing Kyle every day doesn't sound like a hardship. It's what happens *after* those two months that should worry me. What happens when we both go home? I guess we can drive back and forth to see each other. I'll have my shiny new car . . .

Christa interrupts my daydream with, "What happens if it doesn't work out and he hooks up with someone else?"

"Oh my God. *Okay.*" I laugh, raising a hand. "You have got to learn how to chill, Christa. I'm not gonna think about ending things when I'm not sure if we're even *together* yet." *Though hopefully that will change tonight. If Christa would just go back to sleep.*

I turn to leave again.

"Ask him about his father!"

And I'm reeled back in. "What do you mean?" I frown. "What about his father?"

She lifts her chin in an indignant way. "No one else around here knows, but *I do*. And that story about the robbery? That was the real lie. Well, technically it was the truth, but he left out the important details . . ."

Something small cuts through the air behind Christa's head and swoops past the cracked door into our cabin, distracting me completely. "What was that?"

Christa pauses. "What was what?"

"I think a bird just flew into our cabin."

"A *bird* . . ." Two beats pass and then Christa's eyes widen. "No! No no no no no . . ." She bolts inside. I run in after her, just as the interior of our cabin is bathed in light. Her sharp gaze searches the ceiling's corners. "There!" As sleeping bags begin to rustle and squinty-eyed faces emerge, she points to the far corner, where a small, wiry black body clings. “It’s not a bird. It’s a *bat!*”

In those few seconds of calm before reality registers and mass pandemonium explodes, I let out a disappointed sigh.

So much for seeing Kyle tonight.

Chapter 9

NOW

"No!"

"Come *on* . . ." David's on my heels as we enter the building after an industry breakfast meeting. "Just lend him to me for the day!"

"Mark is not a damn pen to be passed around!" I take a calming breath as my gaze settles on the cluster of people loitering around the front desk. Visitors, waiting to get signed in. Kyle sits somewhere behind them, taking down information, handing out badges. Offering them polite smiles and banal greetings, with no more familiarity than he has shown me these past two weeks since he started working in the building.

My intelligent, mature self keeps telling me to let it go. That what we had was *thirteen years* ago. We were teenagers then. Stupid kids, really. We're adults now, and complete strangers. If Kyle wants to keep it that way . . . fine.

Except he was the first boy I ever loved—my first in many ways—and he crushed me. How can he keep treating me like I mean *nothing* to him?

I *have* to stop thinking about the mischievous, playful guy from Camp Wawa. The one who was chasing and charming me from the moment he first laid eyes on me. The one who grabbed my attention from forty feet away and seized my heart not long after.

Clearly, that guy is long gone.

Plus, Kyle's *involved* with someone else. I'm not getting in the middle of that.

"Piper!" David's annoyed bark startles me. He asked me a question. What, I have no idea.

"What was wrong with that lady from a couple of days ago? The one with the thick glasses. Carla said she was perfect."

"Who? *Grandma* Ethel?" David snorts derisively. "She called me *dearie* three times during her interview."

I mock-gasp. "Oh, the horror!"

"*And* she flat-out refused to do dry cleaning or coffee runs, or work past four P.M."

The crowd ahead dissipates. As much as I want to stroll right past without glancing, it's impossible. My eyes veer toward Kyle, sitting in his chair—to his chiseled jaw and high cheekbones and his full lips, noting how much thicker and more stylish his hair looks now. He was attractive as a seventeen-year-old boy; he has become dangerously handsome as a man.

And his steady gaze is on me.

"Come on, Piper . . . help me out," David whines. "Just for the week."

"A minute ago, it was for the day!" This is so David, asking for an inch, then reaching for a mile, as if he's entitled to it. "Ask Greta to help you out."

"Are you kidding? Greta doesn't have time. Plus, Kieran doesn't share well."

"Neither do I, so you had better hire someone soon."

David curses under his breath.

"You know you've done this to yourself," I lecture. There's been a steady trickle of potential executive assistants passing through his office door, courtesy of Human Resources's efforts. All vetted, all with extensive experience.

And all problematic, according to David.

"What's with you lately, Piper?"

"What are you talking about?"

"I mean, you've been in a fucking *mood* for the past two weeks."

"There's nothing wrong with my mood," I hiss, feeling Kyle's and Gus's attention on us as we bicker not five feet away.

David drops his voice. "Is this because I'm seeing other women? You're the one who *told* me to go out and find someone. *You're* the one who ended our engagement, remember."

I roll my eyes. "I don't care who you're with. Stop making this about *us,* David."

"Isn't it, though?"

"No! It's about you finding an assistant so you stop torturing mine. You've been a complete *dickhead* to him since day one."

"Okay, seriously, Piper? I'm on my knees begging you for just a bit of help so *I* can nail this project down for *your* company, and you're calling me names? This is what we've come to?" He swipes his badge over the scanner and shoves through the security barrier in a huff, without so much as a nod toward Gus, whose eyebrows are raised.

And I'm left standing awkwardly in front of Kyle, suddenly feeling like the bad guy.

Kyle curiously watches David's retreating back a moment before focusing on me. He's not actually buying David's sob story, is he?

"He broke Mark's windmill!" I blurt out, as if that explains everything.

The corners of Kyle's lips twitch. "Have a great day, Miss Calloway."

I sigh heavily. Strangers it is. I pass through the security gate, feeling his penetrating gaze on me the entire way.

What is he doing?

My gaze trails Kyle's graceful stride as he strolls along the corridor at a leisurely pace, casting nothing more than a perfunctory glance my way. That's the second time today—fifth time this week—that he has walked by a meeting room I've been in. Did Ivan patrol the floors like this, too? If he did, I never noticed him. It's a bit ridiculous, really. I might understand the need for security patrols during the dead of the night, but it's ten A.M.

Mark's elbow gently nudges my arm, pulling my attention back.

To the four sets of eyes steadily watching me.

"Tripp's recommending we go with KDZ for the construction of the Marquee," Mark murmurs softly, a prompt for what I missed while ogling our new security guard.

I feel my cheeks flush as I quickly scan the proposal in front of me again. "I'm sorry, *who?* We're using Jameson for the Marquee. Who the hell is this KDZ Construction Company, anyway?"

"They're from Boston, but they've recently expanded into the area. They come highly recommended, and their contract will be competitive." Tripp smooths his tie down over his belly as he recites what sounds like a planned response. "I've been in talks with them about the Marquee for months now."

I feel my eyes widen. So Tripp has gone from telling the engineers not to bother with the project to now being highly involved, and with a construction firm that he's never mentioned lined up?

What the hell is going on?

When was he planning on looping me in?

"Well, we're *ready* to sign on with Jameson, who has a proven track record with us. So why on earth would we back out now? Especially when we're already behind?"

"You demanded that we tighten the timeline by almost three months. KDZ can deliver on that. They're already working on their proposal. I'm meeting with their president on Friday to review and make the decision."

Tripp has no business offering up a construction contract without approval from both me and my father, and he knows it.

I bite my tongue before I blurt as much out in front of the broader group, and force a patient tone. "As I've said, we are ready to proceed with Jameson, but I'm willing to review this proposal once you have it—"

"Kieran's already given KDZ the go-ahead. If you don't like it, you'll need to take it up with him." Tripp heaves his body out of his chair. "Now, if you'll excuse me, I have another meeting to attend." He strolls out the door, but not before I catch the smug curl of his lips.

It takes everything in me to school my expression, even as I feel heat crawling up my neck. "Mark will send the follow-ups. See you all on Thursday." I wait until everyone has left the room and the door is shut before I snap.

"When's my father back from LA?"

"Thursday, I think. Hold on." Mark is frowning as he madly types an instant message to Greta. "Yeah. His plane lands at five P.M."

I'll have to call him about this. I *hate* confronting my father over the phone. He's that much more abrupt.

I pinch the bridge of my nose. "Son of a bitch." I'm not quite sure who deserves the title more. Is this another one of Tripp's dick moves to save face and make me look like the fool? Or should the blame land squarely on my father's shoulders this time? "What do I have next?"

"A meeting with David and Jim."

"*Great.* Just what I need right now. Another pompous ass to deal with," I mutter.

Mark tucks his laptop under his arm. "You okay?"

I sigh, collecting my things. "Yeah."

"You sure?" he presses, making me wary.

"Why are you asking?"

"Nothing. Just . . ." He shrugs. "You've seemed, I don't know, not yourself lately. *Distracted.*"

First David accusing me of being in a mood, and now Mark? I duck my head as I collect my things, mainly to hide another flush of my cheeks. "I just have a lot going on right now. You know, the Waterway project . . ." *Lie.* "The Marquee." *Lie.* "And this ongoing Tripp bullshit. It's getting worse." *Partial lie.*

Technically, all those things are real and should be dominating my focus and raising my stress levels. *Should* is the operative word. But the truth is, if I'm distracted, it's because my attention keeps getting snagged on the new security guard, my thoughts lingering in the past.

Mark nods slowly, as if understanding. "*Håret i postkassen*."

"Pardon me?"

He offers a shy smile. "Just something my grandmother used to say. It's a Danish proverb. It means 'you've got your hair stuck in the mailbox.' "

"*What?*"

He smiles. "You've found yourself with a tricky problem."

"*Oh*. With Tripp? Yeah, I guess I have. I just don't know what to do about him. He'll clearly never accept me as his superior."

"*Få hul på bylden*."

I wait with raised eyebrows for the translation.

Mark shrugs. " 'You've got to lance the boil.' "

I cringe at the mental image that spurns. "So your grandma thinks that if I poke Tripp with a long, sharp needle, he'll go away?"

He chuckles. "He'd learn to keep his distance."

"It would definitely make me feel better." I sigh, hauling my weary body out of my chair.

"Off to lunch, Miss Calloway?" Gus asks as he tosses his Alejandro's hamburger wrapper into the trash behind him. The man rarely leaves the desk, even to eat.

"And a meeting." I don't mean to sigh as I take

in the empty chair next to him, but it slips out anyway.

"You *just* missed him. He went to check something in the parking garage."

Of course he did. My gaze drifts to the bank of monitors behind the desk, to the screens showing the elevators. It doesn't take a genius to figure out what's happening.

We're at week three and Kyle is outright avoiding me now, bolting the second he spots me on my way down. Off to test an alarm or patrol the building or to pee. Anything to not have to see me, it seems.

My annoyance flares, but I push it aside. "How's it going so far with him?"

"No complaints. He's punctual, disciplined, quiet. Takes his job seriously."

Not at all like the version I knew. "Good. Well . . ." Loitering here talking about Kyle feels awkward. "I'll see you later." I turn to leave.

"I heard he requested a transfer here, from San Diego," Gus says.

San Diego. So that's where he went. Has he been there all this time?

I feel Gus's steady gaze on me, as if waiting for my reaction.

"Makes sense. Lennox *is* a great city. I could see why he'd make the move," I say casually. Why *did* he make the move? For his girlfriend, maybe?

"Not this city. *This building,*" Gus clarifies, wiping his mouth with a napkin. "Apparently, he's been trying to get in here for a while now. Put in a transfer request with Rikell's HR for *this* building."

I frown. "How many buildings in the city does Rikell do security for?"

"Fifteen. Twenty. Something like that." Gus's eyes study me as I try to process this bit of information.

If it were Lennox that Kyle wanted to move to, he'd accept a transfer at *any* of those buildings. So why did he want to work at this one specifically?

Unless . . .

"There must have been *something* about this place that made him want to come here," Gus says, as if reading my mind.

"The architecture," I murmur absently, more confused now than before.

Something.

Or someone.

"Yes. The *architecture*." A knowing glimmer shines in Gus's eyes, but his brow is pulled with worry. "Anything I should know about?"

What would Gus say if he knew everything about Kyle that *I* know? If he knew our entire history?

Would he be so quick to throw out kind words about him?

"Yes. There is." I lean in, as if to share a secret. "These burgers are *terrible* for you. Start eating healthier."

His laugh trails me as I head for the exterior doors, my mind swirling.

Why would Kyle make the effort to move across the country to work in my building, only to then keep me at arm's length?

What the hell are you up to, Kyle?

Chapter 10

THEN

2006, Camp Wawa, Week One

"Okay! So we all learned something important from last night's fiasco," Darian begins, having corralled the entire staff of counselors to the field beside the pavilion. Meanwhile the campers are suitably distracted with pancakes and sausages, and grossly exaggerated versions of the vampiric, winged beast that tried to kill the occupants of Cabin Nine.

She pauses to look around the group, her index fingers pointed outward. It's her signature move before she asks for audience participation. "Who can tell me what it was?"

"Don't run into a cabin full of sleeping kids screaming, 'Run for your lives before the bat kills you!'?" Colin, a tall dark-haired guy, calls out. All the counselors laugh.

All except Christa.

"I did *not* say that!" she bursts with indignation, her face heating to match the color of her camp T-shirt. "That's *not* what happened."

"No. Well, yes, Colin, *technically,* you're not wrong—you should never say anything along those lines. And perhaps there might have been a more orderly way of waking the children to deal with last night's situation," Darian hazards, lifting her hand in the air to stall Christa's next words of defense.

The first eardrum-splintering shriek had come within seconds, as little Teegan looked up to see the wiry black body cowering in the corner directly above her head, a mere two feet away. A chorus of shrill screams soon joined in, as we scrambled to pull all five girls sleeping on top bunks down, to take cover below.

The next few anxiety-laden seconds felt like they were happening in slow motion, as the bat lifted off and fluttered around the cabin for a few laps before swooping toward Christa. Armed with our pillows, we took turns swinging at it until finally it sailed through the open door and toward the trees.

But the damage had been done—ten terrified little girls who took hours to drift off once again, along with disturbed rest for the ninety other female campers who were awoken by the high-pitched alarm. Plus Darian, of course, came speeding across the campgrounds in a golf cart—dressed in an Elmo nightshirt and hiking boots, her short blonde hair standing on end—to find out what was going on.

"Let's take this as an opportunity to remember to shut your cabin door fully when you're going to the restroom at night, okay?" Darian says. "Simple mistake, I get it! But guess what, everyone? We're in the woods, and bats live in the woods! It's part of nature. It's fine. We can coexist in harmony, as long as they don't get into our cabins."

My eyes flash to Christa before averting them to the grass. When Darian asked for a rundown of *exactly* what happened, I was bracing myself for trouble. I assumed Christa would rat on me for sneaking out to meet up with Kyle.

But instead, she went along with the lie, nodding vigorously when I explained that I saw the bat fly in just as I was coming back. Maybe she felt partly responsible, because *she's* the one who left the door open. Either way, at least she didn't throw me under the bus the first chance she got.

There's another dramatic pause from Darian, another index-finger point. "And why don't we want bats in our cabins at night, besides the obvious creepiness?"

Avery lets out a yelp and then, "Ew . . . gross, Eric!" Heads spin to see Eric hovering over her shoulder from behind, a frothy white substance dripping from his mouth and onto her shirt. There's another round of laughter around the group.

"Because bats carry rabies," Kyle offers innocently, as Eric holds up a can of whipped cream and then swallows. And grins at Avery.

"How did you get . . ." Darian shakes her head. "Never mind. Yes, Kyle, you are correct. Bats *can* carry rabies, and while the cases are rare, we can't have bats hanging around our sleeping kids. Bats have very small teeth and it's possible the kids won't realize they've been bitten, especially as deep as they sleep after their days here. We're feeling pretty confident that none of the girls came into contact with our furry little friend last night thanks to quick action by our counselors—"

"Run for your lives!" that Colin guy calls out.

"But," Darian spears him with a warning glare, "had they not noticed it right away, it would have spent all night in there with them."

I shudder at the thought.

"Then we'd be dealing with a very different situation, involving calls home and a lot of shots. So please remember, keep your cabin doors closed, report any tears in the window screens, and let's all start doing visual checks around our cabins before lights-out from now on, just to be on the safe side. Okay, everyone?"

Mumbled agreement sounds.

"Great. *Also* . . . I happened to notice that one of our golf carts was missing last night. Y'all know that the golf carts are not to be used at night for anything except emergencies. I'm not aware of any *other* emergencies last night, so whoever forgot that rule and borrowed it," her sharp blue eyes float between Eric and Kyle, who are studying their shoes, “please don’t do it again. Okay!” Darian claps her hands. “Time to finish up with breakfast and get a move on! It’s gonna be another hot, sunny day!”

The counselors disband at a leisurely pace, the promise of sweltering heat not as motivating as Darian seems to think it should be.

Kyle hangs back to fall in line with me, his walk more a swagger, his thumbs looped casually into his shorts pockets. “Sounds like you had way more fun than I did last night.”

“If that’s what you want to call it.” My eyes are sore from lack of sleep and I’m sure my bags match the ones under Christa’s. “I tried to sneak out after Christa fell asleep.”

His chest lifts with a deep sigh of relief. “That makes more sense,” he murmurs, and then smiles.

I frown. “More sense than what?”

He shrugs, nudging his shoulder against mine. “I thought maybe you changed your mind.”

“About what? Jumping off a cliff at night?” I mock-gasp. “Never.”

He dips his head, and a shy smile touches his lips. “That, or . . . I don’t know, about *this?*”

This being us.

I can’t help but laugh at the suggestion. Does Kyle *not* feel my gaze glued to him whenever he’s in my line of sight? Does he not notice the stupid grin that takes over my face every time our eyes meet?

He lets out a soft chuckle and then shrugs. "I don't know. I was standing there, waiting for you, and I started thinking, and . . . yeah . . ." Beautiful molten eyes meet mine again, and in them I see a vulnerability I hadn't before. Or perhaps it wasn't there before. Perhaps it took him standing on the path in the dark, waiting for me, for doubt to seed itself.

Had our roles been reversed, had *I* been the one waiting, and he didn't show . . . A hollow pang stirs in my stomach with just the thought. And that tells me two things: one, that I'm already falling hard for Kyle.

And two: that it's not just me.

My pulse begins to race as I reach out to trail my fingertips over his forearm. "No, that's definitely not it. I was just trying to avoid getting grilled by Christa." I add, more to myself, "Which I failed at spectacularly."

His hand slips around to smooth over the small of my back, ever so quickly, before falling to his side. "What did she say?"

My eyes drift to the pavilion, to Cabin Nine's candy-floss-pink picnic table. Christa stands over the campers, hands on hips, evaluating their plates to decide if they've eaten enough. She said a lot last night, but what was most unsettling, what I haven't been able to gain more information about yet, is what we ended with. "That you lied about that robbery."

"What?" He smirks, and his gaze flips to her. "She doesn't know what she's talking about."

It's more calculating than curious, I realize, studying him closely, his brow pinched with wariness.

He's wondering what she knows.

Which means there's something *to* know.

I watch him as I say, "She also told me to ask you about your father."

He can't hide his reaction fast enough—the way his smirk falls and panic flashes in his eyes—before smoothing his expression.

"What did she mean?" I ask as casually as I can.

His jaw hardens with tension as he stares at Christa from across the way. She must sense it because she glances over at us, her own eyes narrowing on him in a quiet challenge before she averts her gaze.

"What else did she say?" he asks quietly.

I toy with the idea of playing dumb but decide against it. Kyle's too smart for that and I doubt he'd appreciate it coming from me. "That she's the only one here who knows the truth about you."

His shoulders sink.

An unsettling feeling begins to take over. "All right, I'm officially starting to freak out. What's going on? Did you *do* something?"

"No, *I* didn't do *anything*. It's just . . ." He shakes his head and sighs again. "It's my family."

"What about them?"

"They're . . ." His throat bobs with a hard swallow. "They're not like yours. Or anyone else's here, I'm guessing." Kids are beginning to get up and carry their dirty dishes to the nearby trolleys. Soon they'll come charging out. "Look, can we talk about this later?"

"I guess. As long as you tell me what's going on." Because now that the questions are out there, not having the answers will drive me insane.

He sighs. "Meet me on the path tonight. I'll tell you everything." There's no missing the resignation in his voice.

I watch him trudge away toward his kids, his head hanging.

What could be so wrong with his family?

I don't bother trying to sneak out this time.

Seven minutes after lights-out, when the last girl has drifted off, I slip down the ladder and pull on my sweatshirt.

Christa's flashlight is shining on her open book, but I feel her gaze on me.

"I'm going to talk to him," I whisper, and walk out, pulling the door shut behind me.

She doesn't stop me.

I rush along the path, my arms curled around my weary body. The camp is eerily quiet at night, the spruce and hemlock trees casting ominous shadows against the property's lights.

Kyle is waiting where he said he would be, leaning against a tree, a cigarette burning between his fingers. "Hey."

Butterflies stir in my stomach. I'm feeling oddly shy all of a sudden. "Hey."

I expect him to pull me into him and lay a teasing kiss on my lips, but he hangs back. "Did Christa give you problems again?"

"No."

"Good. Come on." He nods to his left and I notice the golf cart.

"I thought we weren't allowed to use those after lights-out."

"You want to walk all the way up there?" He points toward the dark, wooded path.

I shake my head and slide in. "Is there *any* rule you actually do follow at Wawa?"

"Uh . . ." He appears to be thinking hard. "Let me get back to you on that. I can't think of any at the moment."

I laugh as we take off, rounding the same winding path through the trees, the only light provided by the dull headlights. The trip to the cliff isn't nearly as long as it seemed the first time. We're parking and climbing out in minutes. Kyle uses one of the camp's battery-operated lanterns to guide us up the narrow footpath, until we reach the same large rock from our last time here. He sets the lantern on a higher crop of stone, allowing it to bathe the area in dim light.

It's eerily quiet here at night. I much prefer the daytime, I decide. Though I'd sit here in a torrential downpour if it meant being with Kyle.

He slides another cigarette into his mouth.

"You know smoking is bad for you, right?"

"So I've been told." I catch his smirk in the flash of his lighter as he lights the end.

"No cliff jumping tonight?"

"You wanna go?" he asks through a puff, his intense gaze on me. "We can go."

I take in the inky sky, the moonlight dappled through the clouds. As terrifying as it was in the daylight, I doubt I could dig up the nerve to leap into the darkness. "Did you actually jump last night?"

"Nah. Wasn't much in the mood."

Because he was waiting for me. Because he thought I'd ditched him.

Awkward silence falls over us, this wedge that Christa managed to slide between us effective.

"So . . ." Where to start this conversation, so I can put my mind and nerves to rest? "Your dad's a government spy. Is that it?"

He chuckles softly. "That'd be cool."

"Assassin?"

"That'd be even cooler."

My thoughts have been lingering on this all day, as I tried to work out what would make Kyle's smile fall so fast when I mentioned his father. Whatever it is, it can't be good.

"Is he alive?"

"Yeah." He adds more quietly, "Unfortunately."

There's only one other thing I can think of, one thing that might make Kyle ashamed to tell me.

I swallow. "In prison?"

The long stretch of silence answers me.

I reach for him, setting my hand on his forearm. "Whatever. It's not a big deal."

"Right." He chuckles darkly. "Would you say that if *your* father were in an orange jumpsuit right now?"

That gives me pause. First, I can't imagine my father behind bars. Has he ever done anything to deserve to be? No, I can't imagine so. He's *always* going on and on about principles and morality.

"So, what's your father in for?"

"Does it matter?"

"Yeah. I mean, my dad's friend got nailed for fudging financials at his company to get more money from the bank. It was dishonest, and of course no one will go into business with him now, but I still see him around sometimes. People still talk to him." Not my father, mind you, but I don't need to share that part. "And people end up in jail for causing car accidents that kill people. It's horrible, but it's not the same as someone who, like, killed ten people and ate their organs. I mean, that'd be *bad*."

"Yeah, about that . . ." Kyle is silent. For too long.

"Oh my God." My stomach falls.

"I'm kidding." He reaches out to squeeze my thigh. "Seriously, I'm kidding."

I give his side a gentle elbow, but groan with relief. "So then, what's he in for?"

"Let's see." He takes a long puff of his cigarette. "He stole a bunch of equipment from the construction company he worked for and resold it. Mainly tools."

"That's not *the worst*. I mean, no one got hurt, right?"

"I'm sure they had insurance," he agrees. "But it was that scam where he robbed a bunch of senior citizens of their life savings that *really* seemed to piss the judge off."

I cringe before I can help it. "He robbed old people? But, that's just . . ."

"Up there with stealing medication from sick children. Don't worry, you can say it." Kyle kicks at a loose stone. "My dad is a lowlife."

I try to imagine the kind of man who would do that—what he looks like, how he talks, what you'd see when you look into his eyes—and I come up empty. I've never knowingly met someone that vile. "When did this happen?" I ask quietly.

"Seven years ago. I was ten. It was the last time I came here. Couldn't afford it after that."

Ashley did say that he and his brother stopped coming. I guess I know the reason why now.

Kyle has burned through one cigarette already. He lights another. “We were living in Albany at the time. My mom was working at IHOP. She got fired because the owner figured she must have known what my dad was doing. He said he couldn’t trust her.”

“Did she? Know, I mean.”

“She’s never admitted to it, but she definitely had to know he was doing *something* shady. I remember this one day he came home on a Saturday night with this fat wad of cash. She had a big coffee can where she stuffed it in, then put it in the cupboard above the fridge. I asked her why she didn’t just put it in the bank. She laughed and said sometimes you have to hide your money. So yeah, I’d say she knew. But did she know he was stealing from old people?” He shrugs. “She acted all horrified when news started spreading, but I’m thinking it might have been an act. She visits him.” He studies a cut on his index finger. “She finally stopped trying to make me go, though.”

I don’t know what to say so I say nothing, and instead smooth a tentative hand over his back. His tension practically vibrates beneath my palm. He *really* must not like talking about this.

“Before my dad got busted, things were okay. After, though, everything turned to shit. We got kicked out of our house a few months later, for not paying rent. We moved to Poughkeepsie,

’cause that’s where my mom grew up and it’s actually closer to Fishkill, where my dad’s at. We stayed with my grandparents in their tiny bungalow for a few months until my mom landed a job working reception at a tire shop. Now we’re in this apartment, above a Seven-Eleven. You know, in one of those strip malls.”

“I’m so sorry.”

He chuckles softly. “About living above a Seven-Eleven?”

“No! I mean yes, but about *everything*.”

“Yeah. It sucks. That’s why I like coming to Wawa. It’s peaceful here. I can be someone different. Someone who doesn’t have half their family in prison.”

I frown. “Half?”

“Oh, yeah. I forgot the best part, didn’t I?” His gaze wanders out to the black skies. “My two older brothers are in jail for trying to rob a fucking *bank*.”

My mouth drops open in shock. I’m thankful for the darkness. “Are you . . . is that for real?” Or am I unwittingly playing another round of two truths and a lie?

“Look it up. *Poughkeepsie Journal*. They did a nice, big front-page spread with the three of them pictured side-by-side. It’s titled ‘Criminal Gene Runs in Family.’ ” He swipes a hand through the air in front of him dramatically; his voice is thick with bitterness.

He'd only mentioned a little brother before. "But I thought you said—"

"Yeah, I lied. I'm sorry. I've got three brothers. I just like to pretend that two of them don't exist." He butts the rest of his cigarette out against the rock.

"So that story about being in an armed robbery the first night—"

"Was true. I *was* in an armed robbery. I just left out a few key details. Like, the part where my two idiot brothers told me to stay in the car while they went inside to take care of some bills and how I didn't listen. Big surprise, right? But it was January and it was cold, and the heat in that car barely works, so I said fuck it and I went inside, and found the two of them with pantyhose over their heads, pointing guns at the tellers. I knew it was them right away by their voices. It was surreal . . ." He shakes his head slowly, as if replaying it in his mind. "They started yelling at me for not listening. Apparently they needed me to wait in the car so I could drive it away when they came running out." He snorts. "*Then* they yelled at me to watch the security guard to make sure he didn't do anything funny. The poor guy was sixty-seven years old and they'd taken his gun from him as soon as they came in. He wasn't gonna do anything.

"I told them to get the hell out of there before they got themselves into more trouble. They wouldn't listen . . ." They wouldn't listen. "I don't know what their plan was, but it went to shit, fast. Someone triggered the alarm for the cops and the place was surrounded in no time. They surrendered."

"Oh my God! That's *insane,* Kyle!"

He studies the ground. "Yeah, that's one word for it."

I try to picture Rhett standing in front of a teller with a gun in his hand—or something equally crazy—but I can't. "What was going through your head during all this? Were you scared that they'd hurt someone? I mean, they're your *brothers*."

"Honestly?" His chuckle is low and sounds sheepish. "I remember wondering where they got those pantyhose from. Like, if they went out and bought them or took them from our mother's dresser."

I burst out laughing, and he joins in, releasing some of the tension in the air around us.

"So, what happened after?"

"The cops figured I was in on it, so they arrested me. *That's* when I got scared. I thought I'd end up in jail, too. But they dropped the charges after they reviewed the security tapes and witness statements."

"And your brothers?"

"They just got sentenced a few weeks ago. Nine years. They'll be getting out around the same time as my dad. Max will be thirty, Ricky will be thirty-two."

"Just think, if you hadn't gone in when you did, you would have driven the car away." If they'd been caught, Kyle would be an accessory to an armed robbery. He would have ended up in jail, too, or juvenile detention, given his age.

I wouldn't be sitting here with him right now.

A sigh of relief runs through me.

"So now you know why I pretend they don't exist," he mutters wryly.

Even Rhett seems like a saint right now, despite the havoc he has caused in our family. "Did they at least apologize?"

He shrugs. "In their own way. But they really fucked up things for Jeremy and me. Now every time there's a theft around school or the neighborhood, fingers are automatically pointed our way. We've even had the cops come by our apartment saying that so-and-so saw one of us in the area at the time. Thankfully we had proof that we weren't. Not sure what's going to happen the next time, when we don't." He sighs. "So, now you know the kind of lowlife trash I am, Piper. We're *that* family. Every town has one of them. The ones you can't trust, that you know it's only a matter of time before they pull some shady shit."

"You're not like your father or your brothers, though," I rush to argue.

He laughs, but there's no mirth in the sound. "How do you know I'm not?"

"I just do," I say with conviction, shoving away that tiny voice in the back of my head that wonders if I could be wrong.

His hard swallow carries in the quiet night as he fumbles with his cigarette pack, pulling another one out. He brings it to his lips but simply holds it there, unlit. "I found a dead cockroach in the box of Cheerios, the morning that I left to come here. I'll bet you could never say that."

I turn away to hide my cringe. I've never even seen a cockroach, alive or otherwise.

He casts his free hand toward the ground. "I'm wearing these shitty running shoes because I can't afford new ones until I get paid. My bumper is being held up by duct tape. And the best thing about coming to camp? I'm not eating peanut butter sandwiches and ramen noodles five days a week." Finally he gives in and lights the cigarette. His third.

I wish I knew what to say to comfort him, but I haven't the first clue. He speaks about a world I am entirely unfamiliar with, and it's not what my mother deems "normal" life.

It's being outright *poor*.

I swallow my pity, because I know he doesn't want it. "Does anyone else here know about your family?" Ashley doesn't, or she would have said something. Does Avery?

He shakes his head, his gaze off in the dark distance. “I didn’t even tell Eric. It was nice, you know. No one knowing *anything* about me. I liked it that way.”

And now *I* know something big.

“I won’t say a word to anyone. I promise.”

He examines the end of the burning cigarette perched between his fingers. “Doesn’t really matter anymore, now that Christa knows. She doesn’t live too far away from me. She must have seen that news article and put two and two together.”

“I don’t think you have to worry about her. She didn’t even want to tell me. She actually held back.”

“Wow. Christa holding back her opinion. That’s a first.” His voice drips with sarcasm.

I feel a twinge of guilt. “She covered for me last night, too. With Darian.” Though the bat fiasco wouldn’t have happened in the first place had she not tried to stop me.

His lips twist in thought and when he speaks again, his tone is much softer. “She must really like you.”

Kyle might not want pity, but I can’t help but offer comfort. “Don’t worry so much about people finding out. No one’s going to care.” I nudge his shoulder with mine. “I know I don’t.”

“Really?” He tips his head to peer at me, and I can barely make out his face in the dim light.

"The girl who dated the captain of the rugby team doesn't care that her new guy is basically white trash?"

I sigh with exasperation. "Stop saying that! You aren't *that*." I frown. "And did you forget that my ex was a giant douchebag? Having rich parents doesn't automatically make you a better person."

"Fair point." He kicks a loose stone away. "But what would your mom say if she knew you were out here right now with me?"

"My mom? She already knows I'm—" I cut that sentence off, feeling my cheeks flush. My mother saw me fawn over Kyle. *So it's going to be the boy with the Mohawk, is it?* she said, and she wasn't at all perturbed by that. Then again, she didn't know about his smoking habit or his tattoos, or that half his immediate family is behind bars. "She wouldn't care."

"Right . . ." Kyle murmurs, as if reading the doubt in my thoughts. He hesitates, and when he speaks again, his voice is soft. "Does it make you wish you'd never taken my dare the first night here?"

When I announced that I'm crushing hard on Kyle in front of everyone.

"Not even a little bit. Is that why you didn't want me to know about this? You thought I wouldn't want to be with you anymore?"

He bows his head and mutters softly, "Something like that."

"Well then . . . you can't read people nearly as well as you think you can."

He lets out a slow, long sigh of relief, and then leans toward me.

My heart begins to pound in my chest.

But he stops himself. "I'm sorry." He holds up his cigarette.

"I don't care." I press my mouth against his with determination—to prove how much I don't care. I revel in the softness of his lips, even tinged with tobacco.

He pulls back suddenly, to drop his cigarette to the ground and grind it out with his toe.

And then he's moving for me quickly, turning his body, one hand sliding around to cup the back of my neck, the other one gripping the side of my waist.

There is nothing tentative or teasing about this kiss, his mouth smashing into mine with a hint of desperation. He beckons my lips to open and slips his tongue inside to move with mine, a deep moan rumbling from somewhere inside.

All day, I've had to restrain my hands, but I no longer have to, letting my fingers smooth over his body, familiarizing myself with the lean body I've been aching to touch freely for days.

He sucks in a breath as my fingers slip beneath his shirt, reveling in the warmth of his skin. Hooking a hand under one of my knees, he pulls me onto his lap to straddle him. The stone beneath my shins is hard and uncomfortable, so I wriggle my body to put my weight on his thighs. It earns his soft groan and a deeper kiss, his hands sliding down over my backside, the tips of his fingers trailing the hem of my shorts, teasing my thighs. I fist his T-shirt, itching to yank it off, my mouth working harder against him, my body aching for more.

He pulls me closer, until our chests are flush. His heart beats hard and his response presses against me farther down.

On instinct, I roll my hips against him, and the ache in my lower belly flares with even more need. All hesitation, all restraint is gone, that voice of reason silenced.

He groans, his hands sliding up beneath my shorts to grip each cheek. He squeezes as he pulls my hips against his.

And I want more. I want all of him.

Our mouths break free of our lip-lock at the same time, as if both of us suddenly realized how far and fast this could go tonight, right here atop this rock, if we don't show some control.

"Whoa." He laughs.

I giggle. "I know."

He leans in to press his forehead against mine, his hands now finding a safe place on the rock beside him. "We have all summer."

I trail his jawline with my fingertips. "Yes. Definitely."

“And this isn’t the most comfortable place.”

“No, it isn’t.” I flick his lip ring with my tongue and he moans softly. “My mom was right. I *am* going to *love* being a camp counselor,” I whisper, earning his throaty laugh.

He cups either side of my face and presses a sweet kiss against my lips. “And it’s only the beginning.”

Chapter 11

NOW

Mark knocks on my office door at six P.M. I beckon him in with a wave of my hand.

"Need anything else before I head out?" He'd stay here until midnight if I asked him to, and likely never utter a complaint.

"I'm good, thanks. I'm leaving soon anyway, to meet my brother for dinner."

He hesitates. "Any follow-ups for me after your call with Kieran?"

Yeah. Start looking for a new job for the both of us. I plaster on a fake smile. "Nope. All good." I called my father in LA and point-blank asked him if he gave Tripp the go-ahead to work a deal with this unknown KDZ company. "I told Tripp to see what they had to offer," was his answer. For a split second, I felt immense satisfaction, knowing Kieran Calloway would tear a strip from Tripp's hide for misrepresenting his wishes.

And then he proceeded to tear a strip out of *me,* for letting Tripp walk all over me.

By the time we ended the call, I was wavering between running home to hide for the rest of the day and hunting down Tripp to wrap my hands around his stocky neck.

"All right, then. Good night." Flashing one last smile, Mark throws his satchel over his shoulder and strolls out.

Finally alone on this corner of the floor, with nothing but the soothing hum of white noise to keep me company, I fold my arms across my desk and lay my forehead on top.

And release a loud groan.

What the hell am I even doing in this job? Maybe Tripp is right! Maybe I am just a twenty-nine-year-old spoiled tart. Maybe my father has indulged me for far too long.

It's always been that way. At six years old, when I asked him if I could design our new house, he sent me off with a box of crayons and a pad of paper. Of course, *my* design was grossly off-scale and a few things weren't practical—the seven stories, the slide from the top floor to the kitchen, the pool in the living room, the dolphin tank in the main bath—but he took my better ideas and transformed them into my childhood home, the house my mother still lives in. She has always said that if Kieran Calloway has a weak spot, it's me, and I'm beginning to think she's not wrong.

He should have left me quietly managing projects for the next ten or fifteen years, until I was old enough, experienced enough, to perhaps deserve a place among the men.

It's a silent admission that curls my stomach with disgust.

A knock on my door has me snapping upright, my mind spinning with excuses as to why it might appear that I was napping at my desk.

Until I see Kyle standing on the other side, a brown package in one arm.

Smirking at me.

Every one of my problems evaporates as my heart begins pounding and my lips curl into a sheepish smile. I wave him in, the revelation from Gus lingering in my mind.

"This just arrived for you." He still has that slight swagger, I note, as he strolls forward to set the box on my desk, where my head was resting. It lands with a dull thud, marking its weight as substantial.

I clear my throat, not trusting my voice. "Security isn't expected to hand-deliver packages. But thank you."

"Your assistant was leaving for the day, so I said I'd bring it up." His gaze roves my glass office—the framed pictures and degrees sitting atop my filing cabinet, the purses dangling from my coatrack, the extra pairs of heels I keep at the office, in case I feel the need to switch.

I frown curiously at the label on the box. It's another package from Rhett. I'm meeting him in an hour. What did he feel the need to send me ahead of time? "When do you finish your shift?" I ask, running my pair of scissors across the seams of the box.

"I'm done now. Heading home."

Home to his wife? His girlfriend? He hasn't come out and said it yet, and I don't have the nerve to ask. Or, more likely, I don't want to. It's easier to deny reality that way.

The small, rectangular name badge on his shirt catches my eyes. "So it's Stewart now?"

"Yeah. My mother's maiden name. I thought it was a good idea given my family history." His jaw muscles tense, his gaze flickering to my Persian rug.

"Right. I guess that makes sense," I murmur, digging into the box. How much do Gus and Rikell know about Kyle's family? Are Kyle's brothers and father still in prison? I can't remember how long he said they'd be away. I have so many questions to ask, I wouldn't know where to begin. My instincts warn me off asking any of them. For now.

He's finished his shift and yet he lingers, watching me.

"What the . . ." I feel my brow furrow as I pull out the wood-and-metal contraption. It's a lamp, quite obviously, made of industrial pipes and a wire cage, the hefty base a block of wood. There's a card included, with my brother's store logo at the top, and a list of where the various materials were sourced from. "Wow. This was part of a railway tie." I tap the wooden base.

There's another small box nestled safely inside,

containing a vintage Edison bulb. I fish it out and set to screwing it in. "My brother made it."

"The one who took off to Thailand?"

"I . . . yeah. That one." A wave of nostalgia washes over me. "You remember that."

Kyle's gaze is now out the window, on my view of the downtown core. "Gus mentioned it."

Somehow I doubt that. Gus is a lot of things, but a gossiper is not one of them. I decide not to challenge him, though. "I'm meeting Rhett for dinner tonight," I say, gingerly unwinding the twisted black cord. "He's back now. From Thailand, I mean. He and his wife live an hour outside Lennox. They opened up this little store that sells up-cycled things. And some days I *really* envy him." I'm babbling now.

I feel Kyle's eyes on me as I map out the best way to plug in this desk lamp.

"Here." He drops to his knees in front of my desk and takes the plug's end from me. Our fingertips graze for just a moment, sending a shock of awareness through me—those hands that spent *a lot* of time on various parts of my body, oh so many years ago—and then he's feeding the cord through the electrical opening in the top right corner and down to the plug panel beneath. "There's one open plug left," he murmurs, and I hold my breath, hyperaware of how close he is to my bare legs beneath the desk, with my skirt reaching just above my knees.

His head pops back up. "Try it now."

And I'm momentarily lost in his beautiful golden eyes, staring back at me.

I clear my throat and flip the simple silver toggle switch. The bulb explodes with light. "I guess my brother actually knows about electricity." I settle back into my chair to admire it.

Except I can't keep my gaze there for long. I never could, on anything else, not when Kyle was around.

Kyle stands, smoothing his uniform's shirt collar, though it's perfectly straight.

Can he hear my heart pounding right now? I feel like I'll explode if I hold the question in any longer. "Why did you request to transfer here—" I begin to ask at the same time that Kyle asks, "You and Tripp Porter don't get along, do you?"

"What? . . . No. We don't, actually." I frown curiously. "Why? What have you heard?"

His lips twist as he seems to consider explaining. "I was behind him earlier today, when he was heading down to the parking garage. He was on the phone, talking to a guy named Hank about a contract that's as good as his. He said he has Kieran Calloway's ear and not to worry about you sticking your—" Kyle purses his lips together, cutting off whatever words he was about to repeat. "That you won't be blowing up this deal."

My ears begin to pound. *"Really . . ."* This

must be about the Marquee. But who the hell is this Hank guy? On impulse, I quickly type "Hank KDZ Boston" into my search engine. And shake my head as a profile of the president of KDZ Construction—Hank Kavanaugh—appears. "Son of a bitch. What the hell does he think he's doing?" I mutter, more to myself, feeling my cheeks burn with rage.

Kyle folds his arms over his chest. "How aboveboard is this Tripp guy?" he asks in a way that makes me think he has an opinion.

"I haven't had reason to suspect he isn't. Why?"

"Because, just before he ducked into his car, I heard him say he wanted his five hundred in the account the same day the ink dries or he'll kill it." Kyle watches me calmly as I process his claim.

"Five hundred . . . What five hundred? Is he talking about money?"

Kyle gives me a knowing look.

"Are you saying that Tripp's taking a *kickback* for this contract?" My voice is eerily steady in contrast to the storm brewing inside me. *Five hundred . . . thousand?*

"I'm telling you what I heard. Thought you'd want to know what he might be trying to pull behind your back. For what it's worth coming from me . . . yeah, he's definitely up to something."

And Kyle always had a knack for distinguishing between fact and fiction.

He moves for the door. “I’d really appreciate it if you don’t pull my name into this. I doubt it would help with credibility, if you take this to your father.”

“No . . . probably not.” How would my father react if he knew Kyle was working in our building?

Kyle opens his mouth to say something, but then seems to change his mind. “Have a good night, Piper.” He’s out the door and strolling along the hall before I notice that he finally called me by my first name and not “Miss Calloway.”

“’Night, Kyle,” I whisper into the silence.

As if hearing my words, he turns to catch me staring at him, and then he disappears.

Leaving me to figure out what the hell I’m supposed to do with this information. If Tripp is lining his pockets with money by securing this construction contract for Hank Kavanaugh, why was he dragging his feet on getting the Marquee off the ground less than a month ago?

Something doesn’t add up.

Also, I never got an answer to *my* question.

Why have you come back into my life now, Kyle?

“You’re not as smart as I’ve given you credit for.” Rhett sucks the edamame beans out of the shell before tossing it into the discard bowl.

“How so?” I swat his hand away as he reaches

for another helping. He showed up to this trendy tapas-style vegetarian restaurant—that *he* chose—twenty minutes late, and now he's eating double his fair share.

He leans back in his chair with a grin, brushing aside his blond hair. It's perpetually six months behind for a haircut—intentionally. The guy is the epitome of ease and in stark contrast to me, right down to his worn metal concert T-shirt and frayed jeans, his Birkenstocks, and the fair trade satchel made from recycled bike tires and plastic bottles that dangles from the back of his chair. "Come on, Dad probably has a series of prerecorded messages so he can run the company postmortem."

I shoot my brother a glare.

His hands go up in surrender. He knows I don't like death jokes, especially after Dad's heart attack. "All I'm saying is, he's not going anywhere anytime soon. Not by choice, anyway. And he's going to run his company the way he always has, even with you there as his sidekick. It's worked well for him so far."

"And for *you*." I give him a pointed glare. Rhett can afford to spend his days making functional art out of trash *because* of Dad's unrelenting work ethic and tenacious drive to succeed.

He rolls his eyes but then acknowledges my point with a sigh and a nod.

"Anyway, if it were up to me, I'd fire Tripp's

ass tomorrow. It makes my blood boil that he could be so disloyal to Dad."

"Do you really think the guy would take a bribe for a construction contract, though?"

"It *would* surprise me," I admit. But Kyle's confidence is hard to ignore. Though maybe it's because I *want* to believe him. Maybe that would be the silver lining to Tripp's deception—a stepping-off point for Kyle and me to begin talking again.

To what end, though?

"Sounds like you've had quite the day." Rhett's hand moves fast, snatching three bean pods as if it's a game.

He doesn't know the half of it. "I can't go to Dad with this. He's already thinking he made a mistake promoting me."

"Kieran Calloway doesn't make mistakes like that." Rhett smiles sympathetically. "He wouldn't have put you there if he didn't *know* you could handle it."

I snort. "You didn't hear him shred my eardrum over the phone earlier. I think maybe he's changed his mind."

"Doubt it. And, besides, you're his only option if he wants to keep the business in the family."

"Yeah. Thanks for that, by the way," I mutter sarcastically, stabbing at a deep-fried cauliflower bite. There are days where I am envious of my brother's laid-back lifestyle. Days where I sit in my office and wish we could swap roles, so he could take the burden of continuing our father's legacy off my shoulders, even just for a little while.

But the truth is, I wouldn't gain any more satisfaction from weaving electrical wire through pipes to make things light up than Rhett would at the helm of the team that's going to build a thirty-two-story condominium.

We are both exactly where we're meant to be.

"Please. If I told him tomorrow that I wanted back in, he'd tell me he'd rather dissolve the company than give me a chance. And I don't, by the way, want anything to do with that world."

"That's because you're too busy smoking pot and playing with silver spoons."

He grins. "Mock me all you want, but do you know how many of those phone holders we've sold? Probably enough to pay for a pair of those ridiculous, overpriced shoes." He waves his fork toward my Manolos. "What were they, a grand? Two?"

"Funny, I seem to recall a time when you only dated girls who wore ridiculous, overpriced shoes."

He smirks. "And then I saw the light."

My brother used to be the archetypal wealthy city-boy type—stylish gelled hair, a taste for expensive clothes, fast cars, and high-society blondes. Moderately entitled, but tempered by my mother's influence; quick to anger when he didn't get his way, though he was for the most part disciplined and eager to please my father. He was interning at CG during his summers, being groomed for an executive position.

And then it was like he woke up one day with a new personality and a one-way ticket to Thailand. In truth, there were probably signs that he would one day snap, but the six-year age gap between us made it hard for me to see them.

"Yes, that light is awfully blue and sparkly." I stare pointedly at the signature robin's-egg-blue Tiffany bag peeking out from his satchel. It contains a diamond pendant that Lawan had been eyeing online one day but would never dare ask him to buy for her. "I wasn't mocking you, by the way. I loved the spoon sculpture. And the lamp that just arrived."

"Yeah?" His eyes twinkle with delight. "And what'd Dad say?"

"He . . . uses it daily."

Rhett bursts out in laughter and I can't help but grin. He's always had a big laugh, but somewhere along the way, it evolved into a hearty, booming sound.

"I hesitated too long, didn't I?"

"You're a shitty liar, Piper."

"It did grab his attention, momentarily, if that means anything."

"Whatever. I gave up on pleasing him years

ago. And I'll tell you, it was liberating." He sighs heavily. "Okay, enough about Dad and that place. Tell me what else is going on in your life, so I know you have a good excuse for not coming out to visit us for *eight months*."

I cringe. "Has it been that long?"

"Since our store's grand opening. Lawan's trying not to take it personally."

"I'm sorry, really. It's just been so busy with work, and then the whole breakup and moving and all that . . ."

He tips his bottle of Corona toward me. "Best decision you've ever made, shedding those two hundred pounds, by the way. Not gonna lie: I may have cracked a bottle of champagne after Mom spilled the news." To say David and Rhett did not click is an understatement. The moment we pulled up to their house in David's Maserati and David stepped out in his polished leather shoes and suit for a casual weekend, Rhett had made his mind up. David only validated his opinion of him when he point-blank told Rhett he was an idiot for not signing a pre-nup to protect his money from Lawan, an especially prickly thorn in my father's side as well.

It's the only time I've ever seen the pre-Thailand version of my brother: seconds away from knocking my fiancé's teeth out.

"How's the condo?"

"Besides the psychotic Siamese cat that was

sitting on my nightstand watching me sleep the other night?" I fill Rhett in on my new living situation.

"I really need to meet these camp friends one day."

"If you weren't already married, I'd be setting you and Ashley up. You'd be perfect together."

"*Happily* married," he corrects with a warning look.

"Whatever. Just make sure you let me know when Lawan runs off with the gardener and half your money." A scenario my father offered up when trying to convince my brother to sign the pre-nup his lawyers had drafted, the day before their wedding.

I'm only teasing, of course. I've never seen a more content and loving couple than Rhett and Lawan. He makes her tea every night and drives to a bakery one town over every Saturday morning for her favorite almond croissants; I've never even heard him raise his voice to her.

Rhett takes a swig from his beer. "And what about you? Dating yet?"

"Not yet." It's funny, just a few weeks ago, that answer would have been more along the lines of "Hell no," and punctuated with a bitter laugh. Now, though, the second Rhett asked, my mind instantly veered to the lobby at work, and to the man behind the security desk.

"Don't worry, someone decent will come along

soon enough." He adds in a grumble, "Preferably as opposite to Worthington as possible."

"He definitely is that," I mutter under my breath as I take a sip of my wine.

Too loudly, it seems.

Rhett leans back in his chair, folding his arms across his broad chest. "Okay, spill it. So there *is* someone?"

"No . . ."

"An architect."

"No."

"Investor."

"No."

"Tennis pro?"

I cringe.

"Masseuse?"

"Stop it."

"The gardener?"

I laugh and joke, "I don't want Lawan's sloppy seconds."

Rhett's knowing eyebrows arch as he waits expectantly. Another Calloway trait he's inherited is tenacity. As in, the rest of our dinner will be hijacked by this one topic until I give in.

I groan. "Okay, but don't tell anyone. Especially not *Mom*."

I wait to get his nod of agreement.

"Do you remember that guy I was with at summer camp? I'm sure Mom must have told you about him. Kyle?"

"I don't think . . ." His mouth curls with a frown and his brow tightens with concentration as he struggles.

"He was from Poughkeepsie." I hesitate. "His father and two of his brothers were in prison."

"Oh yeah!" Recognition fills his face, as I knew it would eventually. "Daddy's sweet Princess Piper got caught with her pants down on the wrong side of the tracks that summer. Finally took some of the heat off me. Especially when you got fired." He starts humming Billy Joel's "Uptown Girl."

I roll my eyes at him. "*Anyway,* I kind of ran into him." I explain.

"He's working as a *security guard* at Calloway?"

"Yeah."

"Wow. That's *something*." He frowns. "If I remember correctly, you guys got into some serious trouble together. Wasn't there some kind of accident with a kid?"

"With one of the counselors, yeah." My stomach tightens with the memory of that night, with how lucky we were, how bad it *could* have been.

Rhett's fingers draw along his chin, scratching at the day-old scruff, as he processes. "Does Dad know this guy is working there?"

"No." I shake my head to emphasize this.

A wide grin slowly splits Rhett's face. "So, are you two—"

"No."

"But you want to?"

"I don't know what I want." Is that even true?

My brother's curious frown tells me he knows it isn't.

"I want to know why he disappeared like that on me. It was a jerk thing to do."

I want to know when exactly he stopped caring. Was it right away or over time? Or did he never really feel anything at all?

Was I just being naïve?

I grind my teeth with the thought that Kyle might have fed me adoring lines and intimate touches to get what he wanted from me before summer was over.

"Huh. Small world, I tell ya," Rhett murmurs.

"That's the thing." I relay what Gus told me about Kyle requesting the transfer to our building. "What do you think that means?"

"That he wants back in your life. *Obviously*. And damn, wouldn't that be something. Daddy's princess with the building *security guard?* One with a bunch of convicts for a family?" He chuckles. "I might be back in Kieran Calloway's good books once he finds out."

"So glad you're entertained," I mutter. "But he doesn't want to reconnect. He's been avoiding me for the most part. Plus he's living with someone."

His lips purse with thought. "So what are you gonna do, then?"

"I don't know! But he keeps getting into my head, messing up my day. I can't concentrate." Heat climbs up my neck. "It's embarrassing! I'm all wrapped up in this. In *him*. It's like I'm sixteen all over again." Except I'm not. I'm twenty-nine years old and getting sucked into nostalgia when I should be focusing on my career, on these projects worth billions of dollars!

"So then there's only one thing to do—you confront him." Rhett shrugs, like it's no big deal.

"You make it sound so easy."

"You're kidding me, right?" He squeezes the bridge of his nose like he's in pain. "Didn't you once walk out of a meeting owning a building that the guy didn't even want to sell?"

I roll my eyes. "That idiot couldn't negotiate worth a damn." A perfect example of where a guy had no business inheriting Daddy's empire and was too stupid and arrogant to realize it.

"And didn't you sit in a lecture hall and lob argument after argument for an hour straight until your professor finally yielded to you?"

"He was a misogynistic ass! I mean, who debates a room full of women about women's reproductive rights? And how do you even know about that?"

"Mom. She was so proud of you, she forgot about the time difference and woke me up in the middle of the night to tell me about it. My point is, you're Piper Fucking Calloway! So get this security guard in a room and get your answers. Because there *is* a reason for him wanting to work in your building, and it *has* to do with you. And hey," he raises his hands in a sign of surrender, "say what you want about making unfair assumptions, but given this guy's family and who you are, there's fair reason to be worried."

"Kyle's not there to hurt me."

Rhett gives me a flat look.

"I guess I could ask him to meet—"

"Ask? No, you *tell* him to meet you. Because you are *Piper Fucking Calloway*." He emphasizes each word with a jab at the table's surface, earning my laugh.

"Fine, I will."

"Good. Let me know how it goes."

"I will. *But*. . . ." I lift a finger in warning.

"I know, I know." He rolls his eyes and mock-zips his lips closed. "Have you talked to Mom lately?"

"A week ago. She's redecorating at Martha's Vineyard." *Again*.

" 'I'm glad to see she's still enjoying the fruits of *my* labor,' " Rhett murmurs, imitating our father's bitter, deep tone.

"Right?" I shake my head. "I can't even remember them ever *liking* each other anymore."

Mom ended up doing a lot of "thinking" over that summer while I was at Wawa, with the help of a twenty-nine-year-old tennis instructor. The affair ended whatever meager efforts my father might have been making toward reconciliation and instead earned his wrath. They've been officially divorced for twelve years now. As much as I dreaded the inevitability at the onset, as much as I despised the both of them for their roles in tearing apart our family, by the time the ink was drying on the legal paperwork of the ugly, high-profile divorce, what I felt more than anything was relief that they'd finally go their separate ways, until the wounds healed and civility might arise. Maybe even friendship.

I've long since let go of that delusion.

The last time my parents were in the same room was five years ago, at Rhett's wedding at Naka Island in Thailand. It took months of me needling to convince my father to make the trip, a seeming victory that turned into a living nightmare when he arrived at the hotel with a stunning twenty-eight-year-old model who he'd met at a fund-raiser just weeks before. Clearly a woman who served only one purpose there. Well, two, if my father's intent was to burrow deep under my mother's fifty-two-year-old skin. And, boy, did he ever, if her toast, delivered after too many glasses of Cristal and with at least a dozen not-so-subtle jabs thrown his way, was any indication. Poor Lawan got a good glimpse of the family she'd married into and an even better understanding of why my brother chose to stay on the other side of the world for as long as he had.

The server comes to clear our plates and deliver the tab, which Rhett grabs before I have a chance to even reach for it. "I'm so glad we did this, Pipes."

"So am I. You know, you're the only one I can talk to frankly, about *any*thing," I murmur. "You never judge."

"I'm a huge stoner, remember? Stoners don't judge." He winks. "What are you going to do about this security guard?"

I sigh heavily. "I don't know, but I have to do something and soon. Like, *tomorrow*." I can't continue on like this, my mind muddled with the past. Otherwise I'm going to start deserving whatever belittling nicknames Tripp wants to label me with. "Any advice?"

He grins. "You're Piper Fucking Calloway."

Arriving to work at seven A.M. has its advantages.

Namely a quiet lobby, ripe for confrontation.

"I'm Piper Calloway . . . I'm Piper Calloway . . ." I mutter under my breath as I march toward the security desk, my heels clicking with purpose, my chin held high as I stare straight ahead.

"Morning, Miss Calloway," Gus croons. "How's my boy Rhett doing?"

I clear the sudden nervousness from my throat.

"He's good. He asked that I pass along his greetings."

Gus's faces splits with a wide grin. "I hope he makes it in here again one day. It's been a long time. He was still in college, the last time I saw him."

"I'll be sure to let him know." I shift my focus to Kyle, who's leaning back in his chair, watching the exchange through curious eyes. "Good morning, Kyle."

"Good morning, Miss Callow—"

"Please meet me on the eleventh floor, in conference room C, at ten A.M."

Something unreadable flashes in his eyes—resignation, maybe?—and there's a few seconds' pause before his golden gaze shifts to Gus. "Is that okay?"

"No problems here." Gus holds his hands up. "What the boss lady says, we do. Gladly."

Kyle sighs heavily and then nods once. "Okay," he mumbles, reluctance in his tone. "I'll see you later."

"Ten A.M. sharp. Eleven C," I repeat. "You know where it is; you've been pacing past it enough times." With that, I wave my badge and head to my office, trying to ignore the rush of nerves churning in my stomach.

Mark's eyes are on me the second I step into the executive wing, his brows raised in curiosity. No doubt because of the email I sent him last night, asking that he be in as early as possible, seven A.M. at the latest. I've never asked that of him.

I'm not in the mood for exchanging pleasantries right now. "I need you to find out *everything* you can on Hank Kavanaugh from KDZ. Where he lives, who he's married to, where he went to school, their construction projects, *everything*. I want to know *how* Tripp knows him, and every meeting they've had. See what Jill can tell you. On the down-low, of course."

Mark eagerly jots down notes, his mouth working over questions he's dying to ask but knows better than to, just yet. Finally, he dares murmur, "So you have a plan?"

"*Oh,* I have a plan." I can feel the vicious and defiant smile stretch across my lips. "We're going to lance a giant boil."

Chapter 12

THEN

2006, Camp Wawa, Week One

"He's, like, *in love* with you!"

"Oh my God, no he isn't!" My cheeks burn even as I grin, my eyes darting around us, making sure no one else heard Ashley's enthusiastic hiss. Thankfully everyone's attention seems to be on the screen ahead or on their nearby friends' giggles, or on stretching their sleeping bags out on the grass as they prepare for *The Parent Trap*. Night Four of camp is "movie night" every week—barring rain—and I'll admit, the sea of small, squirming bodies over the soccer field is impressive.

The image from the projector flickers a few times before it finally fills the screen, and the opening score blares through the speakers and carries through the calm, warm night air.

"*Please.* His eyes are, like, *glued* to you." She drops her voice. "Did you two hook up last night?"

"No."

"I don't believe you."

I can't stifle my wide grin fast enough.

"I knew it!" Ashley starts giggling hysterically. "What was it like?"

"We just kissed. That's all." That's a lie. There's nothing "just" about kissing Kyle, I've decided. My lips were still puffy when I woke this morning, with a content sigh despite the early hour and lack of sleep, and the sound of Christa's voice, urging everyone on their feet.

I've been on a high all day, my body humming with life and expectation every time I catch a glimpse of him. Nothing has been able to dampen my mood—not the sight of Izzy's bloody knee when she tripped over a log, not the icy temperature of the lake when we went swimming, not the overdone and unappealing fish sticks that landed on my plate for dinner.

"You're coming out tonight, right?" Ashley asks.

"Of course." I've been anxiously counting down the hours since my eyes cracked open.

"Wear your bathing suit. We're going night swimming."

I shudder.

"It'll be fun. Trust me." She adds in a coy voice, "I'm sure Kyle will be going."

My gaze wanders over to where he sits, ten feet away, behind his campers. He's laughing at Eric, who's furiously brushing his hands through his blond curls.

"Glitter," Ashley explains with a giggle.

"The kids must have stolen it from the arts tub and played a joke on Eric. That or Kyle did it. They're such jerks to each other sometimes."

Midway through a laugh, Kyle turns my way and I feel the shy smile curl my lips, memories of his mouth against mine still firmly emblazoned in my mind.

"See? He can't keep his eyes off you! You're like a magnet."

"Stop!" I elbow her, but I'm grinning.

Kyle seems to pick up on the gist of our conversation because he reaches into a bowl of popcorn and tosses a kernel at us. It misses us entirely, pinning Christa in the head.

The soft strum of a guitar and laughter carries and the day's warmth lingers in the air as Ashley and I approach the lake, our bathing suits on beneath our clothes. My campers were asleep before hers, leaving me to pace around the girls' restroom, waiting for her to arrive. Christa didn't say a word when I clambered down the steps and grabbed my things.

The way things are going, I doubt we'll ever see eye-to-eye on *any*thing.

People are already in the water, trading splashes, though it's too dark to identify anything beyond a few silhouettes.

Someone has carried a metal firepit down and settled it in the sand. Flames now dance within it, toasting the marshmallows held close while illuminating the circle of faces that surrounds it. Avery and Maria sit on either side of Colin, seemingly lulled by his throaty voice as he sings the chorus to "Wonderwall" by Oasis.

"You guys coming in?" Eric calls out from somewhere in the lake. I can only assume Kyle is somewhere out there, too.

Ashley kicks off her sandals and drags her toes through the shoreline.

"It's amazing. Get in here, Freckles!"

She sheds her clothes where she stands, earning a loud whistle of approval as she adjusts her green bikini bottoms. Wawa has a one-piece-only rule for swimming attire, one of the few dress code rules that Darian makes sure everyone adheres to. "Coming, Piper?"

I follow suit, a swirl of nervousness and excitement stirring in the pit of my stomach as I reveal my own prohibited two-piece—a simple but elegant black bikini that my friend Reid swears makes my breasts look twice as big.

I grit my teeth as we slowly wade in, though the temperature is more bearable now than it was earlier today, the contrast to the air less dramatic.

"Oh, this is *nice!*" Ashley skims the top of the water with her fingertips. "I *love* night swimming."

I suck in a breath, bracing myself against the cold. "I don't know if I'd go as far as to call it *nice*." My skin is covered in gooseflesh.

The next few moments happen in a blur. Water churns and a dark figure charges at me, then I feel wet, strong arms wrap around my thighs and hoist me up.

"No!" I shriek as my body tips over Kyle's shoulder. My fingers glide across his wet skin as I grasp for purchase on his bare back. He's barreling forward, deeper into the lake, his hands gripping my hips tight, his intent clear. "Kyle, don't you dare—"

He only lets go after my body is fully submerged.

"I hate you!" I sputter through my laughter, though I'm quickly warming to the temperature of the water.

"No you don't," he teases, lingering a few feet away, immersed to his neck.

My fingers itch to touch his bare skin. I glide toward him and he begins moving backward, just out of reach, drawing me out deeper and off to the right, away from Eric and Ashley and the others. He only stops when the water level sits at my shoulders and we're alone. The sand feels weird out here. I scrunch my toes against the lake's silky bottom.

"Hey." He stoops in the water to meet me at eye level. His strong hands find my waist and he pulls me closer to him, fitting me in between his parted thighs.

"Hey." My voice is a whisper as my fingers

curl around his biceps, reveling in their shape and strength. My heart hammers inside my chest, memories of his pliable lips against mine last night flooding my mind, exploding my anticipation of a repeat.

"Did you like the movie tonight?" I ask.

"What movie?" He bows his head to settle his forehead against my temple, the tip of his slender nose grazing my cheek. "I wasn't watching any movie."

"It almost put me to sleep." *Lie*. As if I could ever drift off with Kyle in the vicinity.

"You weren't paying attention, either." I hear a smirk in his voice.

"How would you know?"

His hand curls around to skate up my spine, stalling at the fastening of my bikini top, one finger casually slipping beneath it. "Because I was watching you."

"That doesn't sound creepy *at all,*" I tease.

He chuckles. "The way you look in *this* . . ." He slides one strap of my bikini top down and replaces it with his mouth, leaving a trail along my skin, hot against the cool air. I can't tell if it's the metal of his lip ring or just *him* that sends shivers through my body. "No wonder they don't let counselors wear bikinis. My entire cabin would be hiding their hard-ons in the lake."

"Oh my God! They're like, *twelve!*" I cringe through my laugh.

"Exactly. Trust me. You wouldn't believe the stuff they talk about." He swallows hard and then, sliding the strap back in place, shifts away. "Sorry."

"For what?"

He sighs. "I just don't ever want you to think I'm pressuring you."

Because of what I said about that pig Trevor the first night here.

I can't help but laugh. If Kyle were Trevor, he'd have his tongue shoved down my throat and my top unfastened by now.

"What's so funny?" he asks, a touch of wariness in his voice.

"Nothing. Just . . ." Kyle may have figured out that I'm a virgin, but I'm beginning to think he also assumes I'm *entirely* inexperienced. Beneath the water, I smooth my hands first over his chest, and then downward, admiring the cut of his lean torso. "I'm okay with this. With *whatever*."

"With *whatever?*" I can't see his face in the dark, but I can imagine his thick eyebrows arched with amusement.

I let my hand drift farther down, my palm flat as I slide it over the front of his shorts, enjoying the hard form against my palm a moment, letting him know that I'm not *that* delicate or inexperienced.

Kyle's breathing wavers, and the sound of his swallow catches my ear. "Got it." He cups my chin with his palm and leans in to kiss me—not as fervently as last night—before letting his hand slide down over my throat, across my collarbone, and farther, slipping beneath the water to skate over my breast. His touch is tentative at first, but it quickly turns confident as the pad of his thumb draws circles over the soft fabric of my bikini, over my pebbled nipple.

I grip his waist and wait for him to push the material aside, to slip his hand beneath, to feel his touch against my bare skin. Just the thought of it has heat pooling in my lower belly.

"All right, counselors! You've had your little bit of fun," Darian's voice suddenly calls out from the shoreline.

"Shit," Kyle mutters, his hand stalling, his breathing ragged.

A round of groans carries through the night.

"Oh, I know. You guys need to learn to be more quiet if you want to get away with this. Come on, get to your cabins now!"

Kyle sighs.

"Tomorrow?" I murmur against his lips, letting my hand drift down over him once again.

The strangled sound coming from his throat makes me smile.

"Darian is going to *murder* you two!" Ashley whisper-squeals as Eric and Kyle coast up the pathway, one after another, in the camp's golf carts. It's after eleven at night, and the ground is still soggy following an afternoon of heavy rain that kept the campers cooped up in the rec center and under the pavilion. Despite the two-hour-long dance and camper awards ceremony tonight, it still took almost an hour to get them settled—their last night at Wawa—too much unspent energy coursing through their little limbs.

Much like the counselors, it would seem.

"Nah, her lights are off. All those cheesy dance moves tired her out." Eric eases off the path and pulls up next to Kyle's golf cart. "First one to the badminton course wins. Whichever route you want, but grass only."

"You are *crazy*." Ashley shakes her head but trots to take a seat next to Eric, grinning.

Kyle gestures to the vacant spot beside him.

This is probably a bad idea, I note as I slide in, huddling close as if I'm chilled, though the night air is sticky and warm. *"Hey,"* I whisper, pressing my lips against his cheek.

He turns toward me, stealing a kiss. "Miss me?"

"*So* much." Even though we were never more than ten feet apart all afternoon—by coincidence or by design.

He smiles and releases a low groan that I feel deep inside.

The whir of Eric's golf cart sounds.

"Hey!"

I squeal and grab the cart's frame as we lurch

forward. Kyle chases Eric, veering off the path and onto the grassy field, bumping and jostling us both as we try to get around him. Ashley peers back at us, her hair a frizzy halo, as she eggs Eric on. "Faster! Faster!" she calls through her laughs.

It's not a surprise that they beat us to the badminton court.

"That wasn't even remotely fair," Kyle chides.

Eric throws his hands in the air. "Maybe if you stopped sucking face for two minutes . . ."

Kyle rolls his eyes but smirks. "First one to the kayak rack?"

"You're on."

"I'm driving!" Ashley proclaims.

Eric gestures over himself in the sign of the cross.

"Oh, shut up." She smacks his hand, then nods toward me. "It's our turn, right?"

"I guess so?" Part of me wants to cross myself, too, and not in a joking way. "I've never driven one of these, though."

"It's easy. Here." Kyle grabs my waist and hoists me with seeming ease onto his lap, giving me a thirty-second push-this-pedal-to-go-forward-and-turn-this-wheel-to-steer lesson, all while I'm acutely aware of the feel of his growing need against my backside.

"Ready?" Ashley chirps, already in position to drive, her fists gripping the black wheel with purpose.

“Hold on.” We shift places so I’m settled in the driver’s seat.

“Okay. So . . .” Kyle leans in and drops his voice to a low murmur. “They’re going to go that way.” He nods to the left. “But there’s a better way, around the other side of the totem pole.”

“Down the hill?”

“Shh . . . Just to the right of it. I’ve done it before. Trust me. Eric won’t think of it, so pretend you’re following them until we reach . . .” I listen intently as he gives me directions, trying to ignore the feel of his lips grazing my ear as he tries to hide our plan from our competitors.

“What’s he saying?” Eric calls out, his eyes narrowing with wariness.

“To drive safely,” I answer, with mock innocence.

We take off at the same time, with Ashley squealing and Eric shushing her. We’re far enough away from the cabins to keep from waking the campers, but not *that* far away from Darian’s cabin.

“Now!” Kyle demands and I veer off to the right, the cart bouncing over the divots in the grass. “Around that tree!”

I grit my teeth to keep from squealing, too, as I bank around an enormous oak and then speed down the hill and across another stretch of open space toward the lake, a mix of terror and exhilaration coursing through my veins.

“There they are. We have to get to the path by the lake before them.” Kyle points at the other cart, speeding toward us, its dim headlights flickering with each bump. “Shit, they’re gonna beat us!”

“The hell they are.” I jam my foot down on the cart’s pedal, goading the cart to its maximum speed, which isn’t that fast, but in the dark, on rough terrain, I may as well be racing my mom’s Porsche.

“Piper . . .”

“We’re going to make it.” My hands tighten around the steering wheel.

“Shit, shit, shit . . .” Kyle grips the cart’s frame, bracing himself.

“Oh my God!” Ashley shrieks.

I cut in front of them and swerve onto the path, earning Kyle’s “Holy shit!”

And that’s when it all goes to hell.

The path cuts more sharply to the right than I expected, and I’m going too fast to try to correct us.

We crash into the lake.

Darian’s Elmo sleeping attire isn’t nearly as comical tonight as it was the night of the bat incident.

Maybe it’s because she trudged out in her rubber boots just in time to watch Kyle, Eric, and two guys who were by the beach at the time of the accident pull the submerged golf cart out of the lake.

Or maybe it's because the four of us are lined up against the rec center wall like it's some kind of firing squad drill and I half-expect Darian to pull out a rifle and end us. Her normally peppy personality has been replaced by a hard jaw and a stern glare.

"Do y'all realize how much each of those carts costs?" Her arms are crossed over her chest. "*At least* six grand each. At least! And *maybe* this one will run after it dries out and we assess the damage, but it's likely going to need new parts! And think of what *could* have happened!"

Eric holds his wrist gingerly in front of him. He slammed it against the golf cart's frame when Ashley maneuvered to avoid crashing with the maniac—me—who was barreling toward her.

"Go to the kitchen and get some ice on that," she says in a clipped tone.

"It's fine—" he begins to say.

"Now!" Darian barks.

Eric flashes wide eyes our way before ducking his head and trudging into the kitchen.

Ashley and I exchange a look that confirms what we both know—we are in *deep* shit.

Darian takes an exaggerated, calming breath. "Okay. Tell me *exactly* what happened."

I open my mouth to take full blame.

"It's my fault," Kyle blurts out. "I bet Eric I could beat him in a race and I lost control."

I glare at him. Is he nuts? He's not taking the blame for this. "No, it was—"

"I convinced him to take the carts out of the lot," he says over my voice, his hand grazing the small of my back. "I'm sorry. I screwed up, Dare."

I turn to look at Ashley. She stands there, petrified, her lips pursed together.

Eric reappears. "This is all I could find," he mutters, holding a bag of frozen peas.

"No!" Darian's face pinches with annoyance. "We need those for dinner."

"Ugh. Really. Peas?" Eric grimaces.

"Did you check the freezer in the back?"

"No. But this will work, won't it?"

"No, it's our food, Eric!" They begin bickering.

It gives me a moment to turn to Kyle. "You are not taking the fall for this."

"Yeah, I am," he murmurs under his breath. "This is my fault. None of this would have happened if it hadn't been for me."

"No! I'm not—"

"I know how to deal with Darian. Just shut up and let me, okay?" He slips his fingers into mine, to squeeze them once.

"Go and put those peas back before they spoil." Darian points toward the kitchen.

Eric drags his feet back inside.

"You two—" She gestures at Ashley and me. "Get back to your cabins right now. You, a word." Her eyes narrow at Kyle.

"Go. I'll take care of this," he whispers, giving the small of my back a gentle push.

"Now!" Darian yells.

We scurry away, leaving Kyle and Darian to face off.

"I warned you about keeping your nose clean this year, Kyle," I hear her say.

He dips his head. "You did."

"You know what *this means*. You know I can't allow counselors who behave like this to stay. And dragging those girls into it? I know this was not their idea."

"We are *so* stupid," I mutter, my feet moving slowly as I watch the exchange—seeing Kyle's head hanging and Darian's hands waving dramatically, her head shaking furiously—over my shoulder.

"They don't think when they get together," Ashley whispers.

"No, all of us!" *I'm* stupid. I should have known better. *I* know Kyle's situation. If she fires him, he'll have to go back to that cockroach-infested hole. Unlike me, he really needs this job. Why would he risk all that? "We can't let Kyle take the blame, Ashley."

"Maybe she'll cool down and we can talk to her tomorrow? Darian always gives those two a pass."

"I'm not so sure it's going to happen this time." I pause behind a hedge to watch the rest unfold.

Eric comes out with what appears to be an appropriate ice pack against his wrist. Darian's hands are on her hips as she lectures them some more. Both of them tip their heads back. They're saying something, but she just keeps shaking her head.

No, no, no . . . it's saying.

Finally, she waves them away, toward the boys' cabins.

They look at each other once before they walk away, dragging their feet. Kyle's hands are locked together against the back of his neck.

Darian takes a seat at the nearby picnic table and braces her forehead in her hands. Her body language oozes resignation.

What if Kyle has finally run out of passes?

Dread fills me. I can't imagine the summer here without him. I won't last a day.

"Are you coming?" Ashley whispers.

"I'll catch up." I double back.

Darian turns to regard me when I'm about ten feet out, the gravel crunching beneath my shoes. Even in the poor lighting, she looks exhausted. "Piper, I told you to go back—"

"It wasn't Kyle and Eric driving. It was Ashley and me," I blurt out. *Sorry, Ashley.* "And I'm the one who put the cart into the water, because I was racing Ashley and going too fast."

Darian sighs. "And you two came up with the idea to race golf carts all on your own?"

"Yes."

I get a knowing glare in return. She doesn't believe that for a second.

"Please don't fire them."

"Kyle and Eric took those carts out, knowing that they were explicitly told not to. More than once."

I shake my head firmly. "No, I took them. So punish me."

Her eyebrows arch. "You took both of them?"

I make a sound of agreement, dropping my gaze to my shoes.

"You're willing to take *all* the responsibility from those two hooligans?"

Three, technically, if you count Ashley. "Yes." Because the truth is, me losing this job won't affect my future. It won't deprive me of spending money next year. It won't limit my college application or future career. All it'll do is bruise my ego. And my parents'. I'm not sure who it would hurt more—my nostalgic mother or my prideful father.

"I'll pay for the damages. It won't cost the camp a thing, I promise." My stomach tightens at the prospect of that phone call with my mother. "Please don't fire them," I ask again, in a more pleading tone.

"I don't *want* to. Losing counselors the first

week of camp throws everything off." She drags her fingers over the picnic table. "Get to your cabin."

I bite my bottom lip, hesitating. "So, you're *not* going to fire them?"

"I don't know. I need to give this some thought. I will let you guys know tomorrow morning. Now go on."

I trudge back through the dark, quiet campground, preparing myself for a sleepless night, but holding on to hope.

Chapter 13

NOW

My left heel wobbles a touch as I step out of the elevator. I'm two minutes early and Kyle is already in the meeting room, seated and waiting, his back to me, his attention on his phone.

For just a moment, I lose my nerve and reach back to hold the elevator door. For just a moment, I tell myself this is crazy and that I need to let go and move on before I humiliate myself further.

I don't know the cool, reserved man sitting in that room; I only know the wild boy he used to be.

But then that familiar thrill stirs in my stomach, the one that Kyle has *always* stirred inside me like no one else—not even David in our early days. And I can't dismiss that.

Taking a deep breath, I push through the glass door.

Kyle doesn't shift or turn; he waits until I'm towering over him to peer up at me. His golden eyes are wary and resigned. That gaze flickers down, over my slate-blue silk blouse—the collar plunging but not unprofessionally so—and then back up. It's a quick look, but I don't miss it.

"Is this about that Tripp guy?" he finally asks.

I settle into the chair across from him, putting us at equal level. "No."

He nods slowly, as if he knows what I'm going to ask. I'm guessing he heard my question yesterday, after all. He chose to pretend he didn't.

Do I go in hard or do I try a more subtle approach?

His eyes trail my hands as I clasp them on the table.

"How is everything?"

The smallest smirk touches his lips. "No complaints."

"Are you liking things here so far?"

"Yes."

"And you like Lennox?"

"Yes." He's answering as if he's being questioned in an interrogation. And maybe that's what this is.

"Do you like it more than San Diego?"

His smirk falters a touch.

"Gus told me that's where you moved from."

He nods slowly. "I figured it was time to come home."

"Home?" I repeat lightly. "I thought home was Poughkeepsie. Or was it Albany?"

"Both, actually." His lips twist in thought. "You remembered."

"Of course I did. I remember *everything,* Kyle." I hear the vulnerability in my voice and I hate it.

I clear my throat and attempt to steel my nerve. "Unlike you, I've *never* forgotten."

"I haven't forgotten anything," he says quickly, sharply, piercing me with a look that is somehow both hard and soft. "Not a second of it."

The air in this meeting room has suddenly turned electric.

So then why the act? I want to ask, but I bench that question for the moment.

"When did you move to San Diego?"

He shifts and settles back in his chair, as if to get comfortable. "Two weeks after I left Wawa."

With not so much as a call or email or anything to me?

He drums his fingertips over the table's smooth surface in an unhurried tempo, his gaze never leaving mine.

Waiting for me to ask my next question.

My phone vibrates in my pocket with an incoming call. I ignore it. This exchange between Kyle and me feels so much more important than anything else at the moment. "How is your family doing now?"

He sighs heavily, his eyes drifting to the window behind me. "Fine, I guess. I don't have much to do with them anymore."

"Are they out?" I don't need to elaborate.

Kyle turns his head, as if checking the hall behind us to make sure there aren't any eavesdroppers hovering by the door. It gives me a sublime view of his profile—of that long, slender nose that used to nuzzle against my neck, of those full, soft pouty lips that spent many nights against mine. Does he still kiss like he used to, I wonder, or has that changed along with the rest of him?

"Yeah. Well, my dad and Ricky are, anyway. They were released a few years ago. Max got into some trouble while inside, so his sentence got extended. He gets out in a few months." Kyle doesn't say anything for a long moment, and I assume that's all the information I'm going to get. But then he offers, "They were living in Albany for a bit, but they decided to move to San Diego. Last I heard, my mom and dad are back together, and Dad and Ricky were working construction. Probably looking for their next scam."

"You don't think they've learned?"

"*Oh,* I'm sure they've learned. They've learned *all kinds* of things being behind bars for that long. Like, how not to get caught next time," he mutters sarcastically, his gaze shifting to the table again.

His opinion of his family hasn't changed much, I note. In all fairness, I've never met them, so it may be true.

"Do they know you moved to Lennox?"

He shrugs nonchalantly, but then shakes his head. "I didn't tell them. Maybe my little brother did. If not . . . I'll find out when I call my mom at Christmas."

What must it be like to have such a dysfunctional family? Not that the Calloways are a poster child for family ideals. Dad and I do dinner and drinks on December twenty-third so he can pass along whatever gift Greta chose for me before he jets off to his yacht in the Cayman Islands. I spend Christmas on Martha's Vineyard, sipping berry cosmos and listening to Elton John's holiday tracks while Aunt Jackie gets bombed and Mom admires the twenty-foot designer-decorated tree. Though, now that Rhett and Lawan are in America, maybe we'll break out the ugly Christmas sweater tradition again.

What are Kyle's Christmases like? Obviously he spends it with this woman he's seeing. Likely with her family, too. Do they lounge around in matching ugly sweaters and woolen socks, getting drunk on spiced eggnog and playing board games? Do they draw names for Secret Santa and playfully argue over who gets the task of peeling potatoes?

Who even *is* Kyle anymore?

And why did he come here?

I watch him closely.

It's a moment before his gaze lifts to meet mine. That perpetual shadow lingers in his eyes, one that I never saw that summer at Wawa. Maybe it has come with his wisdom and pain.

Or maybe it was always there and I only see it now, because of *my* wisdom and pain.

"Why did you request a transfer to this building?" I ask evenly.

His jaw tenses. I wait several long moments, but he doesn't answer.

"You knew this was my building, didn't you?"

He swallows, his gaze averting to his folded hands on the table.

"Gus told me you put in a request to come *here. Why?*"

Silence.

"I need to understand, Kyle. Otherwise I'm going to have to give Gus details about our history and then he's going to have to report it to Rikell, and—"

"I needed to see you again," he blurts out. He looks up at me, nothing but earnestness in his eyes. "I just . . . I *wanted* to see you again."

Such a simple admission, and yet my chest swells with elation. "Why? I mean, why *now?* It's been thirteen *years*."

He sighs and reaches up to rub the back of his neck. "Like I said, Max is getting out in a few months, and from what my little brother told me—"

"Jeremy. That's his name, right?"

Kyle's eyes flash to mine, a flicker of surprise in them. "Yeah."

How easily the minute details about Kyle come back to me, all these years later.

"He still talks to my mom. She told him that

Max is coming to California when he gets out. Apparently he was asking all kinds of questions about my job and if I could get him in." Kyle snorts. "An ex-con working in security. *Right*. Anyway, that's when I started thinking that it was time for me to leave California, cut them off completely. I figured I could come back this way. I knew Rikell has contracts all over the country." He drags his finger across the wood grain of the table. "I was working the night shift, flipping through a business magazine that someone left in the lobby. You know, just killing time and trying to stay awake. There was this big write-up about these father-and-daughter real estate business tycoons." His lips curl into a knowing smirk. "And there you were, in this long, black dress, standing on a stage."

"The *American Entrepreneur* article." They used a candid shot from the night of my big promotion announcement, of my father and me standing side-by-side in our formal wear, toasting to another good year.

"It was a good article. I mean, I don't read those kinds of things, but I liked reading about you. Where you went to college, things you've said and done—you know, all that." He smiles, more to himself. "It was weird. I kept thinking, 'I knew her way back when.' "

And better than I've let any other guy know me since.

"The article said you were in Lennox, learning the ropes so you could take over the company when your dad retires." Kyle bites his bottom lip, as if deciding whether to continue. "I asked around and it turned out Rikell does the security here. And I thought to myself, if that's not the universe telling me something . . ." A flush creeps across his cheeks, his eyes glued to the table in front of him. "That's when I realized how badly I wanted to see you again. I wanted to see if you've changed."

I swallow at his frank admission. "You could have just called me up, come for a visit. You didn't have to actually get a job here." Then again, that does feel like such a Kyle thing to do—going that extra mile.

He shrugs nonchalantly. "I threw my name in and figured, if an opening came up, it was meant to happen. That we were *meant* to reconnect. I promised myself that if it came up, I'd move here. Why not?"

I can't help but smile. That *is* such a Kyle thing to do. "And something came up."

"Something came up." He grins crookedly. "And, here we are, seeing each other every day again. Just like back then."

"Yeah. You see me passing by you. See me sitting in an office as you walk by. You see me, but you won't talk to me. Remember? 'Let's keep it simple'? Something like that?" My voice is light but tinged with accusation.

He dips his head and rubs at the back of his neck again. “I panicked a bit there, at the start.”

“You were a complete asshole to me.”

He winces. “I know. Seeing you brought back a lot of memories.” His gaze flickers to mine, and in it I see a hint of the vulnerable boy I once knew.

“For me, too,” I say softly, feeling the sudden urge to reach across the table and take his hand. I ball my fist tight to resist. *He’s not yours anymore*.

That’s right. He’s not mine.

“What does your girlfriend have to say about this? She moved across the country with you, didn’t she?” Does she know *all* the reasons why? Because if I were her, I sure as hell would want to know. And then I’d skin him in his sleep for suggesting the move.

Kyle bites his bottom lip again as he regards me evenly. “I live with Jeremy, Piper. *He’s* the one who moved across the country with me, and he was happy to get away from the bullshit back home, too.”

“What? I thought . . .” I stammer, my heart beginning to race. “But you said that you had a . . .” My words drift as I replay the conversation. “No, you didn’t say that.”

“You just assumed it,” he says, adding softly, “and I didn’t clarify.”

“Why not?”

His Adam's apple bobs with a hard swallow. "I don't know. Easier, I guess?" Under his breath, I catch him mutter, "At least, I thought it would be."

My mind is swirling.

Kyle is single. Available.

Not off-limits to me.

Despite how much he hurt me all those years ago, and my irritation with how our reconnection has gone so far, I can't ignore this feeling that I'm about to float out of this chair, that my blood is rushing too fast for my heart to handle.

He clears his throat. "Anyway, I realized as soon as I saw you that this might have been my dumbest idea yet, coming here. But it was already too late—"

"What do you mean? Why is it dumb?"

He chuckles softly. "Come on, Piper . . . We're not teenagers at summer camp anymore."

I frown. What is he saying, exactly? "We're the same people," I hear myself murmur, though I doubt that's true on both accounts.

"You always pretended you were like the rest of us. You can't do that anymore, though. I mean, look at you." His eyes flicker to my shirt again, drawing my own eyes down.

"What? My blouse? What's wrong with my *blouse?*"

"Absolutely nothing. It's definitely not the Wawa red T-shirt, though." That somehow sounds bad, coming from him.

I know what this is about: class and money. Kyle always did seem to have a chip on his shoulder about how much money he presumed my family had, and how little his did. And that was back when he had no idea just who my family actually is.

"Weak."

His lips twitch, and I wonder if he remembers that first day, out on the cliff, when he was taunting me to jump.

"I'm still *me*. You can still talk to me. We can still be . . . friends." The word feels all wrong against my tongue. We were never really *friends*. We were always so much more.

"Right." He smiles. "You're gonna hang out with your building's security guard in your spare time?"

"If I want to, *yes*."

"Your father's going to be okay with that?"

"My father doesn't have a say in my personal relationships."

His eyebrows arch. "You sure about that?"

"I'm a grown woman." It comes out more sharply than I intended. I temper my tone. "If he had a say, I'd still be engaged to David."

"That pompous ass in the Maserati." Kyle grins. "I can't believe you were going to marry that guy."

"Trust me. I know. Thank God I smartened up when I did." I laugh, and my chest feels like it's going to explode with warmth. I'm actually laughing with Kyle again. "This is so surreal."

"I know," he says softly, and I catch a sparkle of mischief in his eyes before it's extinguished, and silence takes over.

I hesitate, but then admit, "I looked for you."

He dips his head but doesn't answer.

"I went to Poughkeepsie, to the Seven-Eleven." There was only one in the whole town, thank God. "There was an old lady in the apartment. She said that you'd moved." I remember not being able to breathe as I knocked and listened to the dull shuffle of feet on the other side. And then, when the woman in the ratty blue robe delivered the crushing news—that she heard the family before her hadn't paid their rent all summer and had skipped town—I thought I was going to throw up, right there on her doorstep. I managed to keep the tears at bay until I was in the parking lot.

Kyle's eyes drift behind me, to the window and beyond.

I still have so many questions. But I start with the most important. "Why did you just disappear like that? Why didn't you ever call me?"

His jaw tenses. "I figured it was better. I mean . . ." Another hard swallow. "We were never supposed to last beyond the summer. It was just supposed to be fun. You knew that."

"No. I *didn't* know that, Kyle." Sure, we'd

talked about it, in the beginning. But things morphed. Feelings intensified. All those stolen smiles, those whispered words, those shared laughs, those heated kisses.

Those nights.

Was I really that clueless?

"Are you saying . . ." I grapple with my thoughts, my rising emotions. "So *everything* you said to me was a lie?"

"No." He shakes his head.

"But you never wanted it to last?"

"*Of course* I did."

"Well then you're not making any sense!" I feel a knot forming in my throat, which only makes me angrier, because I shouldn't still have knots forming in my throat over things that happened *thirteen years* ago!

"Wawa was over for us. We lived hours apart. It just . . . it was never gonna work." His jaw is hard as he spews basically the same line over again.

"Then why are you here?" I temper my volume. These walls are too thin to be speaking that loud. "Why did you come back *now?*"

"I *told* you. I was moving back east anyway."

"And what did you *think* was going to happen when you showed up? What were you expecting? That I would have forgotten how you hurt me?"

He dips his head. "Honestly, I wasn't sure. It's

been thirteen years. I figured you would have moved on."

"I *did* move on!" I snap, because I'm feeling like a fool right now. A sixteen-year-old pining fool.

A fool still in love. But I have to accept that all I'm in love with is a memory.

"You are right. This was a mistake." I stand. "Thank you for coming. You can go back to work now. And maybe you should consider applying for a transfer to another building. Gus can help you with that."

"Piper, I didn't mean—"

"You broke my heart!" My voice cracks, my chest tight with emotion that I'm still grappling to understand. Maybe time doesn't heal all wounds.

I march toward the door, acutely aware of the sound of Kyle's chair banging against the table's leg, the hair-raising ping of metal-against-metal hanging in the air. A moment later, his hand is around my wrist, gripping it tightly, holding me back from escape.

"I'm sorry, Piper. But you don't understand."

"You're right. I don't. Because if all we had was a summer fling thirteen years ago, why the hell would you even give me a second's thought now?" I dare to meet his eyes. "Did you come here for money? Is that what you want?"

He releases my wrist like I've burned him. His nostrils flare. "I don't want *any* of your family's money," he pushes through gritted teeth.

I shrug, but inside, every bit of me twists at the idea. “How do I know that? I don’t know you anymore. Maybe I never did.” I turn to leave.

“He paid me to leave you alone!” Kyle says in a rush.

My feet stall. “What?” I turn to find Kyle’s head bowed, his eyes squeezed shut.

“What did you just say?”

“I never could lie to you to save my life,” he mutters.

A sinking feeling takes over. “Who paid you to leave me alone?”

Kyle meets my gaze, this time with a flat look. “Who do you think, Piper?”

I shake my head. There’s only one person who would do such a thing. The one man who could afford it, and who would be motivated to do so.

“Fifty grand, to pack up and leave, and never contact you again.”

“And you actually took it?”

Kyle flinches. “Your father can be persuasive.”

My pulse begins to race. I can’t believe my father would do this, and yet I don’t doubt for a second that he did.

“When I saw you in the lobby the first time, I couldn’t figure out if you ever found out—”

“*When* did this happen?” I demand.

“That night. When you were leaving,” Kyle admits with a hint of reluctance. “While you were talking to Darian. He told me that someone would be by my apartment within the next day or two to give me money, and that if I was smart, I'd take it and get the hell out of your life for good, before I did something to ruin it." He sighs. "And that if I didn't take the money, he'd find a way to put me behind bars with the rest of my family, where I belonged."

"You're lying," I accuse, even though a voice inside my head demands that I listen. I fish out my phone, intent on dialing my father right then and there.

"He's not going to admit to it."

"Oh, yes, he will." If Kieran is anything, it's self-righteous. *Everything I do—everything I've ever done over the years—I've done only with your best interest at heart. You know that, right?* His words echo in my mind. Is that what Kieran Calloway thought paying the boy I loved to disappear was? In my best interest?

"He doesn't know I'm working in this building," Kyle says, more urgently, with worry on his face. "I'm not sure how he'll react to me showing up here again." He hesitates. "But if you don't care about that, then go ahead and tell him."

If what Kyle says is true, then I have a good idea how my dad will react. Kyle's ass will be out on the sidewalk by this afternoon.

I tuck my phone away, muttering, "He's likely on a plane, anyway." Despite everything, I don't think there's a situation where I *wouldn't* care what happens to Kyle. I sigh heavily.

"So . . . fifty thousand bucks. That's my going rate."

Kyle's eyes are on the thin navy carpet, as if he can't face me. "He made it pretty clear that he'd do anything to make sure you and I were done the second you stepped off Wawa property. I think he actually used the words *over my dead body*. I figured if we were over anyway, that much money would give me and Jeremy a chance to get out of the hole we were living in. So I took it. I thought it was for the best for everyone."

That is a lot of money for anyone, but especially a seventeen-year-old going back to a roach-infested apartment above a 7-Eleven.

"And your mother? What did she say?"

"About the money?" He lets out a derisive laugh. "I never told her about it. She would have taken it and there was no way I trusted her with that much, not when my dad and brothers were asking for cash. God knows she'd find a way to smuggle it in for them. No . . . I decided that if I was gonna take money from your father, I was gonna make it matter. So I hid it. I used what I needed to get a decent car. We were already getting kicked out of our apartment, so I convinced Mom to go to California. We drove for two days straight, found a cheap apartment down there." He shrugs. "I told her I earned the money from Wawa."

"And she believed that?" I ask doubtfully. I remember those pitiful paychecks.

"Of course not. She figured I was doing something shady on the side, but she didn't ask too many questions. She never did. As long as there was money at the end of it." There's no shortage of bitterness in his voice.

I've often wondered what kind of woman gave birth to Kyle and his brothers. Now I'm not sure I ever want to find out.

Uncomfortable silence lingers in the room as I try to process this bomb. "So that's why you disappeared. It wasn't because . . ." My words drift.

"Because I didn't care about you?" He looks steadily at me. "No. That's not why."

And did you ever stop caring? I bite my tongue on that and ask instead, "My father . . . How do you feel about him?" I can't even begin to wrap my head around how *I* feel about him right now, but if what Kyle is saying is true, then I have to wonder if him working here, in my father's building—having easy access to him—is going to be a problem.

And what happens when my father sees Kyle sitting in the lobby?

What will he do if he recognizes him?

I watch Kyle carefully, to see if I can read the lies in his answer.

He surprises me by smiling softly. "You know, it's funny—ironic, actually . . . As much as I hated him back then for making me leave you like that," his somber eyes flash to mine, "that money changed our lives. I got Jeremy away from Poughkeepsie, away from prison, away from *all* of it, before he could get himself into trouble. A fresh start in San Diego turned out to be the best thing for us. Jer has no interest in getting dragged down with the rest of our family, either."

"That's good. I guess." At least something positive came from my heartbreak.

He opens his mouth to speak but then stops.

I have more questions, but right now I need time to think. I need time to calm this inner turmoil down.

"So . . ." He hesitates, watching me through wary eyes, as if trying to weigh my thoughts. "I guess I'll see you around?"

"Until my father recognizes you."

A grim smile touches his lips. "Right."

"Don't worry, though. I'm sure if you play it right, you could make a cool million off him this time around." I say it flippantly, knowing I don't need a harsh tone to hit my mark.

The muscles in Kyle's square jaw tense. He nods once. "Fair enough. I deserved that," he mutters. "But I promise you, I'm never taking another dime from that man again. And if you want me gone, just say the word. I'll put in a transfer request. Hell, I'll quit. It was worth it, just to see you again." With that, he smoothly exits, leaving the delicate masculine scent of sandalwood and musk trailing behind.

I keep my back to the elevator, waiting for the ping of the doors, a storm of emotions brewing inside me.

Am I even angry with Kyle for taking the money? I can't imagine what it must have been like, a seventeen-year-old boy facing off with Kieran Calloway, who was basically blackmailing him. What should he have done?

I know what my sixteen-year-old self would have expected him to do—tell my dad to shove the money up his ass. Or take the money and then tell me what my father had done, so we could hide our relationship from him.

How could my father do something like that, in the name of protecting me? I was an emotional wreck in the months after Wawa. I couldn't get Kyle out of my head. All those nights of falling asleep wrapped in desolation, wondering where Kyle was, what happened to him. Replaying every word, every touch, every promise, wondering what I'd done to make him behave so cruelly toward me. All the anger I learned to wield against happy memories of us, just long enough to help me let go, to heal, to finally move on.

Dad offered me sad smiles and calm hugs, and kept telling me that I was beautiful and smart, and *that hooligan* didn't deserve a Calloway.

My teeth are clenched so tight that my jaw begins to ache. I should have known.

Do I confront my father now, though? Or should I wait until he recognizes Kyle and blows up, sends him packing?

Kismet or not, coming to this building was a ballsy move on Kyle's part, given the risk.

Is he just stupid? Or does he think the risk is worth the potential reward? And what is that reward, exactly? Is it working with me again? A friendship with me?

Or more?

My stomach flutters.

Kyle is single.

He moved here, in part, because he wants to be in my life again.

And the only reason he ever left in the first place is because of my father.

Three truths I need to decide what the hell I'm going to do with.

"You want me to help you *poach* Jack's assistant?" I glare at David in disbelief as we ride the elevator down to the lobby. I was almost successful in ducking out without notice, until David came barreling out of the restroom and crossed my path.

"She doesn't want to work for that stooge," he argues. "She basically told me as much."

"No, she did not." Cheryl is the minutes taker for the Monthly Women's Network meetings I lead at CG and a sweet, single thirty-eight-year-old mom who I suspect is in love with her boss—our CFO, and a married man. Then again, maybe that's why she'd want to move desks—unrequited love is unenjoyable, but especially so when you have to face it day in, day out.

"Just ask her, would ya?" David pleads.

"Why *me?*"

"Because, I can't! *Obviously*. Jack would kill me. And you're . . . you! And a woman, and, I don't know . . ." He throws his hands up in the air, as if giving up. "It's what you women *do!*"

I roll my eyes as the elevator door opens. "See you tomorrow, David."

"Wait. Where are you going?"

"Home."

He checks his watch. "It's only three!"

"I have a headache," I lie, and am saved from further conversation as the elevator doors close, carrying my personal pain-in-the-ass back upstairs. The truth is, I'm going home to curl up under my covers and ponder this morning's revelations. I'm going home to hide from life, and from my father before he gets back from LA this afternoon, until I decide how best to address his deep betrayal.

"You're off early for a change," Gus notes as I push through the security gate, my laptop bag strap already digging into my shoulder.

"Long day." I steal a glance at Kyle, who's occupied with a phone call, his free arm settled across his chest, making his bicep bulge. He was lean when I knew him, but far from scrawny. Now, though . . . what would it feel like to smooth my hands over his sculpted body like I used to do?

Kyle is available, that voice in the back of my mind reminds me, and with it brings that familiar flutter in my stomach.

"Nothing like that's been delivered yet, ma'am," I hear him say politely, his golden gaze settling on me. "Sure thing. I'll keep an eye out for that cookie platter . . ." His lips curl into a smile and, for the first time in years, I see it actually reaching his eyes. Reminding me just how much I always loved feeling his smiles on me. "No, I'll make sure Gus doesn't eat any of them this time."

"What's she goin' on about! I've never stolen anyone's cookies!" Gus sputters, but it's followed up with a sheepish grin. "I may have *sampled* one or two." He winks at me before his brown eyes shift behind me. "Good to see you again, sir. Hope your trip was successful. Where were you this time?"

"Chicago, to look at an investment property," comes my dad's gruff response.

He wasn't supposed to be back for another hour.

And I thought he was in LA?

My heart begins pounding in my chest as I smooth my expression and turn to meet my father's stern face.

Is it true? Did you pay Kyle to break my heart?

I've always known that there is this hard, controlling side to him. I've just been fortunate enough to avoid its wrath. Or so I thought.

"Piper?" He frowns curiously. "You okay?"

I force a smile. I guess this confrontation is happening now after all. Because Kyle is standing *right there*. The boy he paid off is only a few feet away.

I brace myself, waiting for him to look at Kyle, waiting for those harsh features to scowl with recognition when it clicks.

Dad checks his watch. "You meeting someone?"

"No. Headache." My blood is racing with the anticipation of what's to come. What will I do? How will I react?

"Hmmm . . ." His brow furrows. "Go home and get some rest, then."

"Yeah. That's the plan."

He cocks his head curiously at me, but then, as if deciding something, turns his attention away.

To Kyle.

His eyes narrow, and I hold my breath,

preparing myself to intervene before my father causes a scene in our building's lobby.

"There's a panhandler near the east entrance. I'm assuming you can't see him on the security feed and that's why you haven't done anything about it?"

Kyle averts his gaze to one of the monitors on the desk. "You're right. He's in a blind spot."

"Well, would you please help him relocate? *Immediately?*"

"Yes, sir," Kyle says, his eyes still on the screen, his face stoic. Does it burn his pride to call my father *sir,* I wonder?

Dad's gaze drifts over Kyle's sleeve of tattoos, his distaste for them clear. And then he turns to me, dismissing Kyle entirely. "Go home. I'll see you tomorrow." Nodding at Gus, he swipes his badge and marches toward the bank of elevators.

Kyle exhales slowly. He meets my eyes and I can see his thoughts in them. They're the same as mine: Kieran Calloway doesn't recognize him.

Whether it's the "Stewart" on his name badge, or thirteen years and thirty pounds of muscle, or simply the fact that Kyle was nothing more than an ant to squash, a pest for my father to swiftly deal with, I can't say. Likely all of the above.

Either way, Kyle is safe from my father's ire. For now.

I release a lung's worth of air, relieved to have

bought myself some time to figure out how—and if—to confront him for what he did to us.

"You want to kindly escort our friend to another corner, or should I?" Gus peers up at Kyle.

"I've got it," Kyle murmurs, rounding the desk. "See you tomorrow, Piper?" he asks softly, and I hear the real question behind those words.

Do you want to see me here tomorrow?

All I can manage is a nod.

Because the simple truth is that I do.

Chapter 14

THEN

2006, Camp Wawa, End of Week One

Izzy's round blue eyes are watery as she holds out her tiny hand, offering me a ball of hot pink gimp and beads in emerald green and aqua blue.

"For me?"

She nods. "I made it in art. So you can remember me."

I chuckle as I slide the bracelet onto my wrist. It's too loose, but there's not enough slack for two loops. "I doubt I'll ever be able to forget you."

"Will you be my counselor again next year?"

"I hope so!" If Camp Wawa allows counselors who have been on probation back. That was the final verdict Darian delivered early this morning, after last night's golf-cart fiasco. Probation for all four of us—a permanent black mark on our camp counselor employment record—but *not* termination for Kyle and Eric. There is to be absolutely no "shenanigans" after lights-out. We're to be in our cabins with our campers, asleep. If we're caught breaking these rules, it will equal immediate dismissal, no questions asked.

As much as mandatory nightly curfew sucks, it means I still get to spend my summer with Kyle. I had to fight the urge to hug Darian as she delivered our punishment to us.

Izzy's mouth splits into a wide, toothy grin. It's been a mad flurry of activity and emotion at Wawa today, as kids pack up and part ways, in most cases with tears streaming down their cheeks and scraps of papers revealing email addresses and phone numbers, and promises to come back the same week next year.

For these kids, summer camp is over. Meanwhile I've only survived the first week. I have *seven more* to go. Oddly enough, though, the idea of that isn't nearly as dreadful as it was last Sunday, when I stood in this same spot, greeting frenzied children. Much of that has to do with a certain golden-eyed boy, but not all. Camp Wawa has begun to grow on me. The counselors are, for the most part, fun. Spending my days goofing off with them and the campers almost doesn't feel like work. And Mom was right: Russell's chocolate pudding is prison-grade bribery quality.

"Aren't those your parents?" I point to the couple approaching.

"Mommy!" Izzy shrieks, taking off across the field as fast as her little legs can carry her under the weight of her backpack, her sleeping bag dragging across the grass. And just like that, I'm a memory.

"Hey." Kyle sidles up beside me, his fingers discreetly skimming my outer thigh.

I turn to meet his gaze. "Hey."

His eyes drop to my mouth, and I feel that instant urge to press my lips against his.

His smirk says he feels it, too. "Last one?"

"Yeah." I smile, looking on as Izzy drops her things on the ground for her parents to collect and then skips along beside them, her arms gesticulating wildly in the air. "She's so cute."

"You know who *else* is so cute?"

"Eric?" I tease, feeling my cheeks flush.

Kyle chuckles. "Nice."

I hold up my arm, letting the bracelet dangle. "Look what she made me."

"I got some, too." Kyle holds his arm up to display six similar gimp-and-bead bracelets of varying sizes and colors, two of them all-pink. "This one is from Maddie, this one . . ." He goes through each bracelet, identifying which little girl made what.

I roll my eyes. "Are you bragging because you have more than me?"

He shrugs. "I can't help it if I'm well liked."

"Nothing from your campers, though. Hmm . . . that says something."

"Oh, no. They left me with a gift all right," he mutters, tipping his head.

I burst out laughing at the countless specks of iridescent glitter clinging to the roots of his hair.

How could I not have noticed them earlier? "That has to be half a bottle!"

"It's all over my pillow and in my bed, my sleeping bag. I've already had one shower. I'm going to need two more, probably." He sighs heavily and shakes his head, but his easy smile tells me he's not actually annoyed.

"So?" I glance back once, in time to return Izzy's frantic wave before she scrambles into the backseat of her parents' car. The parking lot is mostly empty of camper vehicles. "What now?"

"Let's see . . . Darian will do a half-hour roundup to talk about the past week and then she'll give counselor-of-the-week stars out."

I feel my eyebrows rise. *"Stars?"*

"Every week, three counselors get a star. She's got these big gold stickers"—he holds his hands out in front of him to mimic the size—"and she makes this elaborate production of having the winners tell everyone what they love *most* about being a camp counselor."

"Oh God." I cringe.

Kyle chuckles. "Wait until you hear some of the shit people come up with."

"Have you gotten one before?"

"Yeah. Two, actually."

"Really."

"Probably not gonna get one this year, though." He flashes me a sheepish smile. I sensed the relief pouring off him when Darian told him he could stay, even as Ashley was near tears for what this could mean for her college applications, should they see it.

I feel sorry for her, but we deserve it.

"What's after the star award?" Counselors are supposed to get the afternoon and night off.

He shrugs. "Russell serves up lunch, and then we've got the rest of the day to do whatever we want. Most people catch up on sleep and try to get laundry done. If it's nice out, they swim." He glances up at the gray sky. Rain has been threatening all morning, but it hasn't come to pass yet. It's only a matter of time before the skies open up. "You wanna head into town later? Grab a burger or something?"

I smile. Is that code for our first "date"? "Yeah. Sounds good."

Kyle rests an arm casually over my shoulder, in a way that could be explained away as simply friendly to any casual onlooker. "Before we're on lockdown and we have to do this counselor thing *all over again*."

I groan, though in truth there's nowhere I'd rather be this summer than in this moment, with him.

I'm pretty sure I've never been in a car this old before.

Or one that has its side-view mirror duct-taped in place.

"Shotgun!" Eric charges for the passenger-side door of Kyle's car, testing the handle. It's locked.

"Nice try." Kyle meets his best friend's eyes.

Eric throws his head back in mock-dismay. "Fine. But do you know how uncomfortable your backseat is, bro?"

"Yeah, that's why *you're* sitting in it." Kyle smirks, unlocking his door with his key and folding his seat forward for Ashley. She scrambles in, crawling over the passenger seat to pop a small knob on the other door, releasing the lock from the inside.

God, this is an old car.

"If I make out with him, do you think he'll let me sit in front on the way back?" Eric mumbles, easing his tall body in, then fumbling with the seat's latch to reset it for me. "It's not working, Miller."

" 'Cause you're doin' it wrong." Kyle rounds the car. With one flick of his wrist, the passenger seat snaps back into place.

"Thanks." I smile, his proximity stirring my blood.

"No problem." He backs me up against his car, pressing his body into mine. I bite my bottom lip to hide the goofy smile threatening as I feel *how much* he wants me.

His heated gaze drifts down the plunging neckline of my emerald green tank top before lifting to settle on my mouth.

"You lovebirds wanna get excommunicated from Wawa? Because Darian wasn't kidding around," Eric warns.

"We're not breaking any rules. Read the fine print. There aren't any campers here," Kyle throws back, his eyes lighting up with mischief. "If this is all I get for the week, I need to make the most of it." He weaves his fingers through my hair and tugs gently, just enough to pull my head back and expose my neck. The kiss he sets just below my jawline sends shivers through my body.

"Come on, you can hump each other in town. I'm starvin'!" Eric complains.

Kyle sighs heavily, his lips shifting back to my mouth. "Can we drop them off in town and then leave?"

"It's forty minutes to walk back, isn't it?"

"They could do it in thirty, if they have to run in the rain."

I burst out laughing. "You're terrible."

He grins. "Am I?"

I revel in the feel of Kyle's lips as he deepens his kiss, his hands beginning to wander, one of them hooking the back of my thigh to pull my leg up around his hip, his fingertips skimming over my bare skin, his pelvis pressing harder against me. I can only imagine what tonight could bring, if we can find somewhere private to steal away. The very thought has my own hands wandering, sliding around his waist, pulling his body tighter against me, reveling in the feel of his soft cotton T-shirt as I imagine peeling it off him later.

The sounds of tires crunching on gravel sounds behind us, breaking us free.

"Someone's lost," Kyle murmurs.

I turn. And frown at the familiar black Lincoln SUV with tinted windows now parked beside us.

Eddie, my dad's hired driver, steps out, offering me a curt nod on his way to open the back passenger door.

Out comes my father.

"Dad!" I exclaim, dashing forward. "What are you doing here? Is everything okay?"

"Can't I surprise my daughter?" he says evenly, smoothing the lapel of his typical crisp, tailored navy suit. The fact that it's muggy and warm hasn't stopped him from dressing so formally, and on a Saturday. Obviously he was coming from an important meeting. His cold blue eyes flitter around us, taking stock of the campground, before landing on me once again. My friends back home are convinced that my dad belongs on an afternoon soap opera, not just because his very presence commands attention but also because of his deep, velvety voice.

"Of course. It's just . . . you're hours away." I wrap my arms around his broad shoulders.

He returns the warm embrace, and it instantly brings me back ten years to my six-year-old self, curled up on his lap, watching him read through building proposals.

"I was looking at a potential investment property today that's only forty minutes away, so I figured I'd take the opportunity to swing by."

"You should have called."

"I thought your cell phone doesn't work well out here."

"You're right. Good thing you caught me. We were just heading into town."

"Is *that* what you were doing." His sharp, raptor's gaze shifts to settle behind me.

And with that look, any hope that Dad's attention was engrossed in a report when he drove up—and that he missed the public mauling—withers away.

I feel my cheeks burn as I take a step back and clear my throat. "Dad, this is Kyle. Kyle, this is my dad."

Kyle steps forward, extending his hand. "Hi, sir. It's nice to meet you."

My dad pauses a moment to assess Kyle's face, then his hand, before finally taking it. "I take it you're a camp counselor, too?"

"Yeah." Kyle reaches up to scratch his bicep, inadvertently flashing the ink on his arm.

My dad's eyes narrow but he says nothing, his focus instead shifting to Kyle's car.

"Can't say I've seen a Pinto on the road in quite some time. For good reason, it would seem."

Kyle dips his head to hide his smirk. “It’s my brother’s car. I’m just using it for the summer.”

“And what’s he using?”

“Uh . . .” Kyle seems caught off guard by the question. “Nothing. He went away for a while.”

“Traveling!” I flash Kyle a warning look. Not even a minute and we’ve already somehow stumbled dangerously close to the topic of Kyle’s family situation.

A frizzy head pokes out of the car window then. “Hello, Mr. Calloway. I’m Ashley. It’s nice to meet you! I met your wife last weekend. Would you like to come to dinner with us?”

A glimmer of amusement flashes across my dad’s face before it turns stern again. “No, but thank you for the invitation. In fact, I’m going to steal my daughter for a few hours. If that’s all right with her,” he adds.

As if I could say no.

“I guess I’ll see you guys later?” I try not to sound reluctant. It’s not that I don’t enjoy seeing my father. It’s that I don’t want to lose my one free night a week with Kyle.

“It was nice to meet you, Mr. Calloway,” Kyle offers stoically.

Dad makes a throaty sound. “Yes. Come, Piper.”

He has already decided that he doesn’t like Kyle. My stomach aches with disappointment. But behind that is a flare of anger. He’s not even giving Kyle a chance!

Kyle's gaze flickers to my father, then back to me, and I wonder if he can tell. He shrugs. "We'll be around here later."

"Okay. I'll see you soon." Skating my fingers over his in a fleeting touch, I climb into the back of the Lincoln and settle into the cool leather seat, wishing dinner away.

"You made your mother very happy, agreeing to attend this . . . budget camp of hers," my dad says through a sip of his cocktail, his eyes scrolling over the menu, his lips curled with distaste. For the scant wine list or the lackluster food options, I can't tell. He's already made comments about both. We found what he referred to as the only semi-respectable restaurant in town—an oversized white farmhouse that doubles as an inn, with several room rentals on the second floor. The dining room overlooks the river that cuts through town, which would be picturesque if not for the dilapidated houses and public beach on the opposite bank. My dad has scowled at the view as if it's a personal affront to him. Poor city planning has always been a pet peeve of his.

"You've talked to her?" I ask, hope in my voice. Does this mean they're working through things?

"Briefly, this morning. She called to tell me about the incident with the golf cart and the fact that my daughter is now on probation at her summer job, like some sort of delinquent."

Shit. Darian must have called my mother.

Now this impromptu meeting makes sense. My father wants me to know how disappointed he is in me, and he needs to look me in the eye to do it. My shoulders tense. This is *not* good.

"I don't know what it is with Calloway children putting golf carts into water. You're lucky you didn't break your arm like your brother did," he mutters, shutting his menu and tucking away his reading glasses. "*And* you could have lost your job. That would have been an embarrassment for everyone."

"It was an accident."

"A completely avoidable one, from what I understand. This doesn't sound like something you'd do, Piper."

He's right, it's not. Until you throw a hot guy into the mix and then I'll—literally—jump off a cliff for him.

All I can do is shrug. Shrug, and worry my lip as I wonder what type of punishment he's about to dole out. When Rhett ditched that golf cart in the club's pond, my parents took his car away for three months. I don't even *have* a car for them to take away.

"Was this Kent guy with you?"

"No." Dad's eyebrows spike and I know Mom told him otherwise. "His name is *Kyle,* and it was my fault. *I* was the one driving. But he tried to take the blame for it," I add quickly, hoping to score Kyle some points, seeing as he's already starting off in the red.

Dad's lips press tight. "So he's not bright, but he's chivalrous."

"Dad." I roll my eyes.

The waitress comes by to take our orders and clear our table of menus.

"What do you know about him?"

He's the most beautiful guy I've ever known, and the most adventurous; he makes me feel good about myself. I could kiss him forever. I would be kissing him right now, if not for you. "He's a nice guy."

"His family?"

I knew my dad would ask that question. I knew, and yet I haven't prepared a suitable lie. Shame on me. I buy myself time to think of my answer while taking a long, leisurely drink from my water glass. "He has a few brothers. His parents are married."

"And what does his father do?"

"Um . . . something to do with the prison system." I casually toy with my fork, avoiding his gaze.

"A warden?"

"A guard, I think?" I shrug, feigning a casual, clueless expression. "Not sure, though."

He eyes me for a long moment, and I'm afraid he knows I'm lying. Dad's bullshit meter would put Kyle's to shame.

"I don't want you getting in that car of his. The thing shouldn't even be on the road. Does he have insurance?"

"Of course he does." I hope that's true. "And it's not like I really have a choice if I want to leave camp."

"Funny you should mention that." He reaches into his satchel to pull out a Volvo catalogue and slide it across the table toward me. "You'll need to choose all the details so we can get it on order."

I hesitate, momentarily stunned. *"Really?"*

He smirks. "Your mother *enlightened* me as to your *demands*. I figured this is the easiest way."

I'm not getting punished for the golf cart? Oh, man, Rhett would be *pissed*. He always did say that I could get away with just about anything in our father's eyes.

Dad frowns curiously. "What's wrong?"

"Nothing." I reach for the brochure, unable to help my giddy grin as I flip through the pages.

"Does that smile mean you're finally coming around to my choice of car?"

"If I must. Though I'd still prefer a Corvette."

"And I'd prefer to never have to deal with another rezoning committee again, but we don't always get everything we want," he throws back smoothly, adjusting his tie. "Sixteen-year-olds don't belong in sports cars. O'Connell's daughter drove hers into a concrete barrier within the first week because she couldn't handle it. It's a miracle she walked away from that."

I roll my eyes every time my father uses his friend's daughter as an example. "Becky O'Connell has ridden her bicycle into a park bench. *Twice*."

"And yet she's never put a golf cart in a lake."

"Touché."

He chuckles, always one to enjoy delivering a dig. Settling back in his chair, he clasps his hands and rests them on his small belly. "I can't remember when you and I had a dinner date last."

"New Year's Day. We went for Chinese."

"Has it really been that long . . ." he says absently, as if not looking for an answer.

"You've been busy." *Busy cheating on Mom*. I grind my teeth to keep from saying something that could blow up the rest of our "dinner date." When I first found out about his tryst with the redheaded architect from LA, I was sitting next to my cracked bedroom door, eavesdropping. I didn't need to strain to hear Mom's accusations carrying through their bedroom wall.

I assumed it was a misunderstanding. There was no way my father would fracture our already fragile family for one night with some Californian siren. But I've heard enough fighting through the walls since then to accept that Kieran Calloway is guilty as charged. Also, that he's sorry for it. Flowers have arrived at our doorstep every Friday afternoon like clockwork. All my mother's favorite blooms. Surely ordered by Greta but *still*. And he surprised her with that trip to Paris back in May—a no-business getaway for just the two of them. That she declined.

I've found myself flip-flopping between simmering rage toward him and frustration with my mother, wishing that she'd just forgive him so everything could go back to normal.

I guess that's selfish of me.

He takes another long sip of his drink, seemingly lost in his thoughts for a moment. "So, what have you been up to so far at summer camp, besides trouble?"

"Let me see . . ." Images of Kyle flash through my mind, but I quickly push them aside. "So there was a bat . . ."

"I'm leaving for Tokyo on Tuesday for ten days. If you need anything while I'm gone, it's best you call your mother."

"Do you think you guys will be able to work things out?" I ask, as we turn into Wawa's driveway, the Lincoln's wipers swishing back and forth rhythmically.

"So, you *are* aware of what's going on." Dad's hard, assessing gaze skims over the pavilion and outbuildings, dim in the evening's gloominess, toward the small group of counselors in the field, kicking a soccer ball around, despite the drizzle.

I roll my eyes. "I *am* living in the same house, Dad. And I'm not six years old."

He sighs. "She'll come around."

"Do you really think so?" I hesitate. "After what you did?"

His jaw tenses and I brace myself for a tongue-lashing. "No marriage is easy, Piper, and I am far from the first man to make a mistake. But this is not a topic I'm going to discuss with my daughter." He adds in a more conciliatory tone, "She seems to be in better spirits since getting away from the city. She's been out at the club every day, socializing. And I hear she's on the tennis courts a lot. I think this time to herself will be helpful. It'll give her some perspective. Remind her how good we have it. How my one mistake is not worth throwing the life we built together away."

"I hope so."

He reaches over to pat my knee just as the SUV eases to a stop next to Kyle's Pinto. Just the sight of it—knowing Kyle is here—makes my heart skip.

"This was a nice surprise, Dad." And it *was,* despite my reluctance at the beginning. I wrap my arms around his neck, inhaling his comforting cologne one more time—a scent that he's worn for as long as I can remember, it's now his signature. I wave the car catalogue in the air. "Should I call Greta with my choices?"

"Email her if you can, so it's all written down. First thing Monday morning."

I reach for the handle.

"Before you go, Piper . . ." His steely gaze shifts to Kyle's car. "I don't want you with that boy anymore."

It takes me a moment to process his words, to be sure I heard them correctly. "What?"

"I agreed with your mother that you should experience a summer in a . . . *modest* environment, so you can see how others live and appreciate the privilege you've been afforded. Mainly so you don't end up like your brother down the road, having this sudden crisis of conscience and throwing your life away." He frowns. "But I won't have my daughter getting mixed up with a boy like that."

"You don't even know him!"

"I know what I don't approve of. And the boys I'd consider suitable for you wouldn't be pawing you in public like that. Against a car that belongs in a junkyard, no less."

"He wasn't . . . That was a joke." I feel my cheeks flush, from a combination of anger and embarrassment. Worse, Eddie is listening.

"I didn't find it funny."

"You weren't supposed to see it," I mutter under my breath.

"You can talk to him, of course. You're working together for the summer, so it's not like you can avoid him. But leave it at that."

I shake my head, my fury rising. My dad's

never made a demand like this. Then again, my circle of friends and male interests has always been associated with Breyers Collegiate and the families that can afford to go there. He approved of Trevor before he ever met him, namely because Trevor's father is a high-profile civil lawyer.

If he knew what Kyle's father did for "a living," we'd likely already be on our way home.

I try another angle. "I *really* like him, and Mom's okay with him."

"She won't be after I speak with her."

"Dad!"

"I'm not going to say it again. Do you understand me, Piper?"

And there it is. Kieran Calloway issuing an edict in his calm, cool voice. There's no swaying him when he gets like this. And he expects me to adhere because I always have. No one defies Kieran Calloway, especially not his children.

Tears of frustration prick my eyes. I shove open the door and climb out, into the drizzle.

"Piper." I hear the warning in his steely voice.

"Fine. Whatever."

He sighs heavily, as if *I'm* being the unreasonable one.

A sudden wave of rebellion inflames me. "Just so you know . . . your perfect Trevor Reilly spiked my Coke to get me drunk so he could try to screw me." I slam the door with force and storm off, the cool rain against my face a soothing balm to my anger.

I spot Kyle at the far end of the field, shirtless and deftly maneuvering around another player with the soccer ball to take a shot at the goal. It sails into the top left corner, earning a round of cheers from his teammates.

My anger at my father only intensifies.

I glance over my shoulder to see the SUV's brake lights as it eases around the bend in the road, and then out of sight. He didn't even bother to linger, to see how I'd handle Kyle.

He assumes I'll listen.

I always have.

"Hey, Richie Rich!" Eric calls out from his place in net, his blond curls flattened, his T-shirt sitting in a wet heap by the goalpost, to show off a lanky, sunburned torso. "So, is that, like, how your dad rolls all the time?"

"A lot. Yeah." And for possibly the first time in my life, I'm embarrassed by that.

"Oh." Eric shrugs. "Cool."

A cheer carries from the other end, and Eric's arms are in the air. "Nice! Your boy's on fire!"

Kyle is high-fiving another guy when he notices me there. He waves and, brushing his damp hair back with his hand, begins jogging my way, his lean body rippled with muscle.

My boy. That's right. He's mine. And no one—especially not my dad—is going to decide otherwise.

Normally, I hate the discomfort that comes

with rain—clingy clothes and strands of hair stuck to my face. Now, though, I'm too mad at my father and emboldened by my feelings for Kyle to care.

With a determined smile, I take off running across the field, intercepting the soccer ball meant for the center line, to throw myself into Kyle, knocking us both to the soggy grass.

"What are we doing tonight?" I ask, through our laughs.

"I don't know. Hanging out? It's supposed to rain all night. They're talking about setting up the movie screen in the rec hall." He shifts onto his side, propping himself on his elbow to peer down at me, shielding my face. "How was dinner?"

I roll my eyes. "Fine."

"Yeah?" His finger trails my collarbone. "What'd your dad say about me?"

"That you seem nice."

He gives me a doubtful look. "He doesn't want you near me, does he?" I see a mix of resignation and disappointment in his eyes.

"He doesn't want me with anyone he hasn't chosen." I hook my wrists around the back of Kyle's neck. "But it doesn't matter what he wants. It matters what *I* want. And *I* want you."

"Yeah?" He smiles thoughtfully. "How much?"

I pull him down into a kiss, reveling in his hot, soft lips, mildly tasting of salt from sweat.

Kyle flinches and breaks away when the soccer

ball bounces off his hip, reminding me that we're not alone.

"Are we playing or are we taking a break to watch you two do it right here?" Eric hollers.

"Shut up," Kyle grumbles, turning back to me. "Maybe we can pick this up later, when we're not in the middle of a soccer field?"

"Probably a good idea."

" 'Kay." He dips his head into the crook of my neck with a chuckle. "Shit, I need a minute."

"Why . . . *Oh*." A rush of heat floods my body as I get his meaning.

His hard swallow fills my ear. "Quick, help me think of something *else*."

Something else besides Kyle and me together? Because now that Eric has said it, it's all I'm picturing.

"Eric in a maid's costume. Extra-short skirt and his hairy legs," I blurt out, because yesterday's drama performance had everyone torn between howls of laughter and cringes of mortification.

"Yup. That should do it." With a groan of reluctance, he climbs to his feet, attempting to discreetly adjust himself in the process.

"You gonna be able to run with that?" Eric teases.

"Run . . . kick . . ." Kyle hoofs the soccer ball, sending it straight for Eric's head. "Get back in net so we can finish this." He offers me his hand to hoist me up off the ground. "Ash and Avery and them are in the rec center, making popcorn. Meet you there when we're done?"

" 'Kay." Maybe it's a residual of my defying my father, or maybe it's because of the growing tension between Kyle and me, but I lean forward to graze his earlobe with my teeth, whispering, "Hurry up."

The pained look on his face as I back away makes me smile.

"You're gonna pay for that," he warns.

"I hope so."

Heat flares in his eyes, and I know in that moment we're both thinking it at the same time.

The question isn't *if* I'm going to give myself completely to Kyle.

It's a matter of when.

Chapter 15

NOW

Ashley pounces on me the second I walk through the front door of our condo.

"So, what would you think about"—she slips my bags from my arm—"a party?"

"Uh . . ."

"Like a housewarming party."

"She's already making a guest list," Christa calls out from her seat on the couch, one hand holding the remote as she channel-surfs, the other busy stroking a content-looking Elton.

"You're home early." I plant myself on a bar stool, inhaling the delicious fragrance of apple pie. A golden-crusted dish sits in the center of the island, caramelized juices oozing through the slats of the lattice top. Ashley's handiwork, no doubt.

"So are you." Christa frowns, muting the TV. "What's going on? Is this about Tripp or Kyle?"

I chuckle despite my dark mood. She's always been so adept at reading me. "Kyle. And my father."

Ashley is slack-jawed by the time I finish relaying all that Kyle divulged today about being paid off.

"Wait a second. So Kyle is claiming that your father paid him money to basically disappear?" Christa asks slowly, doubtfully.

"Yup."

Ashley frowns. "Do you believe him?"

"Yeah," I admit with reluctance. "I do." While my father has always portrayed himself to be an ethical man, I know he made a significant financial donation to Brown to help alleviate the concerns that Rhett's grades might not get him accepted. And there was a case at CG, when an employee claimed she had been fired without cause and threatened legal action. My dad paid her a lump sum to make her go away, mainly because he didn't want the hassle that would come with fighting her in court. So do I think he would be capable and willing to pay a boy he deemed "bad news" to get away from his only daughter?

Yes. A thousand percent, yes.

"It's like some horribly cliché plot device in a show about rich people," Christa mutters. "It's crazy."

I snort derisively. "What's crazy is that Kyle could have gotten *way more* money out of my father."

"Oh, to be filthy rich," Ashley murmurs dreamily, her chin resting on her propped arm.

"So, when are you going to confront your father about this?" As always, Christa cuts right to the chase.

"I don't know if I'm going to. Believe me, I *want* to look him straight in the eye and make sure he knows that I know what he did. But, as of right now my father doesn't seem to remember that Kyle ever existed. He didn't recognize him today, in the lobby. Didn't so much as blink at him."

"It's probably better to keep it that way," Ashley says.

"Right? Knowing my dad, he'd have Kyle escorted off the property. He'll probably go after his job." I feel the compelling urge to stop that from happening, and there is one thing I'm sure of—Dad would *never* want anyone to know that he basically threatened and blackmailed a seventeen-year-old boy. There must be laws against that. At the very least, it's shady as hell and wouldn't do well for his reputation.

"Pretty ballsy move, taking a job in the same building. *If* he's telling the truth." Christa still sounds distrustful.

"What else did Kyle say?" Ashley scuttles around the kitchen, collecting small dishes and forks, and a knife. "You know, besides the fact that he moved across the country for you thirteen years later and is still madly in love with you."

"He's not *in love* with me! And he moved as much to get away from his dad and brothers." I feel the smile begin to stretch my lips, unbidden. "But he's single. He's living with his little brother."

"Really?" Ashley squeals at the same time that Christa groans, "Here we go."

"What!"

Christa gives me a flat look. "Forget about the fact that he accepted fifty thousand dollars to stay away from you for a minute. What's going to happen when your dad finds out you're dating the *building security guard?*"

"We're not dating!"

"Yet," she mutters, toying with Elton's ears. "But we *all* know where this is going."

"Who says?"

"History! We were there at camp, remember?"

"Oh, yeah." Ashley's eyes are star-filled as she sets a plate in front of me. "Like horny magnets. Couldn't stay off each other."

I cringe. "That was a long time ago. A lot has changed." Has it, really? Kyle still commands my attention when he steps into the room and distracts my thoughts constantly. From the moment I saw him in the lobby that day, I haven't stopped wondering about him. I'm still so wildly attracted to him, I may as well be a hormonal teenager.

"Is that why you can't look me in the eye right now?" Ashley teases.

"No. I'm just enthralled with this delicious pie," I mutter around a mouthful. "Mmm . . . *so* good. Sorry, what were we talking about?"

"How you haven't stopped thinking about

hooking up with Kyle since you found out he was single," Christa says dryly.

"Or . . . our housewarming party." Ashley stares at me through wide, pleading eyes. "Please, please, please, *please* . . . It'd be a good excuse to invite Kyle."

My heart skitters at the thought of seeing him outside of the office. Somewhere more comfortable, more social. "Shouldn't we have more than a couch and TV set up before we host people here?"

Ashley bites her lip in thought, her gaze skating over the cheap round table in the middle of the room, and then to the empty, white walls, and out to the barren patio behind the glass. "It's just such a waste, to have a place like this and *not* throw a party." Her shoulders sag with disappointment.

"I mean, I guess I could hire that interior decorator who did my office to fill up this place, but I don't have time to field all those questions—"

"I'll do it!" she bursts, putting her hand up as if in class. "I'll take care of everything."

"Really?"

"Are you kidding me? I know your taste; just give me your budget. Questions will be limited, I promise." She grins. "And *then* we can have a party, right?"

I chuckle. "Sure. Okay."

"Perfect." She slides over a notepad with her chicken scratch. "Early list of invitees."

I shake my head with amusement as I scan the list. "My brother?"

"You keep saying we need to meet him."

"I guess . . ." I frown. "Who are George and Harriet?"

"Our neighbors."

"We have neighbors?" There are only two units on this floor and the other one hadn't been sold when I moved in.

Ashley's eyebrows arch. "Yeah, for like *two months* now. She's a teacher at a private school. He's an investment banker. They're nice. Well, *she's* nice. I haven't met him yet. I had afternoon tea with her last week. She has great taste."

Leave it to Ashley to gain herself an invitation to Earl Grey and crumpets.

I keep skimming the list, until one name jumps out at me. *"Eric?"*

"You said Kyle still talks to him." She shrugs innocently. "I'm sure he'd love to see all of us again."

"Right. He missed everyone at Wawa *so* much that he dropped off the planet and never returned your emails," Christa mutters, heaving herself off the couch to stroll over to the kitchen island, Elton tucked in one arm. She leans over my shoulder to scan the party invitation list. "You're kidding me." She shakes her head firmly. "You are *not* inviting Zelda to our housewarming party. No way. No psychics."

Ashley rolls her eyes. "Relax. I'm doing it to be polite. She won't come. But do you think we should invite your dad, Piper? This *is* his place."

"He *definitely* won't come. And no." I would have said that before finding out about the payoff. Now . . . "He's not welcome. Besides, I'm sure he'll be too busy intimidating seventeen-year-old boys somewhere. God, what is that sound?" I exclaim, no longer able to ignore the odd rumbling coming from Elton as he nuzzles Christa's ear.

"He's just happy. Right, Elton?" Christa rubs her nose affectionately against his while she walks away, her voice shifting several octaves to croon, "Who's a good kitty? Yes, *you're* a good kitty."

"He snuck into my room last night while I was in the bathroom, pruned the aloe vera, and then *puked* on my slippers," Ashley offers as proof of the very opposite to Christa's claims. "If there's any chance you've developed a sudden allergy to cats, now would be the time to speak up."

"I heard that!" Christa stops at the hallway that leads to her bedroom. "And Piper? You're not fooling anyone except yourself."

I sigh heavily, stabbing at my pie. "I just don't know what to do."

"Yes, you do. You need to figure out if you

and Kyle can actually make this work in today's world. Is this going to be an epic star-crossed lovers' saga or some tawdry two-hour romance where the heiress to billions is banging the security guard on her desk?"

"I'd read either of those stories," Ashley murmurs through a sip of milk.

Christa rolls her eyes at our romance-obsessed friend. "Figure it out, and decide if you're okay with it."

I sigh. "You're right."

"Of course I'm right." She disappears down the hall.

"So, Shakespeare in Tights has a desperate friend in need of a job, and I'm just supposed to hire her," David mutters. *Thwack.* The tennis ball bounces off the window and back, landing in his grip so smoothly that it seems tethered.

When Mark mentioned a friend who was looking for administrative work and asked if David would consider interviewing her, my first instinct was to ask what she did to make him hate her so much. But when he explained that he gave her the rundown on David, that she has a glass-is-always-half-full attitude, and *is* in fact desperate for a job, the wheels in my brain started churning. This would solve the problem of David—an albeit small problem in comparison to my complications with Tripp, Kyle, and my father—and having David out of my hair is always a good goal to keep.

"She has administrative experience."

"Yeah, at a *truck leasing* company." His voice is filled with disdain as he scowls at the résumé Mark printed out and left on his desk this morning.

"What was that important thing you missed yesterday?" I mock-frown, my index finger to my lip. "Giving a keynote speech, was it?"

"Point taken," he mutters with a huff. "But I'm not promising anything."

"Promise you'll at least give her a fair shot?"

"Well, of course I'll do that. You know me."

"I do. Which is why I'm asking you to *not* be yourself."

He rolls his eyes.

I want to slap him upside the head and tell him to stop being an idiot. But David is much more receptive to having his ego stroked. "Look, you are far too busy a man to be managing these trivial things." I keep my voice calm and soothing. "I need Mark's support full-time and you are not poaching Jack's assistant. Mark has known Renée for years and can vouch for her as being a competent and hardworking woman." More important, Renée has already completed David Worthington 101, a course taught by Mark and one that I can guarantee was not complimentary.

She still wanted to interview.

Mark's smooth voice carries down the hall, announcing their arrival.

"Okay, she's here. Don't be a dick," I warn, turning to watch my sacrificial lamb approach. I struggle to keep my mouth from dropping. "Wow."

Renée is compact in stature, especially next to Mark. I'm guessing five feet tall without the towering heels. She's fit, the navy pencil dress showing off tight, hour-glass curves and muscular legs. Her shock of platinum-blonde hair reaches down past her chest and is poker-straight.

Large, expressive blue eyes take me in as Mark leads her forward, and she bites her pouty bottom lip before realizing it and stopping herself.

She's nervous.

She's also knockout gorgeous.

"She's *hired,*" David murmurs from behind me, watching their approach.

I shoot him a warning look.

"What?" He shrugs innocently. "I've always wanted an assistant who I carry around in my pocket."

As covertly as possible, I elbow David in the ribs before stepping forward. "Renée, it's nice to meet you. I'm Piper Calloway."

For as tiny as she may be, she has a broad smile that takes up half her face, and it flashes now to reveal perfect, white teeth. "I could have guessed.

Mark has told me *so much* about you. He loves working here."

Oh lord, she even has a Southern accent.

David clears his throat and then maneuvers past me with an arm, offering his hand and his signature killer smile. "Hello, I'm David Worthington, vice president of Sales and Marketing at Calloway. You'll be interviewing for a position as *my* executive assistant."

She stiffens in posture. "Yes, of course. Hi, it's a pleasure to meet you."

"Come on into my office." David steps back to give her space to enter, his arm extending in a leading, welcoming gesture. "So, Renée. That's French, isn't it?" His voice fades behind the shutting door.

Mark's nervous gaze is on them.

"So . . . she seems nice."

"Renée? Oh, yeah. She's . . ." He clears his throat. "She's *great.*"

Huh. "And how long have you had a thing for her?"

"What?" Mark's head whips around. "I don't have a thing for her."

"Really? Because your red face would say otherwise," I tease.

He sighs and bows his head in defeat. "Five years now, I think? Basically since the moment I met her."

A burst of laughter sounds from David's office.

Whatever David said must have been funny, because Renée is practically doubled over.

"What have you found on *that person* I asked you about?"

"Oh, yeah . . ." Mark opens his desk drawer to pull out a sheet of paper. He glances around us, then nods toward my office, and my stomach begins to flutter with anticipation. Whatever he has, it's something he doesn't think people should overhear.

"Okay, spill it," I demand as soon as my door shuts.

"So far, I know that Tripp and Hank Kavanaugh were roommates at Minden College. They also played in a men's soccer league together for a few years in their twenties."

"*Really?* That lazy bastard actually chased after a ball?"

"Maybe it was a beer league?" he offers, then hands me a stack of papers. "Here's a printout of his calendar for the last six months. Every meeting with Hank is highlighted in yellow."

I begin flipping through the pages. "A lot of Friday morning golf meetings."

"Those are the ones Jill has a record of."

"What did you tell her?" If I didn't know firsthand Jill's disdain for Tripp, I would never have suggested that Mark reach out to her. Then again, Mark knows nothing of the kickback suspicions.

"I asked her if Tripp's been meeting with a guy named Hank and she sent me all this. Then she offered to comb through his emails to see if there are any from KDZ, though she doesn't remember any coming in."

As one would expect, if he's been working this deal for months, as he claims.

"She knows to keep this between us?" The last thing I need is the administrative grapevine catching wind of this.

"She won't say a word." He pauses. "What are you hoping to find, anyway?"

"Proof that Tripp's up to no good." I know that's a vague answer, but this level of betrayal is far above Mark's pay grade. He's a smart guy, though; he'll figure it out.

Either way, I don't have enough to confront Tripp or accuse him of anything yet. "Keep digging."

Mark nods, and then his gaze wanders back to the office across the hall to watch David and Renée chatter and laugh like old friends. Worry pulls his brow. "Did I just make a *huge* mistake by introducing them to each other?"

I set a comforting hand on Mark's shoulder. "Don't worry. David has too much integrity to sleep with his assistant." *I hope*. There's no doubt David will hire Renée, though; that stupid grin hasn't slid from his face once. At least I can mark off a mental check box next to *one* of my dilemmas and move on to tackle Tripp, and my father.

And Kyle.

Christa's sage advice from last night lingers in my mind. As always, she's right.

I need to figure out if Kyle even fits in my life anymore. And if he doesn't . . . I need to let go of my fond memories and move on.

"Thank *you,*" Renée offers, rushing into the elevator beside me. I used the need to stretch my legs as an offer to walk her down—mainly so I have an excuse to stop by the security desk. "Mark said you made this happen."

"I just set up the interview. And, trust me, this is more advantageous to Mark and me than it is you."

"Are you kidding? Yesterday I was pounding pavement and handing my résumé out at restaurants in desperation, and today I have this dream job!" She looks ready to squeal.

Her interview with David lasted nearly an hour—forty minutes longer than any of his other interviews.

"I hope you still feel that way after your first day. David's expectations of what an assistant should do are a tad *high* at times."

She waves my words away with a broad smile. "Oh, don't worry, Mark gave me the *whole* rundown on David. I'm ready for it. Bruce, my old boss? He used to make me clean his office fish tank every week."

I cringe.

"Yeah. And he made me do recon on the birthday party his ex-wife was throwing for his daughter so I could plan another party for her. And I mean *everything,* from printing the invitations to booking the spa and the food. And it had to be better than his ex's party." She shrugs. "Sometimes these guys are clueless."

I decide that I like Renée. She has an easy, charming way about her. It's no wonder Mark has been pining over her for years. The question is, does she realize his adoration for her? I push that thought aside for now; it's too early to start trying to play matchmaker for my assistant. "You've come to the right place, then. You won't have to make children's birthday invitations for him, but David is definitely clueless at times. I should know—I almost married him."

"Mark *told* me." Her blue eyes widen. "What happened?"

"I smartened up."

"Well . . . I guess I shouldn't be surprised you two were an item. He's *so* . . . I mean . . ." Her perfectly shaped brows pinch together as she searches for a way out of the unprofessional hole she just stepped into. "Oh God." Her manicured hand flies to cover her mouth.

I let her squirm for another second before I

laugh. "It's okay. Yes, he's gorgeous. We all know it. *He* definitely knows it." The elevator doors open and we step out.

"Oh, hey, Piper! I was just coming up to see you." Serge's gaze flickers to Renée, where it sits a moment, his olive skin taking on a pinkish hue.

"You go ahead with your meetings. I'll drop my badge at the desk." Renée reaches out to give my forearm a friendly squeeze. "And again, thank you so much. You're a lifesaver."

"It was nothing. I'm glad it worked out. You should get an email with all the necessary paperwork from HR within the next few hours. If you don't, call Mark and he'll help straighten it out."

She flashes one last beautiful smile and then strolls off toward the security gate, her heels clicking against the travertine.

My gaze catches on Kyle, his attention glued to the security camera monitors. I've lingered around Gus long enough to know those are the ones aimed at the parking garage. He's standing, giving me a full view of that cut body and those muscular arms.

"So I just got off the phone with my guy from Jameson about the Marquee project," Serge says, snapping my attention back to him. "Apparently he tried to set up a meeting with Tripp so we could go over the proposal and Tripp told him that we've decided to go in another direction."

"He did *what?*" It comes out in a hiss, though the voice inside my head is screaming.

Serge takes a step back, as if he can see the rage ignite in my eyes. "I'm guessing you didn't know."

I take a deep, calming breath. "Thanks for telling me. I'll take care of it."

His forehead pulls together. "So that means we *haven't* made any decisions on the construction contract, right?"

I force a wide smile. "That's right. I will call Gary right now and make sure he knows that Calloway Group is still very much interested in their proposal." A third-generation Jameson, Gary is a burly man who has an affinity for cigars and the Vegas strip, but he has always been a reliable partner. I can't imagine the mood in his office right now. We've had dozens of conversations about the Marquee project already and all of them conveyed the same message—that Calloway Group had every intention of signing on with Jameson if the terms lined up.

Does my father know about this?

"Okay, I'll just . . . keep the team working until you and Tripp figure out which direction we're going." There's a hint of annoyance in Serge's voice and I can't blame him; I'm annoyed and I'm not the one managing all the finite details.

"We'll have this sorted soon. I promise."

Musical laughter carries from the lobby as

Serge ducks into the elevator, holding me back from joining him.

Renée is leaning against the security desk, one leg crooked so only her toe touches the tile. Gus has just said something—charming, I'm sure—but her attention keeps shifting to Kyle.

Who is smiling down at her.

Not just a polite "have a nice day, ma'am" smile but that eye-crinkling, lip-curling one that used to make my stomach flip.

That flirtatious one.

Mark's words echo in my mind then, about whether it was a mistake to introduce Renée to David.

Maybe the mistake doesn't involve David at all.

A burn radiates in my chest and grows, as I start playing out a scenario before me—where Renée comes to work every morning, flashing that beautiful smile and saying hello in that sultry Southern accent, lingering at the security desk longer each day, until one Friday she mentions grabbing a drink after work and the next thing I know they're moving in together.

And I've missed my chance.

"Holy shit," I whisper under my breath, standing in the middle of the corridor, an obstacle for the people filing out of the elevator, jealousy gnawing at my insides.

I may not know how—and if—Kyle can fit into

my life today, but I sure as hell know I'm not willing to lose my chance to find out.

The elevator doors open and out comes Tripp, a satchel over his shoulder, looking ready to leave the building.

"Piper. That's a lovely *dress,*" he offers in a patronizing voice, flashing me a smarmy smile.

"Off to sabotage the Marquee project some more?" I throw back before I can bite my tongue.

His bushy gray eyebrows arch. It takes him a moment to process my words. "Excuse me?"

"Jameson."

His lips twist as if working out a bitter taste in his mouth. "He called you? What did he say?"

"Does my father know you've basically set dynamite under our bridge with them?"

"Jameson can't beat the bid KDZ is going to come in at. Kieran will agree with me."

You mean the one that lines your pockets with half a million dollars?

I grit my teeth to hold back from accusing him right then and there. He'll just deny it and without more evidence, I will look like an incompetent asshole.

"If you'll excuse me, *I* have things to do." He sails past me, his head high as he strolls toward the security gate.

Where Kyle is now stealing glances my way, in between Renée's chatter, his sharp eyes narrowing at Tripp as he passes.

As much as I'd like to interrupt whatever is going on over there, I have a project and a long-term business relationship to save.

With that, I take the next elevator up.

Hoping Kyle doesn't fall for Renée's charms too quickly.

Chapter 16

THEN

2006, Camp Wawa, End of Week Two

"Finally, some sun . . . I was so sick of being cooped up inside." Kyle kicks off his shoes and then wanders over to stand on the edge of the cliff and gaze out over the dark blue waters below. The early afternoon sun glimmers off the surface.

I'm not sure which has made the second week of camp harder—the three days of steady rain that forced indoor activities and caused cabin fever for everyone or our ten P.M. lockdown, thanks to our probation. On the plus side, I'm well rested.

"Hate to break it to you, but it's supposed to storm later. At least, that's what Christa said." Though there is nothing more than a few wispy white clouds streaking the sky at the moment.

"And Christa's *never* wrong about anything," he murmurs sarcastically.

A speedboat races past, towing a female wakeboarder behind. Upon closer scrutiny, I realize it's Claire, the waterskiing and wakeboarding instructor.

"She's really good."

Kyle watches her cut through the waves with ease, her muscular legs flexing. "She's got some serious goals, that one. Wouldn't be surprised to see her standing on a podium with a medal around her neck one day."

I hesitate. "What about you?"

"I'm not much into waterskiing." He reaches over his head to pull off his Wawa T-shirt, revealing two weeks' worth of T-shirt tan lines and a smooth, sculpted back.

"No, I meant what are you going to do after high school? Like, do you have any colleges picked out?" Where will Kyle end up next year, and how far away will it be from me?

"Yeah . . . I don't think college is for me." He empties his pockets, casting their contents onto his favorite boulder.

"Really?" I frown. "So, then what will you do?" He must have a goal, *something* to work toward?

"Dunno? Get a job, I guess."

"Doing what?" *What interests you, Kyle?* Besides jumping off cliffs and racing golf carts at night. In the two weeks that we've been here, aside from the topic of his family, our conversations have been light, shallow.

Fun.

But do we even have anything in common?

He shrugs. "Working here, maybe? I can take over Darian's job."

"Seriously?"

"Nah . . . Construction, maybe."

"What, like running your own company?"

He chuckles. "More like hammering nails into boards. I don't really care. I just want to get away from my shitty family. Except for Jeremy. He's cool." He nods, more to himself. "You'd like him."

I quietly absorb his indifference to his future. Is it because he's never been pushed to consider it? Or are things really that bad at home that he can't think beyond the goal of getting away?

"What about you?" he asks with a yawn and a stretch, as if the topic is of little interest to him.

"Brown, probably. It's the Calloway way," I add in a mocking manner.

"Huh . . ." He frowns thoughtfully. "I probably shouldn't follow the Miller way." A wry smile curls his lips as he runs a hand through his Fauxhawk, sending it into disarray. He shifts his focus back to the cliff. "You coming in or what?"

I guess that's the end of any serious talk with Kyle.

"Of course." I shrug my clothes off, stripping down to the teal string bikini I threw on earlier. "So is there anything to do in town?"

"There's a great burger place on Main Street. And sometimes you can catch a good . . ." Kyle's words fall off the moment he turns, his eyes dragging over my bare skin feeling like fingertips. "Is that a new one?"

"No, but I haven't worn it here yet." I adjust the narrow triangles over my chest and test the string ties on my hips, to make sure they're secure. I packed the bikini knowing it's far too skimpy for anything besides tanning in private. And enticing Kyle, apparently. My stomach stirs with butterflies as I stand there, allowing him to look. I've never felt confident being ogled by boys, but with Kyle, I feel a pleasing shiver run through my body. "What were you saying? Something about catching a good . . ."

"Movie," he answers after a long pause, his voice a touch huskier than normal. "At the drive-in."

"A drive-in? Really? I've never been. What's it like?"

"It's fun. Maybe we can check it out tonight." I catch the smile curling his lips before he turns back to the lake, and the rise of his shoulders with a deep breath.

And the way he covertly tugs at his board shorts, trying to adjust himself.

Heat rushes through my core.

Just the two of us, away from here, tucked into his car under the cover of night? Something tells me we wouldn't be paying much attention to whatever's on the screen.

"Nervous?"

My cheeks flush. "Huh?"

He nods toward the edge. "About jumping again."

Oh. "No." Actually, now that I consider the thirty-foot free fall into the lake, I realize that I *am* nervous. *More* so than the first time, when I had little time to think, when I had no experience to recall.

He looks over his shoulder at me and smirks, like he knows I'm lying, his gaze skating over my body a second time.

And then, with a boyish grin, he takes a running leap off the cliff.

Exhilaration swells in my chest as I rush to the edge to watch him resurface.

He wades to the side, his strokes strong and practiced. "Am I going to have to talk you into it again?" he hollers, and I hear the challenge in his voice.

Taking a deep breath, I step back and then charge forward, gripped by a sensation that's both paralyzing and exhilarating as I plummet through the air. By the time my body emerges from the crisp water, a hysterical laugh—of accomplishment and ecstasy—takes over.

Until I realize the rush of water has forced my bikini top clean off me.

I yelp and cover my bare chest with one arm, while using the other to tread water. "Shit . . . my top!"

Kyle swims toward where I plunged in and dives under, only to pop up a few moments later, long enough to curse about murky water. He gathers a deep breath and then he's gone again, swimming deeper into the abyss.

Treading water with one arm is difficult and I finally have to relent, releasing my hold of my chest to stay afloat, wondering just *how* murky the water is, how much Kyle can see from beneath. I have yet to strut around nude in front of him—or any guy, for that matter.

He bursts through the water's surface with a gasp for air. "Sorry, it's gone. It's too deep here and I can't see shit."

"Well, *this* is going to be fun," I mutter, eyeing the steep and rocky slope that I get to try to maneuver up, topless.

Kyle swims toward me, doing a poor job of hiding a secretive smile.

"Don't look *too* upset."

"Sorry. It's just . . ." The small smile morphs into a wide grin. "I was wondering if that would happen."

"And you didn't think to warn me?"

"I *did* think about it." He edges in closer, until our knees are bumping together. "And then I thought better of it."

"You jerk." I smack his chest playfully, before scanning the cliff top. "Where's Eric?" Kyle seeing me topless is one thing. I'm not putting on a show for the other counselors.

"The last I saw, he was heading somewhere with Avery." There's a hint of bitterness in his voice.

"Is he into her?"

Kyle rolls his eyes. "Who the hell knows with him. They messed around last week."

They must have done it in secret, because *nothing* stays quiet long in the counselor circle. So far, Colin's been spotted making out behind the canteen with Jenny and, though no one can confirm they saw Marie and Carlos hooking up, the fact that they both developed a poison ivy rash all over their backs on the same day last week is highly suspicious.

I hesitate. "Is that *weird* for you?" If one of my close friends started dating Trevor after we broke up, that would probably bother me.

"Not the way you're probably thinking. Eric's not serious about Avery. He's just biding his time until Ashley decides he isn't a fool." Kyle chuckles. "That might be a while. I tried to help him out last year by hinting to her that he was into her, and then he pulled the same kind of shit, and Ashley wouldn't give him a chance the rest of the summer. If she hears about him hooking up with Avery, he'll screw his chances up a second year." Kyle shakes his head.

It dawns on me. "Aww . . . You're a hopeless romantic!" I tease.

"Shut up." Kyle grins. "Right now I'm a horny guy with a hot, topless girl in front of me."

The fact that I'm so close to him and naked save for my scrap-of-a-bottom is not lost on me.

Despite the cool temperature of the water, my entire body is flushing with warmth. If Kyle is affected, he's not letting on; at ease in the water, his breath is even and calm.

"You good?" he asks, as if reading my mind.

"Yeah."

He hesitates. "So . . . Shane is going home next Saturday, for the night. He only lives, like, an hour away and he wants to see his girlfriend." Kyle pulls his bottom lip between his teeth and holds it a moment before releasing it, a shy smile touching his lips. "I'll have my cabin to myself for the night. In case you wanted to hang out there with me."

My stomach flutters as I grasp what he's really asking.

"For a few hours . . . or the night." He swallows hard. "Whatever you feel like—"

"Okay," I blurt out, not even pretending to play coy. "I mean, as long as Darian's not going to nail us for breaking probation."

"She said we had to be in our cabins for lights-out with our campers. There *are* no campers on Saturday night." He says it so innocently. "It's our night off to do whatever we want."

Except "whatever we want" means squeezed together in the twin bunk. The two of us in a bed together, alone, *all night long*.

My breathing has turned ragged. Meanwhile, Kyle's breathing hasn't even wavered.

"You're a strong swimmer," I murmur, needing to change the conversation to something less heart palpitation–inducing.

"I should hope so. I did a couple years on my school's swim team." He grins when my eyebrows arch with surprise. "What?"

"Nothing. Just picturing you rocking those little swim shorts and cap."

"Are you mocking me?"

"Never."

He laughs. "I was actually supposed to do the Red Cross lifeguard training program last year." He tosses that scrap of personal information out so casually.

I seize it. "You totally should! It's a great part-time job. I have a friend who's a lifeguard. She makes good money. For a teenager, anyway." Money she doesn't need. She's doing it for her college application.

"Yeah . . . It's like two hundred for the course I was looking at." Kyle's gaze shifts away. "May as well be two thousand."

Two hundred dollars. Less than the cost of the running shoes I bought for this summer. I didn't even blink at setting my credit card on the counter for that purchase. I try to wrap my mind around the idea of not being able to afford something, and I can't. I can't recall a time those words have ever left my parents' mouths.

"But you'll make more than that working here

this summer," I push, keeping my voice light and hopeful.

"I need that money to make it through the year. Clothes and shit like that." His tongue darts out to toy with his lip ring.

"Well, I can lend you the—"

"No, Piper." His tone is sharp. He adds, more softly, "That's nice of you to offer, but . . . no."

Uncomfortable silence falls over us, and I'm desperate to push it away. "How do you tread water like that? I mean, without using your arms?"

His soft sigh skates across my cheek. "Easy. It's called the rotary kick."

"Teach me." Anything to get the conversation away from how different our lives are.

A slight smirk curls his lips. "Keep your arms still and imagine your legs are an egg beater."

I try to mimic Kyle, freezing my arms and kicking my legs how I'd imagine an egg beater would rotate.

I start to sink.

Kyle's hands grip either side of my waist, pulling me back up. "Try again," he coaxes, keeping hold of me this time, our knees knocking against each other's intermittently.

It takes me a few minutes to get the hang of it. " 'Kay, I think I'm doing it."

"You are." He smiles, but he doesn't let go, pulling me in closer to kiss. I let my arms float on either side of me and I close my eyes, reveling in the feel of Kyle's mouth against mine, in his shallow breaths, in the tip of his tongue as it first skates over the seam of my lips, and then into my mouth. He tastes like the spearmint gum he was chewing earlier, and not cigarettes. Though, if he did, I wouldn't care.

Kyle's hands begin to shift upward, ever so slowly, until his thumbs are nestled against the underside of my breasts. And then they're *on* my breasts, tenderly, as if he's memorizing their shape, his index fingers drawing small, teasing circles over my nipples.

I open my eyes, wondering if his are as full of lust as mine must be.

That's when I notice the teal string floating atop the water behind him.

"My top!" I frown a second before realization hits me. My mouth drops open as I reach behind him, to find that he secured it through one of his belt loops. "Kyle!"

With an impish grin, he slips from my grasp and takes off swimming toward the alcove. I chase after him, yelling his name. It's in vain, though; he's much too fast for me.

When I round the corner, I find him sitting on the rocky plateau, leaning back and propped up by his elbows as if basking in the sun, his legs dangling over the edge.

He grins at me, holding out my top. "Sorry, I couldn't help myself."

I yank it from his grasp and attempt to put it back on, quickly abandoning the idea. It's too hard while treading water.

Kyle smirks, like he knows it. "I won't look. Promise." He rolls over to lie on his stomach, facing away from me.

I hoist myself onto the ledge. The rock is almost too hot to the touch. It would be a nice place to relax and rid myself of these hideous T-shirt tan lines. A nice, quiet, private place to linger that can't be seen from the expanse of lake.

"You're not mad at me, are you?" He reaches for a loose stone nearby, to twirl it within his grasp.

"No," I admit. I enjoyed every second of that moment when he was touching me so intimately.

In truth, I wish it hadn't ended.

"Tell me when you're good." He has kept his word, his gaze still on the crop of bushes beyond.

A rash of butterflies explodes in my stomach as I commit myself to my decision. Splashing the hot-to-the-touch rock with handfuls of water to cool it down, I stretch out onto my back and shield my eyes against the blinding sun, leaving my top resting next to my head. "Okay."

With a sigh, he moves to roll back. "I was thinking we should—" His words cut off, his mouth falling agape as it skates over my near-naked body.

"I have these horrible tan lines that I need to

get rid of," I explain casually, closing my eyes and settling my arm down beside me.

Kyle clears his throat. "Right."

I can *feel* his heavy gaze touching my body, and each second that passes makes me crave for his hands to be on me again.

"Did you put on sunscreen?"

Shit. I groan. "No. And my bottle is all the way up—"

"I'll get it."

"You don't have . . ." My voice trails. He's already on his feet, nimbly picking his path up the treacherous hill.

I'm going to need Kyle's help coating my back, I think with a smile, imagining his hands smoothing all over my body, along every inch of exposed skin.

By the time the loud splash sounds a few minutes later—Kyle, leaping off the cliff again—my body is aching with need.

Kyle swims around the bend and pulls himself back onto the rock, my tube of sunscreen firmly gripped in his hand. Droplets of water land on my skin as he shifts closer to me. "Here, roll over," he murmurs as he tries to catch his breath, his eyes skittering over my chest and stomach.

I do, carefully, so as not to scrape my skin against the jagged edges of rock, and rest my chin atop folded arms, silently reveling in the feel of the cool gobs of sunscreen landing on my back.

"You sure ran up the hill fast." His first touch draws a small gasp from my lips.

"Yeah, I guess I just *really* wanted to jump again."

I smile to myself. "Right. Jump."

He chuckles softly.

We fall into a comfortable silence as his hands smooth over my shoulders and down my sides in long, languid strokes, until my entire back is covered. Only he doesn't stop there. He squeezes another dollop onto the back of each thigh and covers the full length of my legs, all the way from my ankles to the edge of my bikini bottoms, his fingertips sliding down over my inner thighs, teasing me, never venturing where I want them to, making the mild ache between my legs morph into a needy throb.

"Your back is done," he announces, his voice low and gravelly.

"Do you mind doing the rest?" I roll over, squinting against the sun as I peer up to admire his stunning features.

He licks his lips as his eyes trail the length of my body. Finally he shakes his head and wordlessly squeezes a glob onto my belly button.

I suck in my stomach from the chill, and he chuckles. He begins smoothing the sunscreen over my abdomen, his strokes even slower than before, his face taking on an odd, somber expression.

"What's wrong?"

"Nothing at all. You're just . . . perfect," he murmurs, shifting his hand upward, over my breasts, his palm cupping each one, the soft pad of his thumb circling over my nipples a few times. "I still can't believe you're here with me. I'm the luckiest guy in the world right now."

I reach out to drag my fingers against his thigh. "*I'm* the lucky one."

"You have no clue . . ." He shakes his head as he shifts his focus, stretching to reach my ankles before moving all the way up each leg, his hands firm and confident. And, once again, he teases me mercilessly, his fingers sliding provocatively as he coats my inner thighs.

I shift my legs apart, just enough that he'll hopefully take the hint.

He definitely notices because his mouth parts and his gaze shifts to meet mine, allowing me to admire the green-and-gold kaleidoscope of his irises.

Finally, Kyle stretches out to lie beside me, propping himself up on one elbow. "You're all covered," he whispers, leaning in to press a kiss against my cheek, his free hand resting on my stomach.

I turn to meet him face-to-face, our noses grazing. "I guess I should do you now?"

He groans and I laugh, angling my head so I

can get better access to his lip ring. I flick it with my tongue.

The hand resting on my stomach slides down over my belly, until his fingers are tracing the top seam of my bikini bottoms, making my blood race and heat pool between my legs. Shifting so that he's hovering over me, blocking out the sun from my eyes, he whispers, "You good?"

I hesitate, reaching up to cup his jaw, my thumb dragging over the light stubble. "I could be better."

A sexy smirk curls his lips as he leans down to give me one of his signature tantalizing kisses. He breaks free long enough to show me his hooded eyes—and maybe to triple-check what I want in mine—before his fingers are slipping beneath the material, and lower.

A slight gasp escapes my lips as I settle my hand on his shoulder and my legs part of their own accord.

Kyle curses under his breath. "God, you're so . . ." His voice trails with a hard swallow, and then he's deepening his kiss as his fingers slip inside me.

I let Trevor venture into my pants only three times while we dated and one of those times, I was drunk. While I can't say I didn't enjoy it, it always seemed like he was marking off a box in the foreplay checklist, with the sole purpose of reaching an end result that got him what *he* wanted. It was all hot hands and fumbling fingers, and never lasted more than a minute before he'd be whispering what he'd *rather* be doing to me and begging me to unfasten his jeans.

It was all about him.

But not Kyle. He's in no rush, and he is *so* far from a fool groping toward the home plate, his thumb dragging over me in soft circles, each stroke bringing me closer to an edge I've never gone over with anyone.

Our ragged breaths mix as his hand works over me, my legs falling farther apart, my inhibitions drifting higher away as my body chases a climax I want so badly to experience with him.

And then a bellow of "Freedom!" carries from somewhere above.

I shut my legs on Kyle's hand and sit up in an instant, the heat of the moment effectively doused just as a loud splash sounds.

A second scream—that of a girl—echoes through the bay as Kyle is slipping his hand from me. Another splash sounds.

I fumble with my top, tying the neck and adjusting the front before the intruders venture this way.

Beside me Kyle lies sprawled on his back, his arms thrown over his face. "I'm gonna kill him," he mutters.

Maybe it's a good thing we were interrupted, I think to myself, as I steal a glance downward, to where his clingy—still wet—bathing shorts leave little to the imagination. The sight drives my need for him, my fingers itching to slip beneath his waistband.

It's only been two weeks and I'm ready to give it all up to Kyle on a hidden rocky plateau in broad daylight. There's no rush, I remind myself. We still have six more weeks together. And we have next Saturday night, when we don't have to worry about anyone invading our privacy.

The ache in my body flares with the thought of what might happen.

For now, though, I settle on dragging my index finger along the thin trail of hair below his belly button in a teasing manner. Checking over my shoulder to make sure Eric isn't in sight yet, I smooth my hand over his hard length, gripping him with my fingers.

"Your turn."

"What?" He lifts his arms to peer at me. "*Now?* Seriously?" His eyebrows are furrowed with doubt, but I don't miss the heat beginning to flare in them again.

I lift up the bottle of sunscreen. "Before you burn."

His arms fall back over his face with a loud groan.

"I haven't received any more calls from your mother, so I assume you're staying out of trouble?"

My dad's voice always sounds especially clipped over the phone. I hate talking to him on the phone because of it.

"No trouble."

"Good. I'm glad to see you finally taking your job seriously."

I roll my eyes.

"Today's your day off, right?"

"Yeah." We saw our third round of campers off earlier. The third week played out much like the last two—tears and amateur gimp bracelets and promises of a reunion next year.

"And where are you now?"

"Just in town, grabbing dinner." Standing next to Kyle's car in the parking lot of Tony's Burgers.

"With who?"

My eyes drift to the green neon sign ahead, and then to the table where Kyle, Eric, and Ashley sit, laughing and picking away at their plates. "Ashley and Christa." It's only half a lie.

"Who drove?"

"Christa." Outright lie. Surprisingly, it rolls off my tongue without issue. It's been two weeks since my father delivered his edict that I am to stay away from Kyle and, thankfully due to his business trip to Japan and my lack of cell phone reception, I've been able to avoid lying to him up until now. The fact that I even have to makes my stomach roil.

"Good. I'm relieved to hear that. I did some checking up on that boy you were with. Did you know his father and brothers are currently serving time in federal prison?"

"What?"

"Of course the little delinquent didn't tell you," he mutters. "His father's a guard, my ass."

He assumes my outburst was shock, and not outrage. I temper the accusation in my voice. "How'd you find that out?"

"I had my guy run the license plate off his car." He admits it so casually, as if that's a normal thing. "I had a bad feeling about him and, as usual, my gut was right. Those plates aren't even valid."

"I just . . . can't . . ." I grit my teeth as tears of frustration threaten to spill. *I can't believe you would do that.*

Kyle glances out the window then. He sees my face and frowns. *Are you okay?* he mouths.

I force a smile and nod, before turning away.

"Did you tell him who we are? Who *I* am?" my father asks.

"No. No one knows." That, I can answer truthfully.

"Good. Because if he's anything like his father,

he'll be trying to extort money from us before long. I have half a mind to call that camp director and report him."

"*Don't!* I mean . . ." I scramble to think of *something* to dissuade him, without letting on that I've ignored my father's iron-willed wishes and am still very much *with* Kyle. In fact, I'll be with Kyle all night tonight, if all goes as planned. His roommate, Shane, drove off right after Darian's weekly star award meeting. "The kids like him, and he's been staying away from me so far. Plus, if what you found out is true, then I'm sure he needs the money. At least he's coming by it honestly."

"Hmm . . . You're right. Perhaps I'm too jaded." He sighs heavily. "But you don't get to where I am without dealing with your share of scammers and extortionists. I've been facing those kinds of people all my life. I'm not about to have my teenage daughter get taken advantage of by some punk."

Because there's no other reason why Kyle would want to be with me, right, Dad?

I could defend Kyle's honor, but there's no point. My father's already made up his mind about him, and clearly the power of money comes before the heart. I swallow the bitter taste in my mouth. "Don't worry, he's already moved on to another girl," I add, piling on the lies.

"Not surprised. A guy like him wouldn't have

any idea how lucky he is to earn a second of attention from you."

I'm the luckiest guy in the world right now.

Oh, he knows, Dad. I feel the vindictive smile curl my lips. *And he's going to know a whole lot more after tonight.*

"Just keep details about our family to yourself and if he tries anything, you call me right away. I'll deal with him."

"I will. Thanks, Dad. Love you." My voice comes out cold and hard.

"Love you, too. See you in five weeks, is it?"

"Yup." I end the call.

"So who am I with now? Please tell me it's the Gasoline Queen."

I spin around to find Kyle standing behind me.

He gives me a sheepish grin. "Sorry . . . I saw your face and I was worried, so I came out. Didn't mean to listen in."

"It's okay."

He slides his hands into the pockets of his jeans. "Everything all right with your dad?"

"Yeah, just . . . It's nothing."

He hesitates. "But you were talking about us."

I sigh. Kyle is the one person I don't want to lie to. "My dad is intense," I begin.

His eyebrow arches knowingly. "Yeah, I got that."

"He ran your license plate. Or he had *his guy* do it, anyway."

Kyle's head falls back with a groan. "My brother's name would have come up."

"It did, and now he knows about him, and your other brother. And your dad . . ."

Kyle curses under his breath. "I have to say, he brings new meaning to the word *over-protective*."

"I know. I'm sorry. I didn't think he'd do something like that, either. But you don't know him. You don't know *who* he is." I hesitate, my father's voice ringing in my ear, explicitly warning me *not* to do what I'm about to do. "My father is—"

"Don't." Kyle's hands go up in the air, stopping me. "I don't *want* to know, Piper. Seriously. Look, I'm not clueless; I'm not gonna pretend that I am. But I like that it's just been you and me here, not your rich parents or my shitty ones. We've been just *us,* together. And it's worked." His brow wrinkles, an earnest—almost pleading—look filling his eyes. "Can we *please* just keep it like that?"

I nod. "Yeah. For sure." My father is *so wrong* about Kyle.

"Good." He reaches for me, taking both my hands into his, pulling me closer. "I don't care if your dad is a freaking *king* of some remote country."

I laugh. "He's not a king—"

Kyle stops my words with a kiss. "I told you. I

don't want to know. Now, can you please come inside and distract me from Eric's disgusting peanut butter burger?"

I cringe. "You're kidding."

Kyle gives me a flat look. *"I wish."*

The sun is minutes from dropping below the horizon when we pull into Wawa's parking lot.

Eric groans as he climbs out of the backseat of Kyle's car, capping it off with an exaggerated stretch, the grease-coated paper bag from Tony's that holds a second peanut-butter-and-bacon burger dangling from his fingertips. "It's a freaking ghost town around here," he murmurs, surveying the silent campground. Several of the counselors have taken off for the night—either to go home or elsewhere, needing an escape from Wawa after three weeks straight. The rest are in hiding. Likely sleeping.

"I think Wade said he was going to start up a fire by the lake." Ashley scoops her frizzy hair into a ponytail and secures it with an elastic.

"Good. Come on, Freckles." Eric hooks an arm around her neck and leads her toward the gravel path that will take them to the beach. "Meet you guys there?"

Kyle's eyes graze over mine. "Yeah. In a bit."

"Oh, *right*. Shane's gone tonight. Gotcha. Don't do anything I wouldn't do," Eric tosses over his shoulder.

Meanwhile Ashley grins mischievously at me, giving me a thumbs-up sign.

My cheeks begin to burn. Great. *Everyone* will have heard about this by the morning.

"Don't forget, you're still on probation," Kyle throws back.

Eric waves it away. "It's Saturday! No curfew tonight!"

Kyle sighs, passing me the bag of snacks I picked up at the local grocery store at a fraction of the price of the canteen, before pulling me into his arms. "You need anything at your cabin first?"

"Nope."

He leans down to set his forehead against mine. "So . . . you want to head to mine, then?" he asks softly.

It's been a week of heated glances and teasing touches while in passing. A week of ten o'clock curfews and restless nights, anticipating tonight.

I smile. "Yes. Definitely."

Kyle is quiet as he leads me to the boys' cabins. The boys' and girls' sides are virtually identical—a cluster of ten small brown rectangular buildings set beneath a canopy of leggy evergreens and elm trees, with a separate shower and restroom off to one side.

By the time we reach the one marked "Seventeen" and he guides me inside, my stomach is a twisted mess of nerves.

"Same as yours, right?"

"Pretty much." Musty air that's ten degrees hotter than outside, low ceiling, six sets of bunk beds, ink-covered walls where campers have scribbled their name to memorialize their attendance, the tacky orange-and-brown floral curtains . . . *Check, check, check*. Except . . . My nose crinkles. "It smells like dirty, wet socks?"

"Believe me, it has smelled *a lot* worse." Kyle chuckles, tugging the curtains back and sliding open both windows all the way. "Sorry, I should have done that before we left."

I wander over to the only bed with a pillow and sleeping bag on it. The bag has been unzipped and stretched out to cover the thin, single mattress, the end dangling off to graze the worn wood floor. I gingerly take a seat on the edge, my hand smoothing over the soft blue-and-red flannel interior. "This is you?"

"That's me," he murmurs softly.

Our eyes meet and lock.

"You good?" he asks.

"Yeah, why?"

"Nothing. Just . . . you've been acting weird since that phone call with your dad." Kyle kicks off his shoes. "Thought maybe you were worried about pissing him off."

"No. I'm not. He doesn't get to decide who I'm with." I set my jaw stubbornly, as if the small act of defiance gives weight to my declaration.

Kyle opens his mouth to answer but decides against it, instead tugging his wallet out of his back pocket, to toss onto the floor below his pillow.

Does he have a condom in there, I wonder?

I didn't even think to ask about getting one.

My heart begins to race with the thought of what we're about to do.

Am I *really* ready for this? We've kissed, a lot. We've fooled around, *a bit*.

Branches snap just outside and then a moment later Colin's face pops up in front of the window. "Hey, Miller, you comin' out to—" He cuts off when he sees me sitting on the bed. "*Oh*. Never mind. See you guys later." With that, he's gone, whistling to himself.

Kyle shakes his head. "Would people leave us alone for just one night?"

"It's hard being so popular."

"It is." He drags the curtain closed and smacks the light switch, throwing us into darkness, save for the safety nightlight that each cabin has near the door. "There. Hopefully they'll think I'm already out."

I can just make out his outline as he strolls over to take a seat next to me, the rustic wood frame giving nothing under our combined weight.

He grazes my cheek with the backs of his knuckles. "This night is *all* I've been able to think about, all week long."

"Me, too," I admit, shifting to pull my leg up so I'm facing him.

Only he's already moving with me, guiding me backward. The next thing I know, I'm on my back and Kyle is lying next to me, pressed up against my side, his fingers trailing along my collarbone.

How many times has he been with a girl before? We haven't even talked about that. Shouldn't we talk about that first?

I gather my nerve. "How many times have you done this?"

"Done what?" He says it so innocently.

I roll my eyes. "How many girls have you *been* with?"

"Do you mean—"

"Yeah."

He doesn't answer right away and I start to think he's formulating a lie. But Kyle doesn't seem the type to lie about how many girls he's slept with. So he must be busy counting them all in his head. "Oh my God," I mutter. "Don't tell me—"

"Two."

"Seriously."

"Seriously. Two."

"Who?"

He groans, like he doesn't want to answer. "First was this girl Shannon, when I was fourteen. My brothers threw a party at our place while Mom was away and she was there. She was a couple years older. Never saw her again." He pauses. "And then Avery, last summer."

So they did sleep together.

My jealous flares, and that cynical voice creeps into my subconscious, wondering if I'm just the 2006 version of Kyle's 2005 summer camp experience, if his summer itinerary would read the same—cliff jumping and golf-cart racing and cabin-sleeping—except with a different female lead.

"You're nothing like her. This is nothing like last summer," Kyle says, as if reading my mind. He leans in to fit his face into the crook of my neck. Hot, wet lips graze my skin.

I close my eyes, reveling in the feel. "How is it different?"

"Because I didn't feel this way about her."

"What way?" I push, because I need to hear him say it.

"Like I'm already doing the math on how much gas will cost to get from Poughkeepsie to Lennox when the summer's over. And I'm wondering how much I can set aside in phone cards so I can text you."

"I'll send you cards," I rush to say, my heart swelling as I shift onto my side so I'm facing him, our noses pressed together. "And I'm getting a car in the fall, so I can come out to see you, too. Every weekend. Or almost every weekend. I don't know. I'll try."

"Your parents are going to let you do that?"

I burrow in closer, until we're touching from our noses all the way to our toes and my arm is curled around him. "I don't care. I'm coming."

He presses his lips to mine. "I'm crazy about you, Piper."

"I'm so crazy about you, Kyle." *I think I'm in love with you*. The words are there, on the tip of my tongue, wanting to leap off.

He reaches up to stroke my hair off my face. "We're not going to let things go too far tonight."

"We're not?"

"No. Shane said he's going home next Saturday, too. There's no rush, and I want you to want to."

"I *do* want to," I'm quick to say.

Kyle smiles softly. "I want you to be totally ready."

I can't answer as quickly. Maybe because I know I'm trying to convince myself more than him. I do want to be with Kyle but maybe I need more time. The fact that my body relaxed the second he said that confirms it.

It *has* only been three weeks. Three of the best weeks of my life, but still, only three weeks.

"So what are we going to do, then?"

"I was thinking we could start with this . . ." He gently pushes my shoulder until I'm lying on my back again and then leans over to press his mouth against mine, his tongue sliding over the seam of my lips until I allow him in.

I could get lost in Kyle's mouth for days, the way he kisses—with such focus, as if he'd be satisfied going no farther—intoxicating.

And at the same time frustrating, as my body begins to ache for more.

"Can we pick up where we left off last Saturday?" I hear myself ask.

He answers by working my T-shirt up over my stomach, over my chest. I lift my arms to help him slide it over my head. He's yanking his shirt off seconds after, tossing it in a heap on the floor.

I'm more excited than nervous as I reach up to push the clasp in the front of my powder-blue lace bra. It pops open and Kyle makes a soft sound.

"Wear more of this kind," he murmurs, lowering his mouth over a nipple, the warmth of his mouth sending shivers down my stomach.

Steeling my nerve, I unfasten my shorts and work them down over my hips and legs, shaking them off my ankles.

Kyle's breath catches as he peers down to regard my powder-blue panties. "Have I ever told you that I have a thing for matching underwear?"

I giggle. "No."

"I do." He shifts back to my mouth, to smile against it as his hand travels down over my abdomen, slipping beneath the elastic band. "Anything you want, I'll do it." His lips press against mine at the same time that his fingers skate over me, pulling a gasp from my lungs.

This time, there is no loud camp director shouting at us.

No annoying friend jumping off the cliff.

Nothing to interrupt me from experiencing my first time falling apart beneath a boy's touch.

And when my ragged breathing has subsided, when I've come down from the clouds to Kyle's mouth pressed against my neck, I reach over, gingerly unfasten his zipper, and push his shorts down over his hips.

And I return the favor.

Chapter 17

NOW

"I'll be there in fifteen," I promise, struggling to gather my dress with one hand while pressing my phone to my ear with the other. I climb out of the town car as gracefully as possible, offering a nod in thanks at the driver as he holds the door open for me.

"You're already fifteen minutes late. Hurry up," my father grumbles. "I hate these events."

"Not as much as I do." I end the call before he can deliver a lecture about how I am at the start of my career and had better get used to it, because showing up for these high-society charity galas is critical for Calloway's image and for connections and *blah, blah, blah*.

Normally my tolerance for my father's sermons is high, but since learning that he single-handedly torched my relationship with Kyle, my Kieran Calloway tolerance meter is set at zero.

I've managed to avoid a confrontation with him so far, answering his emails with direct responses to his questions and tying myself up in meetings all day. Some might call that cowardly, but with a man like my father, I need a strategy, one that doesn't result in hellfire raining down on Kyle.

I swipe my card to gain access to our office building, intent on rushing up to my office to grab the silver Manolos I left in the corner.

A man in jeans, a T-shirt, and a baseball cap leans casually against the security desk with his back to me, talking to the guard on duty.

My steps falter as familiar eyes peer over the counter at me.

"Kyle? What are you doing here?"

"Picked up an extra shift from the weekend guy." He stands from behind the desk, his gaze drifting over the silver lace evening gown I chose last minute for tonight's event. "What are *you* doing here?"

I throw a hand toward the bank of elevators. "Forgot my shoes upstairs. I'm just going to run up."

He nods dully. "Okay."

It takes several more seconds before I can break free of my delighted shock and turn my attention to the other guy dressed in jeans. I feel my eyebrows arch in surprise. "You *must* be Jeremy." He's a more slender version of Kyle, but with green eyes and no ink in sight. Still, the resemblance is uncanny.

The guy grins, showing off deep dimples. "And you must be the reason I'm living in Lennox."

Kyle spears his little brother with a flat glare, but Jeremy's not paying any attention, his gaze shifting downward, over my figure-hugging dress, stalling on the plunging neckline, and then on the high side split. He gives his head a shake, as if catching himself, and then takes a few steps and sticks a hand out, his expression more somber. "I've heard a lot about you over the years. It's nice to *finally* meet you, Piper."

Over the years?

My heart flutters as I close the distance slowly to accept his warm, callused fingers. "Likewise. I mean, I heard a lot about you over that summer."

"I can imagine." Jeremy's lips curl into a secretive smirk and it reminds me so much of the younger, playful version of Kyle from camp, I'm left gaping at him.

He turns to Kyle. "What time are you off tonight?"

"Eleven." Kyle gives his brother a tense look. A warning. For what, though?

" 'Kay, I'll text to let you know where we're at so we can meet up."

"Sounds good."

Jeremy takes a step backward. And grins. "Unless you want to swing by and meet Kyle when he gets off, Piper? 'Cause I know he wants you to."

"I . . . uh . . ." I stammer a moment, caught off guard. My gaze flips between Jeremy and Kyle, who looks ready to leap over the counter and strangle his brother. "I have a charity gala thing."

"No worries. Come by our place sometime.

We're at Seventeen Cherry Lane. Number Seven-one-seven. Easy to remember. Seventeen cherries. Seven-one-seven."

"You're kidding me." My memory begins churning. "Kyle was in Cabin Seventeen at Wawa." And the cherries . . .

"Must be a sign." Jeremy laughs at the daggers Kyle shoots from his eyes. "Have fun at your charity gala *thing,* Piper."

"I will. Thank you," I murmur, my gaze following him out. He doesn't have Kyle's sleek walk; his gait is more bouncy. Still . . . "I can't get over how much you two look alike."

"We take after our mom. So does Max. Ricky is more like my dad," Kyle says calmly, as if his brother's gentle ribbing hasn't fazed him.

I glimpse the waiting black sedan outside, reminding me that I have somewhere to be. "I guess I should grab those shoes."

His gaze drifts over me, much like his little brother's did. "You look . . . good," Kyle finally offers in a stilted voice, his throat bobbing with a hard swallow.

And for a moment there, I remember what it felt like to be sixteen, to have my heart flutter from Kyle's undivided attention. His adoration.

"Thank you." A satisfied smile touches my lips as I swipe through the security gate. Suddenly the hours of primping with hair and makeup appointments don't feel like a waste of my time, if it means leaving Kyle nearly speechless.

"*Really* good!" he hollers just as the elevator doors are closing on me, as if finally finding his tongue and his courage.

I rush upstairs to my office, kicking off my heels and sliding on the silver Manolos, excitement coursing through my veins where there was only dread before. This feels like kismet. That's what Ashley would say. It's kismet that we've crossed paths. Kismet that we can't seem to stay away from each other. The universe *wants* us to pick up where we left off, to erase the damage my father inflicted upon our young hearts.

Clearly, I've been spending too much time with Ashley. Yet, I can't deny that any excuse I can find to ditch this benefit altogether and linger in the lobby for the rest of Kyle's shift is tempting.

When I head back downstairs, Kyle is exactly where I left him.

He watches me approach and, I swear, his chest sinks in a long, slow exhale, as if taking a calming breath. "Find what you were looking for?"

I hook a finger along the split of my dress and pull the skirt back to model the crystals on my toes, knowing damn well that the move is flirtatious. My heart races with the thought of flirting with Kyle again. "Better, right?"

His lips part as if to answer, but stall as his eyes drift over my bare leg. He swallows. "*So* much better."

"You can't tell the difference, can you—"

"Not if my life depended on it," he admits, dipping his head with his smile.

"So you're working until eleven tonight?"

"Yeah." His steady gaze lifts to meet mine again. "Why?"

I shrug nonchalantly. "I might have to stop by again later. You know . . . to grab another pair of shoes."

His lips twitch with amusement at my pathetic lie.

Is what Jeremy said true? Does Kyle want to see me later tonight?

It's a long moment before he gives me an almost imperceptible nod. "I'll be here."

"Have fun."

"You, too." A tiny, crooked smile answers me.

With that, I turn and head for the exit.

"You look *really* good," he calls after me.

"You already said that."

I'm grinning as I climb into the town car.

"You're not yourself, Piper." My dad nods at Roy Molson, a hedge fund exec who we've met with on more than one occasion in our hunt for investors. "You've barely said five words to me. You ignored Larry Muntt—"

"Don't worry, he was too busy staring at my breasts to notice," I throw back. That's what the slimy old man—another Wall Street type—does every time we cross paths at these things.

Dad grunts. He knows as much. "And I don't think you've smiled once in the last half hour."

I turn to give him a wide closed-lip smile that is forced and not at all friendly.

His brow tightens. "What's going on with you?"

"Nothing. Tired," I mutter, taking a long sip from my flute of champagne.

"Learn to put on a good front." He waves down a passing server to pluck a shrimp cocktail from the silver platter, before dismissing him entirely. There are times when my father's high-pedigree upbringing translates into shockingly poor basic manners—such as when he fails to acknowledge wait staff as human beings.

The older gentleman holds the platter in front of me. "No, but *thank you,*" I make a point of saying, and then let my gaze wander over the chic art gallery and sea of faces—most familiar, if only by sight—as an excuse to avoid further eye contact with my father.

"You haven't eaten anything tonight," Dad notes with more displeasure.

"I *never* eat at these things. Only men eat at these things." I used to, until I spent thirty minutes smiling and staring into the eyes of a prominent city council member while we talked, acutely aware of the piece of spinach stuck between his front teeth and doing my best not to let my gaze veer downward. He took it as a sign that I was interested and invited me back to his hotel room. Since then I've drawn the line at food and deep talks with politicians.

Dad studies the crowd. From our vantage point in the corner, he can oversee the goings-on of most of the room—who's here, who's talking to whom. Exactly how he likes it. "Gary Jameson left me a message earlier about the Marquee."

"As I expected he would." You can't tell a longtime business partner that you're cutting his company from the equation on a $250 million construction project that you've been discussing together for two *years* and not expect him to go straight to the top.

"You should have called me as soon as you heard." There's accusation in his tone.

"I couldn't. I was busy calling *Gary* to smooth things over with him." A.k.a. getting yelled at for a good twenty minutes before he finally calmed down enough to accept my apology for the gross "miscommunication."

"Well . . . it seems to have worked. He doesn't want to hang me by my skin just yet." Dad peers into his glass a moment before tipping it back. "Good job."

"I'm sorry, what? I must have *misheard* you. Did you just tell me that I did a good job?"

Dad smirks. "Still, I don't think they're going to be able to match KDZ's numbers. I scanned their construction proposal and it looks solid."

I pause mid-sip, blood rushing to my ears. "*What* proposal?"

Dad frowns. "The one Tripp sent us last night. Didn't you get—"

"No, I did not!" I snap before I can help it.

Dad gives a tight-lipped, apologetic smile to a nearby couple who glanced over at my outburst as he digs into his tuxedo jacket, fishing out his phone. "I'm sure he just wasn't thinking," he murmurs, scrolling through his email. "The team is going through the details right now, but Tripp's not expecting them to find anything of concern." He hits the keypad. "There, you should receive it shortly. Review it over the weekend and let me know what you think."

I don't believe it. That son of a bitch stepped *right over* me to go to my father—again—and my father acts as if it's nothing more than a minor inconvenience. Maybe it's my anger with my father over Kyle fueling me, but I find I don't care to choose my words cautiously. "What I think," I pause, struggling to regain my composure, "is that if I'm to earn respect in this industry, then it needs to start with *you* showing respect to me."

My father frowns, and it makes his normally severe expression look downright insidious. "What are you talking about? Of course I respect you. I would never have made you point person for all of Calloway's operations had I not thought you competent."

"Yes, I am *supposed* to be point person for our current projects, freeing you up to focus on setting up the next five to twenty years for us. And yet I have been undermined by Tripp at *every* turn, and part of the reason is because *you* have allowed it." I refuse to look away from my father. "This whole KDZ thing stinks of something, and I'm not quite sure what yet. But the proposal should have come to me. He knows it, you know it, and yet you didn't bat an eye at the idea that he can't show me enough decency to even copy me on the email. It's a two-hundred-and-fifty-million-dollar construction contract, not an invitation to a goddamn corporate barbecue."

Dad opens his mouth, but I cut him off.

"I may still have a lot to learn, but I can't do that if you allow guys like Tripp to treat me like a token figure, like I'm *optional.* This ends right here, right now, or there is no point in me continuing on in this role." Adrenaline is racing through my veins as I brace myself for whatever verbal missile my dad is about to launch at me.

Dad sighs heavily. "You're right."

"I . . ." I frown, replaying those words to make sure I understood them. "I'm sorry . . . what?"

"You're right. I just thought . . ." He shakes his head. "I don't know what I thought. I guess I keep making excuses for Tripp. For years, he reported directly in to me, so I assumed it was just habit. But, even if it is, it isn't right." His jaw tenses. "I will make sure to remind him of the new chain of command when I see him next."

I study him intently, and with confusion.

"Why are you staring at me like that?" he finally asks, irritation in his voice.

"No reason. I've just always wondered, when aliens abduct a human, do they undress them before infecting the host body or were you still wearing your suit?"

Dad shakes his head but chuckles. Sliding his arm around my waist, he pulls me into him in a quick fatherly embrace that he hasn't given me since the night he announced my promotion and future succession.

For a moment, I forget that I'm furious with him.

For a moment, I forget how he broke my sixteen-year-old heart. If I try hard enough, I could probably convince myself that he did it with the best of intentions.

But the road to hell is paved with good intentions, my gramps always said. He had that quote printed and framed on the wall in the living room, above the piano. Mom said he hung it the day my parents announced they were getting married. Gran insisted that was mere coincidence, but the thing about Gramps was, he never cared for wealth and nothing was ever mere coincidence.

As soon as Dad releases me from his grip, I slip my hand into my clutch to check my phone. Eight fifty. Kyle is working for another two hours.

"What? Do you have other plans for tonight?"

"We've paid our five grand a plate and mingled long enough for people to know we were here."

"Right. I suppose you're off the—Oh, before you go," he calls out to a man passing by. "Lloyd?"

The man stops and turns, his gray eyes shifting from my father to me—to linger one, two, three beats before shifting back. "Kieran, it's good to see you again." I'd put him in his late thirties, with sandy-brown hair that's dusted with gray around the temples. He's attractive in a classic way, with a strong nose and a square jaw.

My dad gestures to me, as if presenting a prize display. "Have you met my daughter, Piper?"

I stifle my groan as I realize his intentions.

Lloyd's eyes are back on me. "I haven't, but I've heard wonderful things. Hello. It's a pleasure to meet you." He smiles and holds out his hand.

I plaster a polite smile on my face and accept it.

"Lloyd is a named partner at Sternum and Oakley."

"Really . . ." I feign interest, though it *is* interesting that my father would be trying to set me up with our law firm's main competitor. "So you are . . ."

"The breastbone." Lloyd flashes a bright, easy smile and then winks. "You wouldn't believe the number of jokes I've endured."

"I think I can imagine." He's charming, I'll admit. And if I weren't already spoken for, I would probably be wondering how I could get his number.

Already spoken for.

My God.

But I have already decided.

I want Kyle back.

"Listen, I don't mean to be rude, but you caught me on my way out. I have another function that I have to make a speech at in exactly"—he checks his flashy Rolex—"ten minutes."

I hold my hands up in the air. "Please don't let us keep you, then."

"A pleasure to meet you, though, Piper. I hope our paths cross again. And soon. Kieran." He nods at my father and then continues on.

"He separated from his wife about a year ago, but I hear he's dating again."

"You should ask him out, then. You two would

make a cute couple, and he looks about the age you prefer."

Dad gives me a flat look.

"What's wrong? Finally giving up on my reconciliation with David?"

"Is it likely?"

"Yes, right after I set myself on fire." I tip back my glass and finish off the champagne.

He sighs. "I do want to see you happy."

"As long as it's with a man like David or this Lloyd *Sternum*."

"Well, you'd keep your last name, obviously. The man is smart, successful, and driven. He's the kind of man you'll need in the years ahead—"

"I don't *need* a man."

He rolls his eyes. "What I mean is, when you do decide to settle down with someone, it will need to be with someone self-assured enough to handle being married to a woman as powerful as you will be."

"And what would guarantee that, Dad? A big bank account? A private jet in the family?" My anger with him flares. "God forbid I date a blue-collar worker who just loves me for me."

My dad snorts. "Isn't that too idealistic, even for you?"

"Just because it didn't work out for you and Mom doesn't mean everyone else is doomed."

An unreadable look flashes through my father's eyes. "Your mother never understood the kind of pressure that I faced. She wanted romance and vacations and all these things that I didn't have time to give her. She didn't understand because she didn't grow up in this world."

"But that architect from LA understood, did she?"

He scowls. "That's personal and not a topic I *ever* want to revisit."

"Let's make a deal, then. I'll stay out of your personal life if you stay out of mine."

He gives me a bewildered look. "It was a harmless introduction, Piper! I don't understand why you're so upset."

"Because I don't want you interfering with my relationships, even if you don't approve. So don't *ever* do it." *Ever again.* My voice is calm and low but no less severe. With that I stroll out of the art gallery, my head held high, a small sense of victory humming through my bones. I may not have confronted my father about his past betrayal—yet—but I've made my position on any future ones as they relate to me—and to Kyle—clear.

And now it's a matter of finding out if there even *is* a future.

"Thank you. You can leave," I tell the driver, my gaze on the darkened office windows in the Calloway building. Oddly enough, I've always found the emptiness on the weekends comforting, as if all the weekday guests have left and I finally have the house to myself.

My chest is tight with anticipation as I climb the steps. My stomach stirs with hope as I swipe my card to gain access through the exterior doors again.

My nerves electrify as I try not to appear too eager strolling toward the security desk. I don't know what to say, but I hope I don't say the wrong thing.

Kyle flashes me a smile that makes my feet falter. It's a smile I've seen many times before, but not in years. "Come back for those other shoes?"

"A pen, actually," I say with mock seriousness. It's the first—lame—thing I could think of.

"A *pen,*" he repeats, setting his book facedown. "That must be one hell of a pen."

"It's one of those gel pens. You know, the ones that glide smoothly over paper." Instead of stopping at the front of the security counter, I round the desk and settle into Gus's chair, collecting my dress so it doesn't get caught in the wheels. "Good book?" The cover depicts a blurred shadow of a person with a palm held out, as if pressed against a windowpane. A thriller, if I had to guess.

"Good enough." He sinks back into his chair, his legs splayed. "So your charity gala thing's over?"

"I went, I mingled, I drank, and then I bolted the second I thought no one would notice."

Kyle chuckles. "I don't even know what a gala is, but you make it sound like pure hell."

"Honestly? It can be. If I could get away with *never* going to another one of these things, I'd be more than too happy." I slip off my heels with a sigh, feeling Kyle's eyes fall to the split in my dress that's creeping up my thigh to a risqué level. Though I know I probably should, I don't adjust it.

"You know, I'm not supposed to let anyone back here."

"Really?"

"Really." He smirks. "I could get in a lot of trouble for it."

"Well . . ." I pull the lever on the underside of the chair and adjust it to sit higher, and then push off against the cold marble tile with my sore toes and let the chair spin once. "It's a good thing I'm not just *anyone*."

"No, you definitely aren't." He smiles secretively as he reaches for a ballpoint pen. He always liked fumbling with things. Usually it was a cigarette.

"Do you still smoke?" I haven't smelled tobacco on him.

"Nah. Well, maybe once in a while, if I'm at a party. But I don't go to too many parties."

"I'm glad you quit. And speaking of parties,

Ashley's planning a housewarming at our place. You should come."

He nods slowly. "I'll think about it."

Not exactly the answer I was expecting. I hesitate. "Do you mind that I'm here?"

"No," he answers without missing a beat, but says nothing else.

Where did my easygoing, carefree boy go?

"Is anyone else in the building?"

"Just you and me. Well, this guy's trying really hard." He leans over and hits the cursor on the keyboard twice. One of the monitors flips to the back of the building, to where a black squirrel is perched. "He got in through a vent last week. Set off a bunch of alarms for the night guys."

Awkward silence falls over us, with nothing but the white noise and the sound of Kyle clicking his pen repeatedly to keep us company. And for a split second my insecurities soar, convincing me that I've misread everything about Kyle so far. Maybe he isn't as perceptive as I give him credit for; maybe he's only now cluing in to the fact that I'm not *just* here for a friendly chitchat.

Maybe he's wishing he hadn't told me that he's single.

Maybe he's wondering how he's going to get himself off the hook.

"God, this is *so* boring," I finally blurt out.

Kyle laughs. "It can be." He glances at his watch. "Just under two hours left."

That's two hours for me, with Kyle.

To talk about nothing. And everything, if I can get him to open up. I plan on taking every second that I have to try.

"I'm hungry. You hungry?"

He frowns. "Didn't you just come from dinner?"

"A five-thousand-dollar-a-plate one." I grab my phone. "I'm ordering us food."

"I can't believe you have a burger joint in your favorites," Kyle mutters, biting into a french fry.

I hold my phone up so he can see the list, while leaning over the plastic container to take a sizeable bite out of my burger.

He frowns at my screen. "Them and every other restaurant within a five-mile radius, apparently."

"Don't judge!" I mutter, shielding my full mouth with a hand. "I work long hours, so I don't have time to cook. I end up ordering in."

"But you know how to cook?"

I consider a clever answer as I finish chewing and swallowing. "Does boiling eggs count?"

Kyle shakes his head, laughing. "Boiling eggs does not count."

I shrug. "I usually grab a salad or something from Christa's, but at least once a month I get a craving for Alejandro's. And . . . hmmm." I moan through another bite. "*So* worth it."

He watches me a moment, a pensive gleam in

his eyes, as I suck a glob of ketchup from my thumb. I'm wearing a $3,000 dress and devouring a greasy fast-food meal.

"I look absurd, don't I?"

"You've never looked absurd a day in your life, Piper. You're incapable of it."

I roll my eyes. "Well, then why are you looking at me like that?"

"It's just . . . you realize how weird this is, right?"

"What? You and me, sitting here together after all these years?" *Because I think it's amazing*.

He holds his burger up. "Naming a burger joint Alejandro's."

Oh. "It is," I agree. "But they have all these different toppings, like breaded poblano peppers, and pico de gallo, and chimichurri. Can't remember what else."

"Peanut butter?"

"What?" I cringe. "Nobody puts . . . Oh my God. That's right!" I press my hand to my mouth as a wave of nostalgia hits me. "Eric does that!"

"He swore it brought out the flavor of the bacon. He put it on his pancakes, too. That and mustard." Kyle shakes his head. "Fucking guy. Used to love grossing me out."

"Does he *still* do it?"

Kyle inspects his remaining fries. "I don't know. I haven't had a burger with him in years."

"You know, I caught Ashley doing that the other day. Mustard on her pancakes."

He cringes. "How is Ash, anyway?"

"She's good. She's substitute teaching, and trying to get a full-time position. And she's a wannabe event planner. She also sells hand-knit blankets, but it takes her months to finish one."

Kyle nods slowly. "She always was artsy."

"Still is."

"And kind of scatterbrained."

I laugh. "Still is. I like living with her, though. She brings a happy energy to our place." I feel a nostalgic smile touch my lips. "You know, I always thought she and Eric would end up together. But he never responded to any of her emails."

"Yeah. He was never good for keeping in touch."

"It's too bad. Maybe she would have ended up with him instead of this asshole named Chad." I give Kyle the rundown.

He's chuckling by the end of the story. "Sounds like this psychic might have done everyone a favor by convincing her to buy that pee couch."

"I think you might be right." I devour my last french fry as I consider this. "So, what about you?"

"I don't believe in psychics."

"No." I chuckle, sensing his intentional diverting of topic. I avert my gaze to my dinner remnants, slowly packing them up. "Girlfriends? Wives?"

"There've been a few."

"A few wives?" I raise my eyebrows.

"Girlfriends, yes. Wives . . . no. I was close once," he admits.

It feels like a punch to my stomach, hearing that Kyle actually considered marrying another woman. That I was engaged to David doesn't temper my jealousy. And yet I also want the intimate details. I want to know everything there is to know about all the years of Kyle's life that I missed—the good, the bad, the painful. "What happened?"

"She wasn't—" He cuts himself off abruptly, and then sighs. "She wasn't what I was looking for. What about Christa? How's she doing?"

"Running a high-end steak house a few blocks from here. Single. Continuing to be right about everything."

He bursts out laughing and I grin. I forgot how much I like making Kyle laugh.

"But she's good. She's my cynical voice of reason most days."

His lips twist in thought. "And what would that cynical voice say about you sitting here with me?"

I bite my tongue, unsure whether I should just lay it all on the line right away. But this is Kyle, I remind myself. We were always honest with each other. "Basically, that we need to figure out what we mean to each other in today's world because Wawa is in the past."

He nods slowly, as if considering that. I can't read his thoughts, though, and I hate it.

"You're a lot more direct then I remember you being," he finally says.

"I've learned to be. I kind of have to be, in my world."

"Yeah, I guess." His brow furrows.

What's he trying to say? "Is that a bad thing?"

"No, not at all. It's just different from how I remember you." He leans back in his chair, his gaze drifting up to the grandiose arching design of the building's lobby. "You know, it's funny, I remember thinking how tough life was that summer. But some things were a lot easier back then."

"Like what?"

"Like . . ." A slow, nostalgic smile curls his lips. "Finding the nerve to ask the hot girl at summer camp to jump off a cliff with me."

I feel my cheeks flush. "*You* definitely didn't lack confidence back then."

"I thought I had the world figured out." He begins fumbling absently with his leather wrist cuff, similar to the one from camp. The one he gave me, which has been tucked into the bottom drawer of my jewelry box for safekeeping all these years.

"Are they still there?" I nod to his wrist. "The numbers."

He opens his mouth as if to answer, but pauses, his tongue sliding out to skate over the lip ring scar. And then he stretches his arm out to rest his hand on my knee—palm up—and quietly waits.

Like he did so many years ago.

As if offering me the excuse I need to touch him.

I take it without hesitation, gingerly unfastening the leather cuff from his wrist, my cool fingers trembling slightly as they slide over his hot skin; over the two rows of numbers, with several decimal points following each.

"Still your favorite place?" I ask softly, my thumb smoothing back and forth over it, reveling in the fact that I am touching Kyle Miller again.

"It's hard to say yes, after what happened to Eric."

"I know. I had nightmares about that day for months after. But he ended up fine."

Kyle bites his bottom lip, his gaze settling on the numbers. "I still feel guilty sometimes."

"It wasn't your fault. He doesn't blame you, does he? Because if that's the case, it was just as much my fault. And Ashley's fault."

He swallows, his gaze on the desk. "No. He's never blamed anyone."

Kyle makes no move to remove his arm from its resting spot over my lap, and so I take the opportunity to study the inside of his sinewy forearm. "When did you get the rest of this done?" His skin has become a canvas of artwork since I last saw him, with shades of green and blue and charcoal gray.

"Over the last couple years."

It takes me a moment to realize what I'm looking at.

"Is this . . ." My fingers roam unabashed now, shifting his arm to get a better angle. On the meaty part of his forearm is a pool of water. Within it is a lone figure, bobbing, only the back of his head and arms showing as he looks upward. Waiting.

I push Kyle's shirtsleeve up, over his muscular bicep, revealing the rocky cliff and the girl who stands at the edge, her long, dark brown hair billowing around her as if caught in a gust of wind, the teal string bikini showing off cartoonish curves.

My heart skips a beat and then begins racing.

"Is that—?" I cut myself off, not wanting to presume too much. But when I meet Kyle's eyes—the questioning gaze in them—and hear his sharp intake of breath, I know without a doubt the answer.

His jaw tenses, but then he smiles. "Favorite place in the world. Favorite summer." His eyes flash downward to my lips. "Favorite girl."

My heart is pounding, when a beep sounds and

the exterior door opens. The night-shift security guard strolls in, throwing a hand up at Kyle.

He removes his arm from my lap and glances at his watch, frowning. "That went fast."

"It did." Too fast. My stomach clenches with disappointment. I could sit here talking to Kyle until the sun rises. I still have so many questions. Some, I think I've already found the answers to.

He crumples our fast-food wrappers into a ball and, rolling backward in his chair, tosses everything into the trash can. "Thanks for dinner. And the company."

"My pleasure." I tuck my feet into my heels and collect my purse.

"Do you need a car?" He reaches for the phone.

"I'll walk. I'm only three blocks away."

He stands and stretches as he watches his replacement approach. "I'll walk you, then. If you're okay with that." He peers down at me, and again I see glimmers of the boy I once knew in the man before me—the longing, the anticipation.

"Yes." A simple answer for so many questions he could ask me right now.

Do you still want me?

Do you still think about me?

Are you willing to see if this can work?

Yes.

Yes.

Yes.

The arriving security guard eyes me curiously

as he comes around the desk. “Good evening, Miss Calloway.”

“Hello . . . Carl,” I read off his name tag. I’ve seen him here, the odd weekend that I’ve come in, but I’ve never exchanged anything beyond a smile and polite greeting. “Hope you have an uneventful night.”

Kyle gives him a quick update and then, collecting his jacket and a navy backpack stowed in a deep drawer, he leads me out of the building and into the bustling night.

The Calloway building is on the north side of King Street, a main artery for downtown Lennox. It’s busier during the week, but even now, there is a steady stream of headlights and frequent blasts of horns.

“Which way?”

I briefly consider leading us in the wrong direction just so we have to make a large loop around the block, to give me more time with him, but decide against it. My feet can’t handle that. “Right.” We fall into step side-by-side at a leisurely pace.

The temperature has dropped, leaving a light chill in the air. I curl my arms around my body. Kyle notices and wordlessly drapes his jacket over my shoulders, his fingers skating over my bare skin, sending electric currents through me.

“Thanks,” I murmur, pulling it close around me. I can smell his cologne lingering faintly on the material. “So, your brother Jeremy . . . I remember you being worried about him. He seems like he turned out okay.”

Kyle kicks a loose stone with his boot, sending it skittering along the sidewalk. “I was on him a lot, especially when he got in with a shitty crowd, right when we got to San Diego. But he smartened up fast, graduated high school, and did almost five years apprenticing under an electrician until he could write his exams. Now he’s out on his own, makin’ way more money than me.”

“That’s great. Well, not the money part.”

“It’s okay. I make him pay more rent.”

“You do *not*.”

Kyle grins. “Nah. I don’t. I tried, but he’s too smart to fall for that.”

“And you? Ever end up changing your mind about college?”

He shrugs. “Never worked hard enough in high school to get the grades. Luckily I didn’t need college for this job. I started at Rikell as soon as I graduated. Been with them over twelve years now.”

“Do you like it?”

He pauses, as if to consider my question. “No stress. It’s not hard and it pays the bills. I get to walk around and talk to people, keep things in order. Better than sitting at a desk all day. No offense,” he adds after a moment.

I laugh. "None taken." If there's one thing I've never heard anyone describe my job as, it's "sitting at a desk all day." "Have you ever thought about joining the police force?"

"Thought about it. Briefly."

"But . . ."

"I guess I just figured they'd do a background check and decide I was too much of a risk."

"That's not true. You should look into it."

"I've had more than my fill of the legal system, anyway."

"Fair enough." I hesitate, my gaze cutting to his sleek form. "Though you'd look good in that uniform."

"Are you flirting with me?"

"Just stating important facts."

I get a lopsided smile in return, his eyes lingering on me a moment. "What about you? Ever thought about doing anything besides working for your father?"

"No. Well, that's not true. I went to visit Rhett in Thailand the summer after I graduated high school and he almost had me convinced to defer college for a year and teach English. He had a house right on the beach. I woke up every morning to the sound of the ocean." I groan at the memory. "It was incredible."

"Why didn't you do it, then?"

"Oh, my dad would have *murdered* me. Like legit flown out to Thailand and tied a noose around my neck. Then he would have killed Rhett." I sigh. "But sometimes I wonder what would have happened had I done it."

Kyle doesn't say anything for a moment. "You still need your father's approval, don't you?"

I frown, his words coming off sounding like a slight. "I don't *need* it. But I want it because . . . he's my *dad*."

Kyle nods, his gaze on the sidewalk ahead. "I guess I don't know what that feels like."

Silence hangs between us as we approach my street. "We turn right up here."

"Wow," Kyle takes in the one-way cobblestoned street ahead, bordered by wide paved sidewalks and a canopy of oak trees—all part of the old-world design of Posey Park. The newly built four-story row houses with decorative detailing and steep stone stairways mirror one another on either side—a nod to the famous brownstones of Manhattan. Even with the busy street to the south of us, the tall buildings and narrow corridor provide quiet cover.

"I remember the first time I saw the design for this project. I was in love."

Kyle's eyebrows arch. "You guys built this, too?"

"Calloway Group, yeah. These houses and those two buildings." I point to the luxury condo buildings that tower over us up ahead, designed to complement one another and the row houses but to also stand out on their own. "We were going for eighteen-hundreds European charm within an urban center."

"I don't know eighteen-hundreds *anything,* but I'd say you nailed it," he murmurs, reaching out to touch one of the replica gaslight-lantern lampposts that run the entire length of the street, adorned by planters bursting with vibrant red geraniums and petunias. Ornate park benches are interspersed evenly. In the wintertime, it's all dressed up in white lights and red bows. "Is there anything your father hasn't had a hand in around here?" he asks, and I could be mistaken, but I sense a touch of resentment in his voice.

"Honestly? Not much. Not in this city, anyway. And once the Waterway project is realized, he's going to own the downtown skyline." The massive project, with two condominium towers overlooking the water, flanked by a river boardwalk and surrounded by several square blocks of retail shops and restaurants, is expected to become the new downtown "it" spot for shopping and nightlife.

Kyle opens his mouth to say something, but he seems to decide against it. "Have you decided what you're going to do about that Tripp guy yet?"

I groan. "I don't know. I can't just come out and accuse him and, no offense, but my father's not going to take your word for it. But I have my assistant, Mark, digging up information. So far I know they went to college together, and they've played golf together. A lot."

"Does he use a company phone?"

"His cell? Yeah."

"You should be able to pull the records for it, then. See how often he's been talking to this guy. I can tell you exactly when I overheard them, so you can pinpoint the number. Also, see if they can pull the records for any deleted texts. He's arrogant enough to use his company phone for shit like that."

"Can they do that?"

"They should be able to. Upwards of a year, possibly. And it's your company phone that he's using. I'm sure you can talk your way into getting hold of the records."

"Yeah. Maybe I will. Thanks for the suggestion." I throw a casual hand at the stately building entrance ahead. "This is me."

Kyle's head tips back as his eyes draw upward, showing off the sharp jutting curve of his neck and that long, slender nose that I used to drag my finger along. "You at the top?"

I can't peel my eyes from his profile. "Yeah."

Those lips that I've kissed a thousand times—what feels like a thousand years ago now—curl in a soft smile. "Figured as much."

"When did you take it out? Your lip ring?"

"When I started working for Rikell." His eyes remain on my building for another long moment before lowering to settle on me. "They don't allow piercings or ink on your face. So far they haven't said anything about my sleeve."

"Too bad. I always liked it." My fingers itch to touch the small scar in the corner of his mouth.

His chest rises with a deep inhale, and I'm hyperaware of just how close we're standing. "Please don't look at me like that, Piper."

"How am I looking at you?"

He chuckles. "You never were any good at playing dumb. That's one of the things I always loved about you."

My stomach tightens with anticipation. "Come up to my place?" I hold my breath, slipping my fingers through his.

He squeezes my hand once before releasing it. "I think that's a bad idea." His voice is hoarse.

"Why?"

"Seriously, Piper? Christ, look at us!" He holds his hands out and laughs. "I'm in a security guard's uniform! You know, for my job in *your* family's high-rise office building. I've been working double shifts and saving every spare dollar for the past ten years, and I'm still five years away from ever being able to afford a down payment on anything. And here we are, literally standing in the middle of your family's billion-dollar empire, with you in a *ball* gown like some sort of fairy-tale princess, after *not* eating at a five-thousand-dollar-a-plate party."

"I don't care about any of that."

Kyle shakes his head. "Maybe not right now, but you will, when you realize that I don't fit into your world. And I don't think I can go through that learning curve with you. I thought I could handle it, but the second I saw you I knew I can't. I can't stand the thought of having you and then losing you again." He frowns deeply, as if pained. "There *was* a place where you and I worked, but it was thirteen years ago and we can't go back in time, Piper. Believe me, if we could, I would. For so many reasons." His eyes are full of earnest as they settle on mine, drifting to my mouth. "I'd go back in a heartbeat."

"But . . ." My objection fades on my lips, as my mind searches for words that will convince him that this *is* worth trying. That *I* am worth trying for.

I listen to what he's telling me, though—that I wasn't the only one with a broken heart when we left Wawa that summer. That brings me an odd shade of comfort, even as my chest aches with frustration.

Is Kyle right?

Am I still clinging on to a past that can never exist in the future? In *my* future?

We fall into silence as a man strolls past us, his poodle pausing to sniff the nearby park bench and then lift its leg against it.

"It's an evening gown, by the way," I mutter.

Kyle frowns curiously. "What?"

I slide his jacket from my shoulders, holding it out for him. "My dress. It's called an *evening* gown, not a ball gown."

He smirks, his eyes flittering over the plunging neckline as he closes the distance to accept his jacket from my hands. "See? I can't even tell the difference between dresses." His gaze locks on mine, and in it I see an odd resignation. "All I know is that you'll always be the most beautiful girl I've ever seen."

I can't resist any longer. Just like on that first day atop that rocky cliff, surrounded by empty packets of candy, my lips stained red from cherry powder, I lean in to press my lips against his.

It's a quick kiss—a test, really—long enough to revel in the feel of his lips against mine again, and then I pull back, to hold my breath and wait for his reaction.

Terrified of his rejection.

"Piper . . ." His throat bobs with a hard swallow. "We still have feelings for each other."

"I know, but—"

"But we're supposed to pretend we don't? We're supposed to pass each other in the hall as we go and date other people? I'm supposed to be okay with perky little Renée hovering around the security desk until you ask her out?" I shake my head, my frustration swelling. "No, I'm sorry. That's not happening—"

Kyle's lips crash into mine, cutting my words off. His hands are on me in an instant, one settling on the back of my bare neck, the other curling around my waist, to pull me flush into his solid body. It takes me a moment to realize that I'm kissing Kyle, and when I do, I reach for his shoulders for support as much as because I simply need to touch him.

This feels every bit as euphoric as I remember it being at sixteen, and yet different. *He* feels different. Thirteen years different. His body is stronger, his hands more assured as they smooth over my skin, his lips more demanding as they ply my mouth open to allow room for his tongue. His stance is different as he pulls me hard into him, not bothering to shift to hide his arousal.

Relief surges inside me.

This feels like coming home, after thinking I'd never see home again.

"Who could have guessed *this* was going to happen," comes a familiar voice nearby, breaking Kyle and me apart.

Christa strolls up the sidewalk, her white Nike runners in stark contrast to her simple black skirt and plum-colored blouse. She stops in front of us. "Kyle . . . Long time, no see."

He frowns, as if trying to place her. "*Christa?* Is that you?"

"Oh, good. You remembered *my* name at least."

He brushes aside the dig. "You look so different. Good. Just . . . different."

"It *has* been thirteen years."

"Yeah." He scratches the back of his head in wonder. And then, as if catching himself, he steps forward to envelop her in his arms. "It's good to see you."

She stiffens and glares at me, as if surprised, but eventually returns the embrace—with that awkward hand-pat-on-the-back move, the only kind of hug that Christa seems capable of giving. "Okay, well . . . this is weird on many levels." She practically shakes him off. "I'll see you upstairs, Piper? When you're done mauling each other like a couple of teenagers on the sidewalk outside our building."

"Yeah, sure," I mutter absently, my mind already moving forward—to the fact that Kyle just kissed me.

"She's changed, but she hasn't," Kyle murmurs, watching her disappear into the lobby. "She still hates me."

"*Hate*'s a strong word. More like eternal dislike. And she's not too big on showing affection. Unless you're her cat."

"How did you end up becoming friends again?"

"She was there for me, after . . ." *After you.* "She and Ashley. My other friends didn't get it." Ava and Reid came back from Europe with tales of marathon shopping on cobblestoned streets and all-night parties on yachts and scandalous nights with French men. They couldn't grasp the appeal of my summer camp boyfriend and they didn't show much sympathy with each day that passed without word from Kyle, as my hope slowly crumbled.

It was a moment of desperation that made me call Christa, who was going to college an hour north of Lennox. We may not have seen eye-to-eye, but we'd shared a cabin and responsibility for dozens of girls.

Half of me expected her to say "I told you so" and crush whatever was left of my spirit. Yet, she did something I didn't think her capable of—she listened. And she commiserated, and she even came with me to Poughkeepsie, to try to find Kyle.

Then she told me "I told you so" and highlighted all the ways I was better off without him. But it was what I needed to hear at the time, to help me move on.

Christa's appearance definitely dampened whatever moment Kyle and I were having. Before I can angle to recapture it, Kyle takes a step back.

And another one.

"This was a mistake."

"Kyle—"

"You may not want to admit it, but you will *always* seek your father's approval."

"That's not true. I ended things with David. And he *loves* David."

"So you'll find someone else he approves of." Kyle gives me a sad smile. "But I will never be it."

"I don't care—"

"Please don't make this harder for me than it already is." Genuine pain fills his eyes.

"Then don't leave." I hear the pleading in my voice and it shocks me. When have I ever wanted a man to stay this much? "You're just scared."

"Terrified, actually." His jaw tenses. "Good night, Piper." With that he turns and walks away, a lone dark figure in a black uniform along the picturesque street, his head bowed.

I watch until he disappears around the corner, barely feeling the air's chill, wondering what thoughts are going through his mind.

Wondering if he's right and there is no going back to what we had one summer, so long ago.

Chapter 18

THEN

Camp Wawa, 2006, Week Four

"She *really* has no idea how big of a dork she is, does she?" Eric stands beside me in the corner of the rec center, his long, lanky arms crossed over his chest, a wide grin on his face as we watch Darian moon-walk across the makeshift dance floor to the Michael Jackson tunes blaring over the portable stereo system.

"More like she doesn't care," Kyle says from my other side, and there's a hint of admiration in his voice.

It's Friday night of Week Four. Dance night. Every week is the same, just with different campers. They call it a "dance," but really it's an opportunity to stuff a horde of bodies into the rec center, feed them popcorn and Kool-Aid, and blind everyone with a disco light that sometimes short-circuits. Darian forces the more extroverted counselors into the center to dance to her own personal CD collection, sprinkled with terrible eighties songs that charted when none of us were alive. Eventually, the small groups will break free from their boy-girl segregation and join in, for no other reason than to top one another's goofiness.

Except for the few older campers who have found first love, of course, and are clinging to each other for their last night. Darian makes us float around, pulling them apart.

Tomorrow, these kids will all leave, with glossy eyes and lofty goals of talking to one another every day, or as much as their parents and phone bills will allow.

I wonder how many will hold fast to their promises, and for how long. Eventually they'll settle back into their reality—school friends and everyday life—and their week at Wawa will become a fond memory, something to look back on, something to look forward to next year.

What will it be like for Kyle and me?

That's the downside of pining for our Saturdays. With each one that races past, we're that much closer to the end of our summer.

My stomach twists with that thought.

"The Time of My Life" comes on, signaling the last song of the night.

"Oh, *hell.* Not this song again." Eric groans. "I need to go to sleep just so it can be tomorrow. We're hitting up Provisions to stock up, by the way, bro."

"You want to get fired?" Kyle mutters.

Eric waves it away. "It's Saturday. There're no rules on Saturday."

Kyle just shakes his head at his friend.

"*You* did this to him." Eric jabs an accusatory finger at me. "He's whipped."

I roll my eyes. "Which one of you has ID, anyway?"

Eric nods toward Kyle.

"Max is twenty-one and we look a lot alike." Kyle slips his hands into mine and walks backward, leading me onto the dance floor.

"No!" I drag my feet.

He grins. "Come on, humor me."

"Fine, but no stupid dance moves," I warn him. Claire and Simon reenacted the *Dirty Dancing* movie last Friday, after practicing the choreographed steps all week in drama.

Kyle chuckles, twirling me once before pulling me into him, close enough that our chests bump each other. "No stupid dance moves. Promise. Put your arms around me."

I comply, roping my arms around his neck. He settles his hands on my hips, gripping me tightly, and we begin swaying as the tempo to the song picks up. "I can't dance to this. It's horrible."

"Pretend it's a different song, then."

"What song?"

He leans in, pressing his mouth close to my ear—the cold metal of his lip ring tickling my lobe—and begins humming in my ear.

A shiver runs down my spine. "What is that?"

"You like it?"

I can feel campers' curious eyes glancing our way and I know we should disentangle ourselves, but he feels too good. "Yeah. But what's it called?"

"It doesn't have a name."

"It has to have a name."

"It doesn't."

I pull back far enough so he can see me roll my eyes. "Just admit you don't know."

"Oh, I know it." He flashes a crooked smile.

I raise my eyebrows, waiting.

An unreadable look passes through his beautiful golden eyes then. "It's called, 'I Think I'm Falling in Love with You, Piper Calloway.' "

A flush of adrenaline courses through my body as I absorb those words, playing them back to make sure I heard them right.

My heart is pounding inside my chest, the blood rushing in my ears as I try to keep the stupid grin from my face. "I'm *so* in love with you," I blurt out, curling my arms tight around his neck, inhaling the smell of his soap as our bodies press into each other. I knew it from the moment I saw him. Others—sane people—would call it infatuation. But I knew.

Kyle's mouth trails over my neck and down to my collarbone.

From the corner of my eye, I spot Darian approaching us. I peel myself away just as she reaches us.

"You two like to test me, don't you?" Her short blonde hair is damp from sweat and disheveled.

Kyle groans. "Come on, Dare . . ."

"Relax. You're not in trouble. *Yet*. But here." She thrusts a basketball into Kyle's hands. "If this doesn't fit between you, you're dancing too close."

He laughs. "You're kidding me, right?"

"Do I *look* like I'm kidding?" Darian points at her rosy face, her expression stern. "And do me a favor: think about this basketball tomorrow night, when you two are *not* doing the things you *shouldn't* be doing, so you *won't* remember to *not* protect yourself so you *don't* end up with a more uncomfortable and serious ball between you. The kind that cries. Got it? Good." With that, she's gone.

I frown. "Did we just get a sex talk from Darian?"

"I think it was more a 'don't get pregnant' talk." Kyle cringes. "That was somehow *way* worse than the one my mother gave me. You?"

"Definitely. And my mother used the word *deflower*."

Kyle tips his head back and starts howling with laughter just as the song ends and Christa flicks on the lights.

"Okay!" Darian claps her hands. "Cabins one through five and eleven through fifteen, it's turn-in time. You have fifteen minutes. Go!"

I sigh. "I guess I'll see you tomorrow?"

Kyle checks over his shoulder to confirm that Darian's attention is occupied and then leans in to kiss my lips.

"You really like taking risks, don't you?" I tease.

"If it means getting another moment with you? Darian can whip me for all I care." His eyes sparkle mischievously as he steals another kiss, which I happily grant him.

"I wish these nights would last longer."

His gaze drifts from my mouth back to my eyes. "We can make tomorrow last forever if you want."

Forever in our memories.

I swallow. And nod. Because I know I'm ready.

I'm still smiling as one of my campers, a little redhead named Suzie, slips her hand in mine and tugs me toward the door.

I walk along the path toward Cabin Seventeen at three in the afternoon, with that same exhilaration coursing through my veins that always does when I'm about to see Kyle. The faint sounds of shouts and splashes carry from the beach, as most counselors—including Christa—cool off in the water. There's not a sound on this end of the camp.

"Kyle?" I call out, knowing that if he's there, he'll hear me through the open window.

"Yup," comes a croaky response.

I step into the dim, stuffy cabin, to find him shirtless and stretched out in his bed in his swim trunks, his arm cast over his forehead, a sheen of sweat coating his skin. "Were you sleeping?"

"Trying to. It's *so* hot."

"Everyone's out in the lake." All the rain from the past two weeks has moved on, a heat wave trailing in behind it. Christa, who has taken it upon herself as "lead counselor" to know the seven-day weather forecast at all times, promises temperatures of close to 100 for the next week.

"I just needed a rest."

"Took you a while to clean the pavilion, huh?" I struggle to keep my annoyance from my tone.

He groans. "You won't believe how many of those little assholes stick gum to the underside of the picnic tables."

"Darian made you scrape those off, too?"

"Yup. Why am I friends with Eric, again?"

"I don't know, honestly." I shake my head. "But you two are lucky that's all you got for starting a food fight." By the end of breakfast, the cement floor was littered with pancakes and bits of sausage. More than one kid ended up heading to their parents' cars with syrup in their hair.

He rolls onto his side, his eyes showing worry. "You still mad at me?"

I sigh heavily. "No, but only because you didn't get fired."

"It was a heat-of-the-moment thing." He yawns. "How was the Laundromat?"

"Uneventful." I drop his basket of freshly washed and folded T-shirts, shorts, and boxers that I offered to run while doing my own laundry. Even though I was pissed at him.

"Thank you." He grins, his sleepy gaze dragging over my tank top and cotton shorts. "You want a nap?"

I laugh.

"Can you lie with me anyway?" he asks softly.

"I can, but it's *really* hot, Kyle."

He toys with the drawstring of my shorts. "Maybe not if you take that off."

Something about the way he says it—his voice, his gaze, the touch of longing in his words—makes my body shiver in the most pleasant way.

I swallow against my sudden nervousness.

Under his watchful eye, I shrug off my clothes until I'm standing in nothing, his eyes absorbing me. I don't feel the least bit self-conscious, which is a far cry from how I was only weeks ago.

Lifting his hips off his bed, he slides his swim trunks off and casts them aside.

The stifling air in the cabin has turned electric with promise as I lie down atop the sleeping bag next to Kyle. Our uneven breathing tangles for a moment as the only sound to be heard, and then Kyle rolls over, fitting himself between my thighs, resting on his elbows as he peers down at me for several long moments.

"I'm so in love with you, Piper."

I smile, reaching up to toy with strands of his spiky hair. "I love you, too, Kyle. I can't even describe how much."

Another moment passes and then he reaches next to him for his wallet.

The next thirty minutes will be ingrained in my memory forever—I don't know how they possibly can't be. Watching Kyle fumble with the condom to ease it on, tasting the salt on his lips from the hot summer day as he kisses me, feeling our hot, slick skin pressed against each other as he prods at my entrance, feeling him sink deeper and deeper in, past the painful pinch.

Hearing him whisper in my ear over and over again how much he loves me as our bodies rock back and forth against each other, finding a blissful rhythm in the dim, stuffy camp cabin on a sweltering summer afternoon.

Chapter 19

NOW

"It feels like forever since we last lunched. When was it, Mother's Day?" My mom smooths her hand over her sleek blonde ponytail and then busies herself laying a cloth napkin over her lap to protect her cream-colored pants. She is the only woman I know who dares to wear cream-colored pants to an Italian restaurant.

"I've been busy. And you haven't exactly been around, either." We have a standing lunch date in our calendars the first Sunday of every month. We've taken turns canceling on each other the last two.

"I know, darling. I was hoping to have all the renovations finished by now, but this contractor does not seem to know what he's doing. I won't be recommending him." She smiles. "But, I have to say, you are glowing. Is this about David?" She glances at my left hand, no doubt to check for the engagement ring.

"David and I are *over*. We will *never* get back together," I say as slowly and firmly as I can, because neither of my parents seems to be able to let go of that dream.

"Well, who is it, then?"

"Who says it's about a man?"

The waiter swings by to drop off a bottle of sauvignon blanc, saving me from having to discuss last night's knee-buckling kiss from my first love. I tossed for hours in bed pondering it, my body a live wire, thoughts of Kyle churning in my mind, the wish to have him lying next to me overwhelming.

"So what are you doing in the city, anyway?" I rush to move the topic off me for the moment. "You said you were visiting someone?"

"Just a friend." She brings her glass to her lips, letting it linger there a long moment, her eyes roaming the menu.

I make a point of holding my glass in the air. "Cheers, *Mom*."

"Oh, right, of course." She laughs, following suit to let our glasses clink. "I forgot."

Cocktail etiquette is second nature to my mother. She never forgets. Which means she's either lying or hiding something.

"A *male* friend?" I push.

She hesitates. "He is male, *yes*." Another long moment passes and then finally she dares to meet my gaze, her rose-painted lips pursing with a small, knowing smile.

"Are you dating someone?" I whisper excitedly.

"I'm not exactly sure. We're taking things slow."

Lord knows it's time. After her affair with the

tennis player that summer I was at Wawa and the ensuing ugly divorce, there was a lengthy dating blackout period in Mom's life, where she wouldn't even broach the thought. There've been a few men since then—one who even managed to slip a ring on her finger for all of a week before she politely returned it.

It's been at least two years since she last mentioned anything that sounds like a date, though I'm sure there's been no shortage of suitors lurking.

"Who is he? What's his name? What does he do?" I rifle off question after question.

She holds a perfect, manicured hand up in the air to quiet me. "It's still in the early stages."

"You have to tell me *something!*"

"Well. He's . . . a man," she begins.

I roll my eyes.

"He's age-appropriate."

"More than I can say for Dad, so thank *you* for that," I mutter through a sip. While my mother could easily pass for a decade younger than her fifty-seven years, I've had enough of my parents dating people closer to my age than their own.

She smirks. "He's unexpected. And surprising." Her blue eyes twinkle. "And that's all I'm comfortable with saying at this point, so please don't push. I don't want to jinx it."

"Wow. It sounds like you *really* like this guy."

"Honestly?" She lets out a shaky sigh. "I

haven't felt like this in *forever,* Piper. He brings out something in me that I thought I'd lost. Well, anyway, I'm really hoping this works out, yes." She laughs. "Listen to me. I sound like a giggling, foolish teenager! Never thought I'd be revisiting those years."

I snort, and nearly choke on my wine. *You and me both.*

"So? What's new with *you?* You mentioned in your message that you wanted to talk about something."

"Yeah." I groan. "Dad."

She holds a smile, but it turns tight. Forced. "What did he do now?"

"Not now, but I think he did something really shitty thirteen years ago."

Leaning back in her chair, drink in hand as if arming herself, she mutters, "Go on."

"Do you remember that guy from camp? Kyle?"

"Oh. *Yes.*" Her eyes widen knowingly. "You were a mess over that boy for your entire junior year, if I recall. Wallowing in your room for hours on end. You lost ten pounds that you didn't have to lose, not eating. As if I'd ever forget about him."

"I was in love with him, Mom. And only sixteen," I remind her, my cheeks flushing with embarrassment. "And there was *a lot* going on back then, if you will recall. Marital affairs, a divorce—"

"Yes, I suppose," she cuts me off, intently focused on her bracelet's clasp for a moment. It took her a year to admit her indiscretions to me, long after the illicit high had faded and the lifelong regret had set in.

"Well, I found out that Dad *paid* Kyle to go away."

The flash of recognition in her eyes answers me right away.

My jaw drops. "Are you *kidding me?* You knew!"

Her gaze flitters around us to make sure no one heard my outburst. "I didn't know about it at the time. He didn't tell me until months later. I swear, Piper. The tears, the moping, the not eating . . . it had been going on for so long that I finally mentioned maybe hiring one of your father's *people* to track this boy down and get you some closure. That's when your father told me the truth."

"And you didn't think to tell me then?"

"Why would I? Honey, he took the money! He chose money over you. Why would I want a boy like that in your life? No, I was furious with your father, but I didn't disagree that this boy didn't belong with our daughter. And don't shake your head at me like that; you'll understand one day," she mutters through a sip of her wine, the glass already half-finished.

"Of course he took the money! *You knew* what

kind of life Kyle came from. What that money could do for him and his family."

"Yes, but—"

"And you *also* know Dad better than anyone else. He *threatened* Kyle, Mom. Can you imagine what it would have been like for seventeen-year-old Kyle to face *that?*" Just thinking about it now incites a deep burn of fury inside me.

She sighs with resignation. "Why are we even talking about this?"

"Because I ran into Kyle recently and he told me."

"Really . . . Here, in Lennox?" She keeps her expression smooth, but I hear the wariness in her voice.

"Yes."

"How's he doing?" She watches me through shrewd eyes.

"He's doing well. He was in San Diego, but he moved here recently. He's working full-time. Security." I intentionally leave out the part about *where* he's working security, until I can figure out where my mother's head is at with this. "He's basically cut off all ties with his family, except for his younger brother, who has made something of himself."

"That's . . . good." She pauses and then feigns casualness to ask, "So, is he dating? Or married?"

"No, Mom. He's single." I meet her steady gaze with my own.

"I see," she murmurs quietly. "I guess that explains this effervescent glow." The waiter passes by to take our orders and collect our menus, stalling the conversation. "Does your father know about you two . . . reconnecting?" she asks when we're alone again.

"We haven't yet. Not *exactly*." *Our mouths have reconnected and it was euphoric*. "And, no, after what Dad did, I don't plan on telling him anytime soon. I want to see if Kyle and I can salvage what we had before I have to deal with that problem."

"I don't know if there will be any dealing with your father about this." She lets out a derisive chuckle. "He's still holding out hope that you'll come to your senses over David. At least I assume so, if I know your father at all."

"Oh, no, he has now moved on to ambushing high-rolling lawyers at galas." I tell her about last night's guerrilla-style Sternum introduction.

She groans. "I swear, that man . . ." She traces the rim of her wineglass with her fingertip as she considers me. "Do you still care about Kyle?"

"I haven't been able to stop thinking about him," I admit.

"And are those feelings mutual?"

I smile, thinking about the feel of his body pressed against mine last night. "Yes. But he's convinced we can't work, and he's not willing to try. He says he can't handle losing me again." Which only makes my heart ache for him more.

Her blue eyes drift out the window, past the sun-soaked boardwalk and milling pedestrians to the river, as if searching for an answer out among the sailboats floating in the distance. "Piper, you know that *I* understand, better than anyone, that a bank account shouldn't determine who you fall in love with," she says carefully, a worried look on her face. "But you are going to be running Calloway Group one day."

I roll my eyes. "I've already heard this from Dad."

"And now you can hear it from me. You're going to be running Calloway Group *and* you're a woman. Right or wrong, you will *always* be dealing with men who think you are lesser, simply because you are a woman."

"I'm fully aware of *all* that, Mom."

"I know you are. Just . . . keep it in mind when you choose who you have standing beside you in life, because as hard as it may seem now, the weight on your shoulders when your father is no longer in the picture is going to be tremendous. You'll need someone who can hold you up when that weight gets to be too much. Someone who's there to catch you when you fall, and help you get back up." She reaches out to pat my hand affectionately. "Maybe Kyle is it. Though it sounds like he already has low expectations for you two lasting, and I'm not sure that's the right foot to be starting off any relationship on, forget one with you."

"He's scared."

She purses her lips. "Then be sure that what you're feeling is real. I wouldn't want you getting hurt a second time by him."

"Kyle didn't hurt me the first time. Dad did."

"Fair enough. Still . . ."

"Dad's making me *so* angry lately." I break off a piece of flatbread and nibble on it, savoring the potent rosemary and oil drizzle. "Though he surprised me last night, by admitting to being wrong about the way he's handling Tripp."

"Yes, I've heard you're having problems. I talked to Rhett," she adds when I give her a questioning look.

I should have known. At least the little gossip kept his mouth shut about Kyle.

Mom smiles softly. "You know, you're more like your father than you'd like to admit. You're both hardworking and tenacious. And sometimes you get so wrapped up in your big, lofty plans that you lose sight of the little things that are just as important to you. Take some time to remind your father of that. He'll come around, eventually. Oh!" she manages through a sip, her brows curving ever so slightly—either from recent Botox injections or her own natural impulse to keep facial expressions to a minimum, to avoid needing further Botox treatments—"speaking of Wawa, since you brought it up . . . Jackie told me they shut it down."

"Seriously?"

"I know!" Her voice is full of dismay. "Ruth was going to send Robert this summer but when she went to register, they said it was closed."

"They must be so upset." My mom's older sister, Jackie, and my cousin, Ruth—eight years older than me—all attended Wawa in their youth. Robert would have been the third generation of my mother's family to attend. "Do you know why?"

Mom shrugs. "Time to move on, maybe? I've asked my agent to keep an eye on the property, in case they put it up for sale." She smiles secretively behind a sip of her wine. "Wouldn't that be something? I could buy it just to spite your father."

"Not a bad idea." I clink my glass with hers. "Maybe we can go in on it together, so if I end up back with Kyle and I'm forced to leave Calloway Group, we can run the camp." Dating a starving writer was one thing; Dad would never be able to stomach his daughter settling down with our building's security guard, let alone one with the Miller gene pool's rap sheet lingering in the shadows.

"I really hope it doesn't come to that." Her lips purse in thought. "I know it sounds harsh, but I think you need to consider the positives about what your father did. You were only sixteen and you still had a lot of growing up to do. Think about it . . . Brown, then Wharton, and the internships to get you where you are now. How would you have managed keeping your priorities straight while carrying on with a boy like this Kyle? I mean, you were *fired* from your summer job because of him, Piper."

"Don't blame Kyle. That was as much my fault as it was his. And what's going on with you? It sounds like you're making *excuses* for Dad's shady behavior."

"No." She holds her manicured hand in the air. "I most certainly am *not* excusing your father's behavior. I'm just trying to help you see past your anger and think about this logically." She offers me a sympathetic smile. "We're your parents. We only ever want you to be happy. But we're also human and have our own set of experiences that have shaped how we see life. Our own pitfalls that we've tumbled into. Sometimes it's hard to stand by and let your children learn the hard way. And sometimes we screw up. But I promise you, whatever your father did, it wasn't through selfish or malicious intent. He has always had *your* best interests in mind." She shrugs. "And it sounds like his methods, however twisted they may have been, helped this boy in the long run, too."

"Yeah, they did," I admit reluctantly. Kyle *did* say that he doesn't hold a grudge against my father, that the money changed his life for the better. Knowing that does temper my anger a touch. Just a touch, because there would have been better ways to help a boy in need than to threaten him.

I sigh. "I can't just move on. Not without knowing whether we could work."

Mom seems to mull that over. "You two weren't ready for the kind of feelings you'd fallen into back then, but maybe you are now."

I frown. "You're confusing me. Are you suggesting that Kyle and I *should* be together?" Because everything she's said up until now has sounded like the exact opposite.

"It is confusing, isn't it? Life? To be so sure of something in your head but unable to ignore what's in your heart." Her eyes narrow on her fork tines in thought. "I think that if you and this boy . . . this *man,* now . . . really want this to work despite the challenges, then you'll find a way." She offers my hand a reassuring pat. "You *are* your father's daughter, after all. And when he married me, I didn't have two pennies to rub together."

"But your looks and your charm were priceless."

Her soft, musical laughter soothes me. "If I remember correctly, this boy was rather cute, despite the funny hair. How did he turn out?"

"He turned out just fine." I give her a knowing look.

"A security guard, you said?" She smiles secretively through a sip of wine. "Do they use handcuffs?"

I cringe. "Mom!"

"Seventeen Cherry Lane. This is it." The cab driver squints as he peers over his steering wheel to take in the condominium, the six o'clock evening sun bouncing off the windows. It isn't one of the buildings we developed, but it's nice, all the same.

Seventeen cherries.

I hand the driver a wad of cash for the fare plus a healthy tip for putting up with the stops we made on the way here. "Just wait here a minute, in case they're not home, okay?"

"You got it."

I slide out of the backseat of the taxi and make my way through the glass doors. The intercom is to the left. I promptly punch in 717.

And wait.

Disappointment begins to swell as it rings three . . . four . . . five times, until a male voice answers on the sixth ring. "Yeah?"

I can't tell if it's Kyle or Jeremy. "Hey . . . It's Piper."

There's a long stretch of silence.

And then a buzz and a click sound, as the interior door unlocks.

I give the taxi the thumbs-up and then head in.

The interior is attractive—trendier than some of the family-friendly ones in the area. There is a small cubby to my right where a security guard would sit, but it's empty. I'm not surprised. We're in the suburbs, a generally safe and quiet area. Most condo boards have opted for security camera systems and part-time staff to save on budget.

I clutch my purse to my side as I ride the elevator up to the seventh floor, my stomach a fluttering mess of nerves. I'm more nervous for this than I have been for any board meeting or investor presentation I've lived through. Maybe it's because this is personal; the end result means *everything* to me.

When I round the bend in the hall, Kyle is waiting for me, leaning against the door frame, barefoot and wearing track pants and a plain white T-shirt that clings to his torso without being too tight. His hair is damp and pushed back, reminding me of afternoons in the lake, when he'd slide a hand through it to keep it from falling onto his forehead.

He watches me approach, his eyes drifting over my outfit—a casual navy-blue-and-white striped cotton jersey dress that hugs my curves and makes me think of warm summer days at Martha's Vineyard.

"You found me," he murmurs with a crooked smile.

"Jeremy was right. It's easy to remember." I stop just in front of him and inhale the scent of soap and cologne that wafts around him. "You smell good."

"I was just getting out of the shower when you buzzed."

Thoughts of Kyle answering my call in nothing but a towel hit me, and heat begins crawling along my skin. "It's okay that I've surprised you like this?"

"Yes." Not a hint of a waver in his voice.

An electric charge is building between us. His deep inhale tells me he feels it, too.

"Come in," he murmurs, gesturing with an inviting hand. He closes the door softly behind us.

It's a modestly sized but nice place—with an all-white galley kitchen and floor-to-ceiling windows off the living room, letting in plenty of light. Sliding frosted glass doors on either side lead to two bedrooms, where neither bed is made.

"Where's your brother?"

"Out with some new friends."

"Sounds like he's settling in well."

"He does well anywhere. He's a social guy."

"*You* were a social guy."

"Why are you here, Piper?" Kyle's gaze drifts to my mouth.

He knows *exactly* why I'm here.

Swallowing my anticipation, I reach into

my purse. "I just happened to be out shopping earlier and look what I found." I hold up a fistful of cherry and razz apple flavored Fun Dips—ten packs in total, which took visits to five different convenience stores before I found them.

Kyle grins. "I haven't had one of those since Wawa."

"Me neither. So I was thinking it was time for a little game of two truths and a lie."

"Fine." His eyes settle on mine, suddenly serious. "You go first."

Okay. I take a deep breath. "I didn't really need a gel pen on Saturday night."

He chuckles and I feel the sound deep in my chest.

"I haven't stopped thinking about you since you came to Lennox." I hazard a reach up, to skate my fingers over his cheek. "And I will jump off any cliff you ask me to, no matter how frightened I am, as long as it means you're waiting for me at the bottom." I let my hand fall to his shoulder and my thumb drag along his bare collarbone, reveling in the heat of his skin. "What's my lie, Kyle?"

He swallows hard. "That's a trick question."

Because they're all truths.

"You always were too good for this game."

"My turn." He steps forward, guiding me backward until my back hits the door. "I knew you didn't really come back for a pen." His hands find my hips. "I've measured every girl I've dated since Wawa against you and they've all failed miserably." His golden eyes lock on my mouth. "And I'm an idiot for being too scared to do *this*." My head hits the door as his lips crash into mine, but I don't feel the throb, meeting his mouth with my own fervor, as thirteen years of pent-up pain, love, and lust releases between us. Our hands roam urgently—tugging at clothing, learning new curves, reveling in each other's familiar heat—as if we have only minutes to accomplish all that we want to do.

He breaks free long enough to reach back and yank his T-shirt over his head, tossing it to the hardwood floor, and then his lips are on me again—on my mouth, my throat, my collarbone, his warm breath trailing along my skin.

My fingernails drag over his shoulders and my eyes shut, as I revel in the feel of both new and old.

I barely notice Kyle pushing the straps of my dress off my shoulders, and then the material is pooling at my ankles and I'm stepping out of it. He wastes no time peeling off the rest and, within minutes of stepping into this condo, I'm still at the front door but I'm naked. His skin is hot against mine as he pulls me into his arms, our bodies smashed together.

I don't hesitate, sliding my fingers beneath the elastic band of his track pants and easing them down over his hips, momentarily surprised by the lack of boxers beneath, but quickly distracted when his pants hit the floor.

"I never thought we'd be doing this again." He grabs the back of my thighs and hoists me up into his arms, guiding my legs around his hips. The door is cool against my bare back as he presses me into it once again, his mouth dipping down to wrap around a pebbled nipple this time, sending shivers skittering to my core.

"I don't think we ever did *this,*" I manage to get out around a soft moan, his hard length pressing against me, my body aching to feel all of it. Everything back then seemed so new and tentative. I remember a lot of fumbling, a lot of nervousness; a lot of Kyle hesitating, not wanting to pressure or rush me.

While *this* moment with Kyle is also uncharted territory, there's nothing tentative about him letting me know what he wants.

And I'm perfectly fine with giving it to him, except for the fact that he has a brother who may come home at any minute.

"Your bedroom. Now," I demand, my arms linked around his neck, my lips against his ear.

His mouth is still on me as he carries me to the room on the right, groping blindly for the door handle to slide the door shut before falling into bed on top of me. "I've thought about doing this every morning since you walked in through the front doors."

"Even while you were ignoring me?" I tease, my fingers curling through his damp hair, sending it into disarray as he grinds his hips against mine.

"Especially then." His teeth skate across my neck as his mouth edges downward, his arms braced on either side of me, the muscles in his broad shoulders straining beautifully as he lifts and holds himself over me, his eyes taking a long, leisurely look downward, over my naked body beneath him.

I follow suit, reaching down to grip him, parting my legs in an inviting way.

He inhales sharply. "If I wait any longer, I'm going to explode," he whispers.

"Don't, then."

I marvel at this new body before me as he rushes to fish a condom from an unopened box in his nightstand, as he tears the packaging and rolls it on.

And then he's curling his fingers within mine and pressing my hands above my head to pin me down.

I happily give up control, allowing him to fit himself between my thighs and push into me without hesitation.

Exhilaration and an unexpected sense of peace surges through me.

• • •

The front door creaks open around eight P.M.

"We left our clothes out there," I whisper into Kyle's bare, sculpted chest, my body warm and relaxed and splayed on top of him. I could stay like this all night.

"It's fine."

"Your brother is looking at my underwear right now."

"Hope they're clean."

"Shut up!" I smack his abdomen playfully and his muscles flex with his laugh. "Of course they are. I changed them before I came here."

"*Someone* sure had high hopes," he murmurs.

"Keep it up and you'll be doing nothing but hoping for a *long* time," I throw back, dragging a fingernail around his nipple and down, over the thin trail of hair past his belly button.

He sucks in a breath as my hand grazes his sensitive flesh. "I might need a few days to recuperate as it is."

"You *were* a little bit eager the first time."

"And the second time."

"And the third."

He shifts our bodies, allowing him to roll onto his side to face me. He runs a fingertip along my jawline. "This is crazy, isn't it? Us, like this, again?"

I lean in to touch his nose with mine. "Crazy, but in the best way," I whisper, my lips grazing his. "Are we going to do this?"

His lip curls with a sexy smirk. "I think we just *did* this."

"That's not what I mean."

Kyle's throat bobs with his swallow. "Aren't you worried about how it looks at work?"

"Why? Are you embarrassed of being seen with me?"

He chuckles, but when he pulls back to look into my eyes, his are filled with earnestness. "There's a lot of outside factors that could make things difficult. We need a game plan."

Really there's only one outside factor—a sixty-seven-year-old man in a three-piece suit.

I hadn't planned anything beyond showing up on Kyle's doorstep to tell him how I feel and seeing what might come of it. But he's right; we do need a game plan. One that keeps the workplace gossip mill at bay and my father blissfully unaware for as long as possible. "We should keep things quiet for now. Because if people find out, then my father finds out. And, I swear, Kyle, his opinion of you doesn't matter to me—"

"You're right, we don't want him knowing just yet," Kyle agrees.

I smooth a hand over his jaw, coated with dark stubble. "I hate it, but I think that's smart. For now."

"Are you *sure* you're going to be okay with people knowing that the future CEO of Calloway

Group is dating the building's security guard?" His voice drips with doubt.

I press my lips against his in a slow, tantalizing kiss. "I'm okay with people knowing that Piper Calloway is . . ." My voice trails. Could I still be in love with Kyle? I never truly fell out of love with him. ". . . dating Kyle Miller."

"Kyle *Stewart*."

My face pinches. "I can't call you Kyle Stewart. You'll always be Miller to me."

His hand slides over my shoulder and down my arm, dragging the sheet off my body. "Call me whatever the hell you want to," he murmurs, guiding me onto my back, his gaze taking in my naked body as he settles himself in between my thighs, his mouth leaving a trail of moisture as he begins shifting downward along my stomach.

"I'm ordering pizza!" Jeremy calls out from the main room. "Do you and Piper want in?"

"You hungry?" Kyle's tongue teases my belly button.

"Kind of," I admit. The salad at lunch didn't fill me up.

"The usual?"

I frown curiously. "What's my usual?"

"Hawaiian. That's what you'd always go for at Wawa."

"You remember that?"

He rests his chin on my pelvis and looks up

at me. "I told you, I remember *everything* about you."

I smooth a hand over his hair, now dry and wild, while emotion rises in my chest. "How does Jeremy know it's me, anyway? I could have been anyone," I murmur. "That would have been awkward."

" 'Cause Kyle hasn't so much as blinked at another woman since we moved to Lennox!" Jeremy hollers.

Kyle rolls his eyes.

"Do you know he called me Sarah when he first saw me?" I call out.

"My brother's an idiot, in case you haven't noticed."

"Order us a Hawaiian and get the fuck away from my bedroom door, you perv!" Kyle hollers back, glancing over as the shadowy figure strolls past the frosted glass, chuckling.

"You've got twenty minutes. I'll be on the balcony." A moment later, I hear the door slide open and shut.

Kyle groans and rests his head on my abdomen. "This place is too small."

I stroke his hair. "We can stay at my place. My bedroom is down a hall, away from the others." In truth, I have my own wing that might be the size of this entire condo.

"But then I'd have to deal with Christa."

"*And* her psycho cross-eyed cat."

"Why am I not surprised."

"But on the flipside, it's only a fifteen-minute walk to work."

"Hmm . . . that's tempting, seeing as I have to catch the bus at five from here."

"Eww."

"Right? So, you know you're welcome to stay here tonight, but I'll be gone early in the morning."

"It's okay. I have to get home soon, anyway. I have this construction proposal to go through before tomorrow." I should have been combing through it all afternoon, looking for issues to arm myself with in my power struggle against Tripp, not searching half of Lennox for Fun Dip powder packs and tangling in Kyle's sheets.

Kyle lifts his head to regard me for a long moment, a curious look in his eyes.

"What?"

"Nothing. I'm still in shock that you're here, with me."

"I know. Me, too." And it still somehow feels like Kyle and me. We've changed, of course—the man looking up at me now is all muscle and strength, with the finest of fine lines touching his forehead and an entire arm and shoulder decorated in art—and yet there is still something so familiar and boyish about him.

Something that feels so *right* about us.

He bites his bottom lip, his gaze drifting over

my breasts. "So I guess I only have twenty minutes, then."

"For what?" I smile coyly.

I get a knowing smirk in return, and then his sinewy arms are tensing as he climbs up onto me.

Chapter 20

THEN

2006, Camp Wawa, End of Week Five

"Are you still having a good time, honey?" Mom's voice sounds breezy and light. We've been catching up on Saturdays, when I come into town and can get solid cell phone reception, but last weekend she never answered my call. It's been two weeks since I spoke to her—a record.

I smile. "The best time. Really. It's been great."

"I'm so happy to hear that. And that you're staying out of trouble."

"It's not hard. I'm still on probation."

"What about *that boy?*"

I glance over at Kyle, to see him and Eric punching each other in the arm as Ashley draws money from the bank machine. I wonder if my mother would consider me losing my virginity to *that boy* last weekend "staying out of trouble."

"He's fine."

"Piper—"

"How are things on the island?" I ask, to divert the conversation.

"Oh, I'm having a *fantastic* time. It's exactly what I needed."

"But you're coming home in three weeks, right?"

"*Of course* I'm coming home. *You'll* be home."

"So . . ." I hesitate. "Has Dad visited you lately?"

She sighs into my ear. "Your father and I agreed to give each other some real space. That means him *not* coming out here."

It also means they can't work things out. It also means my life may be turning upside down when I leave Wawa. My shoulders sag with dismay. Leaving will already be hard enough. "You haven't been lonely out there, all by yourself?"

"Me?" She laughs. "No, darling. Jackie came out for a few days. And I've been at the club almost every day. My tennis game has improved. This instructor I have now is . . . well, he has definitely taught me a lot I didn't know."

"That's good. Maybe we can start playing singles again."

"Hmm? Yes. Maybe. So, listen, I'm going to be heading off to Paris on Monday for two weeks."

I frown. "By yourself?" How hurt is Dad going to be that she refused to go with him in May, but is jetting off now?

"Uh . . . no. Jackie said she'd come with me," she says, almost as if she's deciding then and there that she'll invite her sister along. "But your dad is in Lennox and not traveling. Should you need anything while I'm gone, you can call him."

"Okay. I guess?"

"Good. Love you, darling. See you in three weeks!"

I hang up, the reminder that the end of summer is looming nearer making my chest ache. Just three weeks left with Kyle, and then we have to figure out how we'll manage a long-distance relationship until we're back here next summer.

Kyle sidles up beside me, roping his arms around my waist. "Why so sad?" he whispers, kissing the side of my neck. This past week has been a test of teenage hormonal fortitude—of seeing him but not touching him, of pretending that we're not aching for another Saturday night.

His hands have been on me since the last camper rolled out of the parking lot today—a thumb stroking the small of my back while Darian presented this week's counselor stars; a palm warming my thigh as we inhaled the grilled cheese sandwiches that Russell whipped up for us; fingers digging deep into the back pockets of my jean shorts before we got in his car.

"There's only three weeks left." I don't hide the dismay from my voice.

"I know."

I steal a kiss. "It's so hard, not being able to do that all week."

He steals one for himself. "Unless we risk it and sneak out at night."

"It's not worth it," I remind him with a knowing gaze. Kyle needs this job.

"Anything that means I get more time with you is worth it." He presses his body into mine.

My cheeks flush. "Wow, you're . . . *ready*."

His chuckle sends shivers down my spine. "I can't help it. That's what you do to me every time I see you . . . or think about you . . . or do this." He kisses me deeply on the mouth, and I forget for a moment that we're standing in a parking lot, with people milling around us.

I can't wait to get back to his cabin. "Do you think Shane's gone yet?"

"Probably." He checks his watch. "We'll head back as soon as Ashley and Eric are done."

"What are they doing?"

"I don't know about Ash, but Eric's buying condoms. Don't worry, we're good for tonight."

I struggle to hide my smile. Never did I think I'd end up with a boyfriend—let alone needing condoms—when my mother dropped me off at Wawa five weeks ago.

"But I thought you liked the ribbed ones, Freckles!" Eric hollers. We turn to see him trailing Ashley out of the convenience store, holding up a box, earning several glances from people nearby. "They're for your pleasure!"

"That must have been Avery," Ashley throws back, giving him the finger before storming toward us, chips and licorice in hand, her cheeks bright red.

I feel my eyebrows pop with surprise. "Did Ashley and Eric hook up?" She would have told me, wouldn't she?

"Nope. And I'm guessing he just officially killed any chance he had. The guy has no tact. What an idiot," he mutters, but he's grinning. "Come on, let's get back."

"I think my parents are getting a divorce." I stare up at the underside of the top bunk in Kyle's bed, my head resting against the crook of his arm.

"Why do you think that?" Kyle asks, then shoves a handful of chips into his mouth.

"Because my dad cheated on my mom and she's not in any rush to forgive him."

He chews slowly. Finally, he swallows and asks, "Do you blame her?"

"No. I guess not. But she's been at our summer house since she dropped me off here, and now she's taking off to Paris next week. And she sounded *happy* on the phone today."

"And that's bad?" He offers me the bag of chips.

I grab a few. "Well, yeah. If she's happier without him, then they're going to divorce and my entire life is going to change. I'm not even sure how, exactly. I already don't see my father much as it is." Will I be taking turns living in their separate houses? Will we keep our house in Lennox or sell it? Oh God, what if they remarry? What kind of stepparents will I end up with?

"If it does happen, you'll adjust and you'll be fine."

"I don't want to have to adjust, though. Why are they doing this? Why did my father have to . . ." I don't want to finish that sentence. Talking about my parents having sex with each other—let alone anyone else—makes me cringe.

"Were they happy?"

I consider that. "I don't know. My dad's never home, so . . ."

"Maybe that's the real issue."

I sigh. "I think you may be right."

When I pass on more chips, Kyle tosses the bag to the floor beside us. A few chips spill out, but he doesn't seem bothered. "When my dad went to jail, I thought my mom would divorce him right away. She keeps saying she will, that we'll pack up and move far away from the whole mess, but . . . she hasn't yet."

"Where would you go, if you could?"

He drags a fingertip along my forearm. "*My* vote would be Lennox."

I smile. "Good choice."

"But she always talks about going somewhere warm, where there's no snow."

"That sounds far." A pang stirs in my chest.

"Don't worry. We're not going anywhere."

I stretch my neck to kiss his jawline. "For what it's worth, try to convince her to move to Lennox. That way we won't have to figure out these three-hour drives." *Where will we even stay on those weekends? I guess I can book a hotel for us on my card. What kind of hotels are there in Poughkeepsie?*

"I'll do my best." He dips his head to capture my mouth with his.

"You're salty," I murmur, running my tongue over his lips before flicking the ring.

He groans. "I love it when you do that."

"What . . . this?" I twirl my tongue around the ring again.

His arm tightens around my body. "Yeah, that. Your tongue on anything, actually," he says, his voice strained, his breathing turning ragged. I can always tell when Kyle is turned on, just by those two things.

I bite my lip as I feel the flush touch my cheeks. Kyle's hooded gaze settles on mine as I reach down to run my hand over him once before slipping it beneath the waistband of his shorts and wrapping my fingers around him.

He inhales sharply and then lifts his hips to push his shorts down, before settling back. He presses his lips against my forehead as my hand sets to work, reveling in the feel of his velvety skin and the way he naturally reacts to me.

I did this for Trevor, but I didn't enjoy it a

tenth as much as I enjoy doing it for Kyle now. Though, Trevor was angling for more than my hand every time. He deserved a damn medal for how hard he tried. I always said no and he ended up pouting.

But the idea of my mouth on Kyle—any part of him—stirs my blood.

I pull myself up and onto my elbow.

"What's wrong?" Kyle asks, his fingers skating over my arm.

"Nothing's wrong. I just want to try something. Okay?"

He frowns curiously. "Okay."

I pull my hair over one shoulder and then shift my body and lean down to take him into my mouth.

Kyle hisses.

I smile sheepishly at him. "I've never done this before, so—"

"Don't worry, you're good. Just keep going. *Please,*" he begs in a whisper.

Chapter 21

NOW

Kyle's intense gaze lingers on me as I approach the security desk on Monday morning. We said goodbye last night just before ten P.M., after gorging on pizza and hearing about Jeremy's recent exploits. Kyle walked me to the taxi and left me with a searing kiss, only to then text me well into the night.

It's been exactly ten hours and seven minutes since his lips last touched mine, and I'm anxious to feel them on me again. In fact it's *all* I can think about.

I'm an addict and Kyle is my drug of choice.

"Hello? You wanted my ID?" the man in front of Kyle says, waving his driver's license in the air, irritation in his voice.

Kyle clears his throat as he collects it. "Uh . . . yeah, sorry. Who are you here to see again?" His eyes flash to me before refocusing on the visitor, his lips curling in a small smile.

"Good morning, Miss Calloway," Gus greets, half his attention on the underground parking entrance monitor. "You sure are sparkling this morning."

"I am?" I glance down to take in my forest-green silk blouse and black pencil skirt. It's then that I realize I'm grinning like a fool, and I feel my cheeks begin to flush.

Gus reaches across the desk to hit a button. On the monitor, the arm lifts, allowing the car through. "Good weekend, I take it?"

"It was amazing, actually. Best one I've had in years," I say, loud enough for Kyle to hear. *Like, thirteen years*.

"I'll bet," Gus murmurs knowingly.

"And you? How was your weekend?"

He shrugs. "The usual. Grandkids, church, poker. Not at the same time."

"Sounds relaxing." I steal another glance at Kyle. He's busy photocopying the visitor's ID, and there are two other people waiting behind that guy. I won't get a chance to talk to him this morning, I realize with disappointment. I *definitely* won't get a chance to kiss him.

"Renée, David's new assistant, is already in. Mark took her upstairs." Gus peels the lid off his paper coffee cup to finish the last drops. "Fifty bucks says she runs for the hills by the end of the week."

"I'd take that bet if I felt comfortable taking your money, Gus. I think she's going to work out just fine."

"If you say so," he murmurs, his voice dripping with doubt.

"Have a great day." I swipe my badge, stealing one last glance at Kyle.

The green light flashes, allowing me through.

"That was some dress, by the way," Gus calls out.

I turn back to give him a questioning look.

"That silvery number you had on this past Saturday. You know, while you were sittin' in my chair, stuffing your face with one of those big, juicy Alejandro burgers you keep giving me so much grief about."

"How did you . . ." My words fade as I peer up at the security camera that's trained on the lobby.

"Sometimes I like to skim the surveillance tapes from the weekend shifts, especially when I've got a newbie working. Want to make sure they're not doing something they're not supposed to be doin'."

Kyle's eyes flash to mine and I see the "oh shit" look of panic in them.

"Well, it's a good thing Kyle is proving to be such a good employee," I say evenly.

Gus makes a sound, something that seems like agreement but could also be otherwise. "Also explains why my chair was all out of whack. Took me twenty minutes to get it sorted this morning."

"Oh, sorry. You know . . . long legs and all."

He chuckles. "Have a good day, Miss Calloway. And don't worry, I won't tell anyone your secret." Big brown eyes flash to me and he waits a few beats. "About Alejandro's."

I know for a fact he's not talking about the burger.

Mark trails me into my office.

"Your morning reports are in the blue folder on the left. I've already summarized the market stats and the PowerPoint deck for your ten A.M. is finished . . ." He goes on and on, briefing me on everything he's done to help me prepare for another long, grueling week ahead.

"Thank you. As always, you're on top of things." Whereas I am not. I plan on hiding in my office and reviewing the rest of this construction proposal from KDZ. "Oh, I need a contact at our corporate cell phone company. Whoever manages Calloway's contract. Not the account handler but the executive at the top of that chain. And I need that number and name ASAP." I'm hoping Kyle's right and Tripp is stupid enough to have incriminating text conversations on his company phone.

Mark nods, his brow furrowed with determination.

"How's everything on that front going so far?" I nod to where Renée sits, her long blonde hair pulled into a chic topknot, scowling at her monitor. She's wearing a tomato-red dress that, oddly enough, reminds me of the Wawa staff T-shirts, only the color is flattering on her.

Mark follows my gaze. "Good so far, but

David's not in yet. Carla from HR asked me if I could show Renée the ropes this morning. You know—her computer, and security pass, and all that. I figure it'll take an hour at most. You okay with that? After I get this contact for you, of course."

"Yes, because the sooner she's up to speed, the sooner David will stop pestering us." I drop my bag and sink into my chair with a heavy sigh as I take in the pile of work already forming for me. More signatures, more approvals, more, more, more.

And then I notice the packet of sour apple Fun Dip in my silver spoon figurine, and I start to laugh. We never did get a chance to eat those last night.

"Yeah, I noticed that on your desk this morning. Do you know who left it for you?"

"I do, actually."

Mark lingers another moment, eyeing me carefully. "You seem awfully chipper this morning."

"Do I?" I can't keep the private smile from curling my lips. *Maybe because I haven't felt this alive and free since I was sixteen years old.*

His gaze flickers to the candy pack again. "So, I guess that person works at Calloway."

He's fishing for details.

"Don't you have a number to find me?" I remind him, though I wink to let him know I'm not bothered by his nosiness.

"Right." He's out the door in a flash.

I type out a text to Kyle's number:

Two razz apple Fun Dips says you won't let me take you out to dinner tonight.

The answer comes almost immediately:

Four says you won't ask me to go home with you after.

I quickly respond:

Meet me at eight at my place. And bring your work clothes with you for the morning.

Two knocks rattle the glass door. I look up in time to see my dad poke his head in.

"David has a new assistant?"

"Yes, he hired her late last week. I'm surprised he didn't tell you."

"He called, but I was preoccupied. So what'd you think of the proposal?"

I sigh heavily. "Good morning to you, too, Dad," I offer, not bothering to hide my annoyance. It's barely eight a.m.

He makes a point of slowly saying, "Good morning, Piper. What did you think of the proposal?"

"I'm still reviewing it."

"But so far . . ."

"I'm *still* reviewing." And still annoyed—at Dad for what he did thirteen years ago, but more at the fact that I'm twenty-nine years old and here I am, hiding my love interest from my parents. "I only just got it late on Saturday, remember? And I was busy yesterday. I had lunch with Mom."

Dad makes a sound, the same sound he always makes when Mom is mentioned—a mixture of disapproval and scorn.

"She's dating someone," I offer, unprompted. "She sounds happy."

"Well . . ." He searches my area rug for something to say. "She's not getting any younger. Maybe this one will stick. I'm sitting down with Tripp this morning at eleven to discuss the Marquee. You should be there if you can make it work in your calendar."

"I can't," I begin to say, but he's out the door and marching to his office.

I groan. My women's network meeting is at eleven and, no, I can't just bump *everyone*. But I also *need* to be in this meeting with Tripp and my father. My father may have acknowledged his own part in sabotaging my importance in the company, but that doesn't mean he won't sign off on KDZ's proposal without me.

"Mark!" I holler, rubbing the back of my neck as tension mounts.

Wishing I were back in Kyle's bed, with his arms wrapped around me and the door to the outside world firmly shut.

"Knock, knock," I announce, strolling into Dad's palatial office at exactly eleven A.M., to see the back of his throne-like leather chair. He's looking out over the view of Lennox's downtown core, his phone pressed to his ear.

"I've got a meeting now. I'll call you later?" he murmurs, and I know without a doubt that it's not a business call. Especially when he releases a low, playful chuckle.

"How old is this one?" I ask, after he ends the call.

He spins around to face me. "I thought we were staying out of each other's relationships."

I settle into the chair directly across from him. "Is she at least older than me?" I dread the day I find out otherwise. The day he becomes that stereotype.

"Have I dated anyone younger than you yet?"

"No. Key word being *yet*."

He regards me evenly. "If I told you she's thirty-five and she makes me happy, would you approve?"

"So she's the same age as *your son*. I wonder if they went to school together. Maybe they *dated*."

"And this is why I don't tell you about the women I see," he mutters, annoyed.

"Hey. If *you're* happy, then *I'm* happy." That's a self-serving declaration if I've ever heard one, but I'll be able to remind him of it in the future, when he finds out about Kyle. It's only a matter of time.

I note with surprise the cell phone spoon rest

sitting on Dad's desk, the twin to mine. The one that Dad sneered at weeks ago and wanted to throw out. I'm about to ask him about it when Tripp strolls in.

"Kieran! Good to see you again! Piper . . . don't you look nice." He barely glances at me.

I struggle not to roll my eyes and give my father the flattest "see?" look I can muster.

"Sounds like you've been putting in some long hours lately," my dad offers as Tripp takes the vacant chair beside me.

"That's because you've raised a slave driver." Tripp chuckles, and it's not the fake laugh that's always directed at me. It's the laugh of a man who is comfortable and pleased. Perhaps because he's been granted an audience with the king again after what I'm guessing he deemed a demotion, having to report into me. Perhaps because he thinks this arrangement with KDZ is a lock.

"That's what I like to hear." My dad winks at me.

I stifle another urge to roll my eyes. *Please tell me Dad's swift enough to see that Tripp is using his weakness—me—to score points.*

"So you've had a chance to go through the contract? It's solid, right? I told you they were coming in strong. They really want this. More than Jameson, based on what I've seen." Tripp speaks directly to my father, as if I'm not even in the room.

"And have you received the updated proposal from Jameson already? Did you forget to send that one to me, too?" I ask lightly, sliding my jab in.

Tripp offers me a forced smile. "No, I haven't."

"Then you'll be getting it soon. Gary said it would be in today."

"They've had plenty of time to deliver. More than KDZ."

"They're reworking their numbers to meet our new timelines," I say, keeping my voice even.

He snorts. "What they're doing is trying to make a rabbit appear out of a hat. I've seen this before, a hundred times. You'll start to recognize it one day, don't you worry."

And there's another condescending jab.

The urge to lean over and punch him is overwhelming. I grit my teeth into a smile. "By the way, how do you know this Hank Kavanaugh?"

"How do I know him?" Tripp shrugs. "I know him like I know *all* my contacts. Through *years* of carefully cultivating industry relationships."

"A lot of golf, I'll bet."

"Yes, well . . ." He chuckles. "That's how things have gotten done over the *decades* that your father and I have been at this."

Well played, Tripp. Position yourself as equal to my father. Keep trying to make me look inexperienced and dumb. I'll admit, I *am* inexperienced when you stack up résumés.

But I am not dumb.

"So that's how you two met? Golfing?" I push.

His eyes narrow as he assesses me a few beats, as if searching for an answer. *Why is she asking me this? What does she know?* "We went to the same college. That was definitely a conversation starter for us."

Actually, you two were roommates. Something I can't blurt out without letting on that I've been digging into Tripp's past. But that he didn't mention it now . . . He's hiding a potential conflict of interest. That's another red flag.

Tripp waits another few beats and, when I don't respond, turns back to my father. "Kieran, Hank is ready to commit today. You know where my head's at on this and I've been around the block a few times."

My dad regards him with his naturally steely eyes. "So have I."

Tripp holds his hands up in surrender. "All I'm saying is, I'm *telling* you, KDZ is the right move for the Marquee project."

Dad's lips twist in thought. I know that look. It's the one he gets when he's about to make a decision.

"I disagree," I blurt out.

Tripp's sigh is poorly concealed.

"Why?" my father asks evenly.

I don't have much choice anymore. Still, I choose my words carefully, keeping my gaze on my father. "Because there is a rumor that KDZ has been known to offer kickbacks to secure contracts."

"That's bullshit!" Tripp bursts. "Where did you hear something like that?"

"A reliable source."

"Who?" he demands to know.

I remain calm. "No one I am going to name at this time."

"And so what are you implying, Piper? What, that *I'm* taking a kickback?" Tripp adjusts his position in his seat, the casual slouch replaced with stiff indignation. "After giving almost thirty *goddamn years* to your family's company, you're accusing me of *that?* Kieran?" He looks with bewilderment at my father.

"I'm *sure* that's not what Piper is implying." My father's cold blue gaze lands on me and there is a distinct warning in there.

Meanwhile, Tripp's face is flushed red with anger. It's so convincing that my stomach sinks with dread. Is Kyle wrong about what he overheard?

What if I just made a horrible mistake?

I clear my throat, mainly to steady my voice. The worst thing I can do right now is come off sounding hesitant. "I have someone looking into the claim right now. If it turns up false, then I'm fine with considering KDZ's proposal."

Tripp sighs heavily, and gathers some level of composure. "Kieran, blowing up a solid contract because *your daughter* heard a *rumor* is a terrible business move."

My dad's eyes shift back and forth between us. "I agree."

My mouth drops open. Did he just side with Tripp, *again?*

Rage and shock bubble inside me.

"But," my father continues, staying my sharp tongue from letting loose something that I'll no doubt regret—like, that I quit—"I don't believe Piper would come forward with an accusation this serious if she didn't have solid intel."

I breathe the softest sigh of relief. And again, that twinge of dread surfaces. Is what Kyle overheard really "solid intel"?

Dad shuffles a stack of paperwork—he still refuses to review presentations digitally. "We need to see Jameson's revised proposal and have the team weigh in before we make any decisions. Hank can talk to me if he has an issue with this. Piper, a word, alone."

Tripp heaves his lumpy body out of his chair and storms off, leaving the door wide open.

"Greta! Door," my dad barks. Moments later, Greta pokes her head in to quickly close it.

"What the hell was that!" Dad explodes in a rare burst. "When did you hear about this supposed kickback?"

My heart begins to race in my chest. "About a week ago."

"A week!" His eyebrows crawl halfway up his head. "Who told you?"

"That's not important—"

"The hell it's not!" He picks up a pen, only to throw it across his desk. "Who is your source?"

"Did you know that Hank Kavanaugh and Tripp were *roommates* at Minden College? And they also played on a men's soccer team, together," I say instead. "That's more than just a conversation starter."

Dad stalls on whatever he was going to say. "So you *are* accusing Tripp of accepting a kickback. That's why you think he's gunning for this contract."

"Not officially." There's no point denying it anymore. "But yes, I believe he has made a deal with Kavanaugh for a five-hundred-thousand-dollar payout."

Dad's angular jaw tightens. "Why didn't you tell me this before?"

"Would you have believed me?"

"No. I still don't."

"Exactly. Which is why I'm doing more digging. I have them pulling Tripp's phone records for all deleted text messages in case there's something there." That required a tense half-hour conversation with the VP of our phone company, who was more than reluctant, citing a need to speak to his legal counsel first, until I asked him to verify for me how much our corporate bill was last year and when CG's contract with them is up.

"He wouldn't be that foolish."

"He was foolish enough to have an open conversation on his phone about it." Arrogance and bitterness make people do stupid things.

"Who overheard him?" he pushes. "Jill? Mark? I know it wasn't David. He would have told me."

I fold my arms over my chest and press my lips together tightly.

He sinks into his chair, pinching the bridge of his nose. "I do *not* like being blindsided, Piper."

"I'm sorry. I was afraid you were about to make a huge mistake by agreeing to this."

He spins in his chair, turning his back to me as he gazes out over the city again. "Let me know what you find. And don't ever say I didn't back you."

I take this as my dismissal, and leave my seat to head for the door.

"Did David tell you about dinner tonight?" He spins back around, and suddenly he looks ten years older than he did when I walked in here.

"No."

"He's meeting with Drummond tonight to try to lock them in."

The anchor tenant for the Waterway project. *Right*. "Okay?"

"I was going to go with him but something's come up for me tonight, and I think you should go."

Warning bells go off. Is this another attempt to get David and me back together? "Dad—"

"This is business, Piper," he snaps. "I don't give a rat's ass if you two screw each other or kill each other after dessert, as long as we have an anchor tenant nailed down before the unveiling ceremony next month!"

I hold my hands in the air, in surrender. "Okay. We will take care of it."

"Good. That'll be all," he mutters, his focus already shifting to his paperwork.

I duck out before he can bark at me about anything else, balling my fists to hide my shaking hands. I don't know that he's ever yelled at me like that before. The news about Tripp's potential deceit must be hitting him hard.

Then again, I can't blame him for reacting that way. The Waterway project is worth well over a billion dollars. He's right; we need to nail this tenant. That he's entrusting me to do it is a big sign of approval. He would never use an important business meeting like that for something as trivial as setting David and me up for a reconciliation. I'm an idiot for thinking otherwise.

I start to laugh.

"Is everything okay, Piper?"

I turn to see Greta peering down over her reading glasses at me, her wrinkled hands paused over her keyboard. I've known the woman all my life. She has a severe gaze and it used to scare me when I was little.

"Yes, it's fine."

Because my dad is finally treating me like a worthy colleague.

With a sigh of disappointment, I pull out my phone and send a quick text to Kyle, to change plans.

"Do you need anything else done today, David?" Renée peers up at him with wide, inquisitive eyes from behind her desk, her pen poised to take notes.

"I'm good, Renée. You've been here since eight? Go home. See you in the morning." He flashes his signature panty-dropping smile—that's literally what I've heard him call it—and then falls into step beside me as we head toward the elevator. With traffic, we'll just barely make our dinner reservation with Drummond.

"You're happier than a peacock in front of a mirror today," I murmur.

"She brought me an apple," he whispers with excitement. "I came in and there it was, just sitting on my desk, like a gift."

"How long before you find *her* sitting on your desk like a gift, I wonder."

David's manicured eyebrows arch with surprise. "Is someone *finally* jealous?"

I laugh. "Just please don't do anything that will earn you a sexual assault allegation."

"Don't worry. I don't shit where I eat."

I step into the elevator with a cringe. "*Nice*. Plus, have you already forgotten?" I waggle a finger between us.

"That was different." He hits the ground-floor button.

"Why? Because of my position?"

"Which one, exactly? I've seen you in so many." He smirks, proud of himself for that tasteless joke.

I simply shake my head.

"What's with Kieran today, anyway? He nearly bit my head off."

"That's my fault."

"What'd you do?"

"I ambushed him. But I can't get into it. What do I need to know about tonight?"

The elevator doors open, letting us out into the lobby.

"Drummond wants to sign, but . . ."

David's words drift as my attention veers to the security desk, to the tall, solid figure leaning against it, talking to Roland, the nighttime security guard who never smiles. It's half past six, well after Kyle's shift change. Still, he lingered. I'd like to think it was so he could see me before my dinner meeting, even though he's coming to my place afterward.

He turns to watch me approach, his eyes drifting down the length of my body, the smile on his lips mischievous.

Flashes of yesterday in his condo hit me—of what's beneath that uniform, of what his hands feel like on me, of what his weight feels like on me—and my body begins to heat.

Just one business dinner and then he's mine again, I remind myself. God, this workday feels as long as the ones at Wawa.

"Piper?" David nudges me.

"Hmm?"

"Did you hear what I just said?"

"No. Sorry. What?"

"We're playing good cop, bad cop tonight. You're bad."

"Why?"

"Because you're terrible at kissing ass."

"Fine." He's right, I am.

He glares ahead. "What's with that security guard?"

My stomach tightens. "What do you mean?"

"I mean the guy just stripped you with his eyes. You didn't notice?"

I feel my cheeks flush. "No. And don't say anything to him," I warn as we approach the security gate. "Good night, guys."

Roland simply nods, his face wearing its usually stony mask.

"Have a good night, Miss Calloway." Kyle's voice is practically dripping with promise, his eyes so heavy on me that I have to avert mine.

"Good night, Kyle."

We've made it halfway to the exterior doors when David's legs suddenly stall. "Oh . . . You have *got* to be kidding me."

"What?"

He cocks his head at me, then looks back at Kyle, who's still leaning against the desk, watching us, then turns back to me, his eyes shining with awareness. "You're screwing the building security guard?" he hisses with disbelief.

Oh, shit. I close my eyes. For such an obnoxious ass, sometimes David surprises me with how in tune he can be.

His head falls back with a bellow of laughter.

"I'm not!" I glance around quickly. Thankfully no one's within earshot.

"Oh give me a break, Piper. We were together for two years. I can practically smell the pheromones pouring off you."

"You're wrong."

"Really?" He mock-frowns. "I think I'll go ask him."

I sink my nails into David's forearm before he takes a step. "*Don't,* David."

"Then start talking. I think I have a right to know before everyone else when my ex-fiancée is rebounding with the *help*." David's amusement over this has faded quickly.

"It's not like that. I've known him for years. And he's not the *help*." I steal a glance Kyle's way. The smile and easy stance are gone, and he's heading this way. I hold up a hand to stall him. Thankfully, he stops.

"So *this* is why Kieran was so pissy today? How is this guy still in the building?"

"No, that has nothing to do with Kyle. That's because of the kickback with Tripp."

This time David's jaw drops. "Come again?"

"We don't have time to stand here and do this right now, David. We're gonna be late."

He glances at his watch. "It's a fifteen-minute cab ride over. Start talking."

I glance back once at Kyle, to see his narrowed eyes. *It's fine,* I mouth. Though I don't know if I believe that. Barely twenty-four hours and we've already been found out, by the one guy who will go running to my father.

Kyle is sitting on the park bench across from my building when my cab pulls up at half past nine, dressed in shorts and a T-shirt, his arm resting on his backpack. The mere sight of him there, waiting for me, gets my blood racing.

I pay the driver and then slide out of the taxi, just as Kyle rounds the back end of it.

"I thought you were going to wait for me inside?" I sink into his firm body, reveling in the scent of his soap and cologne as my hands slide over his side, smoothing over his back. "Did Ashley not let you up?"

"It's okay. It's a nice night out." He wraps his

arms around me. "I wanted to meet you down here."

"I'm sorry. Dinner took way longer than I expected it to." I stretch onto my tiptoes and press my mouth against his, releasing a moan at how soft his lips are. "I have been waiting *all day* to do that."

"I know. Me, too." He pushes a wayward strand of hair off my face. "How did your meeting go?"

"Which one?" I grumble. David forced me to go for a drink with him afterward to grill me on all things Kyle and kickbacks. He knows everything now. My summer at Wawa, the payout from my father, how Kyle overheard Tripp. *Everything*. "We've got our anchor tenant. Contracts are getting signed this week." It took David's silky tongue and me faking reluctance while agreeing to bend on a few minor clauses, but it's as good as done.

Kyle's golden eyes twinkle with amusement. "I have *no idea* what that means."

I pull away, slipping my hands into his. "Well, then come inside and let me teach you *all* about the *thrilling* world of real estate development."

"What was all that with Mr. Maserati in the lobby?"

"He figured it out."

"It?" His eyebrows rise. "You mean us?"

"Yeah. Apparently you stripped me with

your eyes and I was oozing pheromones or something."

"True. And . . ." He grins. "*Definitely* true."

My cheeks flush. "What is with you guys? Honestly."

The humor slides from his face. "So, what does this mean? Do I need to be putting in for a building transfer tonight? Am I going to be escorted out tomorrow?" He swallows, looking ready to say something else, but he doesn't.

"I would never let that happen. And David was . . . *okay* about it." Or at least tolerable. He listened and kept his insults to a minimum. "He promised he wouldn't say anything. That was surprising, actually."

"And you believe him?"

"I don't know, but I didn't have a choice. If he thought you were just some guy I was screwing, there's no way he would have kept quiet. But I've probably bought us a few weeks. Hoping, anyway."

He nods slowly. "As long as you can control those pheromones of yours."

I poke his side, earning his smirk.

"It feels like being at Wawa again, doesn't it? Pretending not to be together all day long?"

"You're right. And I didn't like it then, either." I fall into his body with a groan, marveling at how comfortable I am with Kyle, how easily I throw myself at him after just one night back in his arms, not caring if this needy, emotional version of me doesn't match up with the hard-nosed version that just negotiated a multimillion-dollar rental deal over grilled salmon. "Come on, I've been waiting to get you upstairs all day."

A soft curse slips through Kyle's lips as we step through my front door.

"What's wrong?"

He shakes his head, smoothing his hand over the small of my back. "Nothing. Just . . . this place is nice."

I set my purse on the hallway desk and kick off my heels, sighing with relief as my bare feet hit the cool hardwood. "Make yourself at home. Seriously."

"Is that you guys?" Ashley hollers, and I hear the twinge of excitement in her voice.

"Depends on which 'you guys' you mean," I call back, smiling and slipping my hand into Kyle's to lead him in.

Ashley is sitting cross-legged on the couch, with balls of pink and white yarn scattered beside her, a knitting needle in each hand. Her eyes widen at the sight of Kyle. "Oh my God!" Casting her blanket aside, she leaps up and runs for him, throwing herself into his arms. "I can't believe it!"

Kyle is grinning as they embrace. It's an entirely different response than he got from Christa. "Good to see you, too, Ash."

She pulls away, smoothing her blouse over her hips. “This is crazy, isn’t it? Us, all together again like this?”

He cocks his head, peering down at her with genuine affection. “How have you been?”

She shrugs. “Single and looking for a job. You know . . . living the dream.” They share an awkward laugh. “Oh, hey, Piper, those chairs Marcelle picked out arrived today. Wait ’til you see them.” Her emerald eyes light up. “She’s *so* good.”

Ashley and my interior decorator have hit it off, exchanging dozens of emails a day. Somehow the scope has expanded to include the patio, as well as my home office and the empty sitting area in my bedroom.

Her gaze shifts back to Kyle. “Piper mentioned that you still talk to Eric, right?”

“Uh . . . yeah. ” Kyle nods, ducking his head. “It’s been a while, though.”

She slides her hands into her pockets. “Say hi to him for me, next time, will ya?”

“I will. For sure,” he promises, his eyes solemn. “Do you want him doing that?” He points to something behind us.

I follow Kyle’s gaze to the couch, where Elton is batting at the white ball of yarn that Ashley’s using.

“Hey! No! Don’t you do that!” she scolds, charging for the living room. Elton takes off, skittering across the floor with the yarn, dragging her blanket behind him. "Bad kitty!"

Kyle frowns at Elton as the cat races past us, having abandoned his toy. "What's wrong with his tail?"

"Anxiety."

His dark eyebrows rise. "Cats get anxiety?"

"This one does." I slip my hand into his once again, intent on not letting go for the rest of the night. "Come on, I'll show you around."

"And this is my bedroom." The last room to show him in my condo, with the added surprise of two silver-blue wing chairs and a creamy shag rug now set next to the gas fireplace. Marcelle has exquisite taste.

Kyle hasn't said much through the tour. Now he stops in the middle of the room, tossing his backpack as he takes it all in. His gaze drifts to the French doors. "Is that a different patio than the other one?"

"Yeah. But it's just a small one." I push my bedroom door closed.

" 'Just a small one,' she says," he murmurs, strolling over to the other set of doors. He flicks the light switch on. "*This* is your closet?" His gaze takes in the custom cabinetry and shoe racks.

I sidle up to him to settle my hand on his abdomen. "Yes."

He smirks at our reflection in the bathroom's vanity mirror across the way. "Your closet is bigger than my bedroom."

"No, it isn't," I say, trying to brush it off, though we both know it is.

He looks down at me with odd reluctance in his gaze.

"What?"

"Nothing, I'm just . . . I know this all feels normal for you. But it's *not* normal for me."

"It's just a condo! Ashley and Christa are fine living here."

"They're not dating you. Or whatever we are."

I feel a pinch in my chest. "Is this an ego thing? Because, honestly? I deal with fragile male egos all day long, so please don't tell me you've developed one now, too. I'm tired of it." My voice is escalating, but I can't help it.

"No, you just don't understand."

I fold my arms over my chest. "So enlighten me, then."

He sighs. "Do you remember those shitty little cabins at Wawa?"

"How could I forget. They were hot and stuffy . . ."

"Mine smelled like dirty socks and dead things."

I laugh.

Kyle bites his lip. "Sometimes I wish we could go back for a night."

I reach for his arm, dragging my fingers over the tattoo of the cliff, and us. "So do I."

His jaw tenses. "I already knew you were way out of my league, but there, it felt like we were on an even playing field. Here . . ." His gaze skates over my bedroom again. "I can't even afford standing-room-only with an obstructed view in this stadium."

"But I told you, I don't care about"—*How do I word this delicately?*—"our financial differences."

"Yeah, but *I* do. Because people are going to think I'm with you for your money. That's something my shitty father and brothers would do. But I'm not them and I don't ever want you to think that. I don't want your money, Piper. I *hate* myself for ever taking it from your father."

"Is that what this is really about?"

He bows his head.

"You didn't have a choice. My father threatened you."

"Yeah, I did have a choice, Piper. My options might not have been ideal, but I had a choice. I could have cut you out of my life to get your father off my back but not taken the money. I chose to take it and I'm ashamed of that." He frowns. "And I know that's going to come up again and again."

"No, it's not."

He gives me a flat look and I have to avert my gaze, because he's not wrong. Christa condemned him for it. My mother's opinion of him is low, in part because of the money. Even *I* chastised him for it, the day he told me.

"If my father offered you money now—"

"No." He shakes his head.

"*More* money. Ten times as much—"

"No."

"A hundred times—"

"No." His voice is cold and hard, his jaw set with determination. "I'll never take a dime from him, ever again."

"So then, what are you worried about? What *other* people think of you?"

"No, I don't give a shit what they think about me. But I'm worried about what the people who matter to you think." Resignation fills his eyes.

"If they *really* care about me, they'll accept you." And as I say those words, I know them to be true.

He swallows, then nods, though he still seems unconvinced.

"Remember when I first got to Wawa? How out of place I was?"

"Yeah." His gaze drifts over the length of my body. "You were the hot new girl."

I begin unfastening the buttons of my emerald-green blouse, one by one. I tug the zipper on my pencil skirt and let it slide down and pool at my ankles so I can get to the rest of the buttons. Kyle watches with curious eyes but doesn't make a move. Taking a step backward, I shed my blouse. "I was the girl whose mom drove her to Camp Wawa in a Porsche, and who didn't know a single soul." I reach up to unfasten the clasp to my bra and let it spring free.

Kyle's eyes flare with heat.

"The girl who fell head over heels for a boy the first moment she laid eyes on him." I keep backing up until my thighs hit my mattress. "And every time she caught his eye after that, *every time* he looked at her the way only he did, she felt like the luckiest girl in the world."

Kyle's gaze lifts to meet mine. "That's because he knew he was the luckiest guy in the world for that one summer."

"Money didn't matter to them then." I bite my lip, pushing my lace panties down over my hips, letting them fall to the floor. "*Please* don't let it matter to them now." I let vulnerability fill my voice, a sound that has become foreign to me in recent years, as I've learned to maintain the edge I need to become Piper Calloway.

Here, though, with Kyle, I don't need to wear that armor.

He sighs. "I'm sorry, you're right." He stalks forward, taking my chin in his hands and kissing me deeply. "I just don't know how to fix what I did."

"Start by *always* choosing me—us—no matter what, from now on." I tug at his T-shirt, a sly smile touching my lips. "Starting with right now."

Chapter 22

THEN

2006, Camp Wawa, End of Week Six

"Smirnoff?"

"Hell no. That tastes like ass." Eric cringes. "Absolut, all the way, baby."

Kyle rolls his eyes. "You can't even tell the difference."

"Sure, I can!"

Kyle turns to Ashley and me. "What do you want me to grab you?"

"Mike's Hard Lemonade," Ashley requests, handing him a ten-dollar bill. "I think that should cover it?"

"Piper?"

I shrug. "I don't know. Whatever's good. Surprise me. Just not beer."

"Mike's Hard, Surprise Me, Smirnoff—got it."

Eric smacks Kyle in the shoulder. "Absolut!"

Kyle holds his hand out. "Fork it over, and fast. They close at nine."

"Nah, man, you owe me." Eric waggles his finger between Kyle and me. "Don't think I didn't notice. Seriously? You couldn't leave me just *one?*" he adds when Kyle dips his head, grinning.

Meanwhile, my face bursts with heat. The door had barely shut behind Shane this afternoon when Kyle and I landed in his bed, the week of waiting leaving us pent up with frustration and anticipation. He had two condoms and I accidentally tore one with my nails, trying to roll it on him.

And one apparently wasn't enough for us this afternoon, so Kyle yanked on his shorts and darted over to Eric's cabin to "borrow" the fresh box.

We didn't use them *all,* but we definitely used a few.

"Yeah, fine . . ." Kyle digs out his wallet and thumbs through the few dollar bills in the fold. We just got paid, but he's been saving his money.

"Here." I pull out my wallet and count out ten dollars.

"You haven't cashed those yet?" Ashley frowns at the three Wawa employee checks that are tucked inside.

"Best way to save." It's the truth, but it's also a lie. The fact is, I don't need the money. I have an account that Mom transfers money into plus my Mastercard that she pays off each month. "Here. Just use this for everything." I hand Kyle the credit card. I don't have enough time to get to a bank machine to pull out more cash, and the card will *definitely* cover whatever he's buying for us.

"Dude." Eric's eyebrows rise. "Must be nice."

I ignore him. "Do you think they'll check against the signature?"

"Probably not. This place is small." Kyle studies the card sitting in the palm of his hand a moment, as if considering whether to take it.

"Tick tock!" Eric taps his watch. "Five minutes left."

"All right." He shrugs. "Let's see if this works."

"And grab me another box of condoms, too, you thief!" Eric hollers after him.

"Why? They'll just expire," Kyle throws back.

We pile into the car and wait for him, because a bunch of teenagers loitering outside a store that sells booze on a Saturday night is a touch suspicious.

As it is, I'm wary of bringing alcohol back to Wawa. "Is this a good idea?"

"Darian's chill on Saturdays. And we're not gonna be dumb enough to get caught," Eric says, biting on his thumbnail, his eager eyes locked on the entrance to Provisions. He's the main instigator in this whole plan to get drunk tonight, though we are willing accomplices.

Kyle returns five minutes later, his arms filled with brown paper bags.

"No issues?" I ask when he climbs into the driver's seat after loading the trunk.

"Didn't even I.D. me. I didn't know what to get you, so I grabbed some coolers and Jägermeister. Hope that's okay."

"It's fine." It's not like my mom will have any idea what I bought. Provisions sells everything.

He slides my credit card into my hand and leans in to kiss me. "Thank you."

"Of course. I don't mind at all."

"Let's rock and roll!" Eric drums his hands on the back of the driver's seat.

"Shhh!" Ashley warns as Eric stumbles over his own two feet in the dark and the bottles stuffed into his backpack clang together, the sound unmistakable.

"Shit, I'm not even drunk yet," he whispers, tipping the bottle of vodka back to take a swig of it straight. He smiles through a cringe. "Wait 'til I'm drunk."

My attention veers to Darian's cabin. Light flashes in the tiny window. She doesn't usually venture out on Saturday night, preferring to spend the night in front of her TV. However, a loud and obnoxious Eric might draw her out.

I have to admit, while a part of me wonders if maybe we should just stay in our respective cabins and keep out of trouble, the other part feels the thrill of a Saturday night, having fun with friends. We've been under watch for too long.

“Where are we hanging out tonight?” I ask.

“My cabin, I guess?” Kyle offers. “Unless you think Christa wants to play drinking games with us.”

“Uh, my guess would be *no* to that. So . . . what kind of drinking game are we playing, anyway?”

Kyle and Eric exchange a look.

“The *only* drinking game.”

“Oh, God, have I told you guys how much I *hate* black licorice?” Olivia’s tongue hangs from her mouth as if that will dispel the taste of it.

“Only, like, a thousand times already,” Avery mutters, rolling her eyes.

I grin from my spot sprawled across Kyle’s bed, my body relaxed and buzzing from more shots than I can count. Kyle sits on the floor in front of me, the perfect spot for me to draw lazy circles over the back of his neck and toy with his wild hair, reveling in the feel of gooseflesh sprouting along his skin every time I touch him.

We picked up Avery, Olivia, Colin, and a counselor named Frank—a decent-enough guy whose only fault is his crush on Olivia—on the way to Kyle’s cabin, and the eight of us have been playing Never Have I Ever as the rain softly pitter-patters against the roof and the glow of a camp lantern casts a dim light. Much cozier than the naked bulbs overhead and perfect to hide flushed cheeks and sheepish smiles as the questions quickly turn more risqué.

"It's your turn," Avery prompts Ashley.

"Aren't we done yet?" Ashley whines, falling back into the bunk across from me.

If she's irritated about Eric messing around with the beautiful redhead, she doesn't show it anymore. "*Fine*. Never have I ever . . ." Ashley's nose pinches with thought, "experienced love at first sight."

Colin groans. "Seriously?"

Kyle looks over his shoulder at me, smiles, and then takes a shot.

I follow suit, cringing at the taste of black licorice. I sense Avery's curious eyes on us. I know it's wrong and petty and unnecessary, but I feel somehow victorious, that I have achieved something that she—even with her allure and beauty—could not.

I won Kyle's heart this summer.

"My turn," Eric warns with an impish smile, filling our plastic shot glasses for the next round. "Never have I ever rubbed one off while fantasizing about someone in this room." He tips his head back and downs a shot. Frank and Colin follow almost immediately.

Giggles erupt around the cabin, but slowly, hesitantly, everyone else takes a shot. Kyle casts another knowing glance my way, his eyes hooded and slightly red, as he downs his.

"Okay!" Eric tips the bottle upside down to drain the last of the Jäger. The emptied bottle of vodka has rolled under one of the beds. "Well, that didn't last long. Last question. Never have I ever—"

"Hey, it's my turn!" Colin scowls.

"We brought the booze, we get the last question. You assholes are buying next weekend, by the way. Never have I ever gone skinny-dipping with my fellow Wawa camp counselors!"

They all let out a cheer and down their shots.

"Really?" I whisper, the only one left with a drink.

Kyle gives me a crooked smile. "It was fun."

"So much fun," Eric climbs to his feet, stumbling a step, and then claps his hands, "that it's now tradition!"

A surge of adrenaline courses through the cabin. Everyone fumbles for support as they climb to their feet and then dart out the door, engulfed in a bubble of laughter and excitement.

I let out a nervous laugh. "They're actually going skinny-dipping? *Now?* In the rain?"

"It's barely raining and they're going to get wet anyway." Kyle gets to his feet and holds out a hand.

My stomach flutters.

"Trust me?"

"Of course." I hesitate. And then I weave my fingers through his.

• • •

The light rain is a mere drizzle by the time we reach Wawa's sandy beach, to the sound of laughter and splashes. We couldn't be more than a minute behind everyone else, and yet most of them have already peeled off their clothes and darted into the lake. I catch glimpses of movement from two shadows nearby, but without the glow of a fire it's impossible to identify anyone.

"Oh my—ow!" I stumble a few steps over something—a shoe, I think—and then laugh. "It's dark out here!" And I'm way drunker than I thought.

"That's the idea. No one wants to see Eric's bare ass." Kyle lets go of my hand and I sense him yanking his T-shirt over his head. "Come on, don't be lame," he taunts, the jangle of his belt and the pull of his zipper sounding. "It's tradition."

Taking a deep breath—what the hell! Everyone else is doing it!—I quickly strip off my clothes and follow Kyle's lead into the lake, feeling every inch of bare skin that enters the water as we plunge farther in.

"Where is everyone?" Colin calls out from the distance.

"Over here!" Kyle answers, and I feel his voice deep within my belly as he curls an arm around my waist.

One by one, voices call out, followed by nervous giggles and squeals as people splash and dive.

"Vetter, where you at?" Kyle calls out.

There's no response.

"Vetter?"

Still no response.

I sense the tension creeping into Kyle's body. "Eric, come on."

"Yeah! All good," Eric finally answers.

Kyle's body relaxes against mine. "Is Ash with you?"

"Oh, Freckles is here all right." And there's no mistaking the grin in his voice.

Ashley's giggle follows.

"He's grown some balls. *Finally*." Kyle pulls me flush against him.

My hands skitter over his body as if unsure where to sit idle. I want to touch *all* of him. And maybe it's the alcohol, but a second after I think of sliding my hand down his stomach, and farther, I do it, gripping onto him.

The responding kiss is searing. He reaches down to guide my legs around his hips, shifting so I'm sitting on his thighs, facing him. It's a provocative position. All it would take is me shifting a few more inches forward. "We're not doing that out here!" I warn him in a whispered kiss.

"But we'll be doing it as soon as we're back to

my cabin." He laughs, pulling me tighter, until I can feel him pressed against me. So close . . . an ache swells inside me, the urge to slide him into me overwhelming, even if for just a moment. Maybe we *could* do it out here. What would that be like? No one would know and I'm sure it wouldn't be the first time.

I have had *way* too much to drink.

"Shh! Someone's coming!" Avery hisses suddenly.

We freeze and stifle our giggles, turning to watch a beam of light bob up and down, lighting a path for a lone figure heading toward the beach.

Darian's short blonde hair is unmistakable as she passes beneath the path light. "Is someone out there?" she calls out.

"Shit," someone whispers.

"Shut up," someone else warns.

Kyle cuts noiselessly through the water, moving us deeper just as the beam of light dances over the lake. Others must have done the same, because no one is outed in her search.

She shifts her flashlight to the sandy beach, and the scattered clothing.

"If she finds out we were drinking, we'll be gone tomorrow," Kyle whispers into my ear.

My stomach clenches with the thought. Tonight has been fun, but it's not worth that. Why do we keep getting ourselves into these messes?

Oh, right. Because of Eric and Kyle.

"Huh. Gosh . . . I guess my camp counselors must have forgotten their clothes on the beach when they were swimming here earlier," Darian says loudly. "I guess I'll just bring all of it up and leave it at the pavilion, so they can come and find it tomorrow at breakfast!"

"She wouldn't," I whisper.

Darian bends down and begins collecting everything.

"It's a good thing all my counselors are already asleep in their beds and getting well rested for tomorrow," she goes on, and there's no doubt she is fully aware that we're all out here, watching her.

Has she figured out that we're all *naked?*

My guess would be yes. "We have no clothes to get back to your cabin, Kyle," I whisper.

"None of us do." He sighs. "But at least it doesn't look like she's going to wait for us."

True enough, the flashlight is moving back in the direction it came from. When Darian passes beneath the overhead light, we catch a glimpse of the heap of clothing in her arms. She's left us nothing but our shoes.

Whispers and hisses erupt as we watch her disappear into the distance, heading back for her cabin.

"She's evil!" Olivia declares with a nervous laugh. "What are we going to do?"

"Isn't it obvious?" Eric cuts through the water

with force, not far from us, heading toward the shore. "We're going streaking!"

I gasp. "He wouldn't."

"He *will,*" Kyle counters.

Eric's bare feet slap against the wet sand as he exits the lake. Without a flashlight, there's nothing to see, not until the overhead light catches him stumbling across the path, highlighting his lean body and bare white ass. Several whistles and catcalls sound, followed by laughter.

"Is he insane? If Darian catches him, he's gone!"

"Trust me, Darian is going to hide in her cabin all night to avoid the chance of seeing a naked Eric running across the lawn." Kyle chuckles. "He's a nut case when he's drunk, in case you haven't noticed."

"I'm noticing." I giggle, picturing him doing laps around the cabins. Someone's going to get an eyeful.

"You're shivering," Kyle notes, pulling me closer to him. "Do you want to get out?"

"No!"

He begins moving us toward the beach. "Let's get this over with."

I take a deep breath as nervous flutters erupt in my stomach. "Are we actually doing this?" Both the boys' and girls' cabins are a good five-minute walk in either direction, beneath pathway lights. Five minutes, dressed and sober, that is. Drunk and naked . . . this is going to be a disaster.

"We don't have a choice. She's not bringing our clothes back."

"Maybe we should wait?"

"You want to do this with Colin and Frank?"

"Good point." I've been crouching for as long as possible. Now I stand. The cold air hits my bare, wet skin.

"Ready?"

"No!"

Kyle grabs my hand. "Come on!" We leave the lake and dart up the path. I hold my breath as we run beneath the impossible-to-avoid floodlight and a round of whistles and catcalls sounds out from behind us. "Oh my God!" I giggle, but I'm less bothered by the fact that five other counselors have now seen my bare ass than I expected to be. Probably because I'm drunk.

We run hand-in-hand, my free arm held across my breasts, adrenaline coursing through my veins. Getting to the boys' cabins takes less time than I expected, my breaths ragged as we do our best to avoid all the lights, my eyes scanning the cabin doors and windows to make sure no one's watching.

Thankfully, we make it into Kyle's cabin without a humiliating run-in with any unsuspecting counselors.

"Holy shit." Kyle pushes the door shut, his

chest heaving with exertion. "I'm fucking cold."

Now that we're inside and safe, my teeth begin to chatter wildly and my entire body shakes.

"Here." He grabs his towel and quickly dries me off. "Get under the covers."

I scramble to get into his sleeping bag, shivering violently as I watch him towel-dry himself with frenzied hands. He dives into the sleeping bag in another minute, wrapping his arms around me and pulling me close to him, chest-to-chest. Our ragged breaths and sporadic giggles are the only sound in the cabin for what seems like forever, until our bodies begin to warm and calm, and the fact that Kyle is naked and pressed against me finally moves to the forefront of my thoughts.

"That was fun," I admit. "Even the running-through-the-camp-naked part."

He chuckles. "We won't forget this night anytime soon."

"I won't forget *anything* about this summer anytime soon." I press a kiss against his lips.

"We'll have to do it again next summer. Darian just upped the stakes on the skinny-dipping tradition to include streaking."

"Right." *Next summer*. I try in vain to push aside the dread that comes with talk of next year. It's so far away.

"You warm enough now?" he whispers, his mouth finding my throat.

I let out a soft moan of yes.

"Good." His lips begin moving downward—along my collarbone and over my breasts, pausing to suck on a nipple, the cool metal of his lip ring tickling me. "I need to undo this." He pulls down the zipper on the sleeping bag, opening it up so he can shift freely. He keeps moving downward, his mouth trailing softly against my skin, the nervous flutters in my stomach growing.

He pauses at my belly button, and I giggle as his tongue dips into the center, as his eyes lock on mine.

And then Kyle's shifting farther down.

To let me experience another of so many firsts.

Chapter 23

NOW

I'm absorbed in monthly financial reports when knuckles rap twice against my glass door. I look up, expecting my dad.

When I meet Kyle's golden eyes, I can't help the wide grin that erupts.

"Good morning, Miss Calloway," he says in his calm, professional tone. He holds up a small rectangular box. "You have a package."

I lean back in my chair, taking in the sight of his hard body in that uniform. I watched him dress for work from the comfort of my warm bed at five thirty A.M.—as I have all week. It's become routine—we part with a kiss and then I study the clock all day, counting down the hours until we're home and we can be just Piper and Kyle again.

"Mark just stepped out to grab coffees."

Kyle strolls in casually, coming around to my side of the desk, to set the box down. It bears my brother's store label. "I know. I saw him and Renée leave."

"You could have given this to him to bring on his way back."

"I could have. I wanted to see you, though."

"Really." I can't help but stare at the way he's standing so close to me, his belt buckle and those fitted pants at eye level, the strain behind the zipper taunting. My body begins to stir. I tip my head up to find him peering down at me with heated eyes.

And, I'll admit, as much as I can't wait to be Piper and Kyle at home, playing senior VP and the security guard in the office garners a high level of thrill.

"Busy?" he asks.

"Always."

His eyes flip to the numbers on my screen. "That looks . . . *enthralling.*" The boredom in his voice says otherwise.

I sigh. "This part isn't, exactly. But what all these numbers and plans and meetings turn into at the end is . . . spectacular." Skyscrapers and condo buildings, homes and jobs for thousands. A mark on an entire city.

He eyes me strangely.

"What?"

"You work a lot."

"Yeah. I know."

He bites his lip. "Your ex paid me a visit today."

"What did he say?" I ask warily. It's been four days since David found out about Kyle and me, and he has been oddly subdued. He's made no mention to me about it. He's walked past Kyle without acknowledging him. All in all, he's been very un-David-like, and it's beginning to worry me. "He didn't say anything. He just stood there and stared at me."

"*Stared* at you."

"For ten or twelve seconds, until Gus stepped in and asked if he was okay. And then he left."

I roll my eyes. "I'll see what's going on in that child's brain of his."

Kyle nods slowly. "Are you going to be late again tonight?"

"Probably. I'm sorry. Things are nuts right now."

"Okay. Just let me know when you think you'll be home and I'll come down."

A forty-five minute transit commute home, only to head back down two hours later? I sigh. "Why don't you just bring a bunch of clothes with you so you don't have to keep going back and forth after work? You can use the building's gym. I'll give you a key."

His eyebrows spike. "You'll give me a *key?*"

Unease settles in my spine. "Is it too soon?"

He hesitates. His long eyelashes bat as he blinks. "I don't know. Is it?"

"I don't know," I admit, reaching forward to drag my nail along his thigh. "All I know is that I love being with you every night." There has been no question or hesitation so far. Kyle finishes his shift at six and goes home to work out and change. He's back downtown by the time I'm home from work. It's only been a few days and yet the very idea of Kyle *not* staying a night, of us not waking up with our naked limbs tangled together, makes my chest tighten.

"Same." His voice is husky.

"Okay. So . . . maybe we shouldn't worry about moving too fast or too slow. Maybe we should just do whatever feels right." Because, though it has only been a few days, Kyle and me have been years in the making.

His lips twist into a smile. "I'll bring a few days' worth of clothes with me tonight."

My heart skips a beat. "Good."

His eyes graze my lips. "It's *killing* me not to kiss you right now."

The tension in my office is escalating quickly. For once, I'm glad I'm in a fishbowl. If this were my father's office, we'd likely be on my desk by now.

"Think about it all day and save it for tonight."

His jaw tenses and I chuckle, reaching for my envelope opener, to run it through the sleek brown kraft-paper packaging. "What could Rhett have sent me now, I wonder. *Oh,* also . . . before I forget, I was asked to pass along this message." I pause my unwrapping to reach for my phone and find the text from Christa to read aloud: "If your boy toy is going to be wandering around the kitchen in the middle of the night, can you ask him to put on some clothes. Thanks."

"I had clothes on!"

I give him a look.

He shrugs. "I'll put on track pants next time."

"Thank you." I pick up the note that sits on top of the wrapped gift. *A housewarming gift.* I pull back the tissue paper. And gasp. "I totally forgot about this!" Inside the box I find a picture of my parents, Rhett, and me, on the bow of my father's old yacht. I'm around ten, with bangs and a blue ribbon pulled through my hair. Rhett looks like the token prep school student who he used to be. Dad and Mom stand arm-in-arm. We're all wearing crisp white-and-navy-blue outfits, and grinning.

The frame itself is made of old bicycle chains. Another of Rhett's creations, no doubt.

I set the frame on my desk and smile at it. "Look how happy we were." I sigh. "So long ago now."

"Do you miss having that?"

"Honestly? I forget what it's like . . . But both of my parents are happy with other people, so I guess I should be thankful for that, right?"

Kyle nods, his eyes on the picture but his gaze far off.

"Do you ever miss your family?"

"I miss certain moments with my mom, yeah," he admits after a moment. "It took officially cutting them off to really feel it." He smiles sadly. "Holidays are weird."

I smooth a hand over his hip. "Well, you and

Jeremy are welcome to come out to Martha's Vineyard to watch my aunt Jackie get bombed and let me kick your ass at Monopoly."

"Sounds like fun." His fingers entwine with mine. "Just one kiss and then I'm gone?"

I tsk. "You're still that same little boy stealing kisses, aren't you?"

The crooked smirk he gives me sends my blood racing. "Do I *look* like that same little boy?"

"No. You do not." And yet he's still my Kyle.

I'm about to agree to a kiss when Renée breezes in, announcing, "Grande double macchiato!" in that impossibly charming Southern twang.

Kyle steps back, breaking our touch a split second before she looks up.

"Oh! I'm so sorry. The coatrack blocked you." She cringes. "I should have knocked. That's a bad habit of mine. Mark had to stop on the third floor, so he asked me to deliver."

"It's fine, Renée. Security just came to drop off a package for me."

"And now I'd better keep doing my rounds." He clears his throat. "Miss Calloway." He strolls out, nodding once to Renée.

Her eyes trail him with interest as she watches him go. "So what's his story?"

"What do you mean?"

"I mean, is he single? Is he a nice guy? 'Cause *dang* . . . He's somethin' to behold every morning on my way in."

He's mine.

Clearly she didn't notice Kyle pulling away, and didn't sense the tension crackling in my office. It's not that my office isn't electrified by it. But I'd bet money she would never assume that a woman in my position would be with a man in his.

I force a smile. "He has a girlfriend."

"Is it serious? Like, how long have they been together? Weeks, months . . ."

"Years." *Thirteen years. With a lot of missed time to catch up on.*

"Well, doesn't that sound sweet." Her words are in stark contrast with the way her shoulders sink with disappointment. "Guess I'd better get my nose away from *that* scent, then."

I smile at her choice of words. I'm not surprised Mark is infatuated with her. Renée would be hard *not* to like. "How's working with David going so far?"

"Oh." She waves a manicured hand. "He's a dream." She laughs at my raised eyebrows.

"Between you and me, after what Mark told me, I was expecting a lot worse. Of course, he's a giant man-baby, but he just wants to be taken care of. Lucky for him, I like taking care of needy people."

"Well, then, you are a stronger woman than me, because I have no patience for that man," I murmur, savoring the first sip of caffeine.

"I just have different aspirations, is all. Look at you! You're gonna be runnin' the world soon. You don't have time for that sort of thing. But me . . . I've had my wedding dress design since I was seven. I've already got my three kids' names picked out and the color of their nursery and I *can't wait* to join the PTA. It's my jam." She shrugs. "This is just a job for me. A great job, don't get me wrong! But the part I like most about it is taking care of someone and making his life easier." She pauses and then her eyes widen. "Oh my Lord, it sounds like I'm trying to marry my boss and have his babies, doesn't it?"

I burst out laughing. "It sounds like you know who you are and what will make you happy. I'm impressed." Even if it doesn't look anything like my life plan. To be honest, I don't have names or nursery colors picked. I have "children" penciled in for my thirties—mid to late thirties, the way it's looking now—but that's as far as I've gotten. David and I had talked about starting a family, but it was always more in passing, like, "Sure, we'll have one, eventually, when it works for us." We were both more focused on the Calloway world—the only real thing we had in common.

I have no idea if Kyle wants children, I realize. The topic never came up at Wawa beyond talk of condoms and birth control to avoid having them. We were too young then.

But now, I've jumped off another cliff to be

with him and I have no idea what I've landed in. I'm ready to hand him a key, but what kind of life does Kyle see for himself? He's already making comments about how much I work. What if he wants a Renée?

I will never be a Renée.

"You okay, Piper?" She watches me carefully. "You literally just went from laughing to dead silent, like *that*." She snaps her fingers.

"I'm fine."

She hesitates. "Do you miss being with David?"

"No. Not at all. I was never meant to be with him." I toy with the paper wrapping from the package. It's foolish, but I can almost feel Kyle's hands on it.

Speak of the devil . . . David pops his head into my office then. "Renée, I need you now."

"And *I* need *you* now," I demand.

"I don't have time—"

"Two minutes."

"She sounds like her father," he mutters, handing Renée a folder. "Meet me in my office."

Renée marches out, her calf muscles bulging from her high heels.

"What is it?" David asks, and he has the nerve to sound annoyed.

"What was that stunt earlier today in the lobby?" I ask calmly.

"What stunt?"

I glare at him.

"Oh, so he ran up here and cried to you? What kind of man are you with?"

"David!" I snap. "What were you trying to do?"

He begins pacing around my office, his hands on his hips. "I know I was joking around about it because it was funny at first. Shocking. It didn't really hit me until after I got home and replayed what you said, and how you said it." He stops in front of my desk. "You're in love with this guy, aren't you?"

I purse my lips.

That's answer enough for him.

"Fuck . . ." David sighs heavily. "I guess, I don't know. In the back of my mind I thought you'd be so focused on taking over for your dad that you wouldn't have time to date, and then eventually you'd wake up and realize I'm the guy for you and we'd get back together. I did *not* see this coming. The last few days have been . . . weird for me." He frowns as if replaying them in his head. "I almost told Kieran everything on the green today."

"You *what?*" I hiss, my body going rigid, the urge to run for the lobby, to protect Kyle from what's about to come, overwhelming.

He holds his hands in the air. "I didn't. I wanted to, but I didn't."

I sink with relief into my chair.

"So I want you to know that I'm *not* okay with this, and I'm probably going to be a dick every once in a while because I'm not okay with it." He frowns. "But I won't tell Kieran. I don't want him to do something that would hurt you."

My annoyance with David softens. Words like that don't come easily for a man as self-absorbed as he is. "Thank you for the warning. But please don't harass Kyle. It'll make people talk." Thank God Gus is already aware of our relationship.

"I was just letting him know that if he hurts you, he'll have to deal with me."

Kyle and David are the same size, but something tells me Kyle would win that fight. I bite my cheek to keep the laughter at bay. "You're still an idiot. But that might be the most considerate thing you've ever said to me."

His lips twist as his gaze drifts across the way. "Maybe I should start screwing the help, too."

And . . . he's back.

"I think that's a great idea. She already has your children's names picked out."

"What?" Panic flashes across his face.

"I'm kidding. Now go away so I can work."

Except now my focus is splintered between pie graphs and babies.

"Hello?" I holler, kicking the door shut and slipping off my shoes. I'm exhausted, it's a quarter to ten, and I told Kyle I'd be home two hours ago. The kitchen and living room are empty. He's not in our bedroom, either, I note with dismay.

I'm just about to call his phone when I catch movement on the patio.

I smile. Kyle, Ashley, and Christa are standing beneath a canopy of lights strung from every corner.

"There you are," I murmur, wandering out to wrap my arms around his waist from behind. His cotton T-shirt is soft against my skin. "I'm so sorry I'm late."

His fingers graze mine. "That's okay. Ash put me to work as soon as I got here."

"It looks great." Outdoor furniture, surrounded by gauzy curtains and tall palms, fills the formerly empty patio.

"See, Christa? Piper thinks it looks great," Ashley says, in a way that tells me Christa's had a few criticisms.

"We need to move that end over by a foot," Christa directs, pointing to a far corner, waving the staple gun toward Kyle.

He shifts in my arms and leans down to kiss me. "Your dinner is probably cold by now."

"I know. I'll heat it up in a bit. I need to talk to you first." I hook my finger through his belt loop and tug, leading him inside and down the hallway, all the way into my bedroom.

He smirks. "So, is talking code for—"

"Do you want to have kids?" I blurt out.

Kyle's mouth drops open. "Uh . . ." He pushes my door closed behind us. "Eventually."

"How many?"

He hesitates, frowning. "What's going on, Piper? Where is this coming from?"

I sigh. "Renée."

"Renée knows about us, too?"

"No. We were talking about life and she started talking about her three kids—"

"She has three kids? Wow. You'd never guess."

"No! But she knows she wants them. She's got their names and nursery colors picked out, and everything!"

His eyebrows arch. "Renée sounds a little bit intense."

I let go of his belt loop and begin pacing around my room. "I know. But she made me realize that here we are, falling deep and fast into this relationship. I'm ready to hand you a key after not even a week together, but I don't really know you!" Worries that have been simmering all day bubble to the surface now, and I can't keep the panic from my voice.

"Yes, you do, Piper."

"I don't, though. Not anymore. I'm not talking about the little things, like your favorite color or your favorite song, or that you broke your arm when you were six, or that you love jumping off cliffs." All the small, seemingly important Kyle-facts that I collected over that summer. "I'm talking about the *big* things."

He slides his hands into his pockets. "You know about my family. I don't tell *anyone* about them, Piper."

"Yeah, but it's not even that. I'm talking about the things that will make or break a relationship. Things you don't talk about when you're sixteen and skinny-dipping and racing around in golf carts. And I am terrified that once we start finding out all those things about each other, what if we don't work at all?" What if my mother is right?

Kyle sighs heavily. "Okay." He reaches for the door.

My anxiety flares. "Where are you going?"

"Relax. I'll be back in a minute. Just . . . get changed."

I watch him stroll out the door, wondering if unloading on him like that was the best way to approach this conversation. It's too late now.

By the time I've washed up and pulled on my lounging clothes, Kyle is shifting furniture around the little seating area. I catch the smell of warmed Mexican food and my stomach growls in response.

"Hang out over here with me for a while," he beckons.

Not until I reach the armchair do I see the tattered blue sleeping bag spread out on the ground, the woven flannel interior faded. *No way* . . . "That's not the same one from camp."

"The one and only." He smiles and drops down on his knees on one side. "Don't worry, it's been washed." He holds a hand out for me.

"Who knew you were so nostalgic?"

He peers up at me, sincerity shining in his beautiful eyes. "*You* knew."

I scan the leather band around his wrist, the tattoo engulfing his arm. "Yeah, you're right." I did know that. I settle down next to him, accepting the plate and one of two glasses of red wine. "You drink wine now?"

He chuckles. "Eat, before it gets cold again."

I marvel at the softness of the worn flannel under my bare feet as I take a mouthful of Spanish rice and chew slowly.

"Yes, I would like to have kids." Kyle swallows. "Eventually."

"How many?"

"I figured I'd start with one and see how that goes. Well, unless I end up with twins right off the bat." He eyes me warily. "Do you have twins in your family?"

I shake my head.

"Me neither. So . . . one to start. Then maybe a second, so I can pit them against each other. It'll be fun, I promise."

"You wouldn't do that. Well, maybe you would." I laugh, but I don't miss the underlying message there—he's talking about *us* having kids. Together.

My heart skips a beat. Maybe I'm not crazy to have these thoughts sitting heavily in my mind so soon.

He hesitates. "What about you? Do you want kids?"

"I think so. Eventually. I just don't know how I'm going to fit them into my life."

I get a soft smile in return. "That's because you don't fit kids into your life, Piper. You fit your life around them."

"How, though?" I push my food around on my plate with my fork. "How do I fit building a twenty-five-story condominium complex around soccer practice and school bake sales?"

"I don't know. A supportive spouse? A nanny? Good employees?"

"Like Tripp?"

Kyle shakes his head but chuckles. "I want to knock his teeth out every time I see him. You need to get rid of him now."

I groan. "I'm still waiting on that damn report from the phone company, and who knows if that'll give me anything. I don't want to talk about Tripp right now, though. But my dad . . . I think of how hard he's worked all his life and how hard I work now, and I just don't see how I can manage kids. As it is, *I* feel like a kid playing dress-up at an adult party most days. Like I don't belong in this world." I've never admitted that to anyone. I've always been afraid that someone will agree with me, that saying the words out loud will make them true.

"Security guards hear and see a lot more than people give them credit for." Kyle leans back against one of the armchairs. "Do you know what I see when I'm in that building?"

"Old men staring at my ass?"

"Yeah, not gonna lie—I want to punch a lot of your employees out." We share a laugh and then Kyle's expression turns serious. "But it doesn't happen as often as you think. More than that, I see people sitting up straight when you enter a room; I see their eyes glued to you when you speak. When I hear your name floating around, it's said with respect." He smirks. "Sometimes with a bit of fear." He pushes a strand of hair off my face. "And I see a woman who has *I don't even want to know how much* money to burn, busting her ass all day and coming home exhausted at night to the penthouse condo that she's welcomed her camp friends to live in rent-free, and having conversations about kids with new assistants, and stopping to greet the old security guard at the front desk when everyone else is too busy to look up. Do you know how happy that makes Gus?"

"I've known him all my life, is all."

"No, it's because you're still *you.* You're still the same kind, generous, down-to-earth girl from

Wawa who cares about people no matter where they fit. Hell, you could be sailing around in a yacht, or drinking fucking lattes in a courtyard in Paris or whatever it is you rich people do, and yet here you are, working hard doing something that's important to you, trying to please your father, with bags under your eyes, eating takeout on a Friday night."

"You saying I look like hell?" I tease, cutting off a sliver of the chicken enchilada.

"No, I'm saying I know *you*. I might not know everything you want in life, and everything that's happened to you over the past thirteen years, but you're still the same person in here." His hand settles on my chest, over my heart. "The rest . . . we can figure out along the way."

I nod, the confidence in his words a balm to my earlier panic. Panic that arose, I realize, because I want this—us—to work out so badly.

"So . . ." Kyle's hand falls away. "We both want kids eventually. Sounds like we're okay on that front."

I smile, feeling foolish for how I ambushed him with the topic. Though he doesn't seem at all perturbed. "Sounds like it."

He taps my plate, prompting me to eat. "What else are you worried about?"

"I don't even know. Is there, like, a checklist we should go through? I mean . . . Religious beliefs?" I throw out.

"Love is love." He presses a hand to his chest. "Tom and Doyle forever."

I laugh, recalling the shy and secretive counselors. "Politics?"

"I did not vote for *him*."

"Same. Uh . . ." Worry laced my mood all day, but now that I'm here, talking to Kyle, I realize that I have nothing to worry about. He's right. I know Kyle. "All-inclusive beach resort or tours? Which would you prefer?"

He frowns. "Really? That's a relationship deal breaker?"

"It is if you expect to drag me around smelly, hot cities on all-day bus tours with strangers as a vacation."

Kyle's head falls back onto the chair, the jut of his throat looking especially delicious at that angle. "Well then, I'm gonna go out on a limb and say option A. What else is there? Come on, ask. We've got all night."

"All weekend."

His head flops to the side. "I get you all weekend?"

"If you're good."

I get a cocky grin in return, his eyes alight with mischief. "When have I ever not been?"

"We're recommending that we go with KDZ for the Marquee," Serge says as the last slide of the thirty-minute PowerPoint pops up on the screen, stating exactly that. "The financials are competitive, KDZ's timeline works better with ours, and their record with condo conversions may be short, but it's solid." Three other heads bob along with him.

After combing through and analyzing both construction proposals, the Marquee's project development team of experts is giving their official stamp of approval.

And it's not for the one I want.

I grit my teeth, feeling my father's heavy gaze settle on me.

"Good work, guys. I agree wholeheartedly. Thank you." Tripp smiles and nods, dismissing them.

Serge and the team quietly file out, to give the executive team a chance to discuss this decision.

Tripp adjusts his tie and flashes a smug smile my way before turning to my father. "Kieran, are we *finally* ready to lock on this and move forward?"

My father sizes up the screen ahead, his eyes narrow and calculating. I can practically hear his thoughts. KDZ is the proposal to go with. If not for Tripp and what Kyle told me, I would be leaning toward them, too. Not that Jameson hasn't come in strong. But it's as if KDZ prepared their proposal while sitting inside the walls of Calloway, hitting all our pressure points.

They probably did. From inside the walls of

Tripp's office. Hell, Tripp might have written this proposal himself.

I know my father. He's weighing all this against a "rumor" that Tripp is taking a kickback, while I haven't found any solid proof yet because the phone company is taking their sweet time delivering what I asked for. Maybe he's deciding if he even cares, because at the end of the day, the contract is good for business.

But I just can't stomach letting Tripp win.

"Piper? What are your thoughts?"

My father catches me off guard. That he would defer to me in a meeting is a step forward. For once, though, I wish he'd leave me the hell out of the decision. "I think KDZ looks good on paper and we can come to a decision within a few days."

Tripp throws his hands up in the air. "In case you've forgotten, Piper, we're behind schedule."

"Oh, I haven't forgotten," I snap back. *You're the smug bastard who put us there.*

"I agree with Piper," David chimes in. "We have the recommendation. Let's review, discuss offline, and make a decision by tomorrow." He throws me a wink.

As much as David irritates me, I could kiss him right now.

"Oh, are you two back on again? Is that what this is?" Tripp mutters under his breath, just loud enough that a few hear.

"Piper, come with me." My dad gives a curt nod and, not wasting another second, collects his notebook and phone, and stands.

I guess the meeting is over.

I feel like puking as I fall into step next to him and we walk side-by-side along executive lane, to the end.

"Who's your source?" Dad demands to know the second his office door closes behind him.

"Someone who overheard Tripp's conversation."

"Piper . . ." His hands are on his hips, his jaw taut. "You'd better start talking, because otherwise I'm going to give the green light to KDZ. We have *no* reason not to."

Dammit. I squeeze my eyes shut.

A knock sounds on the door.

"Not now!" my dad barks, but David steps in.

"I don't mean to interrupt—"

"Yes, you do," Dad snaps. "What is it?"

David smirks, but then his expression turns serious. "I ran into John Deveaux on the green over the weekend and he asked me what I thought of Tripp. You know . . . what he brings to the table."

It takes a moment for what David is hinting at to click. "Tripp is putting out feelers." To one of our biggest competitors, too.

My dad's lips purse together in thought. "Deveaux lost his VP of Development. He's looking for a replacement."

"How long have they been in talks?" My mind works over the pieces. What's Tripp's play here? That we agree to going with KDZ, he pockets his cut on the deal, and then bolts? Not that I wouldn't be relieved if he left, but this might explain why he's so adamant that we sign now.

"My guess is, if John is approaching you, they're about to make an offer," my father mutters. "What'd you tell him?"

"The truth. That Tripp has built one hell of a network of connections but he's past his prime, and Kieran, I agree with Piper. He's up to something."

My dad throws his hands in the air. "So you've told David, too."

"Yes, I have, because I know David has Calloway's best interest at heart. And you said so yourself—I need to surround myself with people I trust."

Dad frowns. "What's going on here? Is Tripp right? Is this back on?" He waves a hand between us.

"No," I say.

"And has my daughter divulged this super-secret source to you?" Dad peers at David through steely eyes.

David takes a deep breath and my stomach drops. *One crisis at a time, please*. I'm not ready for the Kyle confrontation. "Give her some more time to find out if this kickback rumor is true. Don't you think it's timely that Tripp's looking elsewhere?"

"Of course he's looking elsewhere. Wouldn't you be, with the way he and Piper have been carrying on?" Dad shakes his head. "Get me something by tomorrow night or we're going ahead with KDZ. Both of you, get the hell out of here now."

David slides out of my dad's office on my heels. "Have I told you how much I love having my ass chewed out by your father?" he hisses.

I exhale loudly. "Thank you for backing me."

"You need to consider that your blue-collar playboy may be wrong."

"He's not wrong," I insist, even as that cloud of doubt swells. *What if Kyle* is *wrong?*

"Then prove it and fast, because I just went out on a limb for you and I have no fucking idea why." He storms into his office.

Mark and Renée share a wide-eyed glance and then Mark is on his feet. "Do you need something?"

"No." I breeze past him but then stop abruptly, my mind spinning. "Yes. I need to know exactly how much Calloway has spent with this damn phone company, when our contract is up for renewal, and what the penalty is for breaking it tomorrow." Because I am not above all-out threats to get what I want.

• • •

I walk through the door at nine that night to the sound of Christa's lecturing tone. "He shouldn't have tried stealing third base."

"But that's what he's known for," Kyle retorts.

"Exactly why he *shouldn't* have done it!"

I round the corner to find the two of them on the couch. Christa's already in her pajamas, Kyle's still wearing his gym clothes, and, unbelievably, Elton is perched on Kyle's chest, his deep rumbling purr carrying across the room.

"The Red Sox lost," Kyle announces, stroking the cat's back. "Christa thinks it's my fault."

"I didn't say that," she retorts, clearly missing his teasing tone.

Despite my hellish day, the sight of the two of them sitting together brings a smile.

And coming home to Kyle here . . . this place is actually beginning to feel like home.

A home that is taking shape, I realize, as my eyes wander the space—to the colorful landscape artwork covering the walls, to the Edgewood Made table and white leather chairs filling the dining area. Ashley and Marcelle have been busy.

I scan the kitchen. "Where's Ash?"

"Out to dinner. With *Chad*." Christa gives me a knowing—and unimpressed—look.

"No . . ." I moan, wandering over to fall onto the couch next to Kyle.

"Why is this bad again?" he asks.

"Because he's an idiot and she's too good for him, but he's come to beg for her forgiveness for being an idiot and she'll take him back because she's settling." I could win a fortune betting on the outcome of this.

"Right. Got it. So Ash needs to meet someone else." Kyle bites his lip. "You should introduce her to Mark."

"Mark's in love with Renée."

"Good luck. Renée's gonna be banging David within six months."

I laugh. "I don't know about that."

"I do," he says with that cocky confidence.

"I can't believe I'm saying this, but what about Eric?" Christa throws in. "She always had a thing for him. Is he still single?"

"Yeah, as far as I know." Kyle's brow furrows. And then he's chuckling as Elton burrows his nose into his ear. "This feels really weird."

"Do you two want some time alone?" I tease.

"I can't help it if he likes me more than you."

"He likes your drying sweat, is all," Christa mutters, tossing the TV remote onto the coffee table with a clatter.

"Ow!" Kyle hisses as Elton suddenly leaps off him and over the back of the couch, to tear across the penthouse. He stops by the French doors and spins around to attack the tip of his tail. "You did that on purpose, didn't you?" Kyle accuses, lifting his shirt to inspect the long, red scratch marks across his ripples of muscle, which are much more defined after being worked at the gym.

"And on that note . . ." Christa makes a point of rolling her eyes as she averts them, but I don't miss the hint of pink in her cheeks before she stands and strolls toward her room.

"You up for a game in Boston if I get tickets?" Kyle calls out.

"As long as you're not coming."

"She's definitely warming up to me," Kyle mock-whispers.

"Make him get off our furniture and take a shower!" she shouts back, disappearing down the hall.

"Have I told you how much *I* love having you here?" I murmur.

He lets his T-shirt fall and takes my hand, pressing a kiss against the back of it. "What happened today?"

I sink into him with a groan—the smell of his clean sweat is intoxicating—and tell him about KDZ and my father's ultimatum.

"Still no luck with those phone records?"

"No, and I spent twenty minutes promising their president that I'd pull our five-million-dollar-a-year contract with them if I don't have what I need in my hand by tonight."

Kyle checks his watch. "It's still technically tonight."

I sigh. "Do you think . . . is there any way that what you heard was wrong?"

"No."

"But, what if—"

"This isn't two truths and a lie, Piper. If there's one thing I'm good at, it's picking up on shady shit." His gaze drifts to the TV, though I can tell he's not watching the sports highlights. "God knows I've had enough experience with it."

"It's too bad Gus wasn't there with you."

"Right. Someone people would respect," he mutters, and I don't miss the hint of bitterness in his tone.

"Kyle, no one looks at you and sees what your dad and brothers did. No one but you." Thousands of miles and years later, and he still can't seem to shake his low opinion of himself. I smooth my hand over his stomach. "*I* respect you."

He gives my hand a squeeze, and then pulls himself off the couch. "I'm gonna take a shower."

I watch him wander down the hall to my bedroom, waiting for him to pause, to turn back, to suggest I join him.

But he doesn't.

Settling into bed with a glass of wine while I wait for Kyle to finish his shower, I open up my laptop and check my email. *Re: Phone Records. Confidential*.

My heart begins to race as I see the subject line in my in-box.

"Please, give me a smoking gun . . ." *Please give me something that will prove Kyle's instincts were right, and that Tripp is a thieving liar.*

There are several attachments. I click on the first one and begin scrolling.

And smile with wicked satisfaction, even as my anger boils.

Kyle has just stepped out of the shower when I storm into the bathroom, a white towel wrapped around his lower half, his hair damp, his chest glistening.

"Get dressed."

He frowns. "Why?"

My adrenaline is racing. "They just sent me Tripp's phone records and you were right. *Of course* you were right." An odd sense of pride swells inside me, knowing that. "We're going to show my father what Tripp has been up to."

Kyle's eyebrows arch. *"We?"*

"Yes. *We.* You are the reason Tripp isn't getting away with this bullshit. We would have signed with KDZ otherwise and that dickhead would be laughing right now." All the way to John Deveaux, half a million dollars richer. Who knows—maybe working with this Hank Kavanaugh could have been advantageous, but I want nothing to do with his business tactics.

"I don't need to take any credit for that, Piper."

Kyle shakes his head. "You go ahead, seriously. I'll be here to celebrate with you when you get back."

"No! You're coming with me. I can't hide us anymore. I don't want to. This isn't summer camp and I'm not sixteen years old. I need to get this all out in the open, confront my father about what he did, and move on with you, whether he accepts it or not."

Kyle's gaze wanders the corners of the bathroom ceiling, his forehead etched with worry.

"Look, I know this isn't going to make our lives easier in the short term. He's going to be difficult." A hint of dread weaves its way through the impending victory over Tripp. *Difficult* may be an understatement. It'll likely end up in a fight and a few carefully launched threats from both sides. But what my father did was wrong, and I'll make sure he's aware. "We need to do this, Kyle. So we can move forward."

Kyle takes a deep breath. "Okay, Piper." He sighs heavily. "You want this all out in the open. So let's get it all out in the open."

I can't help but catch the sorrow in his voice.

Chapter 24

THEN

2006, Camp Wawa, End of Week Seven

"I dare you . . ." Kyle pauses to take a long drag from his cigarette, his gaze on the last bit of daylight as we lie sprawled out in the alcove at the bottom of the cliff. Our place. It's cool and cast in shadow now, after a hot, sun-filled afternoon. "I'm tired of playing this game."

I peer up at him, my head resting against his stomach. "You want to go back to your cabin?"

His head tilts downward to meet my gaze. "Do you?"

Yes, I mouth. *Right now.*

I get a lazy, suggestive smile in return as Kyle's eyes drift over my bikini-clad body.

"Well, *I* want to go. I'm getting cold," Ashley whines, wrapping her arms around herself and exaggerating a shiver.

"You need another one of these, then." Eric holds up a shot of tequila. We hit Provisions early and then came out here to drink and swim under the sun. Hours and too many shots later, the very idea of climbing this rocky hill and walking home is exhausting.

Ashley pushes his hand away with a groan. "No more. I'm going to puke."

"Fine." He lifts the shot glass to his mouth.

"Haven't dared you yet!" Kyle objects, waving an arm haphazardly in the air.

"Fine. I dare me to kiss Freckles." Eric dives down to plant his mouth on hers, spilling half his tequila over the rocks in the process.

"That doesn't count, jackass," Kyle mutters, but he's grinning, as am I, because Ashley hasn't pushed him away. "Finally," he murmurs, his stomach muscles tensing as he sits up, his hand gripping my head as I slide downward. "Let's get this over with. I'm getting cold, too."

We collect the empty bottles.

"Man, we drank *a lot,*" Kyle murmurs, chuckling and stumbling a touch. "Thanks, Piper, for bankrolling all this."

"Whatever." I didn't even think; I just handed my card to him. I also filled his car up with gas and picked up our burger tab. It felt good to do that.

It takes three times as long to climb the rocky hill. Ashley and I are on our hands and knees, laughing, by the time we reach the top. "I just want to sleep now," I moan, inspecting the scratches on my palms from the thorny branches and rocks. I'm going to feel them tomorrow.

Eric stumbles over to the edge of the cliff. "I can't believe we only have one week left here."

"Careful . . . You're drunk," Ashley warns. "I don't want you falling off."

Eric turns to grin at her. "Aw, you finally admitting that you care about me?"

"No." She giggles, her cheeks flushing.

And then Eric leaps over the edge, his "Yahoo!" following all the way down to a splash.

"Shit!" Kyle rushes to the edge, stepping carefully as he peers over. "You crazy asshole!" he bellows.

"Jump!" Eric coaxes from below.

Ashley and I both sigh with relief. "So I can climb back up that hill? Hell no."

"Lame!" comes the response.

"Remember, you're a shitty swimmer. Just get back up here." Kyle backs away from the edge, stumbling a touch. "This is going to take a while." He more falls than sits on the boulder. "I drank too much."

"We all drank too much." I hunker down next to him. Ashley falls into him on the other side. We lean against one another while we wait.

"I think I'm going to pass out," Ashley moans. "Or puke. One of the two. Or maybe both."

"Hurry up, Vetter!" Kyle hollers.

Silence answers.

"Eric?"

Nothing.

"Fuck . . ." Kyle stumbles to his feet and heads for the rocky pathway down. "Hey! Eric!"

"I'm coming . . . I'm coming . . ." comes the answer between ragged breaths. "This was a *really* bad idea, wasn't it?"

Kyle laughs. "Yeah, you're full of bad ideas, asshole." He watches with his arms folded over his chest, as his drunken best friend scales the treacherous path.

It's another few moments before we spot Eric's curly blond hair crest.

"Ugh. Finally. Can we go now?" Ashley pulls herself to her feet.

"Good things come to those who wait, Freckles." Eric stands and grins, his arms outstretched, his chest heaving with his exertion.

He sways backward and stumbles to catch his balance.

And then he's gone.

"Eric!" Kyle yells, scrambling for him.

"Kyle!" I choke out. Ashley and I rush toward the top of the path in time to see Eric tumbling head over heels, over and over, bouncing off the rocks. Kyle tries in vain to catch up, skidding and sliding down the path while somehow managing to stay on his feet.

Eric comes to a stop in a sprawled heap at the rocks on the bottom. Even in the dimming light and with my impaired vision, I can see his leg is bent all wrong. Crimson seeps out all over his skin.

He lets out a bloodcurdling scream.

"Eric!" Ashley cries out, looking ready to run for him, tears pouring from her eyes.

"No! Ash!" I grab her arm. I think I'm going to throw up.

Kyle is halfway down the hill, his eyes wild with panic as they flit between his friend on the rocks and us.

"What do we do, Kyle?" I cry.

"Uh . . . Okay. Go and get Darian *now*. Tell her Eric fell and we need an ambulance. Tell her where we are."

I nod, grabbing Ashley's arm.

I run as fast as I can.

Darian's face is carved with worry as she marches toward us, the air ambulance climbing higher in the sky, two state troopers in conversation nearby, six counselors including Christa lingering near the trees, their expressions filled with horror and shock.

"Is he going to be okay?" Ashley manages through her sobs.

"Well, his leg and arm are definitely broken. That's all we know right now. I'm sure it helped, having *all that alcohol* coursing through his veins," Darian says.

I avert my gaze to my feet to avoid her glare. Regret weighs down on me. *God, we are so stupid.*

"What were you guys thinking, going out

there?" she admonishes. "How much did you drink?"

I steal a glance to my left, to Kyle. His jaw tenses.

What will happen to him if the police find out that he used his brother's ID to buy the booze?

"I *know* you've all been drinking. I can smell it on you. And there's a pile of empty bottles lying here. Where did you get the alcohol? In town? Who bought it for you?"

Kyle bought it, but I paid for it all, on my credit card. There's a record of it, and now Eric is badly hurt and there are cops hovering. What will happen to me?

I swallow my rising fear. "I'd like to call my father." As much as I dread that conversation, if there's a way out of this, he'll know it. Plus, he's going to find out anyway. About this, about Kyle . . .

Darian sighs. "That's a very good idea, Piper. Let's call all your parents. And you can pack your things while you wait for them to come and get you."

"Is that him?" Kyle murmurs, his fingers laced within mine as we sit beside each other at a picnic table under the pavilion, watching headlights approach up Wawa's long, winding road at one A.M.

"Yeah, I think so," I manage to say around the painful lump in my throat. The belongings I arrived with are packed and sitting on the ground next to my feet.

"Mine should be here soon," Ashley murmurs, her voice missing that usual spark.

Kyle's mom said she's not coming, that Kyle can drive himself home. Darian insisted that would be first thing tomorrow morning, when the alcohol has left his system.

I'm sober now. I think I've been sober since the state troopers questioned me about how Eric fell. Once they were convinced it was a drunken accident and not foul play, they lined us up and berated us for a half hour about how stupid and irresponsible we are, how no parent would want their child left in our care at this camp, and then handed us all our fines for underage drinking and left.

Dread takes hold of my insides and squeezes tight as the SUV comes to a stop beside the old green Pinto. I'm not sure which is worse—facing my father or saying goodbye to Kyle.

My father doesn't wait for Eddie to open the door. He slides out from the backseat and, adjusting the collar of his button-down shirt, marches across the dimly lit lawn toward us, his face as stony as I've ever seen it, even from all the way over here.

Darian intercepts him on the way. I'm sure she's filling him in on exactly why I've been fired. And whatever he's saying to her, well . . .

Darian seems to shrink back as my father speaks, looming over her tiny frame.

"Piper!" he bellows.

I climb to my feet and sway, not because of alcohol. "I guess this is it, then." My voice cracks.

A sob escapes Ashley's throat as she throws her arms around me.

My own eyes begin to water as I return the embrace.

"I had so much fun with you this summer."

"Up until tonight."

We share a weak laugh, though there's nothing amusing about any of this.

"Keep in touch, okay?" she whispers.

"Of course." Oddly enough, it's the same thing Christa said when she thrust a piece of paper into my hand on my way out of our cabin, her email address scrawled across it in her perfect bubbly penmanship. Then she hugged me. I was shocked, to say the least.

Kyle is on his feet, my duffel bag in his hand.

I fight the tears but they win, streaming down my cheeks. After seeing Kyle every day for almost an entire summer, this is goodbye. For now. "You'll call me, right?"

"Yes." He reaches up to wipe a tear away with the pad of his thumb.

"I'm so sorry." Not only has he lost his job, but that fine will eat into his savings.

He sighs. "What are you sorry about? This isn't your fault."

"Yeah, but . . . I'm still sorry."

"Piper!" my dad calls again. He begins marching back toward the parking lot, expecting me to follow.

"Come on, I'll walk you." Kyle takes a step forward.

I hesitate. "*There?* To him?"

He shrugs. "What's he going to do, hit me?"

I grab my sleeping bag and pillow, and together we trudge across the front lawn. How long ago it seems now, that early summer day when Mom dropped me off here, reluctant and bitter.

Now I would do *anything* to stay. Anything to see Eric running around—naked or otherwise. Anything to be curled up in bed next to Kyle right now, where I should be.

Why did we have to be so stupid?

Darian is waiting for us where she met my father. Her face is drawn and tight. "Piper, can I talk to you for a minute?" she asks. "Alone?"

Kyle unloads my sleeping bag from my arms and continues on, my anxiety rising with each step that he takes toward the SUV.

Darian hands me an envelope. "This covers your pay up until this morning."

"Thanks." My gaze falls to my running shoes. "I'm sorry."

She sighs heavily. "No . . . *I'm* sorry. Kyle and

Eric were always a handful. I was naïve enough to think I could handle them. I shouldn't have allowed them back this year. Or I should have gotten rid of them after the first incident. If I had, Eric wouldn't be lying in a hospital room."

As much as I wish the same for Eric, I'm glad she let them come back—I can't imagine not knowing Kyle, not having these memories—but I don't voice that.

"Is he going to be okay?"

"I haven't talked to his parents yet. They're still on their way from Erie. It's quite a drive. But he was conscious, which is a good sign." Her eyes drift over to the parking lot. "Your father. He's a tough one, isn't he?"

"Especially when he's angry." And he is facing off with Kyle now. *Oh God*. "I should go—"

"I'm not *that much* older than you guys. I remember what it was like to be young and in love. You can't think of anything else. Nothing else matters. It's all-consuming." She smiles sadly. "And it feels like a part of you dies when you've lost it, a part you'll never get back. But you will."

I frown, wondering what she's getting at. I haven't lost Kyle. Sure, we'll be three hours away from each other, but we'll make it work.

I'll make it work.

"I really wish this had gone a different way, Piper. I'm . . . very disappointed. You are a good counselor. I would have liked to have seen you here again next year."

"I would have liked to have come."

"I hope, if nothing else, you've learned from this." She hesitates, but then wraps her arms around me. "Take care of yourself. And make better choices. That could have been you tumbling down those rocks."

With that, I rush toward Kyle and my father. By the time I reach them, Kyle's face is ghostly white and pained.

"Let's go," my dad commands. "It'll be almost four A.M. by the time we get home."

"I need a few minutes—"

"Piper."

"Just a few minutes!" My voice cracks as I bark back, setting my jaw with defiance, though I tack on a "Please."

His lips are a thin line. "I'll take those." He holds his hands out, staring intently at Kyle.

Kyle hands him my things, which he promptly passes to Eddie.

"You have two minutes to say goodbye." He climbs into the SUV.

I grasp Kyle's hands. "What did he say to you?"

"Nothing I haven't heard before." Kyle smiles, but I know it's forced.

"Here." I reach into my back pocket and pull out the stack of paychecks. "I signed all of them over to you."

He's already shaking his head. "No, I can't—"

"Take it! Please. I don't need it and you just lost a week of pay. Plus, this way you can afford to call me and come visit."

His jaw clenches as he gently pushes my hand away. "I *can't,* Piper. Thank you, though."

This is it. I throw my arms around Kyle's neck, my eyes watering again, panic seizing my insides. "I don't want to leave you," I whisper.

His arms tighten around my waist, squeezing me.

I pull away, just enough to press my lips against his, ever conscious of my father's gaze from the backseat.

Kyle hesitates at first, but then he's the one deepening the kiss.

"I love you so much," I whisper against his mouth, crying now.

He blinks away a sheen in his own eyes. "I love you, too, Piper. *Always*. Remember that."

"You'll call me tomorrow, as soon as you get home?"

His jaw grows taut and he swallows, his gaze flittering to the dark window, to the unseen face looming behind.

"Yeah. Here." He slips off the leather bracelet from his wrist. "To remind you of me."

"As if I could ever forget you." I laugh through my tears. I search my body, coming up empty. "I wish I had something to give you."

"I don't need anything." He smiles sadly and taps his temple. "It's all up here."

With one last kiss, he breaks free and begins walking away, his head hanging low.

Not until I'm seated and we're rolling down the driveway, my thumb rubbing back and forth over the grain of the leather, do I get the eerie sense that that felt like a final goodbye.

I'm staring at the plate in front of me—at the massacred slice of toast, shredded to pieces, none of them eaten—when my father swoops into the kitchen, his navy suit looking fresh and crisp, coffee mug in hand. It's Monday morning, at eleven. He should have been at work four hours ago.

"Your mother is on her way back from Paris. She'll be home in a few hours," he announces. It's the first thing he's said to me since the drive home from Wawa, early yesterday morning. After he told me I can forget about my car for a year, as well as my credit card.

"Did she sound upset that she and Aunt Jackie had to end their vacation early?"

"Is *that* who she told you she's with?" Dad's jaw tightens. "No. She and . . . *Aunt Jackie* know it's time they came home." His voice is dripping with bitterness.

"Have you been able to find out anything about Eric?" I ask, pleading in my voice. Ashley and I have been texting back and forth, but there's no news between the two of us. I emailed Christa yesterday, to see if she'd heard. Being lead counselor, she has more access to the office computer than any other counselors there. Plus, she's the only email address I have besides the Camp Wawa administrative in-box that I used for employment paperwork.

She has no news on him, either.

So, I asked my father yesterday if he could find something out. He always has his ways. He didn't acknowledge my request with anything more than a glare.

Dad chugs the rest of his coffee and then sets the porcelain mug on the counter. "The boy's leg and arm are badly broken and he hit his head a few times, but they're saying he'll pull through."

I breathe a sigh of relief. "Thank you." I hesitate. "I'm sorry for lying to you."

His jaw tenses. "I'm sorry, too, Piper. But I will always do what I know is best for you. Remember that." With that, he's gone.

Leaving me to stare at my phone, the agony unbearable.

Kyle hasn't called.

Hasn't messaged, hasn't texted.

Christa said he left Wawa before anyone woke up on Sunday morning. And yet I haven't heard from him. I keep thinking something horrible happened on his drive home. But when I call his number, it rings on and on. His family doesn't know to call me, but, if something bad had happened, wouldn't a family member answer his phone?

The calls go through; it hasn't died yet, so it's being charged.

So why isn't he answering?

Why hasn't he called?

Chapter 25

NOW

"This is where your dad lives?" Kyle's gaze roams the Tudor-style house ahead as our cab pulls into the driveway. We're in a quiet gated community only fifteen minutes away from the downtown core and five minutes from my childhood home. Nothing's changed about this part of Lennox, which is graced with deep-rooted oak trees and ten-foot cedar hedges for fence lines and two-acre properties.

"Yeah, why?"

"I just expected something more . . . showy, I guess."

"That's not really my dad's style." Despite what he builds. The house is on the smaller size compared to the other houses in the neighborhood, but it has character and charm, landscaped with lush gardens and stone pathways marked by ornate lampposts. "We'll probably be fifteen or twenty minutes," I tell the cab driver.

"You got it, lady." The gruff, unshaven man settles back, leaving the meter running.

There's a silver Z3 parked in front of the garage. His flavor of the month must be here. *Great.* We'll have an audience for this.

As resolute as I was while standing in my bathroom, now I wonder whether this is a big mistake. If I should focus on dealing with Tripp and keep my personal affairs private for a few more weeks—or years—so I can enjoy Kyle without the looming presence of my father.

The fact is, though, there is a constant and growing knot in my stomach with the anticipation of confronting my father over Kyle, a festering dread that I'd rather face head-on.

I march for the front door. "Come on. Let's get this over with."

"Wait," Kyle calls out in a rush, just before my finger hits the doorbell. He squeezes his eyes shut. "There's something I haven't told you yet. About Eric. About what happened to him. About what *I* did." His jaw clenches.

And the hairs on the back of my neck prickle with unease.

"What do you—"

The front door flies open.

"Piper?" My dad frowns, his gaze skittering from me, to Kyle, and back to me. "I saw the taxi pull up. What are you doing here?"

"I . . . uh." I planned a mini-speech on the drive here but I'm thrown off for a moment. "The phone company sent me the records. I have proof. You wanted proof about Tripp, and I have it." I stumble over my words. *What was Kyle going to tell me?*

"This is not a good time," my dad mutters. His shirt collar is crooked, the top three buttons unfastened.

"I can see that."

What did Kyle do? What about Eric?

He cocks his head toward Kyle. "Who are you? You look familiar."

"I work in your building, sir," Kyle says stoically.

Dad's eyes narrow as they take in the sleeve of tattoos. "The security guard."

"Yes, sir."

But Dad's still frowning, deciphering Kyle and wearing that *I know you but I don't know how* expression.

I finally find my composure, handing over my phone to Dad. "I have deleted texts between Tripp and Hank Kavanaugh, with Tripp saying 500k is his asking price, and what would have to be in the proposal to look more appealing than Jameson's. And you know how Tripp said he'd been working this with KDZ for months? That's bullshit. Or partly. Because there are all these other texts from January through May that show Hank Kavanaugh wanted to buy that building but we beat him to it. He was looking to invest and convert it himself. He's old friends with Tripp, so he started pushing him to get us to sell. That's why Tripp was stalling. He figured he'd make the project look like a loser and then, when you'd had enough with the delays and decided to cut our losses, Tripp would come in with KDZ. Hank offered him a cut for that deal, initially. And then when that all fell through, Tripp offered up the construction deal for it instead."

"Jesus Christ." Shock fills Dad's face. "You have all that?"

"Yes, in phone texts. I wouldn't have thought to check, but Kyle suggested it. And he's also the one who overheard Tripp on the phone and told me about it."

"Wait a minute." Dad stares at the man standing next to me, and I watch the recognition finally take shape in his eyes. "*Kyle?* The boy from that camp?"

"He works security in *your* building?" a familiar voice exclaims from somewhere inside the house.

I frown. *"Mom?"*

Dad sighs, flinging the door open, and there she is, standing a few feet away. "You knew about this and you didn't tell me?" He glares at her with accusation.

It dawns on me. "*This* is who you're dating? You're dating *Dad?*" My head feels like it's going to explode. "But you two hate each other!"

Dad doesn't bother to explain, his steely gaze on Kyle. "What the hell is he doing here?"

I reach over and take Kyle's hand. "He came with me."

Dad's eyes flare. "You have got to be kidding me—"

My fingers squeeze tight. "I know what you did, Dad. I know that you paid Kyle to leave. I know that you threatened him if he didn't." My voice is rising with each syllable. We're still standing on the doorstep, giving the cab driver a show, but so be it. "You threatened an innocent seventeen-year-old, who was already traumatized by what happened to his friend that same night." It doesn't take much for me to think back and remember the look of fear and helplessness on Kyle's face as he stood halfway down that hill, peering at Eric's broken body below.

"Innocent seventeen-year-old boy?" My father nearly spits the words out.

"Kieran, calm down." My mother reaches for him, her hand smoothing over his arm with affection. It's a bizarre, foreign sight to behold and I'm sure it'll register in my mind later.

I sense Kyle stiffening beside me as Dad steps forward, my mother's attempts failing. "Did your *innocent* little *friend* tell you about the hundred grand that he extorted from me!"

"It wasn't like that," Kyle blurts out. "And it wasn't for me!"

I feel like someone just punched me in the stomach.

A hundred grand?

Extortion?

"What is he talking about?" My hand slips from Kyle's as I turn to face him, to see the guilt and pain in his eyes.

"It wasn't for me. It was for Eric," he says softly.

My stomach sinks.

"About six months after the *incident* at that camp, I got a phone call at work from *Kyle*"—my father spits his name out—"demanding a hundred thousand dollars—"

"It wasn't like that!" Kyle yells, and I startle. I don't think I've ever seen him lose his temper.

"How was it, then?" my father roars back. "What do you call trying to pin a brain-damaged boy's own stupidity on my daughter?"

"What?" A cold feeling seizes my insides. "*Brain-damaged boy?* You told me he was going to be okay!"

Dad squeezes his eyes shut, maybe to hide the guilt of his lie. Another lie.

It's Kyle who answers, his voice pained. "Eric's not okay, Piper. They thought he'd pull through at first, but then his brain swelled more and the doctors couldn't get a handle on it. His family didn't have much money. When all the medical bills and the air ambulance bill started piling on, they were going to lose their house. I gave them what I could, but I didn't have nearly enough." He's rambling through his words now, as if racing to get them out. "I figured out who your dad was. I knew he'd have the money. So I phoned him one day and I *asked* him to help Eric's family—"

"By reminding me that it was Piper who bought all the alcohol—"

"Because I knew she felt guilty! Just like *I* did! I knew she'd want you to help Eric if she knew how bad it was!"

"You think any of that would have happened if you hadn't been there? It's because of *you* that my daughter got into that mess! She has *nothing* to feel guilty for!" My dad grits his teeth, his face red. "And yet, when I told you to go to hell, *you* threatened to find Piper and tell her about our deal unless I sent more money. That is the very definition of extortion!"

Kyle bows his head. "Because I knew it was nothing to you and that you'd pay, just to keep me away from her."

"Says the son of a man who put six elderly people in the poorhouse," my dad throws back. "Robbing people of their money's in your blood. You can't help yourself."

Kyle flinches as if slapped.

Meanwhile, my knees wobble, feeling ready to buckle from my shock. That the two of them were in contact, that this was all going on behind my back. That neither of them told me about Eric.

That Kyle has been keeping this from me even

now. "I can't believe this is happening." My stomach churns as I look to my mother. "Did *you* know about this?"

She shakes her head, her expression dazed.

"I knew you would want to help Eric, Piper." Kyle pleads with his eyes. He reaches for me, but I step away.

"Why did you come to Lennox?"

"You know why."

"I thought I did, but now . . . Do you want more money? Is that it?"

His jaw tenses. "I told you, I don't want your money."

"You've told me *a lot* of things." But never the whole truth.

"Get the hell away from my daughter, before I call the police." My dad's voice is icy calm now.

Kyle's steady gaze stays on me. "Is that what you want, Piper?"

No, but I want what I can't seem to have. I harden my heart. "I think that would be best. Go ahead and take the taxi home. To *your* home."

Kyle squeezes his eyes shut a moment, his chest heaving with a deep sigh. When they open, they're full of pain.

A lump flares in my throat. "You should put in an immediate building transfer with Rikell," I manage to choke out.

"Don't you dare show up tomorr—"

"Dad!" I bark, throwing him a warning look.

"Talk to Gus, Kyle. I'm sure he can help make it happen swiftly."

I hold my breath as Kyle nods and slowly backs away. "For whatever it's worth . . . if you need my statement about Tripp Porter's phone conversation, Gus will know where to find me." He moves toward the taxi, his head down, his shoulders slouched. Looking . . . broken.

"Was all this really worth it?" I call out, my voice shaky. From the second he applied for a job in my building to the second I reached for my father's doorbell—and every second in between—he knew that once I found out about this, we would be done.

"To get even one more day with you?" He pauses at the open door of the cab and smiles sadly, those golden eyes the color of burnt caramel that entrapped me so many years ago settling on me now. "It was worth *everything* to me." Memory takes over and I see the mischievous, wild boy just about to get into his beat-up Pinto. Then that memory is gone and Kyle is climbing into the backseat of the taxi.

My tears stream freely as I watch the taillights disappear down the street.

"I'm going to phone Rikell and—"

"Oh, shut up, Kieran," my mother snaps, pulling me into her arms and leading me into the house.

• • •

"How satisfying is this for you?" Mark leans next to me against the glass wall to my office as we watch Tripp being escorted down executive lane by a tall, bald security guard, a box of trophies and trinkets and other personal belongings in his arms.

"Not as satisfying as I was expecting it to be, believe it or not." I let my father confront Tripp alone; he may have made my life hell, but it's my father he has truly betrayed.

Tripp didn't even bother to deny it, which made the question of legality around the search of his phone records a moot point.

"Do you think he's done it before?" Mark asks.

That's a million-dollar question. "Who knows. But Gary Jameson would never pay him." He has far too much integrity. And we almost burned that relationship because of Tripp.

"Piper, a minute." My dad, who was watching Tripp's walk of shame as well, heads back into his office.

Mark takes his leave. "Renée and I are going to grab lunch. You want me to bring you anything?"

"No. Thanks, though." I don't remember when I last ate. Late yesterday afternoon, I guess. Before my world imploded because of Kyle—again.

I stare at my father's office door a long moment, deciding if I want to answer his summons. After Kyle left my father's house last night, I fell apart on my mother's shoulder—crying harder than I have in thirteen years, since the first time Kyle broke my heart. My dad disappeared into another room and didn't come out again. I left as soon as I could gather my composure to call a cab.

I haven't spoken to my father since. I don't think I have it in me to do so now.

Not when I'm still this angry, and hurt.

Not when I feel this deceived.

Marching into my office, I shut down my computer, collect my purse and phone, and stroll out.

"Piper." I hear my name when I'm almost to the elevator. I ignore it and keep going, only turning back once I've pressed the button, long enough to see my father standing at his office door, to meet his steely gaze with my own, before I step inside and am gone.

"I called every listing for Vetter in Erie, Pennsylvania, but I couldn't find Eric or his family." Ashley slumps in the chair beside me on our newly decorated rooftop patio. I parked myself in the chaise longue eight hours ago upon my escape from the office and haven't moved, save for a trip to the bathroom. And, while my mood is more suited to hiding under blankets inside during a torrential downpour than lounging in a shady alcove of a rooftop patio on a hot summer's day, I'll admit I've found an odd sense of peace out here, listening to the faint and frequent horn blasts and ambulance sirens coming from King Street and beyond, and Elton's motor-like purr as he sits beside me, oddly content as I scratch behind his ears. If I didn't know better, I'd think he knew I needed comfort. And cared.

I reach over and squeeze Ashley's hand. "Don't worry. We'll find him." Even if I have to go to Kyle's condo and drag the address out of him myself.

"How could Kyle not tell us? I just don't understand!" Tears run down her cheeks. They're far from the first ones to escape since I broke the news about Eric to her last night. "How could we not have heard about it?"

I've been playing the same question over and over in my mind. "You know how it was back then. It was all Wawa, all the time, until you left and didn't see anyone for a year. Eric was all the way in Erie . . . and social media wasn't what it is today. I didn't even have a Facebook account until, like, a year later." And then it was all about keeping in touch with high school friends as I was heading off to college, and then adding college friends. Camp Wawa was a bittersweet memory by that point, one I was trying to move on from. Eric left and never came back, never reached out to anyone—not even Ashley; eventually he became that wild story about the guy who tumbled drunk down a steep hill at Wawa one summer but was okay the last anyone heard, a funny guy for people to remember fondly as everyone moved on with their lives.

A friend we lost track of.

"I found Avery online a few years ago," Ashley admits. "Mainly because I was hoping she had heard from Eric. It didn't sound like she knew what happened, either." She pauses. "Do you think Darian knew?"

"Probably. She *was* the camp director. But I doubt the owners wanted anyone talking about underage counselors drinking and getting seriously hurt. It's bad for business."

But Kyle knew. Every time a mention of Eric came up, he was ducking his head or frowning, or otherwise shifting the topic away from telling me the truth. Was it because he couldn't bring himself to tell me? Because he still felt guilty for his part in how badly things turned out that day for Eric? Or because he didn't want to admit that he'd tracked my father down and asked him for more money?

For Eric, though. Not for himself. If he were a true extortionist as my dad accused him of being, he likely would have been lining his pockets for the past thirteen years.

But why couldn't he have just told me all this from the start? It didn't have to go this way.

Now . . . I just feel sick about the whole thing.

"When your dad said Eric was going to be okay, I just believed it."

"Of course you did." So did I. And then I was too distraught over Kyle to worry about much else except putting Wawa behind me.

"And then he never answered my texts or emails and I just assumed he was being Eric. But I should have tried harder to find him. God, this is so messed up. I feel so guilty!" Ashley rubs her cheeks dry with her palms. "I need to know how bad it is."

"Me, too." My gut tells me it isn't good. I was too much in shock last night to push for details. I've reached for my phone a dozen times, to call Kyle—to demand information. But I find myself stalling each time, afraid I'll break down in tears at the sound of his voice.

And this kind of conversation . . . it can't happen via text.

The patio door opens and Christa walks out, her eyes wide.

Behind her is my father, as stern-faced as ever.

I sigh. I guess turning my phone off doesn't mean I get to avoid him for an entire day. At least I've required him to come to me.

"Hi, Mr. Calloway." Ashley forces a polite tone in greeting before leaving her seat to dart inside. She still addresses my parents formally, no matter how many times I've told her to stop.

"Marcelle has done a good job." His gaze roams the space.

I frown. "How did you . . . Oh, yeah." Mom no

doubt told him. That's a whole other conversation to be had, for another day. Thirteen years of hell—an ugly divorce, the fights, the tension, the emotional strain on me—only to find out my parents are secretly dating again.

I'm going to need a therapist after this.

Shrugging off his suit jacket and laying it tidily across the back of the chair Ashley just vacated, he takes a seat. He frowns at Elton, who, surprisingly, didn't bolt the minute Christa showed up. "Have you phoned Gary yet to let him know we'd like to proceed with the Marquee?"

"Yes," I answer curtly.

"And I assume he's happy?"

"Yes."

He sighs heavily. One-word answers drive him insane. "I received a delivery this afternoon."

"Okay . . ."

"From Kyle. Twenty-five thousand dollars cash, in a navy-blue duffel bag. Half of the money he accepted from me thirteen years ago."

I should feel anger, but all I feel is my heart aching at the sound of his name. "He was at our office? Today?" When I came in this morning, Gus informed me with big brown concerned eyes that Kyle would be taking a personal leave until a more suitable building placement could be found for him.

"I would think so. To the lobby, anyway. Gus hand-delivered the money to me. There was a letter with it, saying that he's trying to get a bank loan for the other half of the fifty."

"That'll take him forever to pay off." And he's been saving his money for so long.

"Perhaps." Dad's phone chirps in his pocket, but—shockingly—he doesn't reach for it.

"Why are you telling me this?"

Dad pauses, as if considering my question. "It surprised me. That he would bother paying it back. Some might call it a respectable act."

"Oh, so what are you saying? That you *like* Kyle now?"

"Far from that." Dad snorts. "Paying *me* back fifty grand to try to get back into your good graces that are worth a thousand times more would be a smart move, and he's not a stupid guy."

"And that's what you assume he's doing? That he can't possibly just be in love with me for me?" Maybe that's what hurts most about all this—the thought that Kyle has been manipulating me all along. That I bought everything he was selling to me like a love-struck fool.

Dad's eyes wander over the evening horizon—a sky painted with pale pinks and golden yellows and hints of mauve, the promise of another hot summer day tomorrow. "No, I'm quite certain that is not the case," he admits with reluctance, then sighs. "He was just a nervous boy, that day Greta put him through to my office line, when he was looking for money to help his friend's family. I could hear the shake in his voice." He smirks. "But the kid had guts, I'll give him that." The smirk falls off as quickly as it came. "And maybe I should have handled things differently. But I was shocked at first, that the little shit would have the balls to contact me. And angry. I assumed it was a shakedown. That's why I told him off instead of listening. And then, when he brought you into it, when he threatened to reach out to you if I didn't pay . . . well, I lost my temper. You were already going through enough, with the divorce. You seemed to be on the cusp of finally getting over that summer, going out with friends again. I didn't want him back in your life. I wanted that messy summer over with. That's why I agreed to help the Vetter family out, on the condition that he disappeared from our lives for good. And I didn't ever want to see him again." My dad's lips twist with disdain. "And then the bastard shows up on my doorstep holding your hand last night. Imagine my surprise over that. What a set of balls."

I sigh. "I didn't know about any of this."

"Because I didn't want you to. I didn't want that accident hanging over your head for the rest of your life, especially for a boy you worked with one summer, and I knew you'd feel responsible."

Aren't I, though? I supplied us—Eric—with *so* much alcohol that day. Far too much. Maybe I do deserve part of the blame for how badly he got hurt. A hollow ache fills my chest.

"So, you helped Eric, right?" There's a hint of a threat in my tone. If he didn't, I'll never forgive him.

"I did." He studies his wrinkled hands. "It seemed like a smart move to head off any problems, in case they figured out who you were and were desperate enough to try to sue us."

I roll my eyes. "How charitable of you." Would the Vetters do something like that? Likely not, but stranger things have happened in the court of law.

"Deny it all you want, but I've dealt with too many of those types of people in my life to try to pretend they don't exist. But the Vetters . . . they aren't like that, at all." A wry smile touches his lips. "His father reminded me of your mother's dad. He refused my money at first."

"How'd you get him to take it?"

"I went to his wife. At least she could see reason. They were going to go bankrupt, and then what good would they be to the boy once he got out of the hospital? So, I cleared their debt and helped renovate their house to accommodate him. Paid for a few other things."

"That sounds like more than a hundred grand."

"It was." His eyes narrow on the patio stones. "I can't tell you how many nights I've lain in bed, thinking that it could have been you tumbling down that hill."

I sigh. He's making it really difficult to stay angry with him. "How bad is it, Dad?"

Instead of answering, he reaches into his pocket to pull out a slip of paper. He hands it to me. It's an address in Pennsylvania. "I've made sure he has everything he needs over the years."

"Except his friends," I mutter bitterly. Does Eric wonder why Ashley and I haven't visited?

Will he even remember us?

I guess I'll find out soon enough. "I'm going to see him as soon as I can. Tomorrow, if I can catch a flight."

"Take the corporate jet. I won't be using it until late next week." Dad stands and, slipping his hands into his pockets, wanders over to the edge of the patio, to study the city below. This rooftop penthouse offers a sublime view. I was surprised that he didn't move in himself when it became available. "I'm retiring at the end of the year."

It takes me a moment to process his words, to make sure I heard them correctly. I couldn't have, could I? The formidable Kieran Calloway, talking about retirement? And in the next six months? Despite my anger with him, panic strikes me. "Are you sick?"

He chuckles. "No, quite the contrary. I haven't felt this good in a long time. It's something I've been giving a lot of thought to lately, since your mother and I reconnected a few months ago. I've worked hard all my life, and now it's time to be with her. To travel with her and eat meals with her. Do all the things she wanted me to do—begged me to do—for years but I couldn't make time for." He studies his bare left ring finger. "I don't want to screw this up again."

He *has* seemed happier, lighter, these past months. "I don't know what to say," I finally manage. "I guess I thought you'd stick around to see the Waterway through."

"I don't plan on dying anytime soon," he mutters wryly. "But that project is years from completion. And I know you can handle it."

Can I, though? Doubt creeps into my thoughts.

"If you think I've been especially harsh on you this year, it's because I was trying to make sure you'd be ready to fill my role." Dad's hard profile softens with his smile. "But I realized, the night of the gala, that you're ready. Or, as ready as anyone could be at this stage in the game. You'll figure the rest of it out with the help of your team."

My team. David, my ex-fiancé who I've come to value more now than ever before, and Mark, my proficient assistant, and the rest of the highly qualified people CG employs, short one lumpy, bitter body as of Tripp's forced resignation today. I've already been reviewing Serge's work history with us. He might be a suitable replacement and more-than-deserving of the promotion.

I may be failing in my personal life, but at least the professional side is on the rise.

And hearing that Dad has confidence in me makes my own confidence soar. Kyle was right—whether I'll admit to it or not, I will always look for my father's approval.

I guess the real question is, can I thrive without it?

"So, this thing with Mom is really serious, then." I can't hide the doubt from my voice. I've witnessed their hatred for each other for too many years to believe a reconciliation is possible.

"This *thing* with your mother has *always* been serious." He peers at me, curiously. "From the very first day I saw her."

Like it was for me with Kyle.

A lump swells in my throat.

Dad checks his watch. "I should be off now. I'm already late to meet your mother and Rhett for dinner."

Oh. In all the chaos of the past twenty-four hours, I forgot about my brother. "Does he know about you two yet?"

"They might be discussing it over cocktails at this very moment." Dad sighs heavily. "I'm not sure how he'll respond to this news."

I'm a huge stoner, remember? Stoners don't judge. I smother my smile over my brother's words. "You can start by telling him you're using his spoon phone holder."

“That ridiculous thing . . .” he mutters, his lips twisting in thought. “I guess it’s not the dumbest product I’ve ever seen.”

“Maybe leave that part out.”

Dad makes a sound that might be agreement as he wanders back to collect his suit jacket. He and Elton share a look of mutual displeasure. “I know you may not agree with how I handled things in the past, but you will understand it one day, when you’ve seen the kind of power our money yields, the ugliness and greed it brings out; when you have your own children and find yourself willing to do anything to protect them against the downfalls of our privilege. Maybe you’ll even find it in your heart to forgive me.” He moves for the patio door.

“But you married Mom, who had no money. And Rhett married Lawan, who *really* had no money,” I remind him. “And look how happy you all are.”

“Yes, but you’re my daughter.” He clears his suddenly hoarse voice as he pauses at the French door. “Your friend Kyle gave about half of that fifty thousand to the Vetters, before he reached out to me to help them. I plan on informing him that his debt to me is paid.”

I remember Kyle mentioning something about that last night. “Why would you do that?”

“Like I said . . . *some* might call it a respectable act.” With that he’s gone.

Leaving me to my heavy thoughts.

Chapter 26

NOW

The Vetter house is a simple brown brick two-story structure on a quiet country road outside of Erie, settled on about an acre of land. A separate garage sits off to the side, a riding lawn mower parked in front of it. Someone must have just used it on the front lawn—the air carries the smell of fresh-cut grass.

Ashley and I both inhale sharply as we take in the wooden wheelchair-accessible ramp that leads from the driveway to the wide front door. In the driveway is a gray van—the kind you use to transport people in wheelchairs.

“I guess that answers that question.” Christa is the only one who seems calm as she pulls up beside the van in our rental car.

When I called and spoke to Eric’s mom, Cindy, last night, to ask her if we could visit him, I didn’t push for details about Eric’s condition. I didn’t want to admit that we’d been kept in the dark by my father and Kyle. Ashley and I agreed that we’d find out when we got here and make sure our smiles stay firmly on our faces through it all, so as not to show him pity. Eric wasn’t the type of guy to look for pity.

But now that we're standing in the Vetter driveway, I'm not sure that was the smart move. Maybe we should have come better prepared.

A tall, thin woman with curly gray hair steps out to greet us. "Piper Calloway?" she calls out, absently rubbing her hands against her cotton shorts.

"Yes. That's me." I step forward, making my way up the ramp.

She meets me halfway, with a smile. One that transports me back to Camp Wawa thirteen years ago and makes my chest ache. Eric has his mother's smile.

After a round of greetings, she leads us inside the modestly decorated home, which smells of freshly brewed coffee and homemade fruit pie and, faintly, antiseptic. To the right of us is what I'm guessing used to be their dining room, but which now houses a hospital bed and a flat-screen TV, along with various medical equipment and a dresser covered in pill bottles.

My dread flares.

"I told him that you ladies were coming and he's been busy all morning, preparing. He's in the kitchen, waiting for you," Cindy says in an upbeat voice, leading us toward the back of the house.

Ashley and I share a glance and I know we're thinking the same thing—what exactly does "preparing" mean?

We step into the kitchen—a bright, sun-filled room of golden oak and yellow walls and clean white appliances—just as a man approaches us from the left, his hand toggling the small joystick that controls his motorized wheelchair.

Ashley does a poor job stifling her gasp.

I struggle to keep my smile firmly in place, as my eyes burn with the threat of tears.

And Christa . . . she can't help but avert her gaze a moment, as we take in Eric, his once tall, fit body now gaunt and huddled within the confines of his chair, his neck supported by a padded attachment, his face drawn, the muscles sagging. His face has changed shape entirely. He doesn't look like our Eric anymore. The only thing I do recognize is his blond curls, and even they are cut short.

One side of Eric's face pulls up and his lips struggle to take shape. Finally, he manages to get out a single word.

"Freckles."

Ashley bursts into tears.

"Eric was always my wild child. Getting into trouble, doing crazy things." Cindy slowly stirs her sugar, the metal spoon clanging against the delicate porcelain. I suspect she pulled out her best dishes for today's visit. It's far too hot to be drinking coffee out on the back deck, but when she suggested that Christa and I step outside and give Ashley and Eric some time to reconnect privately, we were more than happy for the escape.

"He was one of the campers' favorite counselors," Christa offers in response. And it's the truth. They all loved Eric and Kyle. The two of them together were unstoppable when it came to mischief, and kids love mischief.

"He loved that camp so much." She smiles. "His father went there when he was young, before his family moved to Erie. We decided to send him there on a whim, when he was, oh, eight or nine? He insisted on going back every year after that."

I don't know how to approach the topic, but I need to ask. "Kyle Miller told me that this happened because of a brain swell?"

Cindy nods and takes a deep breath, as if preparing to fall into a speech that she's told a thousand times already. "We were cautiously optimistic. He had no spinal injuries; his back wasn't broken. He was responsive . . . There was *a bit* of swelling in his brain, but nothing the doctors didn't think they couldn't manage. And then the swelling got worse. And worse, and they couldn't get a handle on it. For weeks, we weren't sure if he'd survive. He did, but he suffered extensive damage to his motor and speech skills. He has some memory loss, too." She smiles sadly. "And yet he remembers his time at camp like it was just yesterday. And all of you. Especially Ashley. He made me spritz him with cologne this morning and I'm pretty sure it was for her." Her laugh is soft and motherly, and it puts me at ease, even with the tense reunion. "He communicates mainly through his little keyboard and iPad screen. He's gotten pretty good at typing out words using his good hand. Ironically, that's the arm that was shattered in the fall."

Christa, who has been mostly quiet since seeing Eric, now asks, "What have the doctors said about his recovery?"

"With a lot of therapy and hard work on his part, we could still see some more progress. You know . . . movement in his arm, slightly clearer speech, that sort of thing. Small things." She smiles, but it seems forced. "My son is still with us, even if his body doesn't want to fully cooperate. That, I have to be thankful for. That and your father, Piper. He has been . . ." Cindy squeezes her eyes shut and when they open, they're glistening, "a lifesaver for us. Eric would not be nearly as comfortable as he is today. We wouldn't even be in this house. I don't know how we would have managed. I try my best to not take advantage of his generosity. I've already told him time and time again that we know who our son was, and that this was not *anyone*'s fault. Still, he has insisted on more than one occasion, and your father can be, shall I dare say, a difficult man?"

I laugh; meanwhile my chest swells with pride. "For once, it's for a good cause."

"Yes, well." Cindy dabs at the corners of her eyes. "I'm not going to lie—there are dark days, when Eric's spirits are especially low, when he gets frustrated and gives up on the work needed to improve. But we do our best to bring him out of it."

Could having Ashley and me around have helped keep Eric's spirits up, had we been given the opportunity?

My various feelings for my father are at such opposite ends of a spectrum—a pendulum swinging furiously between eternal anger and overwhelming gratitude.

The patio sliding door opens and Ashley steps out, her emerald-green eyes red-rimmed from crying. "Piper, Eric wants to talk to you."

I take a deep breath, steeling my nerve as I stand. "Have my seat," I offer her with an affectionate pat on her back. While Ashley may never have admitted how much she cared for Eric, there was never any doubt in my mind that she wanted more than just friendship. I can't imagine how hard this is for her now.

I step inside. The cool, air-conditioned temperature is soothing against my sticky skin.

"Piper . . ." Eric attempts to say as I close the

door behind me and take the seat next to his chair, still warm from Ashley occupying it.

It's hard for me to meet his eyes without succumbing to tears, but I grit my teeth and fight the urge to break down.

He drags his right arm in his lap to tap the iPad screen, which is sitting in a holder.

A page entitled "Piper" on the top appears, with lines that he's obviously prepared ahead of time.

Been streaking lately? Is the first one.

It's so unexpected, so Eric, I burst out in laughter, even as a few tears slip out. "No. Not since that night." I pause. "I'm so sorry I haven't been here to see you. I didn't know this had happened. I thought you were fine. I thought you had healed and moved on with your life—"

He makes a low, guttural sound, then scrolls down the list, his finger moving slowly to highlight line twenty-one.

I know that you didn't know. Kyle told me. He told me your dad didn't want you finding out. He told me about the money. He told me everything. I get it.

"Well, I still don't, and I'm *so* pissed at both of them."

He shifts his hand to a small keyboard and with painfully slow movements, types out, *Don't be mad at Kyle for asking your dad to help me.*

I frown. "That's not why I'm mad at Kyle. I would have demanded that my dad help you, and if he didn't, *I* would have. I'm mad at Kyle because . . . I don't even know why anymore. Because he didn't tell me all this, I guess." He had plenty of time. Plenty of chances, while tangled in my bedsheets with me, while pressing kisses against the back of my palm, while pretending everything was okay.

I wait patiently as Eric's fingers move over the keyboard once again.

He was afraid to, because he thought your dad would cut me off of more help if he went against him.

"Eric, Kyle took a *job* in my *building!* Did he really not think that I was going to find out about all this eventually?" My dad's right about one thing—Kyle is not stupid.

A strange half-moaning, half-grunting sound escapes Eric's mouth, and I realize that he's laughing.

I know. I dared him to, he types out.

My mouth drops. "What?"

I knew he was still in love with you, so I dared him.

My stomach tightens seeing that word. "But that's . . . He wouldn't risk pissing my dad off over a dare."

Wanna bet? Again, that strange half-moan, half-grunt. *I told him that if he didn't do it, I would email you myself and tell you everything. This way at least he might get a happy ending out of it.*

"There was definitely an ending," I mutter, and, when I catch Eric's curious eyes on me, I have to look away. I don't want him to feel guilty or responsible for that mess. He has enough going on.

Eric scrolls through his list, to highlight an item that makes me pause.

I want to go to Camp Wawa. You, Ashley, me, and Kyle.

A conflicting wave of eagerness and dread washes over me. "They shut it down. I don't know if they're going to sell it or what."

He taps on his screen harder.

I sigh. How can I say no? "Okay. I'll see what I can do." It means driving Eric six hours there, in his van, which means I had better make sure we can get on the property. Whatever . . . this is a challenge I can handle. Being there with Kyle, though, with all the emotions that are bound to rise up . . . I frown. "Why do you want to go back there so bad?"

He slowly types out, *I guess cliff-jumping is out?* and laughs.

"Kyle texted from town. They should be here by now," Ashley announces, smoothing her frizzy hair off her forehead.

My palms are sweating as I pull my mom's Z3—her latest car, which I had no idea she'd even purchased—past the open gate and into the familiar driveway. I'm not sure what I'm more nervous about: visiting Wawa again for the first time in thirteen years.

Or facing Kyle again.

We've arranged this trip mainly through email—Ashley and I emailing Eric, and him in turn emailing Kyle. I know Ashley and Eric have been messaging a lot over the past week, outside of planning for this trip. But Kyle and I haven't exchanged a single word. I figured whatever needed to get out in the open would happen today, here.

I'm just not sure I'm ready for it.

My eyes veer in every direction as the car crawls along the long, winding road, unsure of where to settle first. This feels like coming home after being away from it for . . . thirteen years.

"This is surreal," Ashley murmurs, plucking the words out of my head.

"Look." I nod toward the pavilion. The vibrantly colored picnic tables are all there, sitting empty, the scribbles from last year's campers still visible. The worn Camp Wawa paddles hang from the facing, though one has lost its anchor and dangles haphazardly. The grass around the property is long and unkempt; it likely hasn't been cut all summer.

That familiar buzz I remember—of life and laughter and excitement—is long gone, leaving nothing but an eerie silence.

“There they are.” Ashley points toward Eric’s gray van, parked in the lot. The back is open, and Eric is easing his chair down the ramp as his hired nurse for their twelve-hour round trip looks on. I know they were leaving before daylight broke this morning in order to get here by noon. They must be exhausted.

Kyle steps out from around the other side. My chest pangs at the sight of him, in a pair of black jeans and a pullover, to combat the unseasonably cool weather that blew in over the weekend.

I pull my car up next to them and ease out, avoiding Kyle’s gaze for the moment to focus on Eric, leaning in to place a kiss on his cheek. “Ready to go cliff-diving?” I whisper.

He laughs in response, and gives me a thumbs-up with his good hand.

“So when does the real estate agent get here?” Ashley asks.

“I told them we’d be here at one and it’s,” I check my phone, “noon now, so we have about an hour before we have to come back and pretend I’m interested in buying.” It didn’t take much digging to find out that the property is for sale, and it took even less time for them to agree to show it to me once I gave them my credentials.

Eric’s nurse takes that as her sign to climb into the van and shut the door behind her.

“Let’s go,” Eric says in his garbled speech, then shifts his joystick to round the curb and hop up onto the grass. He speeds away, Ashley jogging beside him, laughing. The oversized wheels on his motorized chair handle the uneven ground with ease.

"Who needs golf carts, right?" Kyle murmurs, coming up to stand beside me as I pull on my sweater.

His gaze is on our friends, allowing me to study his beautiful profile a moment.

I'm not angry with him, I realize.

I'm hurt. *So* hurt that he hid this from me.

But I miss him terribly, too.

"You should have told me everything, right from the start," I manage around the sudden lump in my throat. That's what bothers me out of all this.

"Your father didn't want you to know."

"He also didn't want you anywhere near me," I remind him with a glare.

His jaw tenses. "I wanted to tell you, but I was ashamed. And afraid."

I frown. "Afraid of what? That I wouldn't understand why you went to him?"

"That you'd finally realize that your father's right about me."

"Except that I know he's not right about you. He never has been. It's *you* who can't seem to believe it."

Kyle frowns at his shoes a moment before turning to study me, his gaze flittering over my features. "I'm an idiot, and I should have told you. But, if it's any consolation, you now know *everything* there is to know."

"Until the next time you can't find the nerve to tell me the whole truth."

He sighs, and then, nodding once, sets off toward Ashley and Eric, his head bowed.

Kyle gives the canteen door a tug, but it's locked.

Ashley smiles wistfully at the kitschy signs that still plaster the wall. "Remember how kids used to write secrets on the backs of these?" She reaches for the one that reads, "What Happens at Camp, Stays at Camp" and lifts it off the nail, to flip it over and show me several lines of handwriting on the underside. "Here's a good one: 'I kissed a girl and I liked it. Izzy D. 2012.' "

My mouth drops. "*Izzy?* I think she was my camper!" Though six years older in 2012.

Eric makes a sound, beckoning Ashley to him, to read the iPad over his shoulder as he slowly types.

"Check the 'Go Jump in the Lake' sign, he says."

Kyle trots over to the far end, to locate the square blue metal plaque. He unfastens the screw with his fingers and pulls the sign off. And grins, holding it up for us to read.

"Oh my God, 'Ashley Young has a nice rack'! Who wrote that!" Ashley squeals.

“Who do you think?” Kyle laughs.

“Eric!” Her cheeks flame.

One side of Eric’s mouth lifts in a smile as he types out something else.

She leans over to see what he’s writing. “Check the ‘Happy Campers Live Here’ sign.”

Kyle secures the blue sign again and begins moving away. “We should keep going, if we want to get to the beach before the agent gets here, right?”

Kyle clearly doesn’t want us to see what’s written there, which means I need to see it. I march over to the sign in question and lift it off its hook, flipping it over.

My heart stops. Of all the silly little messages and confessions scrawled on the backside, I recognize Kyle’s handwriting instantly.

I’m going to be madly in love with Piper Calloway for the rest of my life and I only just met her.

I can’t help but meet his steady gaze. He remembers what he wrote on there, all right.

“What does it say?” Ashley asks.

I clear my throat and read another message. “ ‘Eric Vetter touched my boob, Darlene, 2005.’ ”

Ashley rolls her eyes. “You always did have an obsession with that part of the female anatomy.”

Eric laughs, but I feel his gaze shifting between Kyle and me as I hang the sign back on the wall.

Clearly, he also remembers what Kyle wrote on there.

"Where to next, the beach?" Ashley asks.

"Yes," Eric struggles to say.

"Actually . . . I'll catch up with you guys. I have somewhere I need to go." Kyle begins backing away.

I know instantly where he's going. "You are not going there alone."

"Fine." He settles those beautiful golden eyes on me. "Come with me, then."

My heart begins to race. What will it be like to be back *there,* a place that holds both my best and worst memories?

It's probably a terrible idea, but all of my worst ideas seem to always be tied to this boy.

I manage a nod.

The walk past the girls' cabins—the bushes and grass around them overgrown, the exteriors needing paint—and up the dark, wooded path is silent, but not altogether uncomfortable as I quietly reminisce about the many weeks of girls huddling in groups and darting to their next activity, the colorful array of wet towels and bathing suits hanging on the lines. The friendships. I wonder how many of them outlived this place.

We reach the end of Wawa's property line. "Guess they learned their lesson," Kyle murmurs, eyeing the multiple "Trespassing Forbidden" signs that are at least three times the size of the old one, and the stretch of fence that's been erected across the path to cut off access to the cliff.

"How do we do this?"

"This way." He wanders into the woods on the left, to the edge of the fence. "Careful—there's poison ivy in here."

"I think I'll be okay." I peer down at my boots and jeans.

Kyle holds out his hand.

Despite my better judgment, I take it, silently reveling in the warmth and strength of his fingers. And when we round the fence through the woods and make it to the overgrown path on the other side, neither of us lets go.

Blood rushes through my ears the moment we push through the branches and step out onto the rocky cliff. Three more large yellow warning signs are posted strategically: "No Jumping," "Danger: Rocks Below," and another "Trespassing Forbidden" for good measure.

Kyle cringes as he reads them. "They've ruined the view."

"My memories have ruined the view," I mutter, eyeing the rocky path down to the alcove below warily, a hint of nausea stirring.

Kyle releases my hand and wanders over to the edge. The lake is quiet, no one on it save for a sailboat in the distance, nothing more than a white speck against the dark blue water. "Not all of your memories, though, right?" he asks quietly.

It's surreal, seeing him stand there with his back to me again. I've seen him in that exact position so many times—first in real life and then in my thoughts. First as the tall, slender seventeen-year-old boy who stole my heart, then as the one who broke it.

And now as the man who still holds my heart, despite everything.

I move to linger beside him and peer down over the water. It's daunting, even more so now. If I close my eyes, I can still imagine the tomato-red camp counselor T-shirt, still feel the hot sun beating down on me and the mixture of fear and thrill churning in my stomach, still hear my terrified shriek as I plummet through the air.

I can still see the boy I was crazy about from the moment I first saw him, waiting at the bottom for me, taunting me.

"My best memories of my life will always be here, with you," I admit. But is that where Kyle—where we—belong? In our memories?

"Would you still jump if I asked you to?" His voice is soft. "If I was down there, waiting."

"Yes. Probably," I whisper. "Except the climb back up feels like *so much* more work now, Kyle.

And *so much* more dangerous. It's the climb back up that I don't know if I can do again."

When I open my eyes, I find him staring at me, his gaze filled with a mixture of grief and resignation. "It feels *off,* being back here, doesn't it?"

I wrap my arms around my body, suddenly chilled. "It feels . . . sad." It doesn't help that the place is shut down, but even if it were buzzing with children's laughter, it wouldn't be *our* Wawa. It'll never be that again. "We'll never get those days back."

"No, we won't." He smiles sadly as he reaches into his back pocket and pulls out two Fun Dip packs. "For old times' sake?"

I can't help but laugh, and an unexpected wave of relief washes over me. "Yeah. Sure."

I let him take my hand again and he leads me over to the large, flat boulder where we used to sit and talk and kiss for hours. He settles down next to me and hands me the cherry flavor. "Here. You like this one better than I do."

We tear open the packages and set to work.

"I don't think I've ever seen you actually eat one of these properly," I muse, admiring the way he sucks the powder off the stick.

"This hot sixteen-year-old girl taught me how." He smiles, his eyes drifting down to my mouth, watching with intense interest.

"Remember the first time we kissed? It was up

here and I was eating one of these. You lied and told me you were allergic to cherry."

"Yeah, for someone who hates lying to you, I sure seem to do it a lot, don't I?" His gaze wanders out to the lake. "Two truths and a lie?"

"Why not."

"Okay." He shifts closer. "I knew I loved you since that day, sitting up here on the rocks, when you made me own up to our bet." Locking his fingers with mine, he goes on. "I have loved you every day since then." His golden eyes settle on me, and there's a slight sheen to them that makes my heart ache. "I still love you, even if you don't feel the same. Even if you never want to see me again." He swallows hard. "What's my lie, Piper?"

I release a shaky breath and manage to whisper, "That's a trick question," before pressing my lips against his with the slow, tantalizing ease that I remember of our very first kiss out here on this rock, so many years ago.

A kiss that could never be mistaken for goodbye.

Coming here now—with everything now out in the open—feels like the end of something tragically beautiful.

But it also feels like the beginning of something new. Something strong.

Maybe I'm a fool, maybe this is the point where Kyle and I are supposed to part ways and move on with our lives.

But I'm not ready to give up just yet.

"Promise me no more secrets, Kyle."

His body heaves with the sigh of a man who has just had a thousand-pound weight lifted from his chest. "I have *nothing* left to hide."

My phone chirps with an incoming text. I frown as I dig it out of my pocket. "They actually work out here now?"

Kyle points at the cell tower across the lake. Another mar on the peaceful vista.

"It's the real estate agent. He's in the parking lot, wondering where we are." I sigh. I could sit out here with Kyle all afternoon, reliving our stolen moments. But this place isn't for us anymore. It's time we move forward. Together. I slide my hand through his. "I guess we should get back."

"Yeah, I guess so," he murmurs, sounding equally reluctant. "But first . . ." He slips his fingers free of mine, kicks off his shoes, and begins peeling off his clothes, an impish grin on his face.

Epilogue

December

"Where did you find this caterer?" Christa asks, inspecting a piece of lettuce from her canapé with a frown. Whatever's about to come out of her mouth next will not be complimentary.

Ashley doesn't answer, cracking a bottle of champagne and scampering away to top off flutes, even though there are wait staff in tuxedos to do that. She knows that what Christa is actually annoyed at is the fact that Zelda, Ashley's psychic, not only showed up to our housewarming party, but she's perched on the couch—Eric next to her, in his chair—and offering free tarot card readings.

The party that Ashley's been trying so desperately to plan was delayed by a few months thanks to my chaotic work schedule. At some point, it morphed into a housewarming party slash holiday party slash retirement party for my father slash engagement party for my parents slash baby shower for Lawan, who is seven months pregnant. We now have seventy people milling around in evening wear, unsure of what to toast to first, and a violinist in the corner playing modern ballads.

"Seriously, my restaurant would have done a better job with the food," Christa mutters, holding a sizeable vegan meatball on a toothpick up as if inspecting it for hair.

"But then *you'd* have control over what food was being served." I gave Ashley carte blanche over the planning, though I'm footing the bill.

"Exactly."

I pluck the stick from her fingers and force the meatball into her mouth before she realizes what's happening. "Just be happy she finally kicked Chad to the curb for the last time." As expected, Chad tried to worm his way back into Ashley's heart. It was all the conversations with Eric, through his slow typing and struggle with words, that reminded Ashley that she deserves so much more than that chump.

Christa moans her agreement.

"Good food, right?"

She glowers at me, her mouth too full to respond immediately.

I take that as my opportunity to escape, leaving her to grumble to someone else.

I pause to take in the view across the room—of my parents standing arm-in-arm, laughing and smiling—and I shake my head in wonder. I don't remember them being like that at parties when we were growing up, but life looked so different from that angle.

What's more shocking is that my father is

having an actual conversation with Rhett, one where their jaws aren't tense and their postures aren't stiff.

Lawan, a petite woman with jet-black hair and large, dark eyes, stands next to my brother in an aqua-blue evening gown that accentuates her swollen belly, quietly watching the peaceful exchange with the same amount of amazement on her face as I feel.

According to my mom, my dad has been unwinding these past months, as he slowly learns to let go of Calloway Group and entrust it to me. That's not going to happen overnight, of course. "Retirement" to Kieran Calloway really means "semi-retirement," with a seat at big meetings as well as Monday morning calls to update him on the goings-on—mainly so he can lecture me on what I'm doing wrong.

A burst of deep laughter pulls my gaze to the left, where David and Renée are in deep conversation with Jim and his wife, Renée's hands gesticulating wildly while telling a story.

David, beaming down at her.

He pulled me aside last week to finally admit they've started dating. He was sheepish about it, afraid of my reaction, I'd hazard. David, being David, assumed I hadn't already picked up on it. But I saw it coming two months before, when his eyes would linger on her, when their closed-door meetings would last longer, when they started strolling into work together. It was one of the worst-kept secrets in CG history.

I'm happy for him, though it means facing the arduous task of shifting assistants around. Jill, Tripp's old assistant, has swapped desks with Renée, and David is none too happy about that. He'll adjust.

The person I've been most worried about in all of this is Mark, who has managed to keep his head in his job despite dragging his feet around since news broke around the office.

Though I've noticed him stealing frequent glances at Ashley tonight. I think I'll be making that introduction sooner rather than later.

But not right now . . .

I weave through the small crowd, making my way out to the patio, to the lone figure in a suit, leaning over the railing, taking in the city, his broad shoulders hunched slightly. The outdoor furniture has all been tucked away for the winter, but the canopy of lights remains and, with the dusting of snow that falls from the sky, it gives the space a magical feel.

The two glasses of champagne I just guzzled warm my body enough that I don't immediately feel the bite from the cold air against my bare skin. I chose a sleek black satin dress for tonight. By the glow in Kyle's eyes every time they touch me, I'd say I chose right.

"What are you doing out here all alone?"

"Enjoying the view." I hear the smile in his voice, his back still to me.

I sidle up behind him, sliding my arms around his waist. "Who are you hiding from?"

"Lawan."

I burst out laughing. My sister-in-law is a soft-spoken and kind woman who has likely never uttered a single harsh word about anyone. "What did he say now?" I ask with forced patience. My father wasn't happy when I told him that Kyle and I had reconciled, but he wasn't surprised. He's been relatively tolerant of the relationship, with only a few jibes here and there. It's almost as if he's trying to accept the idea of us. That or he's biting his tongue and waiting for us to fail all on our own.

In any case, I haven't forgiven him for the past yet.

Kyle slides his hand over mine. "Besides telling me I needed a new suit?"

"Don't listen to him. You look good." I offered to buy him a Tom Ford but he refused, as Kyle refuses all gifts I try to give him. Which is why I'll be buying him a custom suit for Christmas.

He smirks. "He also told me I should be applying for a supervisory position at Rikell. I took that as his way of saying I'm not a complete idiot, so I bolted before he could say anything else."

I nestle my chin on his shoulder. "Yeah, I'd

say that's a good start. Though, you know he's going to keep pushing you until you're running the whole damn thing, right?"

"That's not likely to happen." Kyle shifts in my arms, allowing him to wrap his arms around my back and pull me into his body, into his warmth. "A supervisor isn't a bad idea, though. I have more than enough years of experience. Maybe I'll look into it." Kyle is working front-desk security at a building six blocks away from mine. As much as I loved seeing him throughout the day, it was a good move. It forces me to get home at a reasonable hour every night, so I can spend time with him. If there's one thing that my parents' mess has taught me, it's that I don't want to repeat my father's mistake of putting the business before my heart.

"Good idea." I press my lips against the corner of his, where the tiny lip ring scar remains. "Maybe you can climb the ladder far enough to change the rules about face piercings and get this redone."

His body shakes with his laughter. And then he's kissing me, and the cold, the people milling in the background, the music . . . *everything* simply melts away.

"I see a lake," a voice calls out.

We break free and turn to find Zelda watching us curiously from ten feet away, her garb—colorful beaded cloth, draped over her body in flowing layers, capped with a brilliant fuchsia overcoat—all the more striking against a snowy backdrop. She's every stereotype I imagined Ashley's psychic to be, right down to the wild mane of graying hair, the deep smoker's voice, the piercing eyes.

"I see a lake," she repeats, "and sunshine and warmth, and enduring love."

"You're telling us about our past." Kyle's arms tighten around me. "I'm more interested in knowing about our future."

Zelda's eyes crinkle with her smile.

Acknowledgments

Coming up with book ideas is sometimes as simple as sitting back and observing everyday life. The idea of a summer camp second-chance romance came to me a few years ago, when I was dropping my kids off at a camp near our cottage. I lingered for a few minutes each morning, watching the teenage counselors joke and laugh among themselves and with the kids. I thought about my own summers as a teenager, and wondered what kind of mischief these counselors might be getting themselves into, so many hours away from parental supervision. Of course, it can't be *anything* like the antics of the Camp Wawa counselors, right?

I hope you enjoyed the dichotomy of worlds in *Say You Still Love Me* and felt the nostalgic pull. Nobody is immune to fond memories of summer love and foolish youth, not even the smart, strong-willed, and capable Piper Calloway.

My main goals with my stories have always been to entertain and to make my readers feel something. So thank you, first and foremost, to my readers, who continue allowing me to entertain you and make you feel (even if sometimes those feelings include anger and frustration).

A special thank-you to the following people . . .

Alyssa Co, Sarah Arndt, Katie Pruitt Miller, Jodi Marsh, Anjanette Rose, and Kara Rickel Conrad, for sharing your crazier summer camp stories with me.

Melissa Krampert Hoppe, for answering my questions on real estate development.

Amélie, Sarah, and Tami, for being daring enough to fly your family to Canada one summer and for bringing that second batch of homemade chocolate turtles because my kids ate the first batch and for always making the effort to connect at signings despite my inability to schedule my time effectively . . . basically, for being you, for six years and counting.

Stacey Donaghy of Donaghy Literary Group, for being my biggest (and most biased) cheerleader.

Loan Le, for taking me and this story on, and for doing it with nothing but encouraging words and astute guidance throughout.

Libby McGuire and the team at Atria Books: Suzanne Donahue, Lisa Wolff, Ariele Fredman, Alison Hinchcliffe, and Lisa Keim, for so beautifully packaging another one of my stories. Thank you to Alysha Bullock, Chelsea McGuckin, and Wendy Blum as well.

Last, but never least, to my family, for appreciating this unique opportunity I've been fortunate enough to be graced with.

About the Author

K.A. Tucker writes captivating stories with an edge. She is the *USA Today* bestselling author of nineteen books, including the Ten Tiny Breaths and Burying Water series, *He Will Be My Ruin*, *Until It Fades*, *Keep Her Safe*, and *The Simple Wild*. Her works have been featured in national publications including *USA Today*, *The Globe and Mail*, *Suspense Magazine*, *First for Women*, and *Publishers Weekly*.

K.A. Tucker currently resides in a quaint town outside of Toronto with her family.

Books are produced in the United States using U.S.-based materials

Books are printed using a revolutionary new process called THINKtech™ that lowers energy usage by 70% and increases overall quality

Books are durable and flexible because of Smyth-sewing

Paper is sourced using environmentally responsible foresting methods and the paper is acid-free

Center Point Large Print
600 Brooks Road / PO Box 1
Thorndike, ME 04986-0001 USA

(207) 568-3717

US & Canada:
1 800 929-9108
www.centerpointlargeprint.com